The Child Without a Home

BOOKS BY ANN BENNETT

The Orphan House

ANN BENNETT

The Child
Without a
Home

FOREVER

NEW YORK   BOSTON

Forever
Hachette Book Group
1290 Avenue of the Americas, New York, NY 10104
read-forever.com
twitter.com/readforeverpub

Originally published by Bookouture in 2022.
An imprint of StoryFire Ltd., Carmelite House,
50 Victoria Embankment, London EC4Y 0DZ, www.bookouture.com

First Forever Trade Paperback Edition: August 2023

Forever is an imprint of Grand Central Publishing. The Forever name and logo are trademarks of Hachette Book Group, Inc.

The publisher is not responsible for websites (or their content) that are not owned by the publisher.

The Hachette Speakers Bureau provides a wide range of authors for speaking events. To find out more, go to hachettespeakersbureau.com or email HachetteSpeakers@hbgusa.com.

Forever books may be purchased in bulk for business, educational, or promotional use. For information, please contact your local bookseller or the Hachette Book Group Special Markets Department at special.markets@hbgusa.com.

Library of Congress Control Number: 2023933344

ISBN: 9781538742136 (Trade paperback)

Printed in the United States of America

LSC-C

Printing 1, 2023

For Helen

The Child Without a Home

PROLOGUE

AGNES

Königsberg, East Prussia, January 1945

All she could feel, as she knelt there trembling on the freezing stone floor, was the sweat and the heat of her brother's hand. They clung together in that low brick cellar that was both their refuge and their prison, as bombs rained down on the city of Königsberg. Every other part of her was numb: her body, her mind, her senses. It was as if she was suspended from reality; as if the horrors she was watching, through that narrow slit in the brick wall of the building, were the unfolding of a nightmare, too bizarre, too cruel, too terrifying to be real.

Bombers screeched overhead, the constant soundtrack to this horror story. She'd lost track of how long they'd been down there, crushed in with dozens of other sweating, desperate people. The hours had gradually merged into one. All she knew was that the bombing had been going on since well before daybreak. Her stomach was taut with hunger, her mouth parched with thirst. She could bear that for herself, but it tortured her to know that Dieter was starving and thirsty too. Each time she glanced down at his little face, it tore her heart out to see his pallid skin stretched over hollow cheekbones, the dark circles under his terrified eyes, his blond hair filthy with brick dust.

Promise you'll look after your brother for me, Agnes. Her mother's urgently whispered words went round and round in her mind. She'd promised Mother passionately that she would, with tears in her eyes, but looking at Dieter now she was racked with guilt at how dismally she'd failed.

The roar of gunfire and the rumble of the bombings was deafening, but Agnes had long ceased to react to the sound. Through the slit she had a view of the city square. Except that the square as she'd known it was disappearing before her eyes. Those beautiful, fairy-tale buildings, the medieval landmarks of this city, were all melting away as she watched. Building after building was hit, crumbling in on themselves, eviscerated into nothingness, like sandcastles dissolving into the tide. It was impossible to believe that this was the place that Mother and Father used to bring them for a treat to see the sights and to ride on the trams. Dust, mortar, and stones sprayed everywhere, billowing across the square in clouds of black smoke, filling the cellars where the terrified people cowered with choking dust. Fire was raging through the ruins too now, devouring collapsed roofs, doors, windows.

Another bomb reverberated across the square, another building crumbled in its wake. Agnes blinked in disbelief. People running from this building were overtaken by the falling walls, disappearing from view, buried in the rubble in a heartbeat. Dieter was whimpering, tears falling from raw eyes. She prized her hand out of his and tried to cover his eyes so he wouldn't see, but it was too late.

Suddenly there were soldiers everywhere, swarming through the square with their rifles, climbing over the rubble of collapsed buildings, firing shots randomly. They were not like soldiers Agnes had ever seen before. These were Russians: the enemy. She knew them from the propaganda posters, with weather-beaten faces, boots and greatcoats and fur hats. The sight struck terror through her. They swarmed through the square in groups, shouting at the tops of their voices, faces ablaze with anger and hatred. Agnes drew Dieter closer, wrapping her arms around him tight. Fear enveloped her now, taking over her mind and her body. She was powerless to stop it.

Within seconds the terrifying sound of crashing and thumping came from heavy doors at the back of the cellar. Then the splintering of wood. A collective scream went up as the soldiers broke down the door and burst into the cellar. Everyone moved away as one, the soldiers crowded in, pressing up against the wall where Agnes and Dieter crouched, crushing them, suffocating them. She waited, rooted to the spot, her arms around her shivering brother as the cellar fell into a horrified silence.

ONE

FREYA

Cambridge, Present Day

The flat was lighter and airier than she remembered. A chilly blast greeted her as she unlocked the front door and propped it open with the box of kitchen equipment she'd been carrying. She looked around at the sun-filled room and sniffed the air. The smell of fresh paint mingled with lemon-scented carpet cleaner.

"It's beautiful, Freya." Her mother, Monica, was a few paces behind her, breathless from carrying a crate of china up the stairs.

"I told you it was a lucky find, didn't I? Here, let me take that."

She lifted the crate from her mother's arms and carried it across the room to the kitchen worktop.

"What a view!" Monica strode toward the deep bay window, where the late-afternoon sun flooded through. "And a writing table, with a view of the river. How will you ever do any work?"

Freya laughed and went to stand beside her at the window, sliding her arm around Monica's waist and hugging her. "Don't worry, Mum. That's what I've moved back here for. So I've got more time to focus on my thesis, so I don't have to commute."

Her eyes wandered to the River Cam across the road and the wide expanse of Jesus Green beyond. Between the narrow-boats moored up on the towpath, families with small children were throwing bread to a gaggle of noisy ducks at the water's edge. Rowing boats filled with day-trippers wobbled about on the water and groups of students lounged on the grass or sat on benches, enjoying the autumn afternoon. They looked like freshmen, so young and full of joy and enthusiasm for their new experience. Freya felt a sudden pang of nostalgia for her own first days here. How long ago that seemed now and how much had changed since then.

They watched the scene in companionable silence for a few moments, then Monica moved back into the room, looking admiringly at the tall high, corniced ceiling, the Victorian marble fireplace.

"These big old houses have so much charm, don't they? And it's nice they managed to preserve so much when they converted it into flats."

Freya was pleased that her mother approved of the place and that her face that had been so tense and drawn lately was relaxed and smiling for the first time in what seemed an age. The past few weeks had been so tough on her mother, who had just lost Freya's granddad after caring for him virtually single-handedly for so many years.

"It's so much nicer than that poky little place you and Cameron had in Grafton Street, darling." Monica was in the kitchen area now, opening cupboards one by one and peering inside, inspecting the fridge, the burners, the oven.

"Shall I show you the bedroom, Mum?" Freya asked briskly, changing the subject.

She wished her mother hadn't mentioned Grafton Street quite so soon after they'd arrived back in Cambridge. It had tainted the pleasure of what was meant to be her fresh start. Even though it was several months since Freya had moved out of the little terraced house, the wounds of her split with Cameron were still raw. It was the place where they'd met and fallen in love and hearing the street name brought it all back with a force she hadn't quite anticipated.

The bedroom was at the back of the house, with a little bathroom opening off it and a sash window overlooking the back gardens of the terrace. Freya wandered over to it and stared down at the narrow garden. Disappointingly, it was completely paved over. There were a couple of benches beside the fence and a covered barbecue near the house. Monica joined her at the window.

"Did you ask if you have access to the garden?"

"Yes, I think the leasing agent said I did."

Freya's memory of the conversation she'd had with the young man who'd shown her round last week was hazy. Places so rarely came up on Chesterton Road and it was so convenient for the town and her college, she hadn't bothered too much with the details.

"But it doesn't matter really either way, does it? There's that huge park opposite, after all."

"Well, it would be nice if you *could* use the garden," Monica persisted. "You might get to know the other tenants."

There was that note of anxiety in her mother's tone that immediately put Freya on the defensive. She bit her nail and looked away, trying not to react. She knew what Monica was getting at. She *had* become a bit reclusive since the split with Cameron. Moving out of the house they'd shared for three years had meant moving home to North London and commuting back to Cambridge for the rest of the Easter term. She'd not wanted to go out much in London over the summer. She hadn't even bothered to get a temporary job, or spend time with her brother Matthew or her old school friends. She'd just stayed in her room, living on her meager savings, doing not much at all, often just surfing the internet mindlessly for hours. Festering. It wasn't as if she'd even done much work on her thesis. Everything had felt pointless. And on top of that, Granddad's death had hit her hard too, though she'd tried not to add to her mother's own grief by burdening her with her feelings.

"The garden all looks very low-maintenance," Monica was saying. "Not like next door's . . . Look! That one's gone to rack and ruin."

It was true. From this vantage point there was an almost complete view of the next-door garden. It was very overgrown. The flower borders were choked with nettles and weeds, the unruly hedges full of brambles. Someone had made a crude attempt at cutting the lawn, leaving lumps of cut grass drying and decaying in rough lines. As they stared, a tall ginger cat emerged from under a large buddleia bush, strutted across the lawn, tail up, then lay down and rolled around on its back. When it got up and stretched, it left a flat patch of grass. Then it bounded toward the house. As it disappeared from view they heard the clunk of a catflap.

"I wonder who lives there . . . it doesn't look like students."

"I'm not sure," Freya replied. "Not all the houses in the terrace have been made into flats . . . look, shall we go and get the rest of the stuff from the car, Mum?"

There were a couple of holdalls on the back seat, a suitcase of clothes and another full of books. Her bike was on a rack on the roof. Freya took the heavier case and Monica followed with one of the holdalls. As Freya struggled up the stairs to the flat, she heard the click of a door opening on the ground floor.

"Hello? Would you like any help?"

It was a male voice. She turned to see a young man with dark hair and a beard emerging from the flat beneath hers. He was dressed in shabby jeans and a shapeless jumper. Freya caught Monica's eye, frowned, and started to mouth the word "no," but her mother's eyes slid away from hers.

"How kind." Monica had already put the holdall down and was shaking the man's hand.

"I'm Finn, by the way."

Freya caught the lilt of an Irish accent.

"Monica Carey, and that's my daughter, Freya. If you've got time, we'd be very grateful . . ."

The man, Finn, said "Hi," and waved in Freya's direction. Freya tried to force a smile, all the time wishing her mother hadn't interfered like that.

He carried the holdall upstairs for Monica, returned to the car, then brought up the other suitcases. It was all done in a few minutes.

"Would you like me to take your bike off the roof?" he asked as he turned to leave.

"I can do that," Freya spoke up. "I put it up there, after all."

"It's up to you." He shrugged and turned to look at her properly for the first time. She saw mocking amusement in his dark eyes and for the second time since arriving she had to bite back rising irritation.

"We'd be very grateful indeed," said Monica. "Now, the kettle's in here somewhere. Would you like a cup of tea afterward?"

"Oh no, thanks all the same, I'm just heading out. I'll leave the bike in the hallway. See you around . . ." he added, nodding toward Freya and leaving the room.

"Mum!"

"What's wrong?" asked Monica, feigning innocence.

"Why did you do that? It was so embarrassing."

"Nonsense, darling. He was only too pleased to lend a hand. You shouldn't be so proud."

Monica filled the kettle and found the box of mugs, tea, and milk. Freya watched her silently. Now wasn't the time for an argument, not just before her mother left to drive back to London, back to an empty house for the first time in however many years, so she bit her lip and said nothing.

As they drank their tea, Monica helped her put the kitchen equipment away in the cupboards. By the time they'd finished, the daylight was fading.

"I suppose I'd better be pushing off," said Monica and Freya could hear the reluctance in her tone.

"Oh, Mum, are you going to be OK?"

"Of course. Back to work tomorrow. There's lots to keep me busy." There were tears in her mother's eyes now and she pursed her lips together. Freya felt a lump in her own throat. She put her arms around her and felt her mother give a couple of quiet sobs.

Monica had put her life on hold to care for her ailing father, reducing her hours at the job as a physiotherapist she'd loved so she could be there for him, rarely going out, getting up in the night to help him whenever he woke or shouted out for help. He'd been in the Polish air force at the beginning of the war, then come to England to join the RAF. He'd never recovered either physically or mentally from the injuries he'd sustained when his plane was shot down over the Channel. He was a difficult invalid, angry and bitter to the end. Even so, Freya knew that her mother would find it hard to adjust to having her freedom back, as well as coping with the grief of her loss.

"I'm so sorry about . . . well, about everything," she said, her arms still tight around her mother.

"Let's put all that behind us now, shall we?" Monica drew away and dabbed her eyes with a handkerchief. "It's been hard for all of us, these last few weeks."

"All the same . . . I'm sorry, Mum."

"All I ask is that you give your brother a call soon. Patch things up. You two used to be so close, I hate to see you at loggerheads."

"All right. I will, I'll call him tomorrow, I promise."

"Good. Now I'd better get going before it gets dark."

Freya stood on the pavement and, fighting back the tears, waved as Monica drove away. She carried on waving until after the car had rounded the bend in the road and disappeared from view. Then she turned to go inside, with a heavy heart.

As she walked toward the front steps she looked up at the next-door house, remembering the conversation with her mother about the overgrown garden. The house was shabby, unlike the others in the terrace, the brown paintwork was peeling and weeds grew through cracks on the front steps. There weren't the usual bikes leaning against the front wall or other signs of student habitation; this house had clearly not been converted into flats like most of its neighbors. Perhaps it wasn't even occupied at all. But as she glanced at the house, the graying net curtains in the front window parted momentarily, then snapped shut again. Whoever was living there had been watching her. Looking away and trying to ignore the chills that coursed down her spine, Freya hurried up the steps and into the house.

Back in the flat, her heart sank at the sight of the boxes and bags still piled on the floor but, steeling herself, she dragged a holdall into the bedroom and started to unpack. She wanted to get everything as straight as she could that evening. She had some work to do on her thesis too. Her tutor had asked to see her in college at nine in the morning and she needed to prepare for that. It was confession time. He wouldn't be happy at her lack of progress, she knew that, but she'd resolved to come clean with him and make a fresh start this term.

Putting her clothes away in the bedroom, her mind

wandered again to her mum, driving home alone. She would be on the motorway by now, probably dreading opening the door to a cold, empty house. Freya felt a pang of guilt at what she had alluded to before she left. It was true, she and her brother had had a misunderstanding and had avoided each other for a couple of weeks, and now Matthew had flown off to Nepal to report on the upcoming elections for his newspaper. Being at odds with him made Freya feel low and unanchored. Her mum was right; Freya and her brother had been close their whole lives. There were only two years between them and when their father had died when they were teenagers, the three of them had all supported each other. It had been them against the world. Until their grandmother died too and Granddad came to live with them. That had changed everything.

She couldn't bear to think about the falling-out she'd had with her grandfather, years ago now, when she was at school; his death was too recent and she was too raw. She knew she'd been in the wrong, but she had thought he'd forgiven her. In recent years he seemed to have stopped being quite so angry with her. When she saw his will though, it came home to her only too painfully that he had never forgiven her and that he had harbored his grudge until his dying day. Although he'd left his savings and the proceeds of the sale of his house to be shared equally between her mum, herself and Matthew, he'd left all his personal effects to Matthew. She knew exactly why he'd done that; it was a direct reference to the reason they had argued. It had hurt her badly but she'd tried to hide her pain.

"Are you going to sort through his things?" she'd asked Matthew after the funeral, eyeing Granddad's wooden chest full of wartime memorabilia warily, recalling with a shudder the arguments they'd had about it.

"Maybe when I come back from Nepal," Matthew had said casually and she'd marveled at his restraint. She was itching to know what was in that box, but it wasn't hers to open.

She'd ended up being frosty with Matthew. She hadn't meant that to happen, it was hardly his fault. But it hadn't been resolved before he'd left for Nepal. It hurt her that they weren't on speaking terms.

Trying to put it all out of her mind, she went through to the front of the flat, grabbed a pastry that her mum had left in the fridge, and rummaged in her bag for her laptop. It was time to get down to work if she was going to get any sleep at all that night.

She sat down at the table and opened the laptop. As it was starting up, she looked out across the river and the green opposite. It was dark now. The houseboats were lit up and the students were melting away in groups, some arm in arm, heading off through the gardens by lamplight. She smiled to herself, a warm feeling stealing over her at being back here. Then she turned to her notes on the screen.

She still had a lot of research to get through for her thesis and it was tough going. She began to scroll through some materials and was just getting into the detail when the sudden sound of loud music interrupted her concentration. She paused and listened for the source of the noise. It was coming through the wall and she recognized the theme tune to the television news. Was it Finn? The music soon faded and was replaced with the booming voice of the newsreader. She got up from the table and tried to gauge whether the sound was coming through the floor. Then she realized. It wasn't Finn at all, it was coming from the next-door house. Irritated, she found her headphones, put some calming music on her phone, and turned back to her work, but the noise was so loud her headphones hardly had any effect. Pressing her hands over her ears, she battled on. She managed to read for half an hour or so against the racket, but after the closing theme tune for the news, the noise was turned up even louder and she could hear the weather forecast only too clearly.

Once again, she tried to get back to work, but the words slid past her eyes and panic began to take over. She needed to make some progress before her meeting with Dan Eastwood, her tutor, in the morning or he would be bound to tell her some home truths about her lack of commitment. She couldn't bear the thought of that. Until the past few months she'd prided herself on being conscientious and on not taking for granted the opportunity she'd been given to study here. How could she have let things slide so badly? And if this racket didn't stop there was no way she would get her thoughts in order for the meeting.

She lost patience. "This is ridiculous!" she said out loud. She pulled her headphones off and got up from the table. She needed to do something about this straight away or she'd never be able to study in her own home. Without giving herself a chance to think twice, she pulled on her boots, grabbed her keys, and clattered down the stairs. Outside on the pavement, she stared up at the next-door house. It looked even more neglected and forbidding than in the daylight. It was in complete darkness but for some chinks of weak light around the curtains in the bay window. It was from that same window that the television noise was blaring. Who would be that inconsiderate? Squatters? She put her hands on her hips, indignant. Then came the thought: how would they react to her complaint?

She didn't want to think too deeply about that, so she went straight up the steps and hammered on the door with the rusty black metal knocker. She waited for a few seconds but the noise didn't abate, so she knocked again. After several attempts, the noise stopped abruptly. She held her breath, trying to calm her nerves. Through the glass panels of the door, she saw a weedy light turned on in the hallway, then the looming shadow of someone approaching the front door slowly. There was a painful wait while locks were fumbled with and pulled back, some more rattling, then the door was pulled open a crack, to the extent of a chain, and a face appeared in the gap. Wrinkles, white hair, thick glasses.

"What do you want? It's late!"

It was a woman's voice. Cracked and old, bristling with indignation. Freya was momentarily caught off guard.

"I said . . . what do you want?"

"I've . . . I've just moved in next door. I'm trying to study. I was wondering if you could turn your TV down?"

"*What* do you say?" The door closed momentarily as the chain was taken off, then it opened wider. The old woman who stood there in the gloomy passage was diminutive and frail. Dressed in dark clothes and slippers that zipped up the front, she leaned on a walking stick. She was frowning deeply, her mouth turned down at the corners. Her head was cocked to one side, as if she was listening expectantly.

"I was wondering . . . if you could turn your telly down a bit," Freya repeated, louder this time, but she was beginning to feel a prickle of guilt.

"All right! All right! I have done this now. You don't need to ask." The old woman was glaring at Freya. "Now, is that all?"

"Yes. Thank you," Freya replied. She was about to apologize for disturbing the old woman, but realized how disingenuous that would sound.

"Well, good night then," she finished weakly and was about to turn away when she caught sight of a picture hanging at the end of the dim passage, behind the old lady. The sight of it made her mouth drop open. It reminded her so forcefully of a similar painting that used to hang in her grandfather's room. It was the only reminder he had of his native land; it showed a fortified farmstead, surrounded by forest, the whole landscape carpeted in snow. This picture was so similar—a fairy-tale castle against a backdrop of snow-capped forests—that she couldn't take her eyes off it.

As she was staring, the front door slammed in her face and, through the glass, the shadow of the old woman retreated down the hallway. Then the hall light went off and Freya was left standing in darkness, reeling from the encounter.

Back in her flat, she spent an undisturbed hour at her laptop, preparing for the meeting with Dan. But every time she paused, her thoughts turned to the acerbic exchange with the old lady and the painting in her hallway of that far-off land. It was the same when she finally got to bed, closing her eyes for the first time in that strange new room. The encounter had unsettled her; she couldn't get it out of her mind. Finally, she realized: there was something in the way the old lady spoke, the intonation of her voice, her simmering anger, that was reminiscent of her grandfather in his last months and years.

TWO

The morning air was crisp and chilly as Freya carried her bike down the front steps of the house. It was colder than London and she was glad she'd wrapped up warm. Mist rose from the river as she headed onto the narrow bridge on her bike. A boat from one of the colleges powered through as she crossed, eight men at the oars, rowing in perfect symmetry, the cox shouting instructions from the stern. She resisted the urge to see if Cameron was one of the rowers and turned away, heading diagonally across the park toward the town center. It was a beautiful morning; the trees were beginning to show their autumn colors and the stone and brick of the college buildings glowed vividly in the October sunshine. She cycled past a group of nervous-looking freshmen, riding slowly together—safety in numbers. She smiled in sympathy; nerves were niggling in her own stomach as she anticipated her encounter with her tutor. Despite that, she was glad to be back here.

She reached the lane at the edge of the gardens and cycled on through the narrow streets of the city center. There were the old familiar buildings she loved: King's College, Trinity

College, the Senate House. Outside Emmanuel College, she locked her bike in a rack and went in through the porter's lodge and into Front Court with its ochre stone buildings, its clock-tower and cloisters. Dan's rooms were on the top floor, up a winding wooden staircase in one of the ancient buildings on the right.

"Freya!" he greeted her warmly. "Come on in. Sit down. How are things? Good summer?"

Dan was a young academic, enthusiastic and bright, trying to make a name for himself in the faculty of modern history. He'd believed in her from the moment they'd first met at her interview for postgraduate studies and she hated the thought of letting him down.

"Good, thanks," she said noncommittally, taking a seat in one of his armchairs. The room was low-ceilinged and cozy, lit by a gas fire in the old-fashioned hearth. Dan sat down opposite her, crossing his long legs. He'd tidied his room a little since she'd last been here, although there were still papers and books piled on the desk alongside several used coffee cups.

"Did you manage to get away at all?"

She shook her head. "I was mostly at home, in London."

"Ah, yes. I remember now, you moved back there last term, didn't you?" He looked down at his notes. "You found the commute a bit of a bind, if I remember . . ."

"I'm back in Cambridge now," she said quickly.

He smiled. "That's a relief. I'm hoping you'll be able to take on supervising a few more first-year students this term. It's a very promising young group we have."

"Of course. I'd be glad to."

"I wouldn't want it to interfere with progress on your own research, of course. How's it coming on?"

"Well . . ." She looked down at her lap, unable to hold his gaze. "I've been able to do some work online over the summer, but a lot of the materials are difficult to get hold of. To tell you the truth, I reached a bit of a stalemate in London, I'm afraid."

The hint of a frown clouded Dan's eyes. "Well, not to worry. Now you're back in Cambridge, no doubt you'll be able to steam ahead with your research. A lot of what you'll need you'll find in the Squire Law Library, failing that the University Library. The assistants will be able to track it down . . . It's a very valuable subject you've chosen."

"Oh yes, I know," she agreed, nodding enthusiastically, but the words sounded hollow. She didn't want to admit it, even to herself, but part of the reason she'd been finding it difficult to focus was because the subject matter wasn't firing her imagination as she'd hoped when she'd chosen it: "The effects of the Inclosure Acts 1604–1850 on rural communities." Her real passion was twentieth-century history and she'd studied it as an undergraduate, but she'd wanted to steer clear of the Second World War when it had come to choosing a subject for her thesis. It was all bound up with her arguments with her grandfather. He hated being reminded of the war and wouldn't have approved. And she hadn't wanted to trespass on sacred ground.

"You know, Freya, if you're having second thoughts, it might not be too late to change direction," Dan said.

"Change direction?"

"People do, you know, on occasion. Start with one thing in mind and end up pursuing a completely different path when they get into the research . . . It happens."

"That's kind of you, Dan, but it's fine. I'll get there. I've just had a few things to deal with."

"Yes, I remember."

There was a pause and her eyes strayed to the flickering gas fire. She was embarrassed now, remembering that she'd dissolved into tears at one of their meetings, shortly after her split with Cameron. Dan was not the sort of person you'd expect to offer a shoulder to cry on; shy and socially awkward,

more at home in a dusty library poring over antique documents
than with other people. But he'd been surprisingly understanding. He listened to her pouring her heart out, insisted on
her taking time off, even stepped in to take some of her tutorials.

"My grandfather died a few weeks ago," she said now, as if
to correct him.

"Oh! I'm so sorry, Freya. That must have been tough for you.
You mentioned you were close."

"We were . . . once."

She bit her lip and looked back up at Dan, suppressing the
emotions that threatened to bubble to the surface; emotions over
the arguments with her grandfather, the rift with Matthew.

"Look, it's fine, now, Dan. *I'm* fine. I just couldn't get much
done over the summer. But as you say, now I'm back here I can
steam on."

"Well, that's good news." His face relaxed and he leaned
back in his chair. "And if you want to run anything by me in
between our sessions, I'm always here, you know. Now . . . let me
find the schedule I've drawn up for your supervision of your first-
year students."

After the meeting, she wandered out onto Front Court
feeling as though she'd let herself and Dan down. Why hadn't
she been more honest with him about how she was feeling about
her work? He'd given her an opening, surely?

She went out through the porter's lodge and, leaving her
bike where it was, set off on foot back through the town toward
the library. As she walked, she thought about Dan's words,
and about how her decision to study something she was less
than passionate about had been influenced by her grandfather.
Jah-Dek, she called him, from the Polish "Dziadek," meaning
Grandfather. He'd been a brooding presence in her life since
he'd moved into their home when Freya was in her early teens.
Although Freya had done her best to help her mother, she'd
seen how her independence had gradually slipped away.

By that time, Janick Kowalski had been in his late eighties and growing weaker and more bitter by the day. He was unable to get upstairs by that time, so the back dining room became his combined living room and bedroom and her mum had a downstairs bathroom installed for him too. From that point on, she had cared for him virtually single-handedly and he wasn't an easy patient. Freya could still hear the growl of his voice and the thump of his stick on the floor. "Monica! Where are you, girl? I need you," and her mother would drop what she was doing and rush to tend to him. That had been ten years ago and, bit by bit, her mum had given up most of her freedoms, her leisure, and her life to care for him. It happened so gradually that Freya hardly noticed at first, but he had become so demanding during those two years before his death, her mum had even talked about giving up her job.

"But, Mum, you love your work," Freya had protested, when the subject was broached.

Monica had wrung her hands. "It's hard to fit it all in. And poor Dad shouldn't be left alone for hours on end anymore."

"I could move back home and help out," Freya had suggested. At that time, she had been working in a bookshop in Cambridge, saving up to study for her PhD and spending as much time with Cameron as she could.

"Oh, I couldn't ask you to do that. You have your life to lead, my darling. And in any case . . . I'm sure he wouldn't hear of it."

"No, he probably wouldn't," Freya had said, dropping her gaze. Monica knew that relations were frosty between grandfather and granddaughter, but Freya had never told her exactly what had happened to sour their relationship.

She still felt the pain of that argument now, walking back past the ancient gateway of King's College. But something had changed over the past couple of days. Now that she was back here, making a fresh start, she felt ready to face it in her own mind.

It had been when she was studying the Second World War

in history at school. She knew that her grandfather had been in the Polish air force, that he'd come to Britain early on in the war and joined the RAF, but he'd never spoken to her directly about it. In those days, she would go into his room with his tea tray when she came home from school. They would chat companionably in front of the fire. He would ask her about her day and they would sometimes play chess or cards. She'd tried to introduce the subject of the war to him on more than one occasion as they sipped their tea but each time his face would cloud over and he would go silent and glower into the fire. She'd persisted, but he'd steadfastly refused to be drawn, although once he let slip that he had kept some mementos from the war in a chest that he'd brought from his old home. Freya had pleaded with him to let her look at them, but he'd refused. Each time she asked he got more and more angry, until one day he'd lost his temper and waved his stick at her.

"That's enough! I don't want to be reminded. Do you hear? Do you hear, girl?" he exploded and she'd backed away, shocked.

But his outburst hadn't dampened her curiosity then; rather, it made her even more keen to find out what was inside that chest. Even all these years later, she still went hot and cold at the thought of what she'd done the next day when her mum had driven him to the doctor's surgery for a check-up. She crept into his room, found the key to his chest in his bedside cabinet, and opened it up. There were his medals on top, a fading photograph of a group of young men, hardly more than boys, standing beside a propeller plane on a windy airfield, and underneath that an old shoebox full of papers and photos. Freya had laid the medals out on his coffee table and was attempting to sketch them so she could look them up online later, when she heard the front door and the stump of his stick crossing the hall. Panicking, she shoved the medals and photographs back in the chest and was trying to lock it with shaking hands when he came into the room.

"Whatever are you doing?" he roared. "That is not your property. I told you before!"

She looked round for her mother but realized that she must have dropped him at the front door and left to look for a parking space. Her cheeks were flaming at being caught red-handed.

"Get out!" he said, waving his stick at her. "Get out and don't come back. You are not welcome here anymore."

Since that day it seemed to Freya that he'd taken against her. When she brought him tea in the afternoons, he was grumpy and answered her curtly. He no longer asked her to sit down for a chat, or for a game of chess. Even worse, if she ever had friends round he would shout out from his room, complaining about the noise in the house, causing an embarrassing scene. She'd never dared mention the war, nor his chest of belongings, ever again. It troubled her to admit the thought, but part of the reason she'd been glad to leave home and come to Cambridge after her A-levels was to be away from his unpredictable outbursts.

Now, she crossed the river on the footbridge and there was the library in front of her, a gray modernist building, all chrome and glass. Thinking about her grandfather had reminded her of her promise to her mother. She found a bench to sit on, pulled her phone out of her bag, and dialed Matthew's number. It went straight to voicemail without ringing. She listened to her brother's message and it made her smile, hearing his familiar voice with its jokey edge. She left a message for him to call her back. As she rang off, she wondered what time it was in Kathmandu.

Inside the library building she found a booth, requested copies of some of the earliest Inclosure Acts, and buried herself in study. Here, it wasn't so difficult to shut out her demons and she found herself drawn into the world evoked by the obscure language of the old documents; a world of Lord and lowly tenant, of desperate poverty contrasted with abundant wealth, the elaborate, convoluted sentences designed to exclude the poorest from the land they had worked for centuries. At the end of the afternoon, after having made copious notes on her laptop, Freya felt herself warming to the subject matter and thought that perhaps, in time, she would be able to find some sort of direction for her work.

As the light was fading, she walked back through the darkening streets to pick up her bike. Instead of heading back to the flat, she cycled the short distance across the stretch of flat grass called Parker's Piece to the narrow streets behind it. They were lined with two-story terraced workers' cottages, many of which were now converted into bijou dwellings. She had to cross the end of Grafton Street and she did so without glancing down it. She'd heard on the grapevine that Cameron had moved out and into a flat nearer to Addenbrooke's Hospital, where he worked; she didn't want to be reminded of those last, desperately lonely weeks that had signaled the end of their five-year relationship.

She pulled up outside the little one-story pub, the Free Press, locked her bike to a hook in the wall, and went inside. There were only a couple of early drinkers at the bar. As she crossed the room, her heart lifted as she spotted her friend, Amber, standing behind it, polishing glasses. Amber looked just the same: spiky blonde hair, lots of makeup. Her face lit up when she saw Freya approaching.

"Hey, stranger. Good to see you! I didn't realize you were back in town."

"I know. I'm sorry, I should have let you know. It was all a bit last-minute."

"Don't worry, it's great that you're back. Can I get you a drink?"

Freya asked for a white wine and leaned at the bar, watching Amber pour it.

"I wasn't sure you'd be here still," she said. "You were thinking about leaving when we last spoke."

"Oh, I know." Amber laughed. "I'm always talking about getting my act together, applying for some graduate scheme in London, and I know I should. But I love the job really. Why give up something you love?"

"You're right." Freya smiled at her friend. Amber had studied history with her and they'd both stayed on in Cambridge after graduation, when most of their contemporaries moved on. Freya had stayed because of Cameron, but Amber had stayed for the love of the place.

"It's not half so much fun now that *you* don't work here anymore, of course." Amber's blue eyes twinkled. "We used to have such a laugh."

"Well, actually, I was wondering if there were any vacancies here, now that I'm back."

Amber's face became serious. "I can ask. The manager's out right now, but are you sure? I mean . . ."

"You mean, it might bring back bad memories? No, I'm over Cameron now. And he doesn't live round the corner anymore, does he?"

"True . . . but he does come in here to drink occasionally. With his mates from the Boat Club or the hospital."

"Oh." Freya's spirits sank. She'd pinned her hopes on coming back here to work a couple of nights a week. She'd loved working here last year alongside Amber, and she could do with the money. She drew herself up. "You know, I don't think that would bother me. I've got to face him sometime."

"Well, if you're sure . . ." Amber looked uncertain. *She's thinking about all those months when she had to help me through my heartbreak,* thought Freya.

"I'll ask for you and text you later," Amber went on. "I'm sure they'd be glad to have you back. We've been short-staffed for a few weeks now."

As Freya wheeled her bike across Chesterton Road and onto the pavement opposite her house, she could hear the television blaring out loud and clear from the next-door house again. She felt her irritation mount. Could she face another encounter with the strange old woman? She'd have to buy some noise-canceling headphones if this was going to go on.

She lifted her bike up the steps, pushed the front door open, and wheeled it through and into the hall. As she leaned the bike against the wall, the door to the downstairs flat opened. Finn's head appeared round the door.

"How're you doing?"

"Good, thanks. You?"

"Not so bad."

She gave him a brief smile as she took the pannier off her bike rack, wondering why he was standing there, staring at her. He stepped into the passage and cleared his throat.

"I heard you talking to the old lady next door last night."

"Oh, did you?" She straightened up and looked him in the eye.

"Yes. Agnes, her name is. I was just going to say . . ."

"Yes?"

"Well, she's very old. And quite deaf. She needs to have the telly up loud to hear it."

"Oh." Freya didn't know how to respond. From the tone of his voice, it felt like a reprimand.

"And she's alone in the world," he went on. "She looks forward to watching the news in the evenings."

"I'm sorry, I just needed to study, that's all."

"She always switches it off, right after the weather forecast."

"OK. Well, thanks for letting me know," Freya said curtly and turned to head upstairs, her mind seething with different emotions. She couldn't decipher them all immediately, but she could recognize among them indignation, humiliation, and shame. But as she let herself inside the flat and looked around gratefully at the comfortable, welcoming room, her heart softened toward the old lady next door. She had a name now:

Agnes. There was something intriguing about her. And, as she lay awake into the small hours, Freya recalled the rasp of the old woman's voice, the hint of an accent so reminiscent of her grandfather's, and the painting of that mysterious land that hung in her hallway.

THREE

The next morning, before setting off to meet her new first-year students in college, Freya dialed Matt's number again. She held her breath, expecting to hear the voicemail message, but instead it was Matt's voice at the end of the line.

"Oh, hi, Freya." His voice sounded far away, but even though it was faint, she could tell from his tone that he was less than enthusiastic to hear from her.

"Did you get my message?" she asked.

"Yeah, but I figured you'd be in bed until now. I was going to call."

There were a lot of raised voices in the background, gabbling in a language she couldn't understand. She pictured him in the midst of a surging crowd in a square surrounded by temples and ancient buildings.

"Look, it's difficult to talk right now. Can I call you back?"

"Will you though, Matt? You didn't before. Can't we just talk *now*?"

"I've only got a couple of minutes. Wait, I'll find somewhere quieter."

She listened to his breathing and the uneven sound of his

footsteps as he walked a few steps away from the crowd. The background voices receded.

"What was it you wanted to say?"

"I just wanted to say I'm sorry. About . . . well, you know. About the misunderstanding we had about Jah-Dek's things."

There was silence at the other end and Freya waited, counting the seconds.

"All right," he said slowly. "But the things you said, Freya . . ."

"I know. I know, I was upset. But I am sorry, OK? That's why I called."

"Let's talk about it when I get back. Like I said at the time, I didn't actually *ask* Jah-Dek to leave me his things."

"I know you didn't. And like I said, I'm sorry for everything I said to you, Matt. Can't you just accept my apology?"

"Look, I have to go now. I think there's going to be some sort of announcement. I've been waiting for hours and I can't miss it. I'll call you back another time."

He rang off before she'd had a chance to reply. She sank onto the settee deflated, an empty feeling welling in her chest. He hadn't accepted her apology and it had been such a difficult conversation. It felt as if there was a mountain to climb to get him to understand. And added to that, he hadn't said the little joke they'd exchanged since childhood whenever they said goodbye—"See you". . . "Not if I see you first!" In fact, he hadn't said goodbye at all. She swallowed a lump in her throat. How could she bear this feeling of distance between them, of being estranged from him?

And he'd said he'd call back, but would he really? How long was she prepared to wait for him to call her back before trying to speak to him again herself?

Glancing at her watch, she quickly packed her bags for college and left the flat. As she hurried downstairs, her heart sank. There was Finn in the hallway, locking his front door. She contemplated pretending to have forgotten something and going back up to the flat—she couldn't face another telling-off from him with the way she felt now—but it was too late, he'd already spotted her.

"Morning!" His voice was cheery today and he was beaming.

"Hi," she said.

"Look, I'm sorry about last night. I was probably a bit short with you."

"No worries," she said, not looking him in the eye, concentrating on fixing the pannier onto her bike.

"Well, I hope you weren't offended. I like to get on with my neighbors."

"Don't worry, I wasn't offended," she said, struggling with the buckle, wishing he would just go away. Couldn't he see that she didn't want to make friends? That she just wanted to keep herself to herself?

"It's just that I've a soft spot for poor old Agnes. She's got a sharp tongue and she's very eccentric, but she's had a tough life. She's been through a hell of a lot."

"Oh?" Freya's interest was piqued. The picture on the wall behind Agnes, the hint of an Eastern European accent.

"Yes, poor thing..."

Freya waited, but he didn't elaborate and her resolution not to get drawn into conversation with him was stronger than her desire to find out more about the strange old lady, so she didn't ask.

"Are you at the university?" Finn ventured after a pause.

"Yes. Postgrad."

"Oh..." He smiled sardonically. Laughing at her with his dark eyes. "No, I didn't take you for a first-year."

"What about you?" she asked automatically, then immediately regretted the question. Hadn't she just told herself she didn't want to be drawn into conversation?

"Me? No, I'm not at the uni. I'm a carpenter by trade. I came to Cambridge five years ago to help on the restoration of King's College Chapel. I got attached to the place and stayed."

He opened the front door for her and she wheeled her bike out onto the front step, hoping he wasn't going in her direction. She didn't want to ride with him and be forced into making polite conversation all the way across the Green. He followed her out of the house and down the front steps, carrying his bike. To her relief he set it down, pointing in the opposite direction to hers.

"Well, nice chatting with you, Freya," he said, swinging his leg over the bike, then heading off across the road. She waved vaguely after him, relieved that their exchange was over. As she set off toward the footbridge, something compelled her to glance back at the windows of the next-door house.

Was she imagining it or had the net curtains twitched, just as they had the other evening? She recalled the old lady standing in her hallway, bristling with indignation about being asked to turn her TV down. Finn's words came back to her. Despite their civilized exchange this morning, she was still smarting at the way he'd made her feel guilty on the night she'd arrived. He'd asked if she'd been offended. It wasn't offense she was feeling, it was downright shame and humiliation.

What had Finn meant when he'd mentioned that Agnes had been through a hell of a lot? Why hadn't he told her? But apart from curiosity, her heart suddenly swelled with pity for the old woman. *She's all alone in the world.* How very sad that she had no family and that she lived alone in that tall, crumbling house with just a ginger cat for company, forgotten and neglected by the world as the years slipped away from her. At least her grand-father had been surrounded by people who cared for him in his last years and months, not left to suffer alone. Even if he'd not always appreciated those closest to him.

Freya cycled across the footbridge. Without thinking, she found herself checking up and down the river on the off-chance of seeing an "eight," a college boat out training on the river, but there were no rowers on the Cam this morning. *What am I doing?* Shaking her head briskly at her weakness, she pedaled on across the gardens toward college.

As she went through the day, she tried to put her conversation with Matt and her unsettling thoughts about Finn and the old lady out of her mind. She had plenty to occupy her; first, she rode to college and met a group of first-year students for an hour, then she walked down to the library to continue with her research. The students, two girls and two boys, seemed impossibly young and earnest. Listening to their enthusiasm for their subject and how bowled over they were with everything about the place, starting out on their new lives, made her reflect as she had the day before on how long ago it was since she was one of those fresh-faced eighteen-year-olds. Their energy was infectious though and just being with them filled her with renewed enthusiasm for being here and for helping them achieve their goals. As she'd left college to walk down to the library, she'd checked her phone a couple of times to see if Matt had called or texted and, as she worked, scrolling through old documents, she couldn't help glancing at it every so often and wondered why he hadn't called her back.

At lunchtime, she bought a sandwich, wandered along the riverbank, and found a secluded bench. The bench was on the "backs" and had one of her favorite views: overlooking King's College Chapel and Trinity College beside it with the wide, slow river running in front of them. She always used to come here if she wanted to be alone to think. Now, as she ate her sandwich, she watched groups of tourists and freshmen glide past on punts, propelled with varying degrees of proficiency. Some of them were shouting and laughing raucously, others relaxing and enjoying the beauty of the scenery.

Seeing them brought back the memory of her first date with Cameron. It was a warm summer's evening in the Easter term of her first year. She'd expected to be going to a pub or for a meal somewhere, but he'd surprised her by bringing her down to the river and taking her out on a punt. She'd been impressed that he was able to do it without wobbling or running the punt into the bank. He seemed so self-assured and impossibly mature for a second-year student, so unlike the gawky boys she'd found herself studying alongside so far. He'd even produced chilled wine and a picnic, which they'd eaten beside the river on Grantchester Meadows. She let out a huge sigh now, remembering that idyllic evening, and wondered if it might be better to avoid places that reminded her of those times. Perhaps she should find herself new places to walk and eat her lunch.

As she headed back along the riverbank toward the library, her phone buzzed in her bag and she snatched it up eagerly, hoping it was Matt. But it was a text from Amber.

Dale would love to have you back at the pub. Can you start tomorrow evening? Six o'clock?

She texted back straight away: *I'd love to. Thanks so much for that. Please tell Dale I'll be there.*

She worked a little later in the library that evening and the light was fading as she cycled back through the town center toward Chesterton Road. It was one of those early-autumn evenings when the smoky twilight hung on the air, creating a magical atmosphere. As she crossed Magdalene Bridge she paused and got off her bike to admire the beauty of the mist on the river.

There was a grocery shop on the other side of the bridge and, remembering that she had barely any food in the flat, she went inside to buy some basics. As she was paying at the counter, she noticed a bucket beside it, holding bunches of flowers. On a whim she picked up a bouquet of bright yellow sunflowers mixed in with star-shaped purple asters.

Outside the shop she stuck them in the pannier alongside the bread and tins of soup she'd bought for supper and rode the couple of hundred yards along Chesterton Road back to the house. As she dismounted and pulled the bike up onto the pavement, she looked up at next door's windows. The curtains were drawn, but there was no loud television coming from the front room.

There's no time like the present.

Instead of carrying her bike up the steps and into the house, she locked it up to the gatepost, grabbed the flowers, and bounded up the crumbling steps next door. Just as she had on the first evening, she knocked with the rusty black knocker, only this time more tentatively. The sound echoed down the hallway. There was no television echoing down the hallway this evening. In fact, the place was completely still and silent. She waited a few moments, listening carefully for any sound from inside, then knocked again. As she did so, the ginger cat appeared on the step beside her and rubbed itself against her legs. Then came the noise of a door opening inside. The hall light went on and there was the outline of the old lady shuffling along the hallway. The same fumbling with locks and chains and then the door opened a fraction. The old woman peered at her through her thick glasses.

"You again!" The cat slid through the gap and disappeared from view down the passage.

"Yes. It's me. My name's Freya. Freya Carey. As I said, I've just moved in next door."

"Well? My television isn't on . . ." The tone was accusatory.

"No, I know. I've brought you some flowers, actually." Freya held them up. "As a peace offering. I'm sorry about the other evening, I didn't mean to upset you."

"Flowers?" The old woman frowned and her mouth dropped open. Trembling hands appeared in the gap and there was some more fumbling with the chain. The door was pulled back and the old lady stood aside.

"You'd better come in." Her voice had lost its imperious edge now. Instead she sounded bewildered.

Freya stepped inside the passage and held out the flowers.

"You're Agnes, aren't you? Do you mind if I call you that?"

"How do you know my name?" Again, there was suspicion in her tone. She didn't take the flowers and Freya didn't know what to do with them.

"My neighbor told me your name. Finn. The Irish guy. Do you know him?"

Agnes' face softened instantly. "Oh, Finn. Yes. Nice boy. Very helpful. Very kind."

She held out a bony hand. "Agnes Peters," she said. Freya took it and felt her own bones crushed as Agnes squeezed her hand and shook it up and down abruptly. "You'd better come on through."

Freya followed her down the passage and into a large living room. The proportions were similar to her own room next door, the same high ceiling with elaborate cornicing, a marble fireplace, a deep bay window, but there the similarity stopped. These walls were papered in an old-fashioned floral design that had faded badly and the paintwork was a dull brown color, every surface including the mantelpiece cluttered with all manner of junk, and in the hearth, one bar of an electric fire cast a weedy glow. The ginger cat lay stretched out on a threadbare mat in front of it, which was already covered in its hairs. The room was untidy and none too clean. Piles of newspapers and magazines were stacked up beside the grate.

"Sit down," the old lady commanded, taking a seat herself on one side of the fireplace. "You'll have to move those things, just put them on the floor."

Freya put the flowers down on a nearby coffee table, on top of a pile of books. Then, obediently, she removed a pile of papers from a brown armchair and put them down on the floor beside it. To her surprise, it was sheet music, Beethoven's "Appassionata," and as she straightened up, she noticed that in the back corner of the room stood a grand piano shrouded in a lace cover.

"Do you play the piano?"

The old woman cocked her head to one side. "Speak up, please. I don't hear so well."

"I asked if you play the piano."

"Not now." Agnes frowned and pursed her lips as if there was a bitter taste in her mouth. She held up her hands. The knuckles and joints were knobbly and misshapen. "Rheumatism."

"Oh, I'm so sorry," Freya said, sitting down. "That must be awful."

Agnes let out a short, humorless laugh. "You young people do exaggerate so. There are worse things in life than rheumatism."

"Of course," murmured Freya, wondering what she meant and how to respond without incurring the old lady's irritation further. "You must have been—must *be* very good at the piano. I mean Beethoven's 'Appassionata'!"

Freya was thinking of her own pedestrian attempts at learning to play the piano at school, how she'd had no feel at all for it and had struggled to sight-read the simplest of pieces.

Agnes was frowning at her deeply. "Music was my *subject*," she stated.

"Your subject? You mean you studied it?"

Agnes inclined her head, still frowning. "The study of music is never at an end. I studied . . . I *still* study it and I taught it too. But my teaching days are over."

"You taught it? Oh . . ." Freya felt color rise to her cheeks. "Here? At the university?"

"Indeed. For many, many years."

"How interesting."

"I used to give concerts too. All over the country, in those days."

"That's amazing. Did you study music here in Cambridge too?"

Agnes nodded. "I came here on an exchange scholarship, in the fifties."

"On an exchange?" Freya was intrigued. Which country had Agnes come from to study here when she was young? She knew she was pushing her luck to ask, but the words were out before she'd had time to ponder. "May I ask where you came from?"

At that moment, the cat got up from the rug, padded over to Agnes, and rubbed itself against her spindly legs, meowing and purring loudly.

"Dear Claus . . ." Agnes' voice was soft now, affectionate even. "I know. It is time for your supper."

She looked back at Freya quizzically, ignoring her question, as if to say, *can't you see I have things to do?* Freya took the hint and jumped up.

"Well, I'd best be going. Very nice to talk to you."

As she left the room, she wondered whether Agnes would remember the flowers, but she didn't want to offend her by reminding her. Agnes followed her, slowly, leaning on her stick. Freya sensed it was a struggle, but also that Agnes wouldn't want her to offer any help. Freya passed the picture as she went down the hallway and she couldn't help her eyes lingering on that magical snowbound castle, those dark, mysterious woods. Should she ask about it? Could she? She sensed not, but wondered if she would ever get another chance. She reached the door and turned round to say goodbye. Agnes was right behind her in the passage. Freya's eyes widened in surprise and as she looked back at the old lady, she realized that she was smiling for the first time.

"Thank you for the flowers, my dear," Agnes said, taking Freya's hands between her own trembling, bony fingers again and squeezing them. "You must come again, soon."

FOUR

AGNES

East Prussia, November 1944

"Play for us, Agnes."

She would always remember those words. It was what her father used to say every evening after supper and her heart would fill with pride every time. It was the family ritual. After she, Papa, and Dieter had helped Mother with the dishes, they would troop through to the little parlor and Agnes would take her seat at the upright piano. Mother and Papa would settle down in the armchairs either side of the fireplace and watch her expectantly.

That last winter, even though it was becoming difficult to find fuel, Papa would always make sure there was a fire flickering in the hearth. Dieter would sit on Papa's knee, Claus, their ginger tomcat, would curl up on Mother's lap, and Agnes would play the opening notes of the latest piece she'd learned. She would take pride in delivering a flawless performance and, although she'd only been learning seriously for a couple of years, she could already rattle off many of Mozart's and Beethoven's sonatas from memory.

It would be just the four of them, in that cozy little room, while the snow from the East Prussian plain swirled outside, or the harsh winds howling in from the Baltic shook the windows. At those moments, totally absorbed in the act of making music, secure in the heart of her family, she would feel the warm glow of belonging. It was as if they were cocooned in their own little world here, completely insulated from the disturbing events that were happening all around them.

And when she'd finished playing and looked up from the keyboard at the rapt faces of the ones she loved, it was easy to forget that war was raging on the Eastern Front just a few miles from their sleepy little village, that refugees fleeing the fighting and the bombings in the cities were tramping past their house every day, begging for any scraps they could spare from the little food the family had, pleading for shelter in their outhouse against the harsh winter. It was possible to forget too that train-loads of soldiers passed through the local station on the way to the front every day and trainloads more of shockingly wounded men passed back that way toward the cities of the Reich.

"Why are we doing this to our young men?" Papa would say, shaking his head gravely. "What's it all for? What a waste of young lives."

"Hush, Jonas." Her mother would shake her head quickly and give him a pointed look. "You mustn't talk like that. You know what could happen."

"I'm in my own home, Helga. I can say what I want here."

"No one is safe to speak freely. You know that."

Agnes could guess why they were worried. Two men from the village, simple farm laborers, had been visited by the Gestapo in the dead of night and marched forcibly from their homes, never to been seen by their families again. They had been careless about what they'd said and to whom. Any friend, neighbor, or colleague could be a potential informer. Dissenting voices weren't tolerated by the local Nazi leaders, who themselves were under the control of the *Gauleiter* of East Prussia, Erich Koch, a brutal man. It was rumored that the two villagers, whose only crime had been to question whether Germany was on the right side of the war in the local *bierhaus,* had been marched to the labor camp a few miles away on the edge of the forest.

From whispered scraps of conversation picked up in shops and in the street, Agnes was aware that there were many camps like that, dotted around the countryside, where prisoners were kept penned up and forced to work. People hardly spoke about them, but most knew what they were for.

"They are full of Jews and Poles," she'd heard one woman say in the local market when she went there once with Mother. "They're our enemies, apparently, but I'm not sure why. They look as if they need help. Anyway, the authorities say that they have to be kept away from us for our own safety." Afterward, Agnes thought about what the woman had said and wondered why too.

Life used to be idyllic. Papa was the schoolteacher in the tiny village school, which both Dieter, aged eight, and Agnes, who was almost twelve, attended daily with twenty other children from the village and the surrounding farms. They knew everyone in their tiny community, from the humblest domestic workers on the nearby estate to the stationmistress, the foresters, farmers, and the local shopkeeper. The children were used to roaming freely across the vast open fields in all weathers and were welcomed into everyone's homes.

This gentle country life was all Agnes had ever known and, although she looked forward to occasional visits to the city of Königsberg, and summer trips to laze on the beach and swim in the Baltic at Zoppot, she was happiest of all exploring the fields,

woods, and backwaters around the village with Dieter and her
friends.

Mother was a local girl and although her own parents were
dead, her brother, Tomas, still farmed the family smallholding a
few kilometers outside the village. Agnes' family would spend
Sunday afternoons at the farm, walking there together along
the country lanes after church. It had been a feature of life
since Agnes could remember and she always looked forward
to spending the day playing with her two older cousins in the
farmyard among the cattle, pigs, and chickens, or in the fields,
climbing trees, wading in ditches, building make-believe homes
in haystacks.

Here, in this easterly backwater of Germany, so far away and
cut off from the rest of the Reich, they'd felt a long way from the
influence of Berlin and from the war. It was something they read
about in the newspapers, that affected people in the cities, not
them. But in the last couple of years, as the war on the Eastern
Front grew closer, the effects began to be felt even here.

Most of the young men in the village had been conscripted
to fight; the family had bid a tearful goodbye to cousins Gunter
and Joachim at the station, knowing they were being forced to
fight for a cause they didn't believe in. Suddenly life began to
feel very different. Food grew scarcer. Mother had to queue at
the butcher's in the nearby market town for the fattiest cuts of
meat and at the market for the poorest vegetables. Agnes was
often hungry; she was old enough to understand that there
wasn't enough to go round, but Dieter would cry if his tummy
rumbled and Mother would often slip him rations from her own
plate.

"He needs it more than me," she would say, but Agnes could
see that Mother was losing weight by the day; her dresses hung
off her shoulders and her previously plump and pretty face was
increasingly drawn and thin.

They still went to the farm on Sundays and Uncle Tomas

and Aunt Hannah would give them what they could spare to supplement their rations. Until recently the farm had produced a plentiful supply of eggs, milk, and vegetables; fresh meat too when they'd slaughtered a cow or a pig. But even that was drying up. Sundays on the farm seemed strange and unnaturally quiet without the boisterous cousins, and Uncle and Aunt were anxious and subdued nowadays.

"We have to feed the army now," Uncle Tomas had said last time they'd visited. "One of those Nazi officials came last week to tell us. He took an inventory of everything we have here. It is reserved for them. We will be punished for using more than our own allocation."

Everything was gradually changing and the old world was slipping away. They hadn't been to Königsberg for over a year. In the summer, news of air raids on the city by the British RAF had filtered through to the village. Agnes pored over pictures in the newspaper with a lump in her throat. The ancient cathedral and the magnificent castle with its museum, where Papa had once taken her to look at paintings, had both been devastated. Papa used to take them to the cathedral too to hear music recitals. As she stared at the grainy picture of the smoldering ruins, she remembered how, sitting there in the nave of the great building, listening to the exquisite music from the orchestra, she'd begun to understand its power over her. The thought that the beautiful, historic building had been destroyed instantly in a violent act of war brought tears to her eyes.

In the early autumn, news began to filter through of German defeats on the Russian front and Agnes picked up a new, heightened sense of fear among the adults around her. One night, she was so hungry she couldn't sleep. She lay wide awake, watching the pattern of the moonlight on the ceiling, listening to Dieter's gentle breathing in the bed beside hers. Mother and Papa were talking urgently, in low voices, but even so they floated to her through the still house.

"We have to leave here, Jonas. It's dangerous to stay."

"Where could we go?"

"Anywhere . . . to your cousins in Berlin maybe? Wouldn't they take us in?"

"No one's allowed to leave East Prussia. You know that. No one's allowed to evacuate. It might look like defeatism. That's the propaganda Erich Koch is peddling."

"There must be a way to get out of here."

"Besides, my darling, I couldn't leave the school. The children need me."

"You might have to anyway. You'll surely be called up to fight soon."

Her parents' fear affected Agnes. She began to worry about the future. None of them had wanted this war, wanted what the Nazis wanted, and yet they would be treated like those who did. If Germany lost, the Russians would come and if they did, they would overrun the villages, steal everything people had, torture and kill anyone they found in their path.

Even when Mutti and Papa weren't whispering feverishly at night, Agnes herself would lie awake, terror coursing through her as her imagination ran wild, picturing the horrors of what the future might hold. A few days after that first conversation, she heard something even more chilling.

"It's true, Jonas, isn't it? People were talking about it in the shop and there are posters up around the village. I've tried to keep the children from seeing them, but they will soon."

"It is true, my love. I heard it from the inspector who came to school today. It's terrible news. We've been led to believe that Hitler's army is invincible, but they've been driven back. The Red Army have broken through into East Prussia . . ."

"And that village? Nemmersdorf. Is it true what the Russians did to women and children there?"

"Hush, Helga. It's a terrible tragedy, but of course the Nazi propaganda machine is making the most of it to stir up fear . . ."

"We need to get out of here, Jonas. Before they come. Even though we are against the Nazis, the Russians won't know that, will they? They will treat all Germans the same: as the enemy."

Agnes lay awake, her mouth dry with fear as the voices became whispers and then the sound of Mother sobbing frightened her even more than the words she'd heard.

But they didn't leave; they couldn't. No one could leave without evacuation papers, and Erich Koch was not allowing any to be issued.

And a fortnight later, the worst happened.

Papa did have to leave to fight the Red Army on the Eastern Front.

That was the day Agnes looked back on as the point at which everything changed irrevocably. Before that, she'd watched as the world she'd grown up in slipped away bit by bit; bad things happened to everyone around them, her school friends, her relatives, but because life for herself, Dieter, and their parents had gone on much as normal until that point, nothing had seemed to truly touch them.

That fateful morning, she and Dieter had walked the few paces to the one-room school, hand in hand, as they always did. They took their usual places cross-legged on the floor; Dieter with the juniors and Agnes with the older children. It was November now and snow was already falling, the temperature close to freezing. Papa had opened up the school earlier to light the great cast-iron stove that sat in the middle of the schoolroom using the dwindling supplies he'd collected from the forest, but the wood was poor-quality and damp, clouding the room with smoke.

He began the lessons and the children sat on the floor and watched him attentively. As Agnes listened and watched her father, she noticed for the first time how sunken his cheeks were, how shabby his clothes, how like Mother's they hung off him because he'd lost so much weight. Her heart bled for this once proud, energetic man, who'd worked tirelessly to bring education to this forgotten corner, who looked now as if he'd almost given up hope.

When Agnes and Dieter got home with Papa that afternoon, a tall man in gray military uniform and polished leather boots was waiting in the parlor, his back to the fire. Mother was standing in the kitchen doorway, her face white and terrified.

"Jonas Kass?"

"Yes?"

"You are required for the *Volkssturm,* the Home Guard. All able-bodied men between sixteen and sixty are required to report. You've had your papers, but you did not report yesterday as ordered."

"I am a schoolteacher. It is an essential occupation."

"Your school is closed as of this moment. All men are needed now to fight in the Führer's name. Pack a bag. You will come with me right now."

There was no time to say goodbye properly. The officer waited in the parlor while Papa went upstairs. When he came down, ashen-faced, carrying his battered little suitcase, he held Mother to him for a last precious moment and whispered something in her ear. Dieter began to wail at the top of his voice as Papa picked him up and kissed him. Agnes was last. She didn't want him to see her tears, but she wasn't strong enough to resist; they spilled from her eyes and streamed down her cheeks anyway. He held her tight for just a second.

"Keep strong, my beautiful girl. And never forget your music."

Then he was gone. She leapt up and knelt on the windowsill, her face pressed to the glass, her heart breaking. Papa was marched off into the snow by the officer, head down, to join a group of other men assembled in the field opposite. He didn't look back. It was then that she knew: things would never be the same again.

"Why did he have to go?" She turned to Mother, her face wet with tears. Hadn't Papa said he would never fight for Hitler and the Nazis? That he hated everything they stood for? So, what had changed?

"You saw what happened. He had no choice, Agnes," Mother said, stroking Dieter's blond head as he clung to her, sobbing.

Dieter doesn't understand, Agnes thought. But Dieter did seem to know, as instinctively as she herself did, that Papa's departure marked a turning point in all their lives.

"Why don't you play for us, Agnes?" said Mother gently, her eyes glistening with tears. " 'Für Elise,' one of Papa's favorites, he would want that. It will take our minds off . . . off all this."

And so she got down from the windowsill, went to the piano, and tried to play, but her trembling fingers wouldn't work properly, and try as she might to put her heart into the music, without Papa there radiating love and approval it just didn't feel the same.

FIVE

The days were long and hard that winter after Papa had been taken away to join the *Volkssturm*.

The morning after he left, Agnes pulled on her school clothes as usual, shivering in the freezing bedroom. She packed her school bag and headed downstairs.

"What are you doing?" Mother asked when she noticed her school bag.

Dieter was already sitting at the kitchen table, eating an egg and a crust of bread. Agnes noticed the fear and anxiety in her mother's eyes.

"I didn't know what else to do."

"You heard what the soldier said to Papa, didn't you? They've closed the school."

"I thought I might walk along there anyway and see what's happening."

"I don't want you out there. Look at all those refugees on the road. Anything could happen."

Mother nodded toward the window. It was true. At that moment, a ragged family, wrapped in blankets and hunched against the weather, plodded past behind a horse-drawn cart, onto which was strapped a wardrobe, bedsteads, and suitcases. Like so many families, they were fleeing from the fighting, heading west. Most had passed through the village by late morning, trying to make it to the next town before nightfall.

A wave of panic washed over Agnes. How could she bear it here without Papa? How would the three of them cope without him? He'd always been the strong one, the one who made everything feel better in hard times. He always gave them freedom. Did his leaving mean the end to that ability to explore, to roam the countryside with her friends? If there was no school, she'd never be able to go out.

"Come and sit down, my love," Mother said, softening. "I had to give the last egg to Dieter, but there's still the end of the loaf."

Agnes sat down at the table and tore a hunk off the end of the homemade loaf.

"You have the rest. I don't want all this."

Mother shook her head. "No. You're a growing girl, you need it more than me."

Agnes spread some dripping from a bowl on the table onto the brittle bread, then bit into it. It tasted stale and was so hard she had to chew each mouthful many times, but her stomach was grumbling and there was nothing else in the house. Even so, she pushed half the bread aside.

"I don't want all of it," she said again, but Mother just stared at the plate. It worried Agnes that Mother had no desire to eat. She'd eaten less and less lately and hadn't touched anything after Papa had left the night before. She'd just sat in her chair by the dwindling fire, staring vacantly ahead. At nine o'clock, Agnes had taken Dieter upstairs and they'd gone to bed without a kiss from either parent for the first time since she could remember.

"What shall we do today?" asked Dieter now, his face bright at the prospect of no school. Mother shrugged. Without Father, she seemed at a loss to make any decisions.

"Why don't I just check what's happening at school?" Agnes put in quickly. "They might have sent another teacher out from Tilsit. Look, there's no one on the road now. The refugees have all moved on for today. I could go along quickly and be back in no time."

Mother sighed. "I suppose so. If you go straight there. Fetch my purse from the drawer. While you're out, you could check and see if they've got any flour at the store. We can make bread later if they have any."

"Can I come?" Dieter asked, but Mother shook her head. "Let Agnes go and check. If by some miracle the school is open, you can go back there with her."

Out on the frozen road, Agnes pulled her coat tightly around her and set off toward the schoolhouse. It was snowing steadily now, but the snow had turned to slush on the road and was churned and filthy from the carts and sleighs of the refugees passing through. Agnes' boots kept slipping on the ruts in the road. There was no one about and the cottages that lined the village street appeared shuttered and quiet. All the remaining men in the village must have been forced to go with Papa to join the army. There hadn't been many left anyway; only old men, a few others in essential occupations, and teenage boys. It was down to the wives and mothers now to look after the children and survive as best they could.

She reached the schoolhouse. As she'd feared, the door was locked. There was a sign in official-looking black lettering pinned to it:

SCHOOL CLOSED UNTIL FURTHER NOTICE.

She stared at the words, thinking of how, for as long as she could remember, Papa had been along here just after dawn to open up and to make the schoolhouse ready for the day. She thought of his boundless enthusiasm for his task and of the love and care he lavished on each and every one of his pupils. Just looking at that sign brought home to her cruelly how the absence of her father would leave a great void in her life. The loss of him was like an ache in her chest that felt as if it would never lift. Her heart twisted with pity as she thought of him tramping across that field in the snow, holding his battered suitcase. By nature a peace-loving, gentle man, he loved books and learning and was completely unsuited to physical work. She shivered at the thought of him having to learn how to shoot a gun and enduring the hardships of army training, let alone being forced to face the brutal Red Army.

"Has your papa gone too?"

Agnes turned to see her friend Liesel, her long blonde plaits caked in snow. Agnes nodded. "And yours?"

Liesel's father was a gamekeeper on the nearby estate. Count von Meyer, the local landowner, a member of the Nazi Party, had managed to keep his estate running by somehow refusing to allow key members of his staff to join up. He'd obviously lost the battle now, though. Tears stood in Liesel's eyes and Agnes put her arms around her friend. Liesel was normally a tough girl and Agnes had rarely seen her cry before. But now, they held each other close and sobbed together.

Afterward they wandered along the deserted road arm in arm to the store and Agnes asked for flour. Frau Eckert shook her head.

"I've nothing in, child. No flour or yeast. Only turnips. And the frost got those."

"All right, I'll take one."

Frau Eckert handed her a gnarled turnip in return for a few pfennigs. Agnes sighed. The turnip was a poor specimen; it was shriveled and looked almost inedible. As she handed the coins over, Agnes wondered how much money Mother actually had in the house. Would Papa still be paid his wages? Would he be able to send money home? She tried to swallow her anxiety, but the foundations of her world were crumbling away. Nothing felt certain anymore.

"What shall we do today?" asked Liesel as they left the shop. "There's no school. We could go and hang around in one of the barns on the estate."

"Maybe later. Mutti's expecting me home," said Agnes, but seeing her friend's face drop, she added, "Well, why don't you come along with me? I'm sure she won't mind."

Liesel smiled and tucked her arm into Agnes' again as they drew parallel with the village station. "Hey, look at that." Liesel pointed to a train that stood at the platform. "It's another one of those hospital trains."

Agnes had seen these trains many times before and the sight of wounded men wrapped in bloody bandages lolling against the windows horrified her. Each time she saw one, she was terrified in case she recognized her cousins Joachim or Gunter among the wounded. The faces of the soldiers inside looked so young, most of them little more than boys, only a few years older than Agnes herself. Once she'd been on the platform when one of these trains had puffed through slowly, the station bell clanging like a funeral knell as it passed. That time she'd been close enough to see the expressions on some of the faces. The numb, defeated look in their eyes terrified her.

"We're going to lose the war," murmured Liesel, her eyes on the grubby windows of the train. "And when the Russians come, they'll kill us all, or worse."

Agnes was silent. She knew what Liesel said was probably true, but the newspapers and radio stations were relentlessly positive. Although the Red Army had broken through to East Prussia briefly and carried out appalling massacres as well as raping and torturing innocent civilians in the village of Nemmersdorf, they'd been driven back by the German army after only a few days. Or at least that was what the Nazi propaganda machine would have everyone in East Prussia believe.

"That could be our papas in a couple of weeks' time, you know."

"Oh, please..." Agnes looked at her friend with tears in her eyes. Liesel had always spoken her mind and now she was only giving voice to Agnes' own unspoken fears.

The carriages suddenly lurched and the train started to move forward. The girls watched in horrified fascination as carriage after carriage packed with wounded men rolled past. As it slid by and gradually disappeared from view, another train appeared on the other side of the track, traveling in the opposite direction: a freight train, pulling long, low wagons stacked with crates and logs.

"Come on, let's go back to my house. Mother will be getting worried."

Agnes took a step forward, tugging her friend's arm, but as she did so, two boys, brothers they knew from the village, ran past them from the direction of the school and into the goods yard beside the station.

"Hey!" Liesel yelled. "Mickel, Franz...Where are you going?"

The older boy, Franz, turned and shouted over his shoulder, "To look for food. Don't tell anyone you saw us," he added breathlessly.

Agnes and Liesel watched, astonished, as the two boys crossed the station yard, ran a few paces alongside the train, and scrambled on board one of the flat wagons as the train gathered speed.

"They're going to get food?" repeated Agnes. "Wherever from?"

Liesel shook her head and they began to walk. After a few minutes she said, "Thinking about it, those trains go on a branch line through the forest. I once saw the tracks when I was walking on the estate with Papa, looking for a horse that had broken loose. He told me that the line goes close to the border with Lithuania. Maybe they're going there. Perhaps it's easier to get food there?"

"I don't suppose their mother knows," mused Agnes, thinking of her own mother, how she hadn't even wanted Agnes to walk along to the school alone that morning. Then she glanced down at the pitiful turnip she was carrying and an idea started to form in her mind.

SIX

The next morning when Agnes awoke, she didn't bother to pack her book bag or put on her school clothes. Dieter was still asleep in the bed beside hers. He'd started to cry the night before, after the miserable supper of watery, stewed turnip, and Mother had taken him onto her lap.

"When's Papa coming back?" Dieter had sobbed.

"I don't know, my darling. But I do know he'll be coming back to us as soon as he possibly can."

But Dieter was inconsolable. He'd wailed for his father for a long time and eventually cried himself to sleep.

Agnes left him to sleep and went downstairs. Mother was sitting in her usual place at the kitchen table, her head in her hands. As she looked up, Agnes saw shame in her eyes.

"There's no food, Agnes. Nothing for breakfast."

"We'll get something somehow. I can go back and try again at Frau Eckert's . . ."

"It might be better to go along to the farm this morning. Hannah and Tomas will give us what they can."

Agnes nodded, skeptical. Hadn't her uncle and aunt explained that they were forbidden from using virtually any of their produce? Everything was monitored by visiting officials on a regular basis. Had Mutti forgotten that?

"They'll probably have at least *something* to spare," said Mother, as if she'd sensed what Agnes was thinking.

Later that morning, after Dieter had got up, and after the last of the morning's refugees had passed through on the road, the three of them set off in the steadily falling snow to the farm. They trudged along the road lined with tall spindly poplars that ran through the snow-covered fields. They walked arm in arm in silence, Mother in the middle. Agnes couldn't help thinking of all the times they'd walked along that road with Papa on Sundays, singing and chatting as they went. She'd never given a thought then to how lucky they were to have each other, how contented she was. Now she wondered how she could ever have taken those carefree days for granted.

Aunt Hannah opened the farmhouse door before they reached it. Her face was blotchy with tears and lined with exhaustion. She opened her arms and embraced Mother.

"Helga! Tomas has gone. Two men came and marched him away yesterday. They have taken him off to fight the Red Army. They're taking all the men now. No one is spared."

"Oh, Hannah, Jonas has gone too," and the two women held each other.

"Come on inside." Hannah beckoned Agnes and Dieter into the kitchen. "You'll freeze to death out here."

They sat round the scrubbed table in the farmhouse kitchen in miserable silence. But the stove in the corner kept them warm and Aunt Hannah gave them some soup and bread. Agnes and Dieter ate hungrily while Mother and Hannah talked in hushed tones about their fears for the future.

"It was such a shock. I don't know what I'll do without Tomas. First, Gunter and Joachim, then all the farm boys. They went months ago. And now him."

"What about your Russian prisoners?"

When Gunter and Joachim had left for the front line, the local party official had arrived in a truck with two Russian prisoners of war to work on the farm. The two men, who looked like professional soldiers, not young conscripts, lived in a hayloft above one of the barns and had been given food and lodging in return for their work in the fields. They had fascinated Agnes, speaking in their mysterious language, and she'd tried to talk to them a few times. But they knew no German, so communication had been difficult.

"They were taken away. The party official said the farm was too small to bother with. They've been taken off to another farm, or a work camp, maybe."

After a short silence, Mother said, "Would you like some help with the farm, Hannah?"

Hannah shook her head. "There isn't much left to farm now. The army came with a truck and took the last of the pigs to slaughter yesterday. They'd already taken all the cattle, except one mangy old cow they didn't like the look of. There's only a few hens left."

"We should try to leave here," said Mother. "I've been saying it for weeks. If the Russians invade, what will happen to us then?"

Hannah reached out and grasped Mother's hand. "God forbid, Helga. Don't even think about it." Agnes saw an anguished but meaningful look pass between the two women.

"Look, why don't the three of you come and stay with me? I don't want to be here alone and we can fend together. There are the chickens, they lay the odd egg. There are probably some potatoes and turnips left in the near field under the snow. And at least we'd be together."

Relief spread across Mother's face. "Oh, Hannah. That's so kind of you. We'd be so grateful. Wouldn't we, children?"

Dieter looked up eagerly from troweling down his soup. "We're going to stay here? So, we can play in the barns?"

"Of course, Dieter." Aunt Hannah smiled indulgently and ruffled his hair.

Agnes nodded obediently. It was the right thing to do, she knew that, but out here, isolated on the farm, she would be further from Liesel and her other friends. And she would miss her piano.

They returned to the village before darkness started to descend over the frozen land, packed their bags, and slept in their own beds for the last time. The next morning, they drew the shutters across the windows, locked the house up, and retraced their steps to the farm, carrying their belongings in packs on their backs.

For the next few weeks, they stayed with Aunt Hannah in the farmhouse. The bedroom under the eaves where Agnes and Dieter slept was even colder than their room at home; Agnes could see her breath in the air as she got up in the mornings, but Aunt Hannah gave them quilts and blankets to keep them warm at night. They would get up early and go down to the kitchen, where Aunt Hannah kept the stove burning low at night. After breakfast, they would all go out to the fields nearest the farm with spades to dig in the snow for stray root vegetables that had been left behind in the last harvest. It was hard work in the bitter weather; chilblains quickly formed on Agnes' fingers and toes.

Aunt Hannah and Mother would make what they'd found into soup for their evening meal and each week, Hannah would risk slaughtering one of the chickens. Sometimes one of the remaining ones would lay an egg, but the corn they were fed on was running out too and their poor diet made them malnourished and stringy, so eggs were rare. If Agnes and Dieter weren't in the fields digging for vegetables, they would tramp across the fields to the one of the nearby thicket to collect wood for the stove.

The days were cold and hard and full of anxiety. As they worked in the fields, they would see the endless stream of refugees on the road heading west, heads bowed against the cold, all their worldly possessions packed on horses, carts, or sleighs. Agnes' heart ached for them, thinking of what those poor people had left behind and wondering what would become of them. Sometimes a straggling family, who'd got delayed on the road and weren't going to make it to the next town before nightfall, would knock on the farmhouse door for water or food, and Aunt Hannah would give them whatever could be spared. Sometimes, they would ask for shelter overnight. Agnes would show them to the loft above the barn, where there were warm blankets and mats for them to sleep on, and their horses would be given hay and water in the stable alongside the two farm horses. These refugees would share stories of the hardships they'd encountered on the road and of the fighting over the border that had come so close to their homes they could hear the pounding of shells and gunfire from inside their houses.

One morning, Agnes was working beside Dieter, digging in the snow for vegetables in a field beside the road. The usual column of refugees was passing at walking pace. Their voices floated across the still field to where Agnes and Dieter worked. Suddenly, a different sound split the air: the sound of aircraft approaching from the east. There were only seconds to react. Agnes grabbed Dieter's hand and dragged him toward a ditch on the other side of the field. She ran as fast as she could, her heart in her mouth as she pulled her brother along with her. They'd just reached the ditch and flung themselves into it as the aircraft burst into view. There were three of them, one after the other. The first two swooped down over the road and strafed the column with machine-gun fire. Something dropped from the undercarriage of the last plane; there was a sickening crash, followed by the sound of wood splintering. Agnes lay in the ditch, gripping Dieter's hand, listening to the screams coming from the road as the sound of the aircraft faded into the sky.

"Go back to the house and get Mutti and Aunt Hannah," Agnes said to Dieter, her voice trembling. She didn't want him to witness whatever horrors had taken place on the road. As he sped off across the field toward the farmstead, Agnes set off in the other direction, toward the column of refugees, her legs shaking with fear and dread.

As she reached the road, she saw the carnage wreaked by the bomb and the bullets. One cart had been hit directly. It was upturned, furniture and luggage strewn all over the road and verge. The horse lay dead on the roadside, its head a bloody mess. Agnes gasped and looked away. People were lying on the ground bleeding, moaning with pain. One man was stretched out on the road, motionless; a woman bent over him, crying.

Agnes had no idea what to do, but one woman sitting on the ground with a bleeding arm beckoned her over.

"You need to stem the blood for me," she gasped, her face deathly white. Agnes glanced around for something to do that with and saw an open suitcase with clothes spilling from it. She grabbed a shirt from the pile, ripped the sleeve from it and wound it round the woman's arm over the wound, securing it tightly.

As she was doing that, Mother and Hannah rushed up with water and towels and knelt down in the snow to help the stricken refugees as best they could.

By mid-afternoon, the horse and the dead man had been buried in the ditch beside the road, the broken cart and debris moved off the carriageway and the convoy of desperate people had moved on, the wounded bandaged up and taken on board another cart.

The event shook Agnes to the core. It was the first time

she'd witnessed the brutal reality of the war first-hand. The enemy would stop at nothing, firing at innocent civilians. Her heart was filled with fear for the future. How could they stay here with the enemy approaching? Shouldn't they be joining the column and heading west too? But if they did, would they ever be safe?

In the evenings, after Mother had put Dieter to bed, Aunt Hannah would turn on the crackly old wireless in the farmhouse kitchen and tune it to the RRG news broadcast, and the three of them would sit around the table and listen anxiously for news from the Eastern Front. The voice of the newsreader was relentlessly positive, triumphal even, and spoke of German victories in driving the Red Army back from the border. Agnes watched the faces of her mother and aunt.

The barking voice of Erich Koch, the *Gauleiter* of East Prussia, came across the crackling airwaves: "Citizens of East Prussia, victory for the Führer against the brutal Red Army is within the grasp of the Wehrmacht. No civilians will be authorized to leave the area. We must all keep the faith with the Fatherland."

"You don't believe what they're saying, do you?" Agnes blurted out one evening. "How can you? They will never tell us the truth. You know how many wounded soldiers come back through here every day, don't you? You've seen those trains."

"Please, Agnes. Please don't talk about our soldiers like that!" Mutti said, going pale and glancing at Hannah. Agnes stopped in her tracks. With all their men away at the front, it was natural that Mutti and Aunt Hannah clung to the propaganda like a lifeline.

An evening came, a few weeks after they'd arrived at the farm, when Aunt Hannah spoke to Mother and Agnes after Dieter was in bed.

"There's only one hen left now and she's our best layer. I don't think we should eat her, we should keep her for the eggs. Perhaps we could slaughter her for Christmas dinner."

Hannah and Mother had both grown noticeably thinner over the weeks at the farm and Agnes' own clothes had started to hang off her shoulders; her stomach constantly grumbled with hunger. She thought back to last Christmas, when Papa had made sure there was a tall fir tree in the corner of the schoolhouse and a smaller one at home. They'd decorated both trees with berries, sweet pastries and ribbons and had sung carols round the piano on Christmas morning. After that, they'd walked through the snow to the farm, still singing. Despite the rationing, Aunt Hannah had cooked two chickens, a mound of vegetables, and a plum pudding, and they'd exchanged simple presents. Mother and Father had given Agnes a solid silver bracelet with her name engraved on the inside, which she'd worn every day since. She knew it had come from Mother's own jewelry box, but was touched that Father had gone to the trouble of taking it to an engraver to make it her own.

How her heart ached to see Papa's smile, to hear his voice telling her stories, reassuring her when she felt daunted or down. She or Mother had returned alone to their house in the village once a week to make sure it was secure and to see if there was any post, but they hadn't heard a word from either Father or Uncle Tomas in all those weeks.

"I think you're right, Hannah," Mother said now. "We can make do with the eggs she lays and the vegetables from the fields for the time being."

"The time being?" asked Agnes. "How long will we be able to last like this? Every day it gets harder to find anything in those fields. We're having to go further and further. Soon there won't be anything left."

"Agnes, it doesn't help for you to talk like that." Mother's reproving eyes were on her. "What do you suggest we do? We just have to manage as best we can through the winter."

"Oh, Mother, you used to be all for leaving East Prussia. Why have you changed your mind?"

Mother dropped her gaze to the table. "You know what they say on the radio. No one can leave, it is forbidden. So, we just have to sit tight."

Agnes didn't reply and the three of them sat in strained silence in the flickering candlelight. There was defeat and resignation in Mother's tone. Agnes knew that she no longer wanted to leave because she was afraid that if she did, it would be acknowledging that the Russians were winning the war and that might mean admitting too that something terrible had happened to Papa; that he might never come home.

The next morning, Agnes got up before dawn and pulled on her warmest clothes. She was down in the kitchen before Mother or Hannah were awake. She scribbled a note and left it on the kitchen table. *Gone for food. I will be back soon. Agnes.*

The weak winter sun was struggling to rise over the distant forest of the estate as she set off along the hard road back to the village and, as she walked on, it broke through, a blazing orange line above the dark, tree-lined horizon. As she walked, she met several families trudging in the other direction, west, with their carts. She had to stand aside on the narrow carriageway and they looked at her with curiosity as they passed. A flock of geese rose from the mist above one of the ponds in a dip in the fields and flew away, honking mournfully in unison.

As she reached the outskirts of the village, daylight was creeping over the frozen land. She let herself into the darkened house and shuddered as she stepped inside. It felt even colder in here than out in the snow, where at least the winter sun raised the temperature a couple of degrees. She went straight up to her bedroom. There, she rifled through her drawers and put anything she could find of value into her knapsack: her collection of wooden dolls, her charm bracelet, a couple of silver ornaments her grandmother had given her. It tore her heart to think of parting with these precious things, but she could think of no other way to feed her family. She was about to embark on a perilous quest for food, catching a train to Lithuania, following in Mickel and Fritz's footsteps. She knew that Liesel would help her, but she would be risking her life and the thought of what she must go through sent shivers down her spine.

Down in the kitchen, she added some silver spoons and forks to her hoard and the knapsack was full. As she walked back to the front door, she noticed her piano. The lid was closed and the polished surface now covered in a film of dust. Putting her knapsack down, she went over to it and sat on the stool. She lifted the lid, placed her fingers on the familiar keys, and closed her eyes. She began to play. The notes of "Für Elise" flowed from her fingers and with her eyes shut, it was as if Papa was there, sitting in the armchair across the room, his smiling eyes on her, listening attentively. And as she played, her heart welled with all the pent-up sadness, the fear and anxiety that had been building since he'd gone. Her eyes quickly filled with tears and they flowed unchecked down her cheeks.

SEVEN

FREYA

Over the next few days, Freya's life quickly fell into a regular routine. She would leave her flat at the same time each morning and cycle over the river on Jesus Lock bridge opposite the house, across Jesus Green, through the town center, to spend her mornings studying in the Squire Law Library. Occasionally, she would bump into Finn as she left the house and each time he would make a friendly attempt to engage her in conversation. She remained polite but distant, hoping he would see her as a lost cause and give up. She concluded that he was either very thick-skinned and wasn't picking up on the fact that she had no desire to be friends, or he was somehow mocking her. As time went on, she decided it was definitely the latter. She often caught that amused twinkle in his dark eyes that had so caught her off guard the first time they met. That only served to make her more distant and less inclined to chat.

She was making steady progress with her research now and the more effort she put into her daily sessions in the library, the more her interest was kindled. The librarians had managed to dig out dozens of Inclosure Acts passed by Parliament. The painstaking task of deciphering them and distilling them into notes brought home to her just how much of rural England had been closed off by landowners during that period. The more she read, the more she was able to envisage first-hand how this had changed the landscape dramatically from wide stretches of open common land to much smaller fields bounded by hedges and fences. She also saw how this process had enriched landowners and forced the poorest farm workers to leave their homes to seek work in the growing towns and cities.

At her weekly meetings with Dan, she was able to reassure him, genuinely, that she was now making good progress with her work and that she was confident of achieving the deadline for completion of her thesis. But despite that—and she couldn't even admit it to herself properly yet—there was a niggling feeling at the back of her mind that she would prefer to be doing something different. Somehow, it all felt connected to the death of her grandfather, the guilt and pain she felt at the way their relationship had foundered in his last years, and her regret for the way she'd invaded his privacy by rifling through his precious papers as a teenager.

This feeling was intensified during the weekly tutorials with her first-year students. Each of them had chosen a subject to research and write a mini-dissertation on and she was mentoring them through that process. She'd given them a free hand to choose their subject matter and during their second session, she asked them what they'd chosen to write about.

The girls were the first to volunteer to speak about their ideas. One had chosen how the Beeching cuts to the railway network had transformed rural communities in the 1960s and another was tracing the impact of propaganda during the Cold War. A third student, one of the boys, wanted to study the repercussions of the First World War in mainland Europe, but when she asked the last—Lewis, who up until that point had hardly said a word—he'd hidden his face behind his laptop screen. He seemed painfully shy. His reply made her pause and stare at him.

"The history of Polish RAF fighters who came to England to fight during World War Two."

"Really?" she blurted and immediately regretted it because he blushed furiously, dropped his eyes to the floor, and began to stammer a response.

"Yes . . . but-but- is that a problem?"

She swallowed and felt the tension in the room. The others, who up until that time had been exchanging ideas freely, fell silent, clearly embarrassed by Lewis' awkwardness.

"No . . . no," she said, trying desperately to put him at his ease. "It sounds like an excellent subject for research. A great choice. I just wondered why you chose it, that's all."

There was an uncomfortable pause, then gradually he lifted his eyes to hers. "There was this old man in our village. He was Polish. I used to help him out sometimes in his vegetable garden. He came to this country as a fighter pilot during the war and . . . well, I'd like to find out more about it, I suppose."

Freya looked back at him, at his eyes shining with enthusiasm despite his shyness, and she was touched by his reasons. She had an image of an old man relating his war stories to this intelligent, thoughtful boy as they pottered side by side in his vegetable garden. It seemed such a contrast to her grandfather, bitter and angry, guarding his secrets to the grave, that it almost brought tears to her eyes. In the same moment, though, her mind flitted to Agnes, alone in her big old house. Lonely and prickly. "You must come again, soon," she'd said, enclosing Freya's hands in her papery, calloused ones. Now, hearing about how Lewis had helped his old neighbor, Freya felt a pang of guilt. That visit to Agnes, when she'd taken her the sunflowers, was several days ago now and she hadn't been back. She'd been meaning to, of course, but just hadn't had the time.

Lewis cleared his throat and she was jolted back into the present. She leaned forward and smiled at him.

"I think that's a great idea, Lewis. And it's wonderful that you've got a personal angle too. That will definitely give you inspiration and keep you motivated. I'll help you draw up a list of research materials."

After the students had left, Freya packed up her things to take across to the library. She thought of Agnes again and the prickle of guilt returned. She should have been back to see the old lady, of course she should. But she'd had no time. Each evening, after rushing back home from the library to shower and change, she'd set off across town in the other direction toward the Free Press to work the evening shift serving drinks behind the bar. But there was no excuse this evening, it was her night off. She vowed to pop in to see the old lady, ask if she needed any shopping or any errands done.

She slung her bag over her shoulder and set off to walk to the library. It would be good to have a night off so she could relax at the flat for once, but she was enjoying working at the pub more than she'd anticipated. From the very first evening it had felt good to be back there among old friends and to slip back into her old routine. She and Amber had immediately revived their old closeness and she realized how much she'd missed having someone to confide in, all those months she'd shut herself away in London.

But as she worked, pulling pints, chatting to customers, she couldn't help glancing at the door every time it opened, half expecting to see Cameron walk in. This had been their local when they'd lived in Grafton Street. In those days, if she was working and he wasn't on night duty at the hospital, he would come in to meet her to walk her home most evenings. While he waited, he would prop up the bar and have a swift pint. But, she reasoned, the pub was quite a long way from where he lived now at the hospital. He was unlikely to come in, knowing that Amber worked there and with all the memories the place must hold for him too.

She was actually relieved that Cameron hadn't been into the pub. It was beginning to feel as if she was getting over him and her old life. It also dawned on her that she could now even walk past the small, terraced house they'd shared for years in Grafton Street without feeling nostalgic.

Later, as she worked in her booth at the library, her mind kept returning to the surprise she'd had at Lewis' choice of subject and how her memories and regrets about her grandfather had come flooding back. Unable to concentrate, she checked her phone to see if Matthew had texted or called her. It was several days now since that painful and inconclusive conversation when she'd spoken to him on that difficult line from Kathmandu. She'd been waiting for him to call back ever since. On an impulse she grabbed her phone, left her workstation, and went outside, dialing his number as she walked.

It was cold outside and a wind was whipping up as she walked under the trees beside the river, waiting for Matthew to pick up. Autumn leaves were floating down from the trees, chased by the wind into little eddies and whirlpools on the path in front of her. She shivered and pulled her coat around her. She was about to give up when Matthew answered. Again, he sounded impossibly far away; further even than on the previous occasion.

"Freya?"

"Matt, where are you?"

"Oh, taking a break. I've filed my story. I'm trekking the Annapurna Circuit."

Freya felt a pang of envy. With his outgoing, adventurous personality, Matt had always managed to do such impossibly exciting things. She felt that old familiar feeling from childhood—

that he was out there embracing life, taking all it had to offer, leaving her standing. But she quickly swallowed the childish thoughts.

"Wow! Sounds exciting," she enthused. "So, how are you?"

"Yeah, good." He sounded breathless. "And you?"

"I'm good, but ... well, Matt. You promised you'd call me back the other day."

"Oh ... did I? Sorry about that. Things were pretty full-on in Kathmandu and I've been out of reception for a few days.... in fact, I'm really surprised you managed to get through now."

"Look, Matt ... we need to clear up that misunderstanding about Jah-Dek. Can't we just let bygones be bygones?"

"Well, Freya, I completely agree ..." His voice disappeared and came back again, even more distant this time. "We do need to talk about it ... it's just that now isn't a good time."

"Look, I said I'm sorry for what happened. Can't you just accept my apology?"

"Oh, Freya, it's not that simple." Again, his voice floated away, then returned, stronger this time. "Look, let's talk when I get home, shall we?"

"No." She was suddenly worried that he might hang up. "I don't want to wait until then. We need to clear this up. I can't stand being at loggerheads with you, Matt. Can't you at least begin to understand why I reacted like I did?"

"Look, let's not get into this now ..."

"I'm sorry, but I need to talk about it. About Jah-Dek's things—"

"Oh, that again." Even on the crackling, wavering line she knew he'd lost patience. "Listen, how about this? Why don't you just have them for yourself? That's what you've been angling for, isn't it? Just take them. It's time to move on, it's not worth arguing about."

"Oh, Matt, don't be like that. I didn't mean—"

"Well, I said it wasn't a good time to talk, didn't I?" His voice trailed off and was replaced by a crackling sound. This time his voice didn't return.

"Hello? Matt? Hello?"

There was no reply and with a heavy sigh, she ended the call. She wandered back to the library, staring at the ground, her spirits dashed. This feeling of not being at one with her brother made her feel as though the foundations of her world were crumbling away. And that painful conversation had just made things worse. Why couldn't he understand? She wasn't jealous that he'd been left Jah-Dek's things. It wasn't the things themselves that mattered. She stifled a sob. Everyone was slipping away from her: Cameron, Jah-Dek, Matthew . . .

Back in the library, try as she might, she found it harder to concentrate than before, so she packed up early and cycled home midway through the afternoon. It felt odd going back to the flat at that time; it reminded her of bunking off school early as a teenager. The house was quiet as she let herself in and propped her bike up in the hall. Up in the flat, she set her laptop and papers out on the table, ready to carry on with her work. She looked in the fridge for a snack, but there was nothing. The past few nights she'd eaten at the pub, in the corner of the kitchen, while the chef bustled round her, chatting and bantering. She smiled, thinking about it. With a sigh, she decided to pop round to the shop on Bridge Street.

As she left the house, she glanced next door and remembered her vow to go and see Agnes. It would have been much simpler just to cycle straight to the shop, but she took a deep breath, went up the next-door steps, and knocked on the door with the rusty black knocker.

It took Agnes several minutes to come to the door again and when she finally opened it in the usual way—peering through the gap, then closing it to release the chain with a lot of rattling—

Freya was shocked at how old and exhausted she looked. Her lined face appeared gray and unhealthy. Agnes stared up at Freya through her thick lenses, frowning as if she'd never seen her before. Freya wondered if the old lady had forgotten who she was.

"Miss Peters? It's me, Freya Carey from next door. I came round the other day, do you remember?"

Agnes frowned. "Of course I remember you," she snapped and Freya felt admonished that she might have implied that Agnes was forgetful. "Come on in, then," Agnes said grudgingly, holding the door open wide.

"I'm on my way to the shops actually. I was just wondering if you need anything while I'm there?"

"Oh. Well, that is kind of you . . ." There was a pause while Agnes frowned, lost in thought. "I need some cat food. And I've run out of bread, too."

"Of course. What sort of bread?"

"Oh, German rye bread, *Volkornbrot*. They sell it in Sainsbury's in Bridge Street. Two loaves, please."

"Oh!" Freya was taken aback. She opened her mouth to say that she'd only intended to pop round to the corner shop near the traffic lights, but Agnes had already turned her back and was shuffling down the hallway. "I will get you some money. My purse is in the kitchen."

"Oh, please don't worry, Miss Peters. It will be my treat," Freya said, gently pulling the door closed and heading off back down the steps to her bike.

The bread was hard to find and by the time she'd located it tucked away in a corner of the store and found the cat food and something for her own supper, there were long queues at the checkouts. She tapped her foot impatiently as she waited, but her irritation softened as she thought about how vulnerable Agnes was living alone.

. . .

Agnes was right behind the door this time when Freya rang the bell and she opened it straight away. She examined the loaves that Freya handed to her with a faraway look in her eyes.

"Thank you," she said at last, gruffly. "They are just right. Now, why don't you come inside? I can make tea."

Freya suppressed an urge to glance at her watch.

"All right," she said, stepping through the door and into the chilly hallway. She followed Agnes down the passage just as she had the other day. Once again there was that magical picture dominating the wall at the end of the passage; the fairy-tale castle on the crest of a hill, surrounded by snowbound woods. Where could that be? It must surely be somewhere in Poland, it was so much like the one Grandfather had had.

"Now, let me put these things in the kitchen." Agnes moved on down the passage toward a room at the back of the house. "How do you take your tea?"

"White, no sugar, please. I can help you make it," Freya said, hovering in the doorway behind her.

"No need. I can manage."

The kitchen was breathtakingly old-fashioned, a museum piece from the fifties or sixties: a white butler's sink under the window with a wooden draining board; no kitchen cupboards, just a tall cabinet with a drop-down cupboard door for a worktop and a scrubbed wooden table in the center of the room. Agnes filled a kettle at the sink and set it to boil on an ancient gas stove with wobbly legs. Then she picked up the loaves from the table, smoothed them down lovingly, and put them in a battered bread bin on the side.

Freya was bursting to find out where Agnes had come from.

"That picture in the hallway . . ." she began.

Agnes froze for a second, then clattered the tin lid of the bread bin down. She didn't reply.

"I was wondering where it was, the castle?"

"Oh, that . . . It's just a make-believe place," Agnes muttered, keeping her face averted. "It doesn't exist."

Freya swallowed and plunged on. "You see, my grandfather had a picture very much like that . . ."

"Your grandfather?"

"Yes. He was Polish. It was a painting of a Polish landscape . . . it's just, they look so similar."

Agnes frowned and shot her a sharp look. "Polish? Well, I can tell you, that picture is definitely not of Poland. Like I said, it's just make-believe."

The warning note in her tone told Freya to back off and not push the point further, but she sensed Agnes was not being straight about the painting. Her eyes wandered to the window and the overgrown garden with its sprouting buddleias, brambles, and elderflowers crowding the flower beds. It reminded her of her first day back in Cambridge and how she and her mother had stood at her bedroom window, looking down into the wilderness in the next-door garden, wondering who lived in this neglected house. At that moment the back door rattled and the ginger cat emerged through the catflap. He rubbed himself around Agnes' thickly stockinged legs.

"You're wondering how I cope in this huge old place, aren't you?" Agnes said suddenly.

"No . . . no . . . not at all." Freya colored, feeling caught out.

"I used to have it just so, you know, when I was younger. When I was working. My students would help out in the garden sometimes. Now there's just young Finn."

"Finn? My neighbor, Finn?"

"That's right. He comes to mow the lawn in summer. And if something needs fixing in the house, he will always do that for me. And he does my shopping. Once a week."

The kettle began to whistle, starting low, building to a crescendo.

"Well, that's very nice of him," said Freya as Agnes took the kettle off the stove. "I had no idea."

"He's a nice boy. Very kind. Only *this* week, I ran out of bread early . . . Your tea? White, no sugar, you said?"

"That's right."

"Sit down, please." Agnes motioned to Freya to sit at the table and, with a shaking hand, gave her a mug of tea. Freya sipped it tentatively, forcing it down. It was far stronger than she was used to. Agnes sat down opposite her.

"You look troubled." The old lady was leaning forward now, scrutinizing Freya's face with her old, rheumy eyes. This was so unexpected, Freya put her cup down suddenly, spilling some tea on the table.

"Do I really?"

Agnes nodded. "You see, I know about pain. I don't know *you* at all, but I do know a troubled soul when I see one."

"Oh, I wouldn't say that . . ." Freya began, disconcerted, having to swallow hard to make sure she didn't succumb to tears. Was it that obvious?

Agnes shrugged. "You look . . . quite lonely, I would say. But no matter."

Freya stared at her. *Lonely? Wasn't Agnes the lonely one here?* She felt the tables turning on her. She pursed her lips, a lump rising in her throat. Agnes was the most unlikely person she could think of to confide in, but she was here and she had asked. Perhaps it would be good to share what was troubling her.

"I suppose there is something . . ." she began, taking a deep breath, and Agnes nodded, her eyes fixed on Freya, waiting for her to go on.

"It's about my brother and my grandfather, Jah-Dek. As I said, he was Polish. Well, Jah-Dek died a few months ago . . ."

And the words tumbled out of her, words she hadn't spoken to her mother, to Amber, or even to herself before. She told Agnes all about what had happened between her and her grandfather, how he had shunned her after he'd caught her looking

at his wartime mementos, how they'd never regained the closeness they'd had before, how they'd grown more and more distant
and how he'd dealt her the final blow by leaving his treasured
personal effects to her brother.

"One of the worst things about it is that he *knew* how interested I was in his wartime story," she finished. "Matt had never
shown any interest in it really. Jah-Dek did it on purpose, to
hurt me. And it worked. And worse than that, now it's caused
a rift between me and Matt. It's just a silly misunderstanding,
but I'm worried it will escalate. He thinks I'm annoyed that
the memorabilia might be worth something. How can he even
think that? It's not that at all, it's so much more complicated than
that."

She stopped and wiped a tear away with the back of her
hand and became aware that Agnes' eyes were still fixed on
her. Slowly, the old lady reached out a trembling hand and took
Freya's.

"You mustn't blame your grandfather," Agnes said quietly.

Freya swallowed hard, trying to control her emotions. "Oh, I
don't blame him. I just wish he hadn't done what he did."

"War does terrible things to people," Agnes said, her eyes
grave. "It makes them bitter. It can change them forever."

There was loaded meaning in her words and Freya knew
that she must be speaking from personal experience.

"But your relationship with your brother is a precious one,"
Agnes went on. "It is *so* important that you don't drift apart
because of this. You *must* make sure that he understands why
you were so hurt."

"I've been trying to, but he's traveling at the moment. It's
really hard to speak on the phone."

"Well then, you must write to him! So much more can be
said in a letter. People are losing the art in today's world. Will
you promise me you will do that?"

Freya looked into Agnes' eyes hesitantly. The old lady was

staring at her, sharp as a button suddenly. What Freya had told her seemed to have galvanized her energy.

"Will you promise me?" Agnes asked again, squeezing Freya's hand. Freya had to suppress the urge to cry out. Where had this passion come from? What had happened in Agnes' own life to elicit such a reaction? Freya's curiosity was stoked even further, but she sensed that now wasn't the time to ask Agnes about her past.

"All right, I will. I'll write to him tonight," she said.

EIGHT

AGNES

East Prussia, December 1944

Agnes closed the piano lid and picked up her knapsack with a heavy heart. She left the house, locking it up carefully behind her. The street was deserted now, but the muddy tracks and footprints left by the straggling columns of refugees served to remind her that this wasn't just another peaceful morning like those of the past, when she and Dieter used to wander down the quiet street to school together.

She walked on as quickly as her feet would take her on the slippery surface, past the shuttered cottages, her knapsack now weighing heavy, past the quiet station, for the time being empty of trains, then on toward the village shop. She might as well try to buy food from here. If there was any, she would not have to make the dangerous journey to Lithuania. The door was shut, but Agnes pushed it open and went inside. She looked around at the empty shelves.

"Who is it?" Frau Eckert's voice came from the room behind the shop.

"It's me, Agnes."

Frau Eckert appeared in the doorway, her gray hair unbrushed and greasy. "Oh, Agnes, my child. I haven't seen you for weeks. I thought you'd all left."

"We're staying with Aunt Hannah at the farm, but we're running out of food."

"I have nothing. I'm sorry, child. I took the pony cart to the market at Tilsit for supplies two days ago. There was barely anything there and what I was able to get has been sold already."

Agnes' heart sank. She'd been hoping to be able to swap some of her precious belongings for food here, but it was increasingly obvious she would have to put her dangerous plan into action.

Frau Eckert wrung her hands. "It's so difficult to cope without my Hermann . . . and now he's never coming home." She sat down heavily on the stool behind the counter and buried her head in her hands.

"Oh, Frau Eckert, what do you mean?" Agnes' heart went out to the old lady. Her husband was in his sixties and suffered with rheumatism, but he'd been forced to join the *Volkssturm* just like Papa and all the other remaining men in the village.

Frau Eckert looked up. "He collapsed and died during training, when they first arrived at the barracks," she said. "I got the letter yesterday. He wasn't strong and the conditions were tough. I'm sure there wasn't enough food. I knew it would kill him."

"Oh, what dreadful news. I'm so sorry." Agnes dropped her bag, rushed round to the other side of the counter, and put her arms around Frau Eckert's heaving shoulders. As she tried to comfort the old lady, her mind began to race with anxious thoughts for Papa. What had become of *him* during army training?

Had he coped with the harsh conditions, the lack of nourishing food? Although he wasn't elderly like Herr Eckert, he was hardly fit for military service and in the hard months before he left, he'd lost a lot of weight. She thought of Joachim and Gunter, Uncle Tomas too. Aunt Hannah didn't talk about it much, but her anxious eyes and her knitted brows spoke volumes. Agnes realized now that every waking moment Hannah's mind must be on her boys; she must be sick with worry for her men at the front.

When Frau Eckert had stopped sobbing, she thanked Agnes for trying to comfort her. "Give my best wishes to your mother and aunt," she said. "At least you have one another. You must stick together always and help each other through these dark times."

Agnes squeezed Frau Eckert's hand, took her leave, and headed on through the village toward the estate. She passed through the imposing stone pillars beside the lodge house and walked on down the drive, which cut a straight line through a deep forest of fir trees. Snow lay thick on the ground and was so heavy on the branches of the trees, they drooped under the weight. Far ahead, at the end of the long drive, at the top of a rise, the landowner's castle, with its Gothic towers and spires and fairy-tale parapets, dominated the horizon. She'd always been fascinated by the place—it held a sort of mystical quality, especially when shrouded in mist in the mornings and lit up in the twilight at dusk—but she'd never even been close to it.

As she walked, she heard the engine of a vehicle approaching behind her and the impatient honk of a horn. She stepped off the road to let the car go past. It was a shiny black Mercedes, the peaked cap of a chauffeur visible through the windscreen. She recognized the car as belonging to Count Meyer, whose family had owned the castle and the surrounding land since the time of the Teutonic Knights. She felt a sudden flurry of nerves as the car got closer. Would the Count stop and question her presence on the estate? She'd no desire to come face to face with a prominent member of the local Nazi Party. The car slowed down and she hung her head as it crawled past, the snow chains on its wheels clanking. Through the steamy rear window, the Count glowered at her from behind pebble glasses and she wished the ground would open up and swallow her, but once it was past her, the car gathered speed and continued on toward the castle.

Liesel's cottage was one of a group of estate workers' homes in a clearing halfway down the long drive. Liesel's mother, Gerta, came to the door when Agnes knocked. As with all the other women, Gerta's face was drawn and anxious. From inside came the sound of Liesel's two young sisters playing.

"Agnes! How are you? How is your mother?" Gerta drew the door back and beckoned her inside.

"Mother is, er—" But Agnes had no time to finish answering before Liesel appeared and threw her arms around her.

"I'm so pleased to see you! Would you like some bread?" she asked. "You look famished. I'm sure we can spare a couple of slices, can't we, Mother?"

"Of course." Gerta beckoned her toward the table, where half a loaf sat on a plate. Agnes sat down and ate hungrily while Gerta brought her some hot milk.

"We are lucky, here on the estate. Although food is getting scarcer now, there is a little left for the families. We at least have flour to make bread."

Agnes couldn't help looking at her with pleading eyes, but Gerta quickly retracted the comment.

"But in fact, I've almost run out of flour now. I *would* give you some to take home, you know I would, but I have to think of the girls . . ."

"Of course," said Agnes, disappointed.

Gerta hurried away to the kitchen and Agnes quickly got to the point of her visit: "Liesel, things are getting desperate at the farm. I need to go on the train to find food from wherever Franz and Mickel went that day we saw them at the station. Do you know where they went?"

"Oh, Agnes, you must be careful."

"You could come with me. We could both go."

Liesel shook her head and glanced at her little sisters playing in front of the fire. She lowered her voice: "I can't. I have to stay here."

"Why?" Agnes was puzzled; Liesel would normally have jumped at such a challenge. In fact, she'd been relying on her doing just that.

"I'm not supposed to say anything," Liesel's voice was a whisper now, "but I'll tell you if you can keep a secret."

"You know I can. What is it?"

"You mustn't breathe a word . . . not to anyone."

"I won't."

"Well . . . Count von Meyer is planning to leave East Prussia and he's going to take most of the families on the estate with him. He's chartering a special train. The word to leave could come at any time. Even today."

Agnes stared at her friend, fear prickling her scalp.

"I don't understand . . . isn't von Meyer one of those people saying that Germany is winning the war? That we must all stay in East Prussia and there's no need to evacuate?"

Liesel shrugged. "What they say in public for the radio and the newspapers is not what they really think. You know that."

Agnes felt anger rise in her chest. "But what about everyone else?" she blurted. "People who don't have a Count von Meyer to help them evacuate without papers?"

Liesel looked down at the table, shamefaced. "I know," she stammered, "it's not right. But there's nothing fair about this dreadful war. Believe me, if I could take you with me, I would."

Agnes got up. "I need to go," she said, stung by the unfairness of all this and the fact that Liesel was just going along with it without protest. Her friend got to her feet too.

"Agnes, please. Don't be like that. I *have* to go with Mother. She needs help with the little ones, I don't have a choice."

Agnes walked toward the door and Liesel followed, tugging at her arm. "Look, I'll show you the railway line where the goods trains pass through. They're heading for Schmalleningken near the Lithuanian border. There's a branch line in a cutting in the middle of the forest, like I said before, and the trains slow down to go through it. You could jump onto one of the trucks there. It's only half an hour to the border."

"How do you know all this?"

"I talked to Franz the other day. I saw him at the station again. I came to see you, actually, but your house was all shuttered up. I thought you'd left without saying goodbye. I was worried about you."

Agnes was wrong-footed momentarily. She turned back, her hand on the doorknob. "I'm sorry, I should have let you know where we were going. Everything happened so quickly."

"I understand," Liesel said, with a sympathetic smile. "So, shall I show you the line?"

Agnes nodded and they left the house. As they went out, she shouted goodbye to Gerta, careful to keep her voice casual, as if this was just an everyday farewell. But as she did so, it came home to her with a jolt that she had no idea when she would see Liesel and her family again.

The girls walked side by side a little way down the drive in the direction of the castle. Then Liesel led Agnes off the road and down a footpath that wound its way between the dense evergreens. The snow was thick underfoot and it was heavy going. Agnes was soon breathing hard, her knapsack weighing heavy on her shoulders. She had to concentrate to avoid falling over. As they struggled along, Liesel related how Franz and Mickel had told her they'd jumped off the train just before the outskirts of the border town. They'd made their way through some woods and into Lithuania, avoiding the Russian checkpoints. A couple of kilometers through the woods was a little town, where there was a small market.

"They've done it a few times, Franz said it was quite easy." Liesel stopped walking and pointed. "Look, Agnes, there's the track up ahead."

They'd reached a break in the trees and the ground descended steeply in front of them toward a long, deep cutting, where a single-track railway line ran. A train must have gone through within the past couple of hours because there was only a powdering of snow on the rails.

"This is it," said Liesel. "It's much safer to get on here than at the station, where people might spot you."

Agnes swallowed hard and stared down the steep bank at the tracks below. Was she really going to do this? Alone? When she'd set out from the farm, she'd been counting on Liesel coming with her. But even as she stared, the track started to vibrate and hum.

"There's a train coming. You need to get down there."

"Liesel . . ." Agnes squeezed her friend's hand and kissed her cheek. There was no time to say goodbye properly. She let go of Liesel's hand and slithered down the side of the cutting, snow filling her shoes and soaking the back of her trousers. When she landed at the bottom, she turned and looked back up at Liesel, who stood there peering down, clutching her hands together anxiously. The tracks were humming now and the air was filled with the roar of an engine approaching around a bend. She pressed herself against the bank, drawing back behind some snow-covered undergrowth; then the great black engine burst into view, filling the cutting, steam and smoke billowing from it, its pistons pumping. Soon it was parallel with her and a blast of heat enveloped her as it steamed past, hissing. Then came the rattle of the trucks that followed it.

The train was traveling slowly, but close up, the trucks looked enormous—far too high for Agnes to scramble on board.

Unlike the train they'd seen at the station, this one was pulling high-sided, rusting wagons. Agnes began to panic as they rattled past her, wondering if she'd ever get on, but to her relief, after them followed low flatbed trucks carrying logs. Here was her chance, there was no time to hesitate. She flung herself forward onto one of the trucks, her legs flailing free. There were a few tense seconds when she thought she would slip off, but she got a handhold on a chain holding the logs in place and managed to heave herself on board.

Once she had pulled herself upright, she realized there was nowhere to sit, so she perched precariously beside the mound of tree trunks, hanging onto one of the chains. By the time she was settled, the train had traveled several kilometers clear of the cutting, but was still moving through dense forest. As it rattled on between the snow-covered trees, Agnes gradually edged herself to the back of the wagon, where she managed to conceal herself and her knapsack in a gap behind some longer logs. There she crouched, as the train bumped and swayed, hanging onto the logs for dear life.

It was another fifteen minutes before the train was clear of the von Meyer estate. Sitting on the wagon staring backward, Agnes got a distant view of the castle perched on the hill as the train rattled on beyond the forest and through open farm-land. The castle was almost mythical in its beauty, shrouded in mist, surrounded by snow-covered forests, but the sight of it now brought tears to her eyes. It would soon be deserted, along with everyone who lived there and who had tended the farm-land, forests, and animals of its vast estate for generations. What would happen to that land and buildings if the Russian army overran the place? And what would happen to Liesel and her family on their long journey west? Would Agnes ever see her friend again?

The train rolled on past pretty villages like her own, with their neat farmsteads, square Lutheran churches, and low stone cottages with long, sloping roofs. She spotted several deserted stork nests perched on rooftops, disheveled straw and sticks hanging from precarious perches, left for the winter as their occupants headed for warmer climes. Agnes loved the beauty and simplicity of the East Prussian countryside and the thought that all this could soon be overrun and destroyed by Russian tanks and troops made her heart heavy with a deep sadness.

NINE
AGNES

The train was rumbling across a steel bridge and Agnes peered down at the stretch of black water below her. This must be the Memel River, which snaked its way from Lithuania all the way across East Prussia to the Baltic coast. A few minutes later, they were passing sheds and warehouses and the roads began to look increasingly built-up. This was surely Schmalleningken, the last East Prussian habitation, just inside the border. There were bound to be Nazi troops in the station, checking trains coming into the town. Agnes knew she had to leave the train now. Her heart thumping, she slung her knapsack over her shoulder, let go of the chains, and shifted herself forward to the edge of the truck. The train was traveling too fast to jump off safely, the ground sliding past in a blur. At last it slowed a little and she took a chance. Throwing her knapsack down first, she flung herself clear of the tracks, landing heavily in the snow on a bank.

She picked herself up and watched the rear of the train disappear off down the track; then, glad that she'd landed unscathed, she picked up her knapsack, dusted the snow off her clothes, and looked around for clues as to where to go. There were no buildings in this spot, just a deserted farm track running alongside the track, bordering a field. Beyond that field was a huge forest of evergreens, like the one she'd just come through. Agnes set off toward the forest, tramping on through the dirty snow, and quickly realized that many feet must have tramped this way before her. Footprints had made a track across the field, which led into the wood.

This forest was less dense than the one on the von Meyer estate. There was space between the trees and snow lay on the ground. Agnes was relieved; she'd been wondering how she'd ever navigate her way through a thick forest, but there was a path to guide her and light from the pale sky above. A few meters in, she disturbed a deer eating bark from a tree. Startled, it leapt off through the undergrowth. She carried on, wondering how far it would be to the other side, but as she walked, she got the sudden feeling that she wasn't alone. More than once she could have sworn she heard the sound of voices on the breeze. She stopped twice to listen, her skin prickling with fear, but heard nothing. She carried on with an uneasy feeling. This was so risky. Lithuania was occupied by the Russians but there was no fighting in this area. Would there be soldiers here? Suddenly she was scared. Why had she taken such a risky step? Surely, if she'd tried harder she could have found food somehow in or near the village, without going to these lengths. Suddenly a figure darted out from behind one tree and ran across the path in front of her. It was a long way ahead and at first, she thought it was another deer, but deer didn't run on two legs.

She froze. Her pulse pounded in her throat and her mouth was dry. Should she turn round and run back to the railway line? It would mean going home empty-handed. She took a deep breath and walked on slowly. She reached the spot where the figure had darted across and looked down at the snow. Sure enough, there were human footprints crossing the path. She swallowed.

"Hello?" she called tentatively. She waited, her heart pounding, but there was no reply. She walked on cautiously, looking all around her, checking back over her shoulder, but the whole forest seemed still and quiet now.

At last, she reached a rough road on the other side. Rolling farmland stretched away ahead of her. Little farmsteads dotted here and there, nestling in the valleys. It looked very much like the countryside around her home. She stepped out onto the road and strained her eyes in each direction, wondering which way to walk. She could just about make out the shape of buildings on the horizon to the east, so she set off that way. It was hard walking through the snow. A couple of farm carts trotted past; the occupants stared at her but didn't stop to offer her a ride.

She was tired by the time the little town came into view. It didn't look much bigger than her own village. Was this the same place Franz and Mickel had found? But as she drew closer, she saw something that made her blood run cold. The road was long and straight, and up ahead, she could clearly see a barrier across it, slung between two oil drums. An armored vehicle was parked up on the verge and two soldiers leaned against it, smoking. Russians! This was a Russian checkpoint. Agnes began to panic, looking around for another way to get into the town. It was surrounded by rolling farmland, blanketed in snow. There was no choice, if she didn't want to go home empty-handed. She plunged into the snow on the roadside, jumped over a drainage ditch, and was soon skirting around the edge of the town across the fields. When she judged she was far enough away from the main road, she cut back toward the town, finding her way onto a quiet street through a farmyard, where chickens and ducks scattered in every direction at her approach.

On the other side of the farm was a quiet street, its houses shuttered against the cold. She had no idea which way to turn but began walking toward what she thought must be the center of the little town. It was so quiet, she began to think it must be the wrong place. Then she turned a corner and there was a little town square with a few market stalls set up around the edge. The farm carts that had passed her on the road were parked up with others on one side and a small crowd of people bundled up in winter clothes milled about among the stalls. Her heart sank when she realized that there were soldiers mingling in the crowd, in greatcoats and fur hats, rifles slung casually over their shoulders.

The stalls were piled with vegetables, potatoes, sacks of flour and loaves of bread, and on a rail above one of the stalls hung rows of chickens. Her heart leapt at the sight, but a new worry set in that had been niggling at the back of her mind since she'd got aboard the goods train. Would she be able to make herself understood? She knew virtually no Lithuanian. And what if one of the soldiers stopped her? Putting those thoughts aside, she took a deep breath and approached the stall selling poultry. The stallholder had a ruddy face and greeted her in a jovial manner, but she had no understanding of what he said to her. She pointed to the chickens, swung her knapsack off, and pulled out two silver spoons. The stallholder's eyes crinkled in mirth.

"Ah! Little German!" he said, smiling broadly, but his eyes flicked to the crowd and he lowered his voice. Through gesticulations and sign language they managed to reach a bargain. He gave her two chickens in return for two silver spoons and a knife. He wrapped the chickens up in paper and Agnes packed them carefully into her knapsack. The jovial man was all too willing to help her, making discreet eye contact with the neighboring stallholder, who was selling potatoes, and ushering her toward that stall. All the stallholders seemed to understand the need to ensure that she didn't come to the attention of the soldiers. After less than half an hour, her knapsack was packed full of food and she'd parted with all the valuables she'd brought with her. Anxious to start the long journey home, stuffing carrots into one of the side pockets in the knapsack, she began to walk away. As she did so, she felt a firm hand on her arm. Shock washed through her, but she looked up into the unshaven face of a roughly dressed farmer.

"You come with me, girl," he said in heavily accented German.

Agnes tried to pull her arm away and shook her head. "I have to go home," she said.

"I need help on my farm," he said gruffly. "I pay good money."

"No. Thank you, but I have to go home."

He scowled, let go of her arm, and shambled away. Agnes hurried on, back along the road to the farm, through the farmyard again, and out of the village across the fields. She was a little shaken by the encounter, but at least it hadn't been one of the Russian soldiers.

The knapsack was heavy and her legs were tired, but her heart was lighter now. She'd managed to get food for the family. The chickens and vegetables in her knapsack would last them a couple of weeks if they were careful. It would take them past Christmas and there'd surely be no need to slaughter their last laying hen. As she walked, she thought about the apparent abundance of food in this little Lithuanian community. What a contrast it was here to just a few miles away, where the Nazi government was bleeding the country dry, taking the produce of the land from the mouths of its citizens to feed its failing army.

As she emerged from the last field, skirting around a farm on the edge of the little town, she peered back down the road, checking for Russian soldiers. Her heart slowed down a little. There was no one around. Turning, she set off along the road toward the wood. All she had to do was to cross that, then she would be back in East Prussia. But she had only gone a few steps when there was a shout from behind her: a Russian voice. Her blood ran cold.

"*Devochka*! Girl! Stop!"

Her shoulder was seized and someone turned her round, and she looked up into the rough, weather-beaten face of a soldier. She took in his fur hat, his trenchcoat, the gun slung casually over his shoulder. He was saying something to her. Something she couldn't understand. His face was stern, his voice angry, urgent. What was he asking her? And how could she say anything without giving herself away as a German? An enemy. She stood rooted to the spot, staring up at him, her eyes wide with terror. This was it. This was the end for her. How could she have been so stupid as to think she could get away with this?

TEN

FREYA

Cambridge, Present Day

As soon as she got home from Agnes' house that afternoon, Freya sat down at her table in the bay window and opened her laptop. She was deeply affected by the entreaty in the old lady's eyes and her passionate insistence that Freya must do everything she could to heal the rift with her brother. As they'd parted at the front door, Agnes had squeezed Freya's hands again, looked at her earnestly, and said, "You won't forget that promise you made me, to write to your brother, will you now?"

Freya had assured her that she wouldn't forget and that she was going straight home to do just that. Agnes had spoken about her writing a letter, but Freya and Matthew had never communicated that way. They normally texted or messaged each other, and birthday and Christmas cards were about the only things they had ever penned and sent through the post. Freya guessed that an email would do just as well and in any case, how long would a letter take to get to Nepal? She had no idea where to address it to. And anyway, the post office in town would certainly be closed by this time.

As the light gradually faded over the river opposite, she found Matthew's email address and started to type. It was tough going. At first, she even struggled to form a sentence—everything she wrote looked so clumsy and insensitive. She made many false starts before deleting what she'd written and starting all over again.

In the end she gave up and deleted everything she'd written. She stared at the screen. Despite her promise to Agnes, she just couldn't do it. She wasn't ready to reach out to Matthew yet, let alone apologize for the misunderstandings and seek his forgiveness. Instead, with a sigh, she turned back to her work. But as she did so, she noticed an email popping into her inbox from her student Lewis Vaughan. She clicked on it, curious:

Dear Freya, I've started my research as discussed at our supervision this morning and am sending some links for you to look at.

She knew she should be getting on with her own research, but she couldn't resist clicking on the links Lewis had sent, and was quickly drawn into the story of the Polish fighter pilots who came to England in 1940. Once she'd started reading, she couldn't stop. She discovered that when German forces invaded Poland in 1939, they overwhelmed the Polish army and air force in a matter of weeks. Many Polish fighter pilots made their way to France, wanting to help in the struggle against the common enemy from outside their own country. When France was itself invaded, these airmen were transported to Britain and absorbed into the RAF, forming two complete squadrons. Freya was astonished to discover that there were over 2,000 of them.

Many Polish fighter pilots distinguished themselves in the Battle of Britain and many went on to stay in Britain and become British citizens.

Freya had been vaguely aware of all these facts, but because of her grandfather's sensitivity about the past, particularly the war, she'd never actually read about it properly before. It made her think of him, proud and bitter to the end, difficult and demanding, putting up barriers so no one could ever see his pain. It was becoming clear to her now what he must have gone through, having to leave his fallen country and fight for it from afar, never returning to the place he'd been born, had grown up, and had once called home. She recalled that when he was still mobile, he would put on his suit on Saturday evenings and go down to the Polish club in the backstreets of Nottingham where he'd settled for several vodkas and to while the evening away with other displaced Polish men of his generation. He would stagger home in the small hours, swearing in Polish, and her grandmother, always sweet and patient, would help him to bed.

After reading those papers about the Polish airmen, Freya had to force herself to turn back to her own research, which suddenly seemed dull and irrelevant in comparison. She spent the rest of the evening poring over some 1850s appointments of commons commissioners and a poem she stumbled upon by an early social reformer, lamenting the enclosure of common land, the depopulation of the countryside, and the pursuit of wealth.

Finn was in the hall the next morning when she came downstairs, unlocking his bike. As usual, her heart sank when she saw him there, smiling up at her. Why was he always so cheerful?

"Good morning! Everything OK with you this morning?" he asked.

Freya nodded grudgingly. "Morning."

"I hear you went to the shop for Agnes yesterday afternoon?"

Irritation began rising inside her. How did he know that already? And what business was it of his anyway? But then she softened, remembering how Agnes had sung his praises.

"Yes, I did actually. She gave me a cup of tea too."

Finn unlocked his bike and moved it away from the wall. "Now, *there's* a turnaround," he said with a twinkle. Freya opened her mouth to retort, but he went on, "Well, you certainly made an impression on her. She couldn't stop talking about you when I popped in with her evening paper on the way home from work."

"Really?" Freya said in alarm, hoping Agnes hadn't divulged that she had confided in her, that she hadn't told Finn that Freya had sat there weeping at her kitchen table.

"Yes, really. She was genuinely touched that you'd thought about her."

"Well, I'm more than happy to help her out," she found herself saying. "She said that you do her shopping, but if you ever need me to step in . . ."

"That's kind, but I can manage the shopping. It's company she needs more than anything," Finn said, opening the front door and motioning Freya to push her bike out ahead of his. "If you could pop in with the evening paper sometimes, she'd love that. I sometimes have to work late at the workshop, so it can be difficult. And she loves to read the news."

"Of course. I'd be happy to do that. I normally come home from the library at six-ish. I can do it this evening, if that would help?"

"That would be great. Thanks so much, Freya. Agnes would love that and it would be a weight off my mind."

They carried their bikes down the front steps together and

set them down in opposite directions as usual. She turned to say goodbye and noticed that Finn was smiling at her, a genuine smile this time, not his teasing, mocking one. His dark eyes were full of warmth. Her instinct was to look away, but something inside told her not to be so prickly. What harm would it do to return his smile? So she held his gaze and smiled back, for a fleeting moment, then turned and pushed her bike in the direction of the bridge.

That evening, she bought a copy of the *Cambridge Evening News* on her way back from the library and dropped it in with Agnes.

Each time Freya went in for a cup of tea, Agnes would ask her if she'd heard from Matthew and it pained Freya to have to tell her that she had not. What she couldn't say, though, was that she hadn't actually written to him yet. Agnes always gave her such a sympathetic, pitying look that she began to dread the question, not just for her own sake but for Agnes' too, because the brother-and-sister rift clearly pained her as well. It pained Freya too that she was lying to Agnes; that she hadn't been able to write the email to Matthew.

It was eight thirty and she wasn't due to meet her students in college until ten o'clock. She had time to pop round and check on Agnes. Agnes took her time answering the door when Freya knocked. She was wrapped in a faded red candlewick dressing gown, her white hair covered in a hairnet, feet clad in stout zip-up slippers. Claus the ginger cat rubbed himself around her legs, meowing. Agnes' face was colorless that morning, her eyes vague and bloodshot.

"Oh, I'm so sorry, Agnes. I hope I didn't wake you?"

"Not at all. I was just getting up. Is something the matter?"

"No. I just wanted to see if you're all right."

"Oh, I'm fine. But why don't you come on in for a minute?"

She held the door open and Freya followed her down the

passage to the kitchen, noting with concern how stiffly Agnes was moving that day and with such difficulty.

"Have you time for a cup of tea?" Agnes asked over her shoulder.

"Of course, but please let me make it."

"No, no, I can manage," Agnes insisted, but she moved slowly, her joints clearly stiff, and Freya could see how painful it was for her to lift the kettle and light the cooker.

When she finally set two mugs of tea on the table and sat down opposite Freya, she asked if she'd heard from Matthew: "There's nothing more important than your family. Especially a brother."

There was a brief silence and Freya looked down at the tan-brown tea in her mug.

"I'm so sorry, Agnes. I haven't been straight with you. I haven't been able to write to him yet. It doesn't feel right, I need more time."

"Oh!" Agnes' face fell. "But you promised."

"I know, I know. And I will do it . . . as soon as I'm able."

Agnes fell silent. "Your bond with your brother is the most important thing in the world," she muttered.

Freya didn't know what to say in response. She so wanted to find about more about Agnes, but she knew how prickly and sensitive the older woman could be. Surely they knew each other well enough now for her to ask? Was now a bad time? No worse than any other, she reasoned. She took a deep breath and took the plunge: "I was wondering, do *you* have any family, Agnes?"

Agnes immediately stiffened, drew herself up visibly, and pursed her lips.

"I have no one now," she said curtly. "I'm quite alone in the world." Her tone discouraged further questions, but Freya wasn't put off.

"I've often wondered . . . you said you came to Cambridge on a scholarship in the fifties, but where did you come from? Which country, I mean."

Agnes turned her gaze on her, frowning deeply, and Freya thought she might refuse to answer, or tell her to leave. Was it really such an impertinent question? Was it really so wrong to ask, when they were getting to know each other as they were? But then Agnes spoke.

"Lithuania," she said sharply. "I came from Lithuania."

"Oh!" So it wasn't Poland then, after all. Freya was surprised. "So that castle . . . the one in the picture? Is that in Lithuania?"

The frown deepened. "That castle is *not* in Lithuania!" Agnes snapped. "Didn't I tell you the other day? Have you forgotten that already? That place, that castle, that country, it doesn't *exist*. I don't know why you keep on asking about it."

Agnes was trembling now. Angry color had risen in her cheeks.

"I'm so sorry, Agnes," Freya said, putting her hand out to take Agnes' on the table, but Agnes snatched hers away. "I really didn't mean to upset you."

Agnes just shook her head and didn't reply. They sipped their tea in silence, listening to the sound of cars and lorries rumbling past on the main road, the birds in the garden. Freya tried several times to move the conversation on, but each time Agnes rebuffed her with a snappy response or a withering look. Once she'd finished her tea, she noticed the time on Agnes' kitchen clock: it was almost half past nine.

"Look, I'm sorry, but I have to go now," she said, getting to her feet. "Are you going to be OK? I'll come back this evening with the paper."

"You don't have to," muttered Agnes.

"But I'd like to." Freya got to her feet. "See you later on."

She got up and left the room, feeling guilty about having let her curiosity get the better of her and asking those questions.

Was Agnes not even going to say goodbye? But as she got to the front door and put her hand on the knob, Agnes shouted from the kitchen: "I'm glad about your brother."

Freya smiled to herself as she called goodbye, hoping that by the evening, her transgression would have been forgotten. But the exchange with Agnes kept returning to her mind all day; throughout her supervision with the students, while they were discussing titles for their dissertations and research ideas, Agnes' bitter face kept returning. Freya tried to be even-handed with the time allotted to each of her students during the discussion and not to let it show that Lewis' subject was dear to her own heart. But while they talked, she couldn't help thinking about the way Agnes had clammed up when she'd asked about her family. Poor Agnes. Whatever had she been through when she was young to elicit that reaction?

Later, in the library, Freya's mind kept flicking back to Matthew. She knew she should write to him, to carry out the promise she'd made to Agnes. She couldn't settle to her work while it was on her mind. Finally, she decided to make another attempt. Then and there in the library. Once she'd made the decision to write, the words tumbled from her.

First, she apologized for all the misunderstandings they'd had over their grandfather's death and his will. She explained why she was so stung by what their grandfather had done, she told Matthew how much she loved him and how important their relationship was to her, how being at odds with him shook the foundations of her world. She asked him to forgive her for anything she might have said shortly after their grandfather's death when she was upset and asked if they could put the whole thing behind them and pick up where they left off. She finished,

> I hope you'll understand that I didn't mean to hurt you, that
> your love and friendship mean far more to me than Jah-Dek's

personal effects. It would mean so much to me if we could make a fresh start and meet up for one of our legendary nights out when you get back.

She signed off, "All my love, Freya."

But when it came to sending the email, she just couldn't bring herself to do it. Her finger hovered over the SEND button, but she didn't have the courage to press it. Again, their bitter exchanges came to her mind. Finally, she gave up the struggle, consigned the email to the drafts folder, and shut her laptop.

She was grateful to Agnes for trying to persuade her to write; she obviously meant well. But why was she so reluctant to speak about her family or her home country? Finn's words kept coming back to her: *she's had a tough life. She's been through a hell of a lot . . .*

Despite her reluctance to get to know Finn, it seemed that they now had a common interest in helping Agnes. Perhaps, now she'd made it crystal clear that she wasn't interested in becoming friends, she could ask Finn if he knew what had happened to Agnes during the war?

When she'd finished in the library, walking back to where she'd chained her bike, Freya called her mother.

"How's it going in Cambridge?" Monica asked.

"Great, thanks, Mum," said Freya and realized as she said it that she actually meant it and wasn't just saying it to reassure her.

"Have you got to know that dishy neighbor of yours yet?"

"Dishy? Oh, give me a break, Mum! We just say good morning when we pass in the hall."

"What a shame. I thought he looked rather promising."

"I know you did, but I wish you'd stop it. And how are you coping at home?"

"Oh, good, thanks. Work's been really busy, I've started yoga on Tuesday evenings and I've even joined a book club. I can't help missing Dad, of course," Monica said wistfully.

"I know, Mum, we all do."

That evening, when Freya knocked at Agnes' door to drop off her newspaper, Agnes was still in her brusque mood.

"Thank you," she said, snatching the paper from Freya's outstretched hand and not meeting her eye. "I'm busy, so I won't ask you in."

"Are you sure you're all right?" Freya asked, peering at her.

"Of course. I'm fine, thank you," Agnes said and shut the door quickly.

Freya stood on the step and sighed. She wasn't surprised at this reception and berated herself once again for asking Agnes intrusive questions.

Amber asked her what was wrong as they worked side by side in the bar.

"You're not looking yourself this evening, Freya," she said. "You're not still hankering after Cameron, are you? I thought you were over him."

"No! You're joking. I'm completely over him. No, it's just this old lady next door I told you about. She's so prickly and difficult. I think I upset her today by asking about her family."

"Oh dear. You said she was quite sensitive before, didn't you? I thought you were getting on well with her now."

"Oh, I was. I mean until today, that is. The fact is, she reminds me a bit of my grandfather. She's got a similar accent and she's difficult and a bit bitter, just like him. At first, I thought she was Polish like he was, but she assured me she came from Lithuania. I just wish she felt able to tell me about her war experiences."

"Perhaps she just wants to forget all about it. Lots of people do."

"Yes, maybe, and maybe it's wrong of me to want to know. I just feel she's bottling it all up, a bit like my grandfather did. I always thought that if he'd been able to talk about what happened to him, he might have been less bitter and angry."

"Yes, but that generation, Freya, they're different to us. They don't like to bare their souls."

"I know . . ." Freya went on polishing a glass. She was mulling over what had happened with Agnes, thinking about what Amber had said, when the door opened and a group of about ten people came in—men and women. They were clearly in party mood, laughing and talking loudly, obviously out on a pub crawl. Freya recognized a couple of Cameron's rowing friends among them and felt her heart race. The next second, to her dismay and confusion, she spotted Cameron himself, looking slightly flushed but fit and bursting with energy. The group settled at a table in a corner and as Cameron passed the bar, he caught her eye. He smiled and gave a half-wave and Freya felt color creep into her cheeks and her hands shaking as she handled the glass she was polishing.

"Are you OK?" Amber asked, her hand on Freya's shoulder.

"Of course," Freya said, swallowing. She'd known this would happen one day, she'd prepared herself for it, but now, it *had* happened, her emotions were all over the place and she had no control over the way she felt.

"Don't worry, I'll serve them," said Amber quietly, squeezing Freya's arm and making her way to the side of the bar that faced the large table.

Two of the men came to the bar to be served, but Cameron remained seated at the table, his back to Freya.

The group stayed for over an hour and Freya couldn't help glancing across at them every now and then, even though the pub was busy and she was kept on her toes serving drinks. What she saw didn't surprise her: Cameron was the center of attention, as he always loved to be, telling stories and jokes while the rest of the group hung on his every word, applauding him, laughing uproariously at his anecdotes. Watching him perform like that made her remember how it had been every time they'd gone out with friends. He craved attention and approval, had to be the ringleader.

Just being with Freya hadn't been enough for him. She remembered bitterly how he'd started spending more and more time with his friends from the hospital and his rowing fraternity and as a consequence had spent less and less time with her. If she wasn't working in the pub, or seeing her own friends, she would spend her evenings alone, doing her research or just watching TV. He hadn't changed one jot, she saw that now. But despite that, it was a shock to see him there. Freya was dismayed to realize that she still felt hurt by the way he'd just upped and left, telling her their relationship had stagnated, that it bored him, he saw no future in it, and that he needed a change.

Just before ten thirty, the group got up to leave. Freya watched as they crossed the pub toward the door. Would he come and speak to her? To her surprise he approached the bar as he left. She felt her stomach churn with nerves.

"Hi, Freya, how are you doing?" His tone was casual and friendly but at the same time gave out the signal that the fact he was speaking to her didn't actually mean anything.

"Good, thanks. And you?"

"Yes, great. We're celebrating a win today for our eight."

"Oh, that's good news," she said flatly.

"Yeah. You look well," he said. "How long have you been back in Cambridge?"

"Since the beginning of term," she said, forcing herself to look into his eyes. How odd it was to be talking like this as if they were strangers when they'd once meant the world to each other, planned a life together. She wanted to tell him about her grandfather, but resisted the urge. Now wasn't the time. His friends were waiting with the door open and a blast of cold air reached her.

"Oh well, I must go," he said. "See you around then."

She stared after him as he left.

"You OK?" Amber's arm was around her shoulders.

Freya nodded.

"Yeah. It was a bit of a shock, that's all."

It was time to clear up and leave for the night, and while she washed glasses and swept the floor, cleaned tables, she analyzed her feelings. It was no use pretending to herself that she hadn't been affected by seeing Cameron. She had to admit that it had left her feeling low and deflated.

"Do you want to come back to mine for a nightcap and a chat?" asked Amber as they left the pub and unlocked their bikes.

Freya shook her head. "I've got some work to catch up on, and I'm really tired. Thanks anyway."

"No worries. If you need to chat, just text me."

"Thanks. You're an angel, Amber. I'm sure I'll be fine though."

She cycled through the quiet streets, past the colleges, eerily beautiful in the floodlights, and across Jesus Green in the autumn mist. As she pedaled, with the cool night air on her face, her spirits lifted. Tonight had been a hurdle she'd had to get over, but now it was behind her, she could move on. If she and Cameron both lived in the same town, they were bound to bump into one another occasionally. By the time she reached the footbridge across the river opposite her house she felt almost normal again.

She crossed the bridge and pushed the bike across the road. She glanced at Agnes' house as she walked toward her own front door. She stopped, puzzled. There were chinks of lights spilling from the edges of the curtains in the living room. That was odd; normally Agnes was tucked up in bed by this time, the house completely dark. Freya bit her nail, wondering. Should she go and check? If everything was all right, Agnes was bound to snap at her, but that didn't matter.

Freya quickly put her bike inside her front hall, then dashed down her own steps and up Agnes'. She knocked on the door and waited, her ear against the glass. Then she saw Claus sitting on the windowsill. She'd never seen him there before. He jumped down and rubbed himself round her legs, meowing pitifully. There was no sound or movement in the passage. She knocked again, harder this time. Perhaps Agnes had gone to bed and forgotten to switch the lights out? That wasn't likely though; she was a creature of habit and had to be careful about money. Freya knocked again, beginning to feel a prickle of panic now.

She lifted the letter box and peered inside. The hall was in darkness and there was no still sound from within. Claus meowed again and scratched at the door. Freya paused, her heart pounding, then made a decision. She ran back down Agnes' steps and back up the flight of steps to her own house. She switched the light on in the hall and listened at Finn's door. Music was coming from inside. He was still awake. She knocked on the door. He didn't answer immediately, so she had to knock again. Then came the sound of the lock and he opened the door a couple of inches.

"Freya?" He opened it wider. His hair looked unkempt, his eyes tired.

"I'm sorry to bother you, but it's Agnes. I'm worried about her. The lights are still on in her front room but she's not answering the door. It might be nothing, but . . ."

Finn's face dropped. "I've got a key. She gave it to me for emergencies. Wait, I'll go and get it."

He was back within seconds, pulling on a sweatshirt, and together they rushed back up to Agnes' front door. The key was stiff in the lock and Finn had to put his knee to the door, swearing under his breath. The cat rushed through the gap in the door when Finn prized it open and they both followed him down the passage to the living room.

Shock washed through Freya and she let out a gasp. Agnes was sprawled in front of the electric fire in her red dressing gown, face-down, motionless, a cup in her hand, a large tea stain spreading out on the rug where she'd fallen.

ELEVEN

AGNES

East Prussia, January 1945

Agnes stood quaking, looking up in terror into the eyes of the Russian soldier. She opened her mouth to speak, but it was so dry she wasn't sure any words would come out. She only knew a couple of words of Lithuanian, but she knew that to utter a word of German would spell disaster for her.

"*As nesuprantu,*" she muttered at last. *I don't understand.* This sent the soldier into another torrent of angry words in Russian. He was pulling her arm, shaking her. She smelled alcohol on his breath. She stared at him, paralyzed. "*As nesup-rantu,*" she said again.

She became aware of the sound of a horse clopping along the road and a cart loomed into view behind the soldier. He let go of her arm and shouted something to the man in the cart. The man pulled the horse up and stopped the cart. Hope flooded through Agnes as she recognized the friendly stallholder who'd sold her vegetables. The soldier spoke to him rapidly in

Russian. There was a brief exchange, then the soldier let go of Agnes' arm and motioned her to get onto the cart. She clambered up on trembling legs and sat down beside the stallholder, who shot her a warning look to keep quiet. Then he slapped the reins and the horse moved forward. Soon they were trotting along the road toward the wood, leaving the soldier behind in the middle of the road. Tears of relief sprang into her eyes.

"Thank you," she breathed.

When they had gone far enough to be out of earshot of the soldier, the man said, in halting German, "He asked me who you were. I said you were from my village and that I knew your family."

Agnes looked at his amiable, ruddy face and was filled with gratitude. Why had this kindly man risked his life for a stranger?

"We like our Little Germans here," he said as if reading her thoughts. "They buy our goods and some of them help out on our farms. And we hate the Russians . . . Shall I drop you at the wood at the top of the hill?"

"Yes, please," she breathed. "And thank you. Thank you so much."

The light was beginning to fade as they reached the edge of the forest and she climbed down from the cart, thanking the man yet again. He waved his hand, dismissing her thanks, and set off with another wave.

Agnes watched the cart fade into the distance, then stepped off the road and, with trepidation, entered the little path that led into the wood. She was still reeling with shock from the encounter with the soldier. She couldn't stop thinking how differently it might have ended had the stallholder not turned up.

At least it wasn't too far to the other side of the wood, she reminded herself, and she knew the way. She began to trudge through the trees, head down, walking as quickly as she could.

All the time, her nerves were taut and her ears primed, listening for the sound of voices or the crackle of footsteps on the forest floor. She kept up a steady pace and she was aware of her heart pumping and her breath coming quickly, freezing in clouds on the air. At last there were glimmerings of light between the trees at the far end of the path, and she sped up. She was almost at the end when someone stepped out of the undergrowth and onto the path in front of her. Her heartbeat surged and in her sudden panic everything around became a blur. She looked down—into the filthy, scrawny face of a boy. He must have only been ten or eleven.

"Where are you going?" he asked in German.

She swallowed, her heartbeat slowing down. This was just a young boy, only a little older than Dieter. How could he be a threat?

"I'm going home," she said. "And I'm in a hurry, so please move out of the way."

"Give me some of your food," he said, looking at her with huge, pleading eyes. "I know you've got some in that bag. You've been to the market in the village, haven't you?"

She looked into his eyes. His face was pinched, his hair matted, his clothes in rags.

"What are you doing here? Why don't *you* go home?"

He shrugged. "Don't have a home."

"What about your parents?"

"Dead. My father was killed in the war, my mother died too. Of starvation."

"Oh, that's dreadful!" Agnes said, her heart filling with pity for this little waif.

"There are a few of us living in these woods," he said. "There's more food in Lithuania and the farmers are kind to us. But I'm still hungry ..."

"Why don't you come with me?" she said, although even as

she said it, she had no idea how they could feed another mouth at the farm.

He shook his head. "No. I'm staying here, with my friends."

Agnes hesitated. How could she just walk on and leave him without anything? Those huge, sad eyes had spoken straight to her heart. She swung her bag off her shoulders and took out one of the two loaves of bread she'd bought at the market. She needed to do this quickly, so she wouldn't have second thoughts. She shoved the loaf toward him: "Here you are. Now, if you're sure you don't want to come with me, I have to get on. It's getting dark."

He grabbed the loaf and darted back into the trees. Agnes hurried on, out of the forest, across the fields, and was soon back at the railway track. She had no way of knowing when or even if a goods train would be traveling back toward her village, so, shouldering her knapsack, she turned in the direction of the river and began to walk along the tracks toward home. And as she walked, she thought of the little boy and other orphans like him, living in the forest like wild animals. And she thought of Mother and Dieter and Aunt Hannah waiting for her at the farm and her heart filled with warmth at the knowledge that she had a home and a family waiting for her there.

TWELVE

It was late evening by the time Agnes reached the farm. She'd had to walk along the railway for an hour or more before a goods train approached along the track behind her and she was able to jump on board for the rest of the journey back to the village. Crossing the river bridge on foot had been terrifying. There was hardly any space to walk; she'd had to take great strides from girder to girder, the black water swirling meters beneath her. She'd felt very exposed out there suspended above the river, but there was little light in the sky by then and with her dark clothes, she hoped she blended into the iron girders of the bridge.

On the other side of the river, she walked along in the middle of the track between the rails, striding from sleeper to sleeper for another few kilometers before she felt the rails vibrating beneath her feet and turned to see the lights of a goods train approaching behind her from the direction of Schmallen-ingken. She waited beside the track until the train was abreast of her, then picked her moment and flung herself on board. The flatbed wagons were empty, so it wasn't hard to find a place to ride for the last few kilometers.

It was dark by the time the train reached the von Meyer estate and, as it rumbled through the cutting where she'd left Liesel that morning, Agnes wondered if she and her family had already left their home and started out on their long trek west. Sadness swept over her at the thought that she might never see her best friend again. She wondered whether to jump off the train here, scramble up the embankment, and find her way through the forest to Liesel's house. But as much as she wanted to see Liesel again, she couldn't bring herself to do that. She was so exhausted from the day's exertions, she didn't think she could walk any further than she had to through the snow. Instead, she lay back on the wagon as it carried on toward the village, staring up at the stars that made tiny pinpricks in the darkening sky. As the train approached the village station, she gathered her knapsack and threw herself off the wagon onto a soft bank of snow.

Mother and Aunt Hannah were sitting at the kitchen table when she got back. Their two anxious faces turned to her in the flickering lamplight as she entered and relief spread over both immediately. Mother jumped up and flung her arms around her, holding her tight.

"Where have you been? I thought something had happened to you."

"Didn't you get my note?" Agnes set her bag down and pulled off her wet boots.

"Of course, but you didn't say where you were going."

She put her knapsack on the table. She couldn't help smiling with pride at her achievement: "Here, this should last us a little while."

Agnes sat down, exhausted, while Mother and Aunt Hannah emptied the bag, exclaiming with delight at the contents.

"You're a wonder, my girl," said Mother, her eyes glistening. "We won't be hungry at Christmas after all."

Aunt Hannah kissed her head and hugged her. "Take off your wet clothes and put them on the stove. I'll bring you something to eat."

When she'd changed, Aunt Hannah put a bowl of thin potato soup they'd saved from the family meal in front of her and Agnes broke into one of the loaves she'd bought at the market. She hadn't eaten anything since the end of the loaf she'd had at Liesel's early that morning and the taste of that soft bread, dipped into the tasteless soup, was delicious.

After that first trip, Agnes made the exhausting and perilous journey into Lithuania to barter for food several times over the following few weeks. The first time, on her way back through the estate to the railway cutting, she looked in at Liesel's home. As soon as she turned off the deserted castle drive toward the cottages, she could tell that they were empty. There were no dogs barking, no lights on in any of the windows. She knocked on Liesel's front door and waited, hoping against hope that Gerta would open it just as before. But there were no footsteps inside, no welcoming voice, no Liesel bouncing down the stairs to welcome her. She pictured Liesel, Gerta, and the two little girls, crowded onto a train with all their luggage, steaming across the snowy plains toward the Reich, and the thought that they'd gone brought tears to her eyes.

Christmas came and, thanks to the supplies Agnes had brought them from the market, there was no need to slaughter the one remaining laying hen left on the farm.

How different this year was from Christmases of the past. Agnes remembered how, even in the last three years when the country had been at war, they'd had enough food at Christmastime and she'd played carols on her treasured piano for the family to sing. This Christmas morning, she awoke in the cold bedroom and stared through the iced-up window at the snowy fields stretching into the distance. It was a beautiful morning and the countryside sparkled in the sunlight, but her heart ached for Papa and for all the little rituals of the Christmases of her childhood. When they woke, she and Dieter would open the presents Papa had left in knitted stockings at the end of their beds. They would all walk through the snow to the little white church with its red roof and steeple, where the whole village would gather to sing carols. And then on to the farm where Aunt Hannah would have cooked them a fine spread and where she and Dieter would play snowballing with their cousins in the afternoon.

There had been no word from Papa or Uncle Tomas, or about Gunter or Joachim. Although Mother and Hannah seemed almost afraid to mention their names, not wanting to voice their fears and their own private sadness, the absence of all their men at Christmas could hardly go unnoticed. Agnes and Dieter chopped a small fir tree down from the edge of the wood and brought it into the kitchen by the stove, but decorating it wasn't the same without the cousins. They exchanged simple presents and homemade cards; Agnes had managed to buy some handkerchiefs for Aunt Hannah and Mother on her latest trip to Lithuania. She was touched when Mother handed her a tiny box containing some silver earrings that she knew she had been given by her own mother and had treasured for years.

The four of them walked together to church in the village, where the congregation consisted mainly of mothers, children, and old men and women. Agnes was surprised to see several new faces among the worshippers. Most of these newcomers looked exhausted and dirty; perhaps they were refugees, pausing to stay in barns and outhouses in the village on their journey west? It felt good to stand and sing hymns in the freezing building, even though the mournful melodies brought tears to Agnes' eyes. The minister preached a sermon of hope and courage for the brave soldiers fighting to defend their freedoms on the front line but, as

Agnes looked round at the faces, all she saw was bewilderment and fear. Afterward, as they crowded out of the church together, Mother suggested they call in at home to collect a few household things.

Agnes had last been back a few days beforehand to gather more trinkets to exchange at the Lithuanian market, but this time as they approached the house along the village street, it was clear that the place wasn't empty. Smoke curled from the chimney, the shutters had been pushed back, and a pair of dirty boots stood beside the front door. Mother and Hannah exchanged looks.

"What's all this?" Mother marched up the front path and Agnes followed close behind. Mother opened the door. "Hello?"

Agnes followed her inside, with Dieter and Aunt Hannah hard on her heels. Their beloved sitting room was filled with smoke. Someone had lit a fire and several grubby-looking children were playing on the rug in front of it. An old man, bundled up in a wooly hat and overcoat, was asleep in Father's chair. A woman emerged from the kitchen, wiping her hands on her skirt.

"Who are *you*?" she asked, her eyes suspicious.

"This is my home!" Mother replied, tight-lipped. "What are *you* doing here?"

"Well, it's ours now. We had nowhere else to stay, our village in Memelland is on the front line. Every building is full of soldiers, there's shelling all day, every day. We had to leave."

"But . . . but you can't stay *here*." Mother's mouth hung open, her face an angry shade of red now.

"Well, we can't go on," said the woman. "Our cart broke down outside this village two days ago. This house was empty, so we stayed here."

"Well, you can get your things together and move on right now."

But the woman stood her ground. "You aren't living here.

We thought you'd left the area. It's a fair assumption. This place is *our* home now."

Agnes' eyes strayed to the fire. She frowned. The orange flames were licking through something strangely familiar. A piece of carved wood. With a gasp of recognition, she realized it was the wooden panel from the front of her piano. She turned round and there was the piano in its usual place against the wall, the front panels stripped off, the keys and strings exposed. It was like a body without skin.

"What have you done?" she screamed. The woman took a step back. "That's *my* piano!"

The woman shrugged. "There wasn't any wood for the fire."

"You will pay for this!" Mother said quietly, her voice shaking. "Come on, Agnes. Let's go." Then, turning to the woman, "This house belongs to the education authority. I'm going to report this to them right away. You won't get away with this."

As they walked away from the house, Mother collapsed on her knees in tears on the icy road. Dieter began to cry too, clinging to her. Hannah glanced at Agnes and they each took an arm and lifted Mother to her feet.

"Come on, Helga. There's nothing we can do now. Come on back to the farm and let's eat that lunch we've been promising ourselves."

Mother barely spoke on the long walk back to the farm. She sat down at the kitchen table silently and when Aunt Hannah dished up the long-awaited Christmas lunch of chicken and vegetables, she pushed her plate away.

"I couldn't touch a thing, Hannah. I'm so eaten up inside," she said.

Agnes felt guilty tucking into the delicious meal, the most nourishing one she'd had in months, while Mother sat there brooding, her eyes faraway. It reminded her of the day Papa had been taken.

"This beastly war," Mother murmured as if to herself. "It has taken everything from us. Nothing will ever be the same again."

Aunt Hannah put her hand on Mother's on the table and said, "On Monday, we will take the horse and cart and go into Tilsit to see Herr Schultz."

Mother's eyes went wide. Herr Schultz was the local *Block-leiter,* or Nazi leader.

"Why would we go to see that man? Jonas would have nothing to do with the Nazis. They've ruined our lives. And what would he do, anyway? No, I will go to the education department."

"They're all the same, Helga," Hannah said gently. "Do you think the education department isn't run by the Nazis too? I just thought, if Herr Schultz won't do anything about the refugees in your house, we could ask him for evacuation papers so we can all leave once and for all."

Mother reluctantly agreed, so a few days later, Hannah harnessed the old horse to the cart and the two women left the farm early one morning to travel the thirty kilometers into Tilsit. Agnes wanted to go with them, but Mother insisted it was safer for her and Dieter to stay on the farm.

Agnes did her best to entertain Dieter while they were gone, to keep him from worrying. After they'd finished their morning chores, they walked across the snow-covered fields to the woods on the edge of her uncle's land, where there was a pond that was covered in ice. There they skidded about, hand in hand. As they played, Dieter's eyes lit up and he roared with excited laughter. Agnes' heart soared to see him happy and laughing again. But the pond was where Agnes and her cousins used to come with their skates on winter Sundays and being here without them made her yearn to hear their laughter again, to be able to turn the clock back to those carefree days of fun and freedom.

It was almost dark when Mother and Aunt Hannah returned, their faces gray with the exhaustion of the journey.

"What happened? Is Herr Schultz going to do anything about the house?" Agnes asked as they came into the kitchen, shaking the snow off their wet coats.

Mother shook her head. "Schultz wasn't at Nazi headquarters," she muttered. "The whole place was deserted. Only an old caretaker left. Schultz and his henchmen have already evacuated back to Berlin, even though they're stopping everyone else from leaving."

"So, what are we going to do?" Agnes looked from Aunt Hannah to Mother. They exchanged anxious glances, then Aunt Hannah dropped her gaze, avoiding looking at Agnes.

"What's wrong?" she asked in alarm. "What aren't you telling me?"

"Tilsit was almost deserted," Mother said. "And . . . well, the battle must be very close now. You can hear guns and shelling from the town."

"So, your mother and I decided on the way back. We will leave here tomorrow," Aunt Hannah said gently. "We would leave tonight, but the horse needs to rest. Go up to your room now and pack your things. Just one bag each. We will take what we can, but the cart isn't very big."

"Where are we going?" asked Dieter.

"We will go to the Baltic coast," said Mother. "We spoke to a few people in the town and that's where people are heading. There are boats going from Pillau and Danzig, evacuating people back to the Reich."

Dieter looked uncertain, but Agnes squeezed his hand. "Don't worry, it will be an adventure, Dieter. You'll see."

"Agnes is right. And we'll all be together. Now off you go and pack. I will go now and slaughter the last hen. We can cook it tonight and take the meat with us to eat on the journey."

· · ·

After a restless night, they all rose shortly after dawn and ate their last meal in the farmhouse kitchen: stale bread left from Agnes' last trip into Lithuania. Then they put on their boots and coats and went outside into the yard, where Aunt Hannah had harnessed the horse to the farm cart once again. She'd piled blankets and cushions in a little space on the back for Agnes and Dieter to sit, between a couple of crates of belongings, the pot containing the cooked chicken, and four suitcases, which were tied to the back of the cart with string.

They all climbed on board, Agnes and Dieter facing backward. Hannah urged the horse on and they pulled out of the yard and onto the icy lane. As they drew away from the farm, Agnes stared back at the little house and its surrounding barns, orchard and fields, with tears in her eyes. This place had always been home to her; roaming around the barns with their sweet smell of hay and the rolling fields was as much a part of her life as breathing. Now they were leaving it all behind. And as they turned the corner in the lane, and the familiar old buildings disappeared from view, she had a powerful sense of stepping into the unknown, that her old life was over and that she would never see the farm or the village again.

THIRTEEN

They traveled for days in that jolting cart, moving through the countryside toward the Baltic coast at a snail's pace. As Agnes stared out at the rolling landscape, the endless hours and days seemed to melt into one. Several times she had the uncomfortable and frightening impression that they'd passed that way before: that the roof of a hay barn looked familiar, or that she'd seen that flock of geese flying over that frozen lake a few miles back. It all looked so achingly familiar—the gently undulating snow-covered fields, the thick evergreen forests, the farms nestled in hollows, the iced-up stretches of water, the picturesque villages, now all but deserted by their inhabitants.

Progress was slow. It became clear, a few minutes after they'd left the farm and approached the main road that passed through the village, that they were about to join a never-ending convoy of families fleeing the war. As they approached the end of the farm lane they could see, above the hedge that bordered the road, the bowed heads of a line of refugees, plodding through the snow, just as they had been doing for months. Only now, there were so many more of them. Some rode on horse-drawn carts as Agnes and her family were, some pulled prams or buggies laden with belongings, others pushed wheelbarrows or handcarts, others staggered and slithered along on the ice with heavy suitcases. They moved in families, carrying their babies on their backs, supporting their children and old people, lugging as many possessions as they could. Nobody had a motor vehicle; they had all been confiscated by the army months ago. The convoy of desperate people on the main road was endless and slow-moving and the road was so congested that it was impossible to make progress faster than the slowest horse-drawn cart up ahead.

"Would you look at that convoy!" Aunt Hannah exclaimed as she pulled the horse up at the crossing and watched for a gap in the tide so she could move out into the road. They had to hang back for several minutes, then Hannah clicked her tongue and the horse moved forward, throwing his head up, startled at the sight of a bent old woman pushing a doll's pram full of colorful clothes that flapped in the icy January wind. Agnes held onto Dieter's hand as they moved forward, looking back at those unfortunates on foot who stood aside for the cart to pass. At first, Dieter seemed content to be sat facing backward on the cart, watching the extraordinary sights unfolding behind them—"Look, there's a doll's house on that donkey," or "Why is that lady wearing three hats?"—but he soon tired of that game and became fractious and bored.

"How much longer? I'm hungry," he kept saying, even before they'd been traveling an hour. Agnes kept telling him that they would be eating some of Aunt Hannah's freshly cooked chicken for lunch, but the seconds seemed to grind by and it felt as if it was still hours until lunchtime.

"Are we going to stop for a picnic like them?" Dieter asked, as they passed a family resting on their luggage on the slushy verge, eating something from newspaper parcels.

"I don't think so," Agnes replied. "We need to make as much progress as we can in the daylight."

"But why do we have to go? Why can't we stay at the farm? I don't understand."

Agnes didn't know what to say. She had nothing to offer her brother by way of comfort. She didn't want to frighten him by saying that the war was on its way, that the Wehrmacht had virtually capitulated and was in retreat, and that before too long the Russians would be here, rampaging through the countryside that had always been their home. She shuddered at the thought of Russian soldiers overrunning their beloved village, destroying homes, setting fire to farms. But she couldn't tell Dieter that, or that they were on the road because anyone who was still at home when the Red Army did arrive would be lucky to survive.

"We're going on an adventure, Dieter," Mother called over her shoulder. "It's exciting. You'll remember this forever. And if we're lucky, we'll be going on a ship from Pillau or Danzig. You've never been on a ship before, have you?"

Dieter's eyes flickered. He clearly wasn't sure whether to believe Mother.

"Will Papa be there?" he asked suddenly.

"Perhaps, my darling!" Mother's voice was falsely bright. "He might well be. Let's just wait and see, shall we? Now, why don't you just enjoy the journey? There's lots interesting to see."

But some of the sights on the road were so disturbing that Agnes frequently had to put her hand over Dieter's eyes. Then he would squirm and cry out and try to push her hand away. Dotted along the route at regular intervals were broken carts and wagons that had collapsed into the ditch at the side of the road, their wheels or axels broken, the contents spilling out, left abandoned by their owners. There were horses too, dead from exhaustion or starvation, lying on the verge, their stomachs huge and distended. Tears came to Agnes' eyes at the sight of these poor creatures and she thought of their own beloved Florian, the fifteen-year-old carthorse who had lived and worked on the farm since before she was born, now plodding faithfully through the ice and snow, carrying them away from harm. She couldn't bear the thought of him perishing in the cold or from starvation and collapsing beside the road. All these dead horses must have meant the same to other families who had been forced to leave them there, unburied and unloved.

Toward late afternoon, Agnes saw something that chilled her even more than the sight of the dead horses. They were traveling along a long, straight stretch of road that rose from a flat river valley toward a village on the crest of the hill, between lines of poplars. It had been a slow and steady climb for several kilometers, the pace of the convoy growing slower and slower as the gradient increased. At the foot of one of the poplar trees was the body of an old woman. She had collapsed sideways from a sitting position as if she'd stopped there under the tree to rest but death had taken her before she could get up again. Her suitcase had fallen open, or been broken open by looters, the contents spilled out all around her. Clothes, china trinkets, books and even a worn toothbrush were scattered around her body.

"What's that?" In her own distress, Agnes hadn't thought to distract Dieter.

"It's just a lady resting there," called Mother from the front, her voice choked with shock. "Nothing to worry about, darling."

"But what about her things? Doesn't she need help?"

"There's nothing we can do, Dieter. Now, why don't you count the trees before we get to the next village?"

After that first old lady, they saw several dead bodies beside the road. They were mostly old people without the strength to survive the freezing conditions, who must have either been traveling alone or whose relatives had no choice but to leave them there unburied and to walk on to save their own lives. Agnes got used to covering Dieter's eyes and pretending it was all a game. But the sight of those poor people who had perished along the route chilled her to the core. The first time she saw a dead baby lying in the ditch, its waxy face as white as the surrounding snowdrifts, the terror and tragedy of their situation hit her hard.

On the first night, they found shelter on an abandoned farm. The farmhouse itself was already full of refugees when they arrived, sleeping on blankets in every square inch of the house, so they pulled the cart into an old hay barn in the farmyard. Hannah fed the horse from the sack of oats she'd packed on the cart, then let him loose in the barn. The four of them slept together inside the cart, under the blankets they'd brought from home, huddling together for warmth. Agnes cuddled Dieter to her and, in a few moments, safe and secure with Mother's arms around her own body, she forgot about the horrors of the day and drifted into a deep sleep.

The days on the road passed just like that first day. Agnes never stopped feeling shocked and sickened at the sight of dead people and horses and the collapsed wagons beside the road, but she learned not to react for Dieter's sake. She was constantly cold and hungry, but never complained to Mother or Aunt Hannah. The meager supply of food they'd brought was running low, so Agnes often gave some of hers to Dieter. It frightened her that Mother barely touched her own portion, often handing part of her meal to Hannah or Dieter. Agnes knew that she and Aunt Hannah were doing everything they could to get them through this and that it fell to her to look after Dieter and keep him distracted from the horrors that faced them at every turn.

It must have been early afternoon on the third or fourth day when Agnes was startled by the sound of frantic shouting and horns blasting from the back of the convoy, and the carts and wagons behind them started moving onto the verge on either side of the road, like a parting tide.

"Something's coming from behind," she yelled to Aunt Hannah, "you need to pull off!"

As the cart lurched off the road and into the soft, drifted snow, the blasting horns behind them grew louder and then, through the chaotic crush of wagons, carts, and pedestrians, the great pipe-like gun of a tank burst into view as the giant vehicle lumbered toward them on its caterpillar tracks. It was the first time Agnes had ever seen a tank, apart from in grainy photographs in the pages of a newspaper. Its sheer size and the sleek brutality of this killing machine close up struck terror through her.

"A Panzer!" Dieter's eyes blazed with delight. He jumped up and waved madly to the soldier who stood in the turret and the soldier saluted him solemnly as the gray-green tank crunched past the cart. Dieter squealed with excitement. There were four other soldiers riding on the back of the tank, in their sage-colored uniforms and caps, looking battered and dirty. As they passed, Agnes caught a look of resignation in their white, exhausted faces. More tanks followed, seven or eight of them altogether, several German soldiers riding precariously on each one, followed by a convoy of armored cars and smaller jeeps, all crammed full of weary-looking soldiers.

"It's the Wehrmacht in retreat," said Hannah as she urged Florian forward again. "We've seen it with our own eyes now, Helga."

"Hush, Hannah, be careful what you say," said Mother as the cart lurched back onto the icy road once again. They all fell silent for the next few kilometers, contemplating what the convoy of German soldiers meant for them, apart from Dieter. He had found a stick on the back of the cart and was training it on people they passed who were struggling along on foot, as if it were the gun of a tank.

More convoys of the retreating army followed at regular intervals and, as the light went from the sky, Agnes caught sight of a line of flickering fires on the horizon behind them. Her breath caught. Was that the Red Army burning villages and farms as it advanced, as the newspapers had warned?

Shortly after one Wehrmacht army column had passed through, above the sound of the cartwheels grinding on the ice, Agnes caught a gentle hum in the sky from the east. It quickly grew louder, building to a loud buzzing sound, and two tiny planes appeared in the sky above the burning horizon, flying side by side, heading toward the column of refugees. The noise grew louder by the second. Screams went up in the carts and wagons behind and people panicked, leaving their vehicles, to run into the fields or take cover in the ditch or under the bushes.

"Whatever's that?"

Agnes had a fleeting glimpse of Mother's horrified face as she turned to the sky, then the two planes were dipping toward the road, flying directly toward them in single file. The breath went from her body as the first plane opened fire, strafing the column of helpless people with bullets. She caught a flash of the white underside of the first plane and the red star on its fuselage. A scream ripped from her and she pushed Dieter down beside her on the floor of the cart. Then came the sickening crash of an explosion ahead, the splintering of wood, the screams of people and animals, and then a second one, further away, as the roar of the planes receded to a buzz.

A wagon, two ahead of them in the column, had been hit, the wagon itself blown to bits, the horse collapsed between the shafts. An old man lay motionless on the ice beside it, his head a bloody mess, and a young woman clutching a baby wandered around on the icy road, dazed. Mother jumped down from her seat and ran toward the scene of destruction, along with several others, who all surrounded the young woman with offers of help.

Agnes held Dieter to her and they sobbed together in fear and bewilderment. Up at the front of the cart, Aunt Hannah was crying too. Behind them, all was chaos. People had been shot down as they'd made a break for the fields, or where they sat on their wagons. The road and verge were littered with bodies, the snow patched crimson with blood.

Mother returned to the cart. "We need to move, Hannah. Florian's feet will freeze to the ice standing here. We can get past the broken wagon by pulling onto the verge."

"What about that poor young mother? Did you say we would take her and the baby?"

"Of course, but she's going on with the people in front. They were neighbors and have room in their wagon. She didn't seem to know what was happening, the poor thing. The old man with her, her grandfather, was killed outright."

For the next three days this horrific scene was repeated many times over. The Russian air force seemed hell-bent on targeting the innocent East Prussians trying to make their escape from the fighting. To add to the horror, progress became even slower than before because of all the broken vehicles on the road. They were forced to pull over many, many times for retreating German tanks and troops. At night they found shelter in abandoned farms or barns, eating the last scraps of their own food and anything they could scrounge from other travelers. From talking to others on the same route, they gleaned that they would have a better chance of being evacuated if they were to make for one of the ports on the inland sea, the Frisches Haff, rather than Pillau, the port near Königsberg.

"They are bringing ships into the ports in the Frisches Haff," a woman who had been told by some passing troops said. "If you make for Pillau, you'll have no chance if you aren't related to an army officer or don't have special evacuation papers. In the other ports, including Danzig, they're taking everyone. Some are going by train, others by boat. That's where we're heading."

Three days later, they reached the port of Rosenberg. The streets of the small town were crammed with refugees just like them, all moving slowly in a great tide toward the port.

"Where are all the ships?" Mother asked, as they neared the empty docks, her voice brittle with fear and exhaustion.

A man walking beside the cart looked up and said, "The lagoon is frozen over, lady. If you want to board a ship, you have to cross it to get to the ports on the other side."

And as they reached the dockside, they could see that people were doing just that. A column of wagons, carts, and pedestrians, hunched against the freezing weather, were setting off to trek in single file across the great expanse of ice.

"I don't like the look of this, Hannah," Mother said. "What if the ice isn't strong enough to hold us?"

"We have to go, Helga. There's no choice. It's that or the Russian army. If the ice breaks, I'd rather freeze to death in the waters of the lagoon than be here when they arrive."

With that, Hannah shook the reins and Florian moved forward, straining in his harness, pulling the cart on toward the dockside and the frozen lagoon. As they reached the edge of the dock, the cart in front of them was just starting out on the ice, following the long line of wagons that had already stepped off into the unknown, onto the track that was carved into the ice by the carts and wagons that had gone before it, crossing the ten kilometers of ice that lay between them and the port of Danzig. Agnes stared back at the town they had left behind. Snow was falling now and as the town receded into mist, the roofs of the buildings were already blanketed white.

Dieter stood up. "Hey, we're on the ice. This is exciting! But what if it cracks? We'd fall through, wouldn't we?"

"Be quiet!" said Mother sharply.

"Sit down, Dieter." Agnes pulled him down beside her and

he fell silent. From the back of the cart they watched the nodding heads of the two horses pulling the wagon behind them. It was eerily still and quiet; the only sounds were the slipping of hoofs, the grinding of cartwheels on ice, the snorting of horses, and the occasional chivvying noise from the drivers. Everyone riding in the carts and wagons was holding their breath, listening out for the sound of the ice cracking, praying that it would hold until they reached Danzig. They passed many people struggling along on foot, hauling their possessions with them, slipping and sliding on the slushy surface. Some were so weak they were barely able to walk. They passed platoons of German soldiers, marching toward Danzig, their heads bowed in retreat, hurrying, like everyone else, away from the Russian advance.

There were bodies too, stretched out where they'd fallen; horses and mules dead from starvation or from the freezing temperatures, people who had given up the struggle and collapsed in the extreme cold, their belongings scattered around them. Several were dressed in the tell-tale striped uniform of a concentration camp. These bodies were like skeletons, their heads shaved, cheekbones visible beneath stretched skin.

"Look, Hannah! Those poor souls," Mother said in hushed tones as they passed the first one.

The trek plodded on in silence, but after a couple of hours they heard a sound they had learned to dread: the drone of a plane approaching from the east.

"Duck!" shouted Hannah, but there was nowhere to go to avoid the approaching bomber. It was upon them in seconds and dived overhead, its engines a deafening roar. There was the crack of an explosion in the column behind them. As Agnes watched in terror, a crater formed in the ice. A wagon had been hit and several people walking were struck down instantly. Shock waves ran through her. From where she sat on the back of the cart she watched helplessly as myriad cracks began to form in the ice and spread rapidly in every direction, chasing the column of struggling people.

"Move, move, the ice is cracking!"

Hannah urged Florian on and the exhausted horse strained forward more quickly, slipping on the ice as he pulled them round past the stationary wagon in front, trotting and skidding forward on the treacherous track. It was as if he knew that the ice was cracking and his instinct for survival was kicking in to save them all. Agnes clutched Dieter's hand, willing the journey to be over, hoping against hope that the bombers wouldn't return. They passed more bodies lying on the ice, including the body of another prisoner in striped pajamas with blood oozing from a wound in his head.

They were about halfway to the lagoon when they came upon the group of remaining prisoners, stumbling along on the ice. They were dressed only in clogs and thin, striped pajamas, their heads bowed, their faces a translucent white. They were being herded by four Nazi officers, prodding the back line of prisoners along with their rifles.

"Look, Hannah! Where are they taking them?" Mother asked in shocked tones.

"Who knows, Helga. Best not to look. They must be Jews or enemy aliens. There's nothing we can do for them."

But Agnes couldn't help looking as the cart ground past these unfortunate souls. Not one of them lifted their head and it was impossible to tell whether they were men or women as they trudged along, the wind whipping their thin clothes. But as the cart drew level with them, one of the prisoners on the edge broke ranks from the group and made a bid for freedom, dashing toward the cart. As he reached it, he lunged toward Mother, who was riding at the front next to Aunt Hannah.

"Take me with you," he pleaded, looking up at Mother with bloodshot eyes. "They're going to kill us all." Agnes was horrified by his face close up: the sunken cheeks, the dark skin under his eyes, the weeping sores on his lips.

"Please!" The man's voice was barely more than a whisper. He tugged at Mother's clothes with bony fingers. In seconds, one of the guards was upon him, seizing the man with black-gloved hands, dragging him backward across the ice, away from the cart. Then he was beating the prisoner with the butt of his gun, hitting him again and again, on the chest, the arms, and the back. The prisoner collapsed onto his knees on the ice, but the beating carried on, his back and his shoulders now.

"Stop that!" It was Mother's voice. Agnes watched in horror as she jumped down from the cart and, skidding on the ice, rushed toward the guard.

"Helga! Don't!" Hannah yelled, but Mother didn't turn back. Dieter began to whimper.

"Stop that, you brute! He's a human being."

The guard flicked his gaze toward Mother, then turned away. He was bashing the man's head now with the butt of his gun. The prisoner had collapsed forward and lay motionless on the ice in a crumpled heap of striped material. Mother rushed at the guard, screaming, pulling at his uniform. The man straightened up and turned his cold eyes toward her.

"Get off, woman. Get back on your cart."

"I will not. This man needs help."

"He's just a Jew. Leave him alone."

Ignoring the guard, she knelt down beside the prisoner.

"I order you, woman! Get up and go back to your cart."

Mother took no notice. It was as if something had snapped inside her; as if the hardships of the past months, the hunger, the pain, the terror had finally got to her. She didn't even glance at the guard. Instead, she began wiping blood from the man's head with the end of her scarf.

It happened in seconds. The guard turned the gun on Mother, bringing the butt down and whacking her on her head.

She cried out in pain. Agnes, Dieter, and Hannah were all screaming. He hit her time and time again, just as he'd beaten the prisoner. She collapsed forward and fell beside the prisoner on the ice. The guard straightened up, slung his rifle over his shoulder. He looked over at the line of wagons and carts, which had ground to a halt while the dreadful scene had unfolded. The white faces of the refugees stared, uncomprehending.

"She disobeyed my order," he said. "We do not tolerate disobedience."

He turned back to the crowd of remaining prisoners, who stood there huddled together, shivering on the ice, watching wordlessly.

"March!"

As they shuffled away, Agnes scrambled down from the cart and rushed toward the spot where Mother lay in a crumpled heap. Her heart was in her throat. She couldn't believe what she was seeing. Everything around her looked surreal. As she ran, she was aware of Aunt Hannah running beside her and Dieter following behind. She and Hannah reached Mother together and both knelt down beside her at the same time. The prisoner, lying next to Mother, was clearly dead, blood staining the ice red, spreading from his head in an expanding pool.

Agnes bent over Mother. Her eyes were flickering. Her head was a bloody mess, blood oozing down her forehead. Agnes was aware of Dieter's distraught screams, but they seemed to come from far away. Aunt Hannah leaned over, put her arms around Mother, and tried to lift her.

"No," she murmured. "Leave me here."

A great sob rose in Agnes' throat. "Mother . . ." The tears were falling now, rolling down her cheeks, dropping onto Mother's face.

"Promise you'll look after your brother for me, Agnes."

"Oh, Mutti, don't say that . . ." Her voice was so choked with tears she could hardly speak.

"Promise me . . ." The words were whispered, but they held such power and significance.

"Of course," Agnes breathed.

There was the faintest flicker of a smile on Mother's lips, then her eyes closed and all the breath left her body in a single sigh.

FOURTEEN

FREYA

Cambridge, Present Day

Freya was shaking all over when she hung up from her call to the emergency services. On the living room floor in front of her, Finn was crouching over Agnes' prone body, performing CPR, frantically pressing up and down on Agnes' chest, stopping every few beats to put his mouth to hers. Freya watched helplessly for a while, but she couldn't stand still and started pacing up and down the room, alternating between flicking the curtains back and staring down the road, willing the ambulance to arrive and striding back to the rug where Finn was trying to revive Agnes. It seemed an age, but it must only have been a matter of minutes before she heard the wailing of a siren outside, blue light strobing through the room, and the green and yellow ambulance came to a halt in front of the house.

Two paramedics, a man and a woman, came in and took over from Finn. As they worked, they asked Agnes' name and details. Finn provided some of the answers, but when it came to her medical history, he shook his head.

"I don't know her that well, I'm afraid. She's a very private person."

"Is she going to be all right?" Freya couldn't help asking as they attached wires to Agnes' body, fixed an oxygen mask over her face.

"She's breathing, but we'll need to take her into hospital." The young woman, dressed in green scrubs, gave her a reassuring smile. "Are you family?"

"No, just neighbors."

"Does she have any family nearby?" the other paramedic asked.

"I don't think so," said Finn. "She told me she has no living relatives."

The two paramedics lifted Agnes onto a stretcher and Freya and Finn followed them out of the house and down the steps to the waiting ambulance.

"Would either of you like to accompany her to hospital?"

"I will." Both Freya and Finn spoke at the same time, then looked at each other.

"Look, you go with her, Freya," Finn said. "My van is parked in the alley behind the house. I can come separately and meet you there."

Freya agreed and, once the stretcher was secured with straps, climbed into the back of the ambulance. She sat on a seat on the other side of the vehicle. The male paramedic carried on working on Agnes as the ambulance took off and sped down through the town, sirens wailing. Freya looked down at Agnes' face anxiously. It was frighteningly gray and sunken-looking, her skin lying in wrinkled folds, her lips two thin blue lines. Freya's heart went out to the old lady she'd just started to get to know and appreciate.

It reminded her so much of when her grandfather had been

taken ill only a few months before. He had collapsed in his room
one morning, an ambulance had been called, and her mother
had gone alone with him to hospital. Freya had waited at home,
listening out anxiously for a phone call, sometimes wandering
restlessly through the house to stand in the doorway of his room.
His walking stick lay at an angle beside the window where he'd
fallen; his half-drunk cup of coffee still stood on the little table
with his newspaper where he'd almost completed the crossword.
He had never returned to his room; he had never come home.
Looking at Agnes as the ambulance sped through the center of
town, Freya hoped and prayed that history wouldn't repeat itself
for her.

The journey took ten minutes. When the ambulance drew
up outside the emergency department, Agnes was unloaded and
whisked inside. Freya climbed out after her and the paramedic
asked her to wait in the waiting room.

"Miss Peters has been taken into intensive care. Someone
will come and speak to you in a little while."

"Do you know what's wrong with her?"

"Not completely sure at the moment, no. It's hard to tell. The
doctors will be able to tell you more."

Freya sat down in one of the plastic chairs in the soulless
waiting room, under the glare of the flickering strip-lights. She
glanced around absently at the other people waiting there: a
young couple with a screaming baby, white-faced with anxiety,
a group of boisterous students, one of whom had a bandaged
leg, a man whose forehead was covered in blood. There were
others like her, sitting alone, clearly waiting for news of loved
ones. She could tell from the way their eyes darted to the swing
doors whenever a member of the medical staff emerged from
the emergency room. Each of them was guarding their own
story.

"You OK?" It was Finn's voice and she felt a surge of relief as
he sat down beside her. "Any news?"

She shook her head. "She's been taken into one of those rooms for treatment."

"Poor, poor Agnes. I wonder what's wrong with her." He buried his face in his hands.

"Me too. It was such a shock."

"It was a good thing that you noticed the light was on in her front room."

"It was lucky really. I just happened to look up at the house by chance when I was coming home from work."

Freya had a sudden feeling that, through exhaustion and shock, she might burst into tears, but she bit her lip and fought them back. Crying in front of Finn was unthinkable. But she couldn't stop dwelling on the guilt she was feeling about how she'd left things with Agnes. Her curiosity had got the better of her again. She'd done just what she'd done with her grandfather—she'd pushed too far for information. Now she was beginning to wonder if she'd been wrong to try to speak to him about his past. After all, that was what had led to their rift. And now she'd risked the very same thing with Agnes.

Why hadn't she learned her lesson?

"How was she in the ambulance?" Finn asked.

Freya shrugged. "Still unconscious, I think . . . there was a mask over her face. I just hope she's going to be OK."

"Look, if you'd prefer to go home, I can call you a taxi. I can stay on here and talk to the doctors if you like?"

Freya shook her head. "No, Finn, I want to stay." And it was true. Even though she was dropping from exhaustion, there was no way she could even think about going back to the flat until she knew that Agnes was going to be all right.

So they sat there side by side. At one point, Finn bought them cans of Coke and chocolate bars from the vending machine. Freya was glad of the comfort of the blast of sugar to her shocked system.

Neither spoke very much, and for the first time, Freya

began to wish that Finn would revert to his normal, cheery conversational mode. The fact that he was uncharacteristically silent was proof that he was as worried as she was. There was a television high up on a wall, tuned to a 24-hour rolling news channel with the sound turned down. Freya found her eyes wandering up to it repeatedly, just to keep her mind from going into overdrive, thinking what might be happening to Agnes. She kept telling herself that Agnes was very old, that she must prepare herself for the worst news, but despite that, she didn't want to give up hope. She couldn't stop recalling Agnes' kindness when she'd poured her heart out; Agnes' intuition about Matt and how, despite her prickly exterior, she had a kind and loving soul. They were just getting to know each other and Freya was sure that Agnes was holding onto a lot of pain from her past. How she would have loved Agnes to find the courage to tell her about it, but perhaps now that chance would be cruelly snatched away from them both.

At last, a doctor in a white coat approached. She was young, exhaustion etched on her face, but she had kind eyes. She asked them to follow her into a side room, where they all sat in upright armchairs.

"I understand you are Miss Peters' neighbors and that she doesn't have a next of kin?"

They both nodded and the doctor looked down at her notes.

"Well, I'm afraid I have to tell you that Miss Peters has a serious heart condition. She is very frail and it has obviously been building up for some time. Our tests have also found that she has untreated diabetes, high cholesterol levels, and dangerously high blood pressure."

"Is she going to get better?" Freya couldn't help asking in a weak voice.

The doctor sighed and gave her a sympathetic smile. "We'll be able to stabilize her and hopefully discharge her in a few days, but she'll need a lot of medication and care. I'm sorry to have to tell you that she probably only has a few months to live."

"Oh!" Freya's hand flew to her mouth. Finn's face seemed to collapse.

"I know, it must be a shock," the doctor said gently. "But Miss Peters is well into her eighties and I'm afraid she hasn't been looking after herself. Our records show that she hasn't visited a doctor's surgery for over twenty years."

"Can we see her?" Freya asked, but the doctor shook her head.

"Not tonight, I'm afraid. She's heavily sedated now. If you call the intensive care ward tomorrow morning, they'll tell you whether she's well enough to have visitors tomorrow afternoon."

Freya and Finn walked side by side out through the waiting room, through the sliding glass doors, and out into the hospital car park.

"My van's over there," said Finn, indicating a battered blue Ford Transit parked in a corner under a streetlamp. "I'll drive you home."

"I didn't know you had a van," said Freya, getting up into the passenger seat as Finn moved a pile of books and newspapers aside for her to sit down. The van seemed very old and smelled of wood polish and paint.

"I usually keep it at the workshop, but I have to make a delivery first thing tomorrow morning so I brought it home tonight, as luck would have it. There's an antique chest of drawers in the back."

The engine roared as he started it up and he turned to her with a teasing smile. "I hope you don't mind being seen driving through Cambridge in an old jalopy like this—it's not very stylish."

She smiled back and saw sadness in his dark eyes. They both knew that Finn was only trying to keep up their spirits, to distract them from the traumatic events of the evening and the tragic news about Agnes. At least his face no longer bore that look of utter despair that it had when they'd been talking to the doctor. But as they drove back through the town, she stared out at the floodlit colleges and had a sudden image of wandering hand in hand with Cameron late at night through these romantic streets when they were carefree students and how all her hopes and dreams from those magical times had come to a bitter end. It was only a few hours since he had come into the pub with all his mates. So much had happened since, it seemed a lifetime ago, but the encounter had shown her that her feelings were still raw.

She was still recalling her shock at seeing Cameron again as they arrived in Chesterton Road and Finn maneuvered the van into the alley behind the house and parked up. They walked through the garden gate, down the long, paved garden, and into the house through the back door. At the bottom of the stairs, he stopped and turned to her: "Would you like to come in for a nip of brandy? It's been a tough evening."

Freya couldn't meet his eye. She knew it wasn't Finn's fault that she felt the way she did and that it was seeing Cameron that had brought back all those troubling feelings. But something inside her was stopping her responding to Finn's friendly overtures.

"No," she said. "Thanks all the same, but I'm shattered. I just need to get some sleep."

He shrugged. "As you like," he said. "I have to go out early for that delivery, but I'll pop next door and feed Claus first and I'll call the hospital when I get a chance afterward."

"It's OK. I'll call them and text you. What's your number?"

He told her and she tapped it into her phone.

"See you tomorrow then," she said, starting up to the first floor wearily. She expected to hear the slam of his door as he went into his flat, but none came and she sensed that he was still standing there, watching her walk up the stairs. But she didn't look back.

Despite her exhaustion, Freya lay wide awake for hours, staring at the shifting patterns made by the moon on the ceiling, thinking of poor Agnes, lying there helpless and alone on her living room floor, her colorless, inert face in the ambulance, and the shock of hearing that she only had months to live.

The next morning, she felt drained, but she got up early and called the hospital. A nurse on the intensive care ward told her that Agnes had come round and been moved to the general medical ward. She would be able to see visitors that afternoon after three o' clock.

"You won't be able to stay long, I'm afraid. A few minutes at the most. She'll get tired very quickly."

"I understand," said Freya. Then she called Finn and they arranged to meet outside the hospital entrance just before three.

"I can pick you up and take you over in the van if you like? I'm just on my way back to my workshop now."

"Thanks, but it's fine, Finn. I can cycle to the hospital. I'm going to the library anyway."

When she'd hung up, she reflected for a moment, wondering why she'd refused his offer of a lift. She'd already decided that she was too tired to go into the library, that instead she would work at home that day; she'd told the white lie to avoid him coming to collect her.

Sighing, wondering at her own reticence, she sat down at the table in the window and opened up her laptop. She'd resolved to get on with working through more Inclosure Acts for her thesis, but there was a tantalizing email from Lewis at the top of her inbox:

Here's an update on the research I've been doing this week. I followed up loads of leads and found this forum for Ex-RAF Polish airmen from WWII. It contains several first-hand accounts of wartime experiences from Polish airmen who came to Britain. It's so interesting. What do you think? Do you think they are usable for my dissertation? Do you have any advice about how to go about verifying the sources?

She clicked on the link in his email and was immediately drawn in, quickly becoming completely enthralled and forgetting about her own work. The time flew by as she read. The accounts were all quite similar and bore out the previous research Lewis had sent her. They were written by men from all over Poland, born between around 1910 and 1920. Many had been attracted by the romance of aviation to sign up with the Polish air force in the 1930s and had joined squadrons up and down Poland. They had been fiercely proud of their country and the professionalism of their air force. Many described their devastation when the Germans invaded Poland in September 1939 and, after a doomed attempt to hold a much stronger enemy off, they'd had to escape to surrounding countries, most fleeing to Romania. The pain at having to leave their homeland and their families behind them with no way of knowing what would happen to them was plain to see. As Freya had read before, many ended up in France fighting against a German invasion, and once France itself was invaded, they were evacuated to Britain, where they were gradually absorbed into the RAF, once again risking their lives to fight against the Germans for the remainder of the war.

Freya already knew most of these facts, but reading these first-hand accounts from the men who, like her grandfather, had lived through those traumatic times, brought home to her just what a terrifying and tragic ordeal it must have been for him to be ripped from his home, having to leave behind everything he knew to be destroyed by the enemy. She read on and on, forgetting all about her own work, drawn in by the details of these young men's plights, getting a clear sense of the upheaval the war must have wrought on them.

Eventually, she came to one account that made her stop in her tracks and read and reread the document over and over again. It was written by Michal Nowak, an airman who had originally come from Warsaw, but had settled in the north of England. At first, his story followed the usual pattern. After the German invasion, he'd escaped via Romania to France and had eventually arrived in England, where he'd joined RAF squadron 301, known as "the Land of Pomerania," becoming a navigator. He described how he and a comrade were flying a bombing mission to Germany when they were shot down over the coast of France, their stricken plane falling from the sky in flames:

> I managed to get out with a few burns, but the pilot, Sgt Janick Kowalski, a Polish air force comrade from my Warsaw days, but originally from Hajnowka, as well as being badly burned, had his leg crushed in the fuselage. We were picked up by a British vessel and taken back to England. Sgt Kowalski never flew again, but he was awarded a medal for gallantry for helping me to safety when the plane went down and for the 100 successful missions he'd previously flown for the RAF.

Freya stared at the words on the screen: *Sergeant Janick Kowalski.* That *must* be her grandfather, it just couldn't be anyone else. She knew that his leg had been wounded in the war, an injury from which he'd never recovered. He'd always found it difficult to walk and it had just got worse as he got older.

So everything fitted with Michel Nowak's account. Freya's heart beat faster as she peered again at the words. Here was a tiny but crucial clue to her grandfather's life before the war. Freya quickly did an internet search on the town of Hajnowka and found that it was on the edge of a great expanse of primeval forest, the Bialowieza Forest, where herds of wild bison still roamed freely. Her mind flew back to the picture of the dense, snowbound woodland in her grandfather's room, the towering conifers that surrounded the remote fortified farmstead. That forest must surely be Bialowieza. What an impression growing up in such a wild place must have made on him. Had he lived in that mysterious farmstead in the picture, or in the town itself? A quick search of the town revealed that it had suffered terrible, devastating bombing raids during the war and that many of its citizens had been killed. How had he felt about escaping that fate? How many of his friends or even family had suffered at the hands of the Nazis and the Russians? Why had he never spoken about it?

She thought about her grandfather's belongings. Would they give up the secrets he'd guarded for a lifetime? Would they confirm where he'd come from in Poland and reveal more about his life before he joined the air force? Something had to explain the bitterness and anger he had taken to the grave. It was clear he'd suffered greatly, just as Agnes had, but perhaps with Agnes there was a chance that she might be able to speak about the terrors of her past before it was too late.

The time flew by and soon it was time to set off for Addenbrooke's. It was blustery as Freya pedaled across Jesus Green, the sky was darkening, and autumn leaves spiraled about in the currents. Raindrops blew in gusts, soaking her face. She didn't mind. She loved the fresh autumn air, the strange, clear light, and the feeling of being out alone in a gathering storm. She was glad to be able to visit Agnes too. What a relief the older woman had survived her attack. When Freya had first seen her sprawled on the living room floor, she'd imagined the worst.

Once she was clear of the gardens she stopped at a florist's shop. She looked round for sunflowers, recalling how pleased Agnes had been with the bunch she'd bought her in those first days. But there wasn't much choice and many of the flowers looked past their best. She chose a bunch of brightly colored flowers, with Michaelmas daisies, cornflowers, foxgloves, and sweet peas.

As she chained her bike up outside the hospital entrance, she saw Finn walking toward her across the car park. He waved as he approached and she saw that he was carrying a bunch of pink roses.

"How was the library?" he asked.

"Oh!" Freya was momentarily at a loss for words but decided to come clean. "Well, actually, I decided to work at home after all. Just couldn't get my act together to go into the library."

Finn gave her a skeptical look but said nothing.

They followed the signs to the general medical ward, took a lift to the third level, and arrived at some locked double doors. A notice invited them to press a buzzer. The door was opened by a smiling nurse who invited them in and showed them through the main ward to a side room. Seeing the flowers, she said, "If you leave them in the sink in Miss Peters' room, I'll find a vase for them later."

Agnes was propped up in a bed beside a window, connected by wires to various bleeping and flashing machines. She turned to look at them as they entered, but her eyes were confused.

"Agnes?" Finn approached the bed first. "It's me, Finn. And Freya is here too. We've come to see how you're doing. We brought you flowers." He held out the roses and Agnes peered at him, then her face cleared. "Finn," she said, reaching out and clutching his hand with trembling fingers.

"How are you feeling?" he asked.

Freya hung back.

"I've been better," she said with a wan smile. "Thank you for coming. Who's that with you?"

"It's me, Freya." Freya stepped forward, took Agnes' cold hand, and held the flowers out for her to see. Agnes focused on the petals. She blinked quickly for a few moments and Freya saw there were tears in her eyes.

"How did you know?" Agnes muttered, looking up at her.

Freya frowned, confused. "Know?"

"How did you know about the cornflowers?"

"Cornflowers?"

"Yes. All over the countryside they were, during spring and summer"—Agnes' eyes took on a dreamy look—"in the ditches, on the banks of the lake where we used to swim on hot days. The national flower . . ."

"National flower . . . of Lithuania, Agnes?"

Agnes shook her head. "Not Lithuania, dear, no. Before Lithuania. It has gone now. The land where the cornflowers bloomed." A tear escaped from the corner of her eye and rolled down her wrinkled cheek.

"Oh, Agnes, please don't upset yourself," Freya said, squeezing her hand.

Freya exchanged glances with Finn and he raised his eyebrows as if to say, "I have no idea what this is about either."

"The nurse said she'd put the flowers in a vase for you later," Freya said, still holding Agnes' hand. "I'll ask her to put them beside your bed."

"Would you do something for me, dear?" said Agnes, gripping her fingers.

"Yes, anything."

"Fetch a photograph for me? From my bedroom? It's important. I have to have it with me."

"Of course."

"It is on my bedside table, in a silver frame. And could you bring it back straight away, please? I can't be without it."

Finn drove Freya back to Chesterton Road, stopped the van outside the house, and handed her the key to Agnes' place.

"Do you want me to come in with you?" he asked.

"It's OK, I'll be quick."

"I'll go and turn the van round and wait out here for you."

She let herself into the empty house and shivered at the blast of cold, damp air that greeted her in the hallway. Claus bounded toward her down the passageway and rubbed himself against her legs, purring loudly.

"Poor Claus. Are you lonely?" She bent down to stroke him. "Finn will come in to feed you later on."

She started up the staircase. Even though Agnes had asked her to come into her house and go into her bedroom, she still felt like an intruder. Unlike in Freya's own house next door, which was clean and bright, this one hadn't been modernized. The walls were papered in floral brown wallpaper, the staircase was mahogany, and the carpet on it threadbare, secured by brass stair rods. She went upstairs, trailing her hand on the wooden banister. The cat followed her to the top. She had an instinct that Agnes' room would be the one at the front with the bay window overlooking the river and she was right.

The heavy velvet curtains were drawn, so the room was in semi-darkness. Freya put on the light and took in the bedroom. Like the rest of the house, this room was a museum, with dark, heavy furniture and a gilt-edged mirror above the fireplace. Freya moved about cautiously, still feeling awkward about being in this most private place. The room was cluttered but fairly tidy, except for some clothes left in a pile in the corner and a stack of books on a chair. She picked one up, a novel, and scanned the first page. She knew just about enough German to recognize the language. Freya fleetingly recalled Agnes' love of German bread. So, was Agnes actually German? From East Prussia, not Lithuania? But why if that were the case would she have said she came from Lithuania?

Beside the bed was a walnut bedside cabinet, a small china pot containing some oddments of jewelry, a half-empty glass of water, and a small, silver-framed photograph. Freya switched on the bedside lamp, picked up the photo, and peered at it. A small boy with white-blond hair stared out at her. He was dressed in old-fashioned, baggy shorts with braces and boots. He was standing in front of a window. Through the window was a garden, with flowering bushes. His legs and arms looked very thin, but he was smiling, his eyes shining into the camera.

Freya flipped the photograph over. On the back was written, in scrawling handwriting, "Dieter, Lithuania, 1945."

Back in the van, she showed Finn the photo. "I wonder who that is?"

Finn shrugged, pulling out into the traffic. "She's always maintained she hasn't got any family but I know she went through hell during the war. She will never talk about it, not to me anyway."

"He was clearly very special to her. A brother maybe? A cousin, or a nephew?"

"Perhaps she'll tell you . . . Hey, why don't you go in on your own this time?"

So she left Finn to drive back to his workshop and went back into the hospital alone. The same friendly nurse let her into the ward and when she entered Agnes' room, she saw that both bunches of flowers were already arranged in vases beside the bed. Agnes looked very small and vulnerable, lying there among all that equipment. Freya went to the bed and handed her the photograph.

"Oh, you brought it. You are a good girl. Thank you." Agnes

took the photograph and held it up to her eyes. She stared at it for a long moment and, as Freya watched, Agnes' eyes filled with tears.

"Oh, Agnes," Freya said gently, sitting down beside her. "Please don't cry. Could you tell me what it is? Who is the boy in the photo?"

Agnes handed Freya the photograph and she propped it up beside the wildflowers. Anxiously, she watched Agnes taking deep breaths, fighting against her tears. She wondered if she should call the nurse.

"It is my brother. My younger brother, Dieter."

"Your brother?"

Agnes nodded. "I have to have his photo. I need him with me. I promised Mutti, you see."

FIFTEEN

AGNES

East Prussia, 1945

Night had fallen by the time they entered the city of Danzig. The streets were full of refugees trying to get to the docks. As the cart moved slowly through the congested streets, Agnes, numb from loss and shock, stared out at the imposing buildings, some decorated with great banners bearing the Nazi flag. The image of Dieter weeping over his mother's body was etched in her mind. It was cruel to tear him away but she could only give him a moment before she knew they simply had to keep moving.

At last they reached the docks and after queuing at a barbed-wire barrier to be checked in by soldiers, they were waved through to wait in a customs shed with hundreds of other hungry, desperate people. At the door, the officer in charge said, "Take your cart down to that disused land and leave it there. No carts inside the shed. Only one suitcase each allowed."

On a patch of wasteland behind the customs sheds, already

cluttered with abandoned vehicles, they left the cart along with many of the belongings they'd struggled so hard to bring this far. They took as many warm clothes as they could cram into their suitcases, together with their remaining scraps of food. Agnes stared at Mother's suitcase, the only one left on the back of the cart, her heart aching and her eyes filling with tears.

"It's terribly hard, I know, my love," Aunt Hannah said as she wiped at her own eyes. "But we'll have to leave that here too." She was looking at Mother's suitcase as well.

It was also time to leave Florian behind and turn him loose to fend for himself as best he could alongside the other abandoned horses already wandering about. Aunt Hannah slipped off his bridle and harness and fed him the last of the oats from the sack.

"Are we just going to leave him here?" Dieter's bottom lip was wobbling again. He'd not stopped crying since they'd left Mother's body on the ice. Agnes put her arm around him. She felt his pain as if it were her own. Having to leave Florian would be severing yet another link with the past and was a fresh blow, on top of losing Mother, that brought home the tragedy of their situation even more starkly.

"We have to, Dieter dear," Aunt Hannah said. "I'm very sad too. But we have no choice."

"But what will happen to him?"

No one knew the answer to that question. Swallowing her own tears, Agnes threw her arms around Florian's neck and buried her face in his damp mane. He whinnied quietly and lifted his head. The earthy smell of him brought back all those summer days on the farm when she used to play with Joachim and Gunter in the barns and stables. Florian was the last link with that life and it was unbearable to say goodbye to him.

When Agnes was finally able to step away from the old horse, Aunt Hannah slapped his rump and he set off at a trot across the wasteland, between the abandoned wagons, heading toward two other horses who were sheltering from the cold beside the wall of the customs shed.

"Goodbye, old friend," murmured Aunt Hannah and tucked her arm into Agnes', and the three of them turned away and walked solemnly back toward the entrance to the shed. Agnes walked in silence, the lump in her throat preventing her from speaking.

The shed itself was full of people just like them, waiting to make their escape to Greater Germany or to Denmark by sea. The sound of hundreds of voices under the echoing roof was deafening. There was nowhere to sit apart from the freezing concrete floor, so they spread their spare clothes and blankets out and huddled together during that perishing, endless night.

Although she was exhausted, Agnes lay awake, her mind going over and over what had happened. Her grief and sadness pressed down on her chest like a heavy weight. Dieter, snuggling beside her, slept fitfully. Every so often he jerked awake with a cry. In the background, Agnes was dimly aware of babies wailing and the coughing and snoring of the hundreds of other refugees who surrounded them.

She thought back over their terrible journey, the horrifying sights they'd seen, the hunger and hardships they'd endured to get this far. The loss they had suffered was hard to comprehend. Her mind was filled with images of Mother, of her kind face, of her constant presence, and of her sacrifice. She thought of Papa too and of her uncle and cousins. Were they still alive? And if they were, would they ever be reunited? She yearned for her home and for her old, secure life, but she knew deep down that that life was gone and nothing would ever be the same again.

In the morning they were awoken before dawn by soldiers blowing whistles, barking orders to everyone to get up and line up; there was a ship already docked and ready to take them to

Keil. They would be safe from the Russian advance there. The three of them scrambled up, rubbing their eyes, and packed up their belongings. Then they shuffled along with everyone else through the doors of the customs shed, along the dockside, already swarming with people trying desperately to board the single ship that was docked there. It took a couple of hours pushing forward in the freezing cold through the press of bodies until they finally arrived at the ship's gangplank. An officer waved them on board: "There are no bunks left. You will have to find a space in the ballroom," he said. "Turn to your left and up two flights."

The ship was huge, an old passenger liner that must have been used as a troopship, judging by how shabby and run-down it was. Virtually every space inside was already taken by desperate people, sitting, squatting, or lying in corridors, filling the decks and stairs. Eventually they found the ballroom, its chandeliers, grand pillars, and corniced ceilings boasting of grander days. It was warm inside the ship; warmer than they had been for weeks. The ballroom was almost full too, but Aunt Hannah found a corner where they could spread their blankets and sit down together. As they settled, the giant engines began to rumble into life, vibrating the floor and making the chandeliers rattle and shake. A cheer went up throughout the ship; all those people who'd struggled for weeks through ice and snow to get here were overjoyed to be leaving East Prussia and the dangers it held. Agnes felt a pang of sadness for everything and everyone they were leaving behind. As she looked around her, she wondered if she was the only one feeling that way.

"Do you mind if I go on deck, Aunt Hannah?" she asked, getting to her feet.

Aunt Hannah looked anxious, her face blotchy with tears from sobbing through the night.

"Please . . . I just want to say goodbye," Agnes began and from Aunt Hannah's eyes she could tell she understood.

"Well, don't be long. And be careful, please."

"Can I come?" Dieter was on his feet too.

"Of course." Agnes took his hand and they began to pick their way over the blankets, belongings, and people lying down.

The icy wind hit Agnes as she left the ballroom with Dieter clinging to her hand. They found a metal ladder that took them up to the promenade deck. There weren't many people on deck, just a few families huddling beside one of the chimneys for warmth and a row of hardy stalwarts bundled up in coats and blankets at the rail. Agnes found a space and stared out at the snowbound city as the ship eased away from the dock wall and the length of choppy water between the dock and the ship grew wider. Then the ship was moving forward, clearing the docks, and sailing out into the Bay of Danzig. She looked back at the land as the shape of the buildings grew less distinct and soon it was just a mass of gray melting into the white sky.

Agnes had never been away from East Prussia before. She gazed back at the land where they had lost Mother and where Mother's body still lay abandoned on the frozen icy wastes. Her eyes filled with tears and her heart filled with fresh grief. How could she bear to go on without her? And would she ever see East Prussia again? She felt overwhelmed with homesickness for her old life and for the only land she had ever known.

Other passengers drifted below deck, unable to bear the sub-freezing temperatures, and soon Agnes and Dieter were the only ones there, clinging to the iced-up rail, staring out at the gray line of land as it grew fainter and fainter. They must have been standing there for more than half an hour. Agnes knew that Aunt Hannah would be worried about them, but she couldn't tear her eyes from that last diminishing glimpse of East Prussia.

"I'm frozen. Can't we go inside?" Dieter kept saying. When the last gray line of land had finally melted into the horizon, they turned to walk toward the doors leading back to the steps. At that moment there was an ear-splitting crash and the ship jolted side-ways, sending them sprawling onto the boards. At the same time a huge spray of water jetted across the deck. The explosion was followed by the sound of screaming and the frantic blaring of sirens. Within seconds came another shuddering crack and the engines juddered to a stop. The air was eerily silent then, filled only with the shouting and screaming of panicked crew and passengers.

The ship quickly began to list sideways.

"We need to find Aunt Hannah." Agnes was trembling, she could barely speak. She grabbed Dieter's hand and made for the steps. But as soon as they'd reached the next deck down, they were swept up in a crowd of frantic people swarming out from the rooms and cabins on that floor, blocking the next staircase down to the ballroom. Women and children were screaming, skidding sideways on the tilting deck, crowding toward the life-boats on the other side. Crewmen were already there beside the lifeboats, pulling off the covers, fixing them to ropes, cranking them out over the edge of the ship.

An officer in uniform grabbed Agnes' arm.

"Women and children first. Come on, let's get you over to the other side. There'll be a space in a lifeboat for you."

"But my auntie . . ." Agnes stuttered. "She's in the ballroom."

The man looked at her, frowning. "You can't go down there now. She'll be evacuated from the next deck down. You'll have to go on your own. Now come on."

Dieter was wailing hard now. Agnes could see his contorted face but she couldn't hear his cries; they were muffled by all the screaming and commotion on the deck. The ship's sirens had started up too, blasting repeatedly, adding to the panic and confusion. His fingers pinching into their arms, the officer propelled them through the crowd to the other side. As soon as they'd reached it, another crewman swept Dieter up and lifted him into a lifeboat. Then he waved Agnes toward it.

"Climb in," he said. "Quickly now."

She put a foot onto the short ladder. The boat was rocking, causing her to stumble as she climbed.

"Hurry, hurry, there's no time to waste," the sailor kept shouting.

The lifeboat was already crowded with women and children, huddling to the sides, their faces white with terror. Some of them were wearing padded lifejackets. Agnes realized with a jolt that no one had given her and Dieter one; in fact, no one in the ballroom had been wearing lifejackets. What if the lifeboat capsized? Agnes herself was a strong swimmer. Dieter could swim too, but she wasn't sure how well. Suppressing these thoughts, she pulled him down beside her on the bench as the boat filled up with more women and children. Two sailors were the last to jump in.

"We're here to row you," one of them said when a woman started berating him.

The little lifeboat jerked and shuddered as it was cranked out on its chains over the side of the listing ship. Each time it jolted, people let out terrified screams. Agnes and Dieter, tight-lipped with fear, stayed silent. As the lifeboat reached the limit of the crane, it paused in mid-air. Agnes gasped as she got a bird's-eye view of the angle of the ship. She knew then how far it had listed over in those few minutes since it had been hit. Then the ropes above moved again and they were descending quickly toward the choppy waters of the Baltic Sea. As they went down, they got a full view of the two gaping holes in the ship's side. Through one of these great gouges, the chandeliers and pillars of the ballroom were visible, now half-submerged under water. Inside the flooded ballroom was the unmistakable sight of bodies floating on the surface. Letting out a squeal of shock, Agnes let go of Dieter's hand and scrambled up on the side of the lifeboat.

"Aunt Hannah!" she yelled. "Aunt Hannah!" But her voice was lost in the wind and the creaking of the ropes.

"Get down, girl!" ordered one of the sailors. "You'll upset the boat."

She shrank back down onto the bench, numb with shock, and the next second the lifeboat splashed down on the icy waves. The two sailors grabbed the oars and began to row furiously away from the stricken ship. Dieter clung to Agnes, shivering, and she stroked his wet hair, trying to comfort him as they pulled away. She stared back at the ship. It was slipping further and further into the water, the people crowding onto the deck, the lifeboats plummeting from the side and hitting the water. People were throwing themselves from the upper decks now too, giving up hope of a place in a lifeboat. Was Aunt Hannah one of those? Had she made it out of the ballroom before the water flooded in? Agnes closed her eyes and gritted her teeth, trying to blot it all out. She didn't want to watch any more. She didn't want to think either; it was all too much to bear.

SIXTEEN

"Wake up, girl!" Someone was shaking her arm. Agnes opened her eyes, momentarily confused. She'd been deep inside a heavy dream, running on a sunlit day through the ripe summer corn in a field near her home. The corn was dotted with poppies. Liesel's arm was linked through her own and they were making for a lake a couple of kilometers from the village. It was surrounded by poplar trees and cornflowers bloomed on the grassy banks. The sun was burning through her skin and she couldn't wait to reach the water to cool off. On the banks of the lake they would take off their dresses and bathe in the delicious cool of the fresh water on the hottest of days.

"Wake up!"

Blinking into the present, she felt the chill, dank air of the army shelter and saw the gloomy concrete of her surroundings. Everything came back to her in a rush. She experienced a moment of groundless despair as she remembered how her world had fallen apart over the past forty-eight hours.

A soldier was bending over her, shaking her, frowning impatiently. Dieter lay on the hard bench beside her, his eyes closed, breathing through his mouth. The inhospitable army shelter was crowded and the air was rank with their collective stale breath. People were getting up now, wrapping themselves up in their sodden clothes, their faces dazed and shaken. The other occupants of the shelter were all women and children. Agnes looked around her at the family groups and it dawned on her that she and Dieter were the only youngsters there without their mother. Most of the other children were much younger; babies and toddlers, many of them, grizzling and bawling in the chilly, damp air.

"You need to get up and walk to the station. There is a train waiting to take you to Königsberg," the soldier barked. "From there, you can get to the port of Pillau, where you'll be evacuated by boat."

She stared at him, her mouth dry, digesting what this meant. The loss of Aunt Hannah and Mutti was fresh in her mind. She could hardly focus on anything except the overwhelming grief she was feeling. But boarding another ship to cross the Baltic that could easily be torpedoed just like the first one? She shivered at the prospect.

"You need to get on that train. It is the last one to Königsberg. There will be no more after that one. There is porridge and water in the next room if you are quick."

Shrugging away her fears, Agnes quickly got to her feet and shook Dieter awake. They had slept in their wet clothes and had nothing else to put on, so they struggled back into their damp coats. The night before, when the lifeboat had washed up on a deserted beach, they'd eventually been collected in an army truck and brought inland to this shelter. They'd been told that it was on an army base outside the town of Elbing. They'd been given water and hot soup, but nothing more. Rough army-issue blankets had been distributed and they'd been told to go to sleep on the hard, wooden benches and bunks in the shelter. Like Agnes and Dieter, everyone around them had been in a state of deep shock from their ordeal. From their traumatized faces, Agnes guessed like them, most of the women must have lost loved ones when the ship went down. Talking to a few of them, she'd discovered that the occupants of two other lifeboats were there too. Her heart lifted in hope then and she'd searched among them for any sign or news of Aunt Hannah. But she'd searched in vain. She asked several of the women if any of them had been in the ship's ballroom when it went down, but they all shook their heads.

It was impossible to get information. None of the soldiers knew anything about other survivors either. In fact, they seemed put out at having to help these washed-up women and children who should have been on their way to Kiev, when they should be preparing themselves to fight the Russians. They dealt with them gruffly and without an ounce of compassion or sympathy.

Agnes' heart was so heavy with loss that she had no appetite for the bowl of lumpy porridge an orderly handed her, but she forced it down, not knowing when she might eat again. In contrast, Dieter wolfed his down. She was relieved to see him eating, but she saw that his lips were now cracked and sore. It must have been from the freezing wind in the three hours they'd spent in the lifeboat exposed on the Baltic Sea. When he'd finished eating, she took his hand and they followed the rest of the women and children out into the freezing morning. They trudged through the snow along a long, straight road past some empty, boarded-up houses to a lonely railway station, where they crammed onto a train that was already almost full. The mothers pushed on in front of Agnes, quickly grabbing the last available seats for themselves and their children. Agnes and Dieter found themselves standing in a crowded lobby beside the doors.

"I want Mutti," Dieter sobbed as the train jerked forward and pulled out of the station. Agnes squeezed his hand. The sadness in his voice and the anguish and pain she herself was feeling for the loss of Mother brought tears to her eyes.

"I know," she whispered. She wanted Mutti too, how desperately she wanted Mutti, but she remembered Mutti's dying words and knew she had to be strong for Dieter so she swallowed her tears.

"Don't cry, Dieter, I will look after you," she said, bending down and putting her arms around him, holding him tight. "I'm going to make sure we're all right."

"But where are we going?"

"We're going somewhere safe, don't you worry. Everything will be fine."

She managed to say those words in such a bright tone that she almost believed them herself. The train gathered speed and she watched through the window as they rolled through the flat, snowbound landscape. They rattled past farms and villages, forests and lakes. The countryside was still beautiful in its shroud of sparkling white, but it also looked forlorn and abandoned. There was nobody around: no animals or farmers in the fields, no pony carts or sleighs on the lanes. Many of the farms had already been bombed out, their jagged roof timbers stark against the white sky.

The lobby was crowded with people. Old men and women, bundled up in coats and blankets, blocked the light from the window on the other side of the train. But when Agnes happened to glance over in that direction, she got an occasional glimpse of the frozen wastes of the Frisches Haff. Once, she even caught sight of a trail of wagons crawling across it in a long line. They were so far away, they looked like a column of ants. It sent chills right through her, remembering their own fateful trek across that ice, and to think that Mother's body still lay on that great frozen expanse where they had left her, only two days before. She turned away, unable to bear the sight, and pointed out some flying geese to Dieter to make sure he didn't look that way too.

The train made many unexplained stops before it reached the city of Königsberg. Often, desperate people carrying bundles and suitcases tried to board at country stations but were pushed away by guards shouting that there was no more room. They ground to a halt on the outskirts of the city and in the momentary silence, Agnes could distinctly hear the rumble of distant shelling. Her skin crawled with fear. Hadn't people said they would be safe coming this way to the port of Pillau? As they continued on through the beaten city, Agnes saw first-hand what the bombing she'd read of in the papers last summer had done. Warehouses beside the railway line had been reduced to piles of crumbling brick, rows of houses without roofs, ruined churches, cratered streets mounded with rubble.

At Königsberg station soldiers with guns and batons ordered everyone off the train. All was chaos. They climbed down onto the platform in a sea of confused people. Everyone was impatient to get to Pillau and onto a ship, and unhappy to be forced off the train here.

"Where's the train to the port?" a woman in front of Agnes asked angrily.

"There are no more trains, lady," one of the soldiers replied. "It isn't safe for them to go to the port anymore. The Red Army has broken through. You'll have to stay here in the city."

They were herded by soldiers out of the station, through the empty streets where the houses were boarded up, abandoned vehicles and trams littered the roadside, and packs of feral dogs rooted in the many piles of rotting rubbish. The sound of the battle was much louder here. Every so often, against the rumble of the shelling, there would be a loud whistling sound followed by the crash of an explosion. Everyone ducked instinctively each time it happened. The bombs were getting closer and closer as they walked, some of them sounding as though they'd landed in the next street. Agnes was sick with fear as she stumbled along, holding Dieter's hand. It was as if she was inside a nightmare from which she would never wake up. She felt so utterly helpless and alone, terrified for herself and for Dieter.

They entered a great cobbled square and Agnes recognized some of the beautiful medieval buildings from her trips to the city with Mother and Papa. How different it looked now with its smashed or boarded-up windows, some of the facades shattered by the shelling. A soldier ahead stopped beside a heavy studded door on the pavement. He yanked it open and motioned the people through.

"There are cellars down there," he said. "Go down and wait until the battle is over. You will be safe from the bombings down there."

Obediently, they went inside. As Agnes went through the door she shivered at the breath of foul, dank air that greeted her. It was cold and dark and, as they went down the steps, Dieter began to cry again.

"Why do we have to go down here? I want Mutti," he wailed.

"We'll be safe here," Agnes told him. "We won't be here long and I will look after you," she went on as they descended into the dark, smelly depths. But the place sent shivers down her spine too and she had no idea whether they would ever get out of there alive.

SEVENTEEN

Agnes was running as fast as her legs would carry her. She was dragging Dieter along beside her, her heart pounding, her mouth dry, her breath coming in great, sobbing gulps. All around them was chaos. Dust and rubble from bombed-out buildings covered the ground they ran on and they frequently slipped and stumbled on the icy ground, dodging piles of rubble, fallen roof timbers, burned-out vehicles. She was running as if her life depended on it—and she knew it did depend on it. She expected at any moment to come face to face with Russian soldiers wielding guns, or for a shot to ring out from one of the buildings that would spell the end to this nightmare.

"Please God, keep us safe," she kept praying fiercely under her breath. It might be easier to die than to face what they were facing, but in her confused state all she could think of was Dieter and her promise to their mother. If she were gone, however would he cope alone?

It had been instinct that had told her to scramble up the bare stone wall and out through the opening in the cellar when the soldiers had burst in through the back doors. It had only taken a moment or two for her to understand what was happening and to make the decision to escape by whatever means possible. From where she and Dieter had stood, crushed behind the press of people cowering away from the soldiers, she couldn't see what was happening near the doors, but she could hear everything. Having been shocked to the core by the newspaper reports about what had happened at Nemmersdorf, she understood only too well.

"*Frau, Frau . . .*" the soldiers were shouting and there were screams as women were dragged away, yelling and fighting. When protests came from the men, shots rang out, followed by thuds as bodies dropped to the ground. Chills of dread went through Agnes.

"Come, Dieter," she said, her voice shaking. "Let's climb out."

She found a foothold in the crumbling stone of the cellar wall and guided his foot toward it. When the people around them saw what they were trying to do, they helped by lifting and pushing them up toward the opening. Agnes went out first, squeezing herself through, grazing her shins on the rough surface, then Dieter emerged a few seconds behind her, pushed out by a kind man. Standing outside in the deserted street, blinking in the dust-filled daylight, Agnes was momentarily confused. Which way should she turn? But in a split second she'd made her decision. Going back into the square was unthinkable; from where she stood, she could still see groups of soldiers with guns kicking down doors, scrambling over piles of rubble. So she turned the other way and started to run, pulling Dieter along with her. She didn't know the city well and it was virtually unrecognizable now as the beautiful, majestic place that Papa used to bring them to, but she had an instinct that the direction she'd chosen would lead them away from the city center.

They ran past the destroyed cathedral and the bombed-out castle, then down a random side street between tall, terraced buildings that appeared empty. Did anyone live here anymore or had they all evacuated ahead of the Russian army? Many of the houses and tenements bore the scars of bombs: broken roofs or blown-away front walls, shattered windows and doors. Others were boarded up. At first, they didn't see a soul in some streets, only packs of skinny dogs running together. Once they almost trod on several large, scruffy rats scurrying toward a broken drain. But after they'd been running a while, they came across a horrific sight. Four or five bloated corpses lying face-down in the gutter. Some were old men, wearing trousers with suspenders, bloodstains on their torn shirts, but there were at least two women, their hair matted with blood, bare legs mottled and bruised against the snow.

Dieter let out a cry, but Agnes forced him on: "Don't look." She stumbled past, her throat choked with revulsion and terror.

Still the sound of shelling filled the air and occasional bursts of machine-gun fire rang out from the other side of the city, but the further they ran, the more the sounds of battle receded. They passed more corpses, some collapsed in doorways, others lying prone on heaps of rubble. At last, in a quiet road, beside an upturned wagon, Agnes stopped. Her legs were refusing to carry her further. She bent over to recover her breath.

"Where are we going?" panted Dieter. "I can't run anymore."

She looked back at him, into his terrified eyes, ringed with exhaustion, at his scarred white skin and his scabby mouth. What could she say to him? Everywhere around held terror; nowhere was safe, there was nowhere for them to go. But the pleading look in his eyes twisted her heartstrings and she became desperate to say something to give him some comfort.

"We're going home, Dieter," she said at last and was gratified that a tentative smile of hope crept into his eyes.

"Home? What, back to the village?" he asked.

"Yes. We will have to walk, but that's where we're going. Come on."

EIGHTEEN

FREYA

Cambridge, Present Day

"And how's the thesis going?" Dan settled into his armchair and peered at Freya earnestly through his pebble glasses. "You seemed to be making better progress with your research last time we spoke."

"Oh, it's going really well, thanks." Freya shifted in her seat, aware that she was forcing enthusiasm into her tone. "I've made a lot of progress. The librarians have unearthed some brilliant material from the archives at the Squire Law Library. I've been getting stuck into some of the early Inclosure Acts."

"Excellent . . . excellent." Dan nodded eagerly. "What a relief, Freya. You know, for a while at the beginning of term, I had my doubts about whether you'd stay the course. It's so reassuring that you're finally finding your feet with your subject matter. Would you like a cup of tea, by the way? I'm about to brew up."

She shook her head. "I'm sorry, but I can't stop long today. I have to get to Addenbrooke's for visiting time."

Dan looked at her with sympathy and concern. "Hospital? I'm sorry to hear that. Anyone close?"

Freya was about to say, "My next-door neighbor," but realized that Agnes was far more than just a neighbor to her now.

"It *is* somebody dear to me, yes. I've only known her a few weeks, but in that short space of time we've become friends. It's the old lady who lives next door. She collapsed a few days ago and another neighbor and I have been visiting her every day to keep her spirits up."

"How very kind of you."

Freya shook her head. "Not kind, really. I *want* to visit her. She's an extraordinary person. You know, eccentric and prickly, but warm and talented too under all that. In a funny way she reminds me of my grandfather."

Dan smiled. "The one you lost during the summer?"

"Yes. They both come from Eastern Europe and have a similar way of speaking. Although Agnes comes from Lithuania and my Jah-Dek was Polish."

"Well, as you probably know, there was a lot of migration across the shifting borders of Poland, East Prussia, and the Baltic states during and after the war. Poles were expelled by the Nazis from Poland after the invasion and later brought into parts of former Germany by the conquering Russians. German citizens in East Prussia evacuated ahead of the Russian invasion and later, and those who remained were left in terrible danger."

Freya sat forward. "I knew it was complicated and that the consequences of the Nazi regime and the Russian invasion for ordinary people were devastating. It's such an interesting period. I'd love to have the time to find out more. And I definitely will, once I've finished my thesis."

Dan smiled and nodded in encouragement, and she went on: "You know, I've been fascinated by the subject chosen by one of my first-year students, Lewis. I told you before, didn't I?

He's researching the Polish airmen who came to the UK during the war and served with the RAF. Amazingly, through what he managed to dig up, I uncovered a connection with my grandfather."

"Go on."

She told him what she'd found out about her grandfather. How she'd discovered which RAF squadron he'd been in, the town in Poland he'd come from, and that he'd been injured when his plane had been shot down over the Channel.

The words tumbled out of her. "It was quite amazing, Dan, seeing his name there in black and white in the other airman's memoir, when my grandfather himself had hardly spoken about it. The war had a terrible effect on him."

"That must have been an incredible find for you—those are the best moments in our line of work, aren't they? When our research turns up something with such a personal connection, that reinforces one's own link to the past so directly."

"It really was an incredible find," she said, then noticed the time on the old brass clock on Dan's desk.

"Oh . . . I'd lost track of the time," she said, standing up. "I have to dash."

"Of course." Dan got up and hurried to open the door for her. "Well, it's been such an interesting conversation. Do keep up the good work. Oh, and Freya—it's great to see you back to your old self."

Freya ran down the stairs and walked across Front Court, out through the porter's lodge. She unlocked her bike from the rack at the front of the college and set off toward the hospital, musing about what Dan had said about shifting populations at the end of the war. She'd hardly considered before what it must be like to be driven from your home, from everything you knew, by a brutal regime or an advancing army. Now she shivered, thinking about it; she pictured columns of people on the march through the snow with all their worldly belongings, not knowing where they were heading, not knowing if they would survive the journey, even. Had poor Agnes gone through something like that? If only she would talk about it. Freya had thought she might open up after she'd brought her the photograph of her brother, but after Agnes had made that revelation she'd clammed up again and she was so ill that Freya hadn't wanted to put her under any pressure. Where was her brother now? Was he the child in that photo?

As Freya arrived at the hospital entrance, she caught sight of Finn cycling up at the same time, the wind ruffling his dark hair, his cheeks flushed in the cold of the November afternoon. As he drew up, he smiled his broad smile. Freya smiled back and realized with a start that she was pleased to see him. They locked their bikes together and walked into the hospital side by side.

It was Agnes' fifth day in hospital and Freya and Finn had made sure that at least one of them had been there to see her every visiting time. The general medical ward was a large, busy place, with nurses and doctors bustling around, the chatter of people's radios and televisions, and families at visiting times. Freya had been worried that Agnes would react badly to being in such close proximity to so many other people—she lived such a solitary life at home—but she seemed content to watch the comings and goings on the ward. Freya had noticed that she did appear unwilling, or perhaps too unwell, to speak more than a few words to either of the old ladies occupying the beds either side of her.

They approached the ward along the final corridor and were about to go in through the double doors when the doors burst open and two people emerged, walking quickly. Freya and Finn stood back to let them pass. At first, Freya didn't recognize the tall doctor in his white coat, his brows knitted together, his face clouded over with irritation, his head held high in an arrogant way. He was clearly scolding the nurse who scuttled along beside him, looking shamefaced.

"Didn't I tell you before to make sure the order from the pharmacy was expedited today? I really shouldn't have to tell you twice..."

Freya caught his eye and at the same instant as she realized who it was, he stopped and turned toward her, his expression changed. "Freya! Oh, Nurse Barratt, you can carry on. There's no need for you to wait for me."

The nurse turned and fled down the corridor.

"Cameron!" Freya was at a loss for words and felt color creep into her cheeks. It was hardly surprising really that she might bump into him here, but the past few days she'd been so busy, what with dashing back and forth to visit Agnes, juggling her job in the pub, and keeping up with her studies and her students, he had scarcely crossed her mind.

"What are you doing here?" he asked, his eyes flicking toward Finn and back again.

"Just visiting a friend."

"Oh." He frowned. "Anyone I know?"

She shook her head but didn't elaborate—she didn't want to tell Cameron about Agnes.

"You must introduce me to your friend," he said, looking pointedly at Finn.

"Finn, Cameron, Cameron, Finn," Freya said awkwardly.

"Good to meet you, Finn." Cameron held out his hand and Finn shook it.

"How d'you do," Finn replied and gave Freya a knowing look.

"So, how do you two know each other? Fellow graduate students?" Cameron asked.

Finn barked out a laugh. "I'm afraid not. I'm just a humble carpenter."

"Oh?" Cameron's smile looked forced.

"Finn and I are neighbors." Freya stepped in quickly.

"Right. Interesting. Look, I must get on, I'm due on another ward. But if you need me to hurry up any of the staff on this ward, for your friend, just give me the word. They'll listen to me. Well, nice to meet you, Finn."

With a quick nod to both of them, he was on his way, striding down the corridor purposefully, already speaking into his mobile phone, his white coat flapping.

"So," said Finn, smiling broadly now, "that's the guy you told me about."

Freya was still going hot and cold with shame and embarrassment. "He's not always like that," she said, but even as she said the words, she was wondering why she was defending Cameron.

"Did you hear the way he spoke to that poor young nurse?" Finn went on.

"I know . . . It was embarrassing. He was so rude."

Finn muttered something angrily and Freya couldn't help smiling to herself.

"Come on, Agnes will be expecting us," she said briskly and they went through the swing doors and began to cross the ward toward Agnes' bed.

"Just neighbors, then, are we?" Finn said as they walked.

"What?"

"You told him we were neighbors."

"Well, we *are* neighbors, aren't we?"

"I was hoping you might count us as at least friends by now, but I can see I've got a way to go before you're prepared to say even that."

They'd almost reached Agnes' bed now and all Freya could do was give Finn a questioning look and shrug helplessly. He smiled back and winked at her to show he was just teasing.

Agnes looked brighter that day. She was sitting up in bed, her hair brushed, reading a library book.

"They say I can go home tomorrow," she said. Freya looked at Finn and she saw from the look in his eyes that he too was wondering how Agnes would cope on her own.

"Don't worry," said Agnes. "They're putting in place a care plan. That nice young nurse told me all about it. People will come in three or four times a day to help me."

"Oh, Agnes, that's wonderful," said Freya, reaching out to take her hand. "I'm so pleased for you. But Finn and I will pop in whenever we can, too."

As Freya and Finn left the ward, to her surprise he said, "Do you fancy going for a coffee or something? We can work out what we're going to do when Agnes comes home."

Freya hesitated. She'd been about to refuse without even thinking about it. She had conditioned that response into her every interaction with Finn, but now she wondered why. When she'd moved into the flat, she'd not wanted to get close to anyone, but circumstances had thrown her and Finn together. Anyway, he'd remained remarkably thick-skinned when she rebuffed him. In fact, he'd taken no notice whatsoever and had just carried on being friendly to her in that half-joking, half-mocking way he had about him. Looking at him now, she realized how much she'd come to rely on his constant presence and relentless cheerfulness, and for the first time she felt a little guilty that she'd treated him the way she had.

"Well?" He was looking at her, his head slightly on one side, that teasing look in his eyes. "Is that a hard question to answer?"

"Sorry, I was just thinking about it. Actually, I'm sorry, but I don't have much time just now. I've got to get back and change and I'm due at the Free Press at six thirty for the evening shift."

"Oh, come on, Freya. It's just a coffee. We could go down to the hospital canteen for ten minutes. What harm could there be in that?"

"Oh no," she said instantly with a shudder, "not there!"

Finn looked puzzled for a second, then his face cleared. "Oh, I get it. You're worried that the dashing doctor might be in there. I see. Well, why don't we stop off somewhere in town instead? I've got to go back to the workshop for a few hours, but there's a great little coffee shop I know tucked away beside the river on Mill Lane. I expect you know it."

"I do," she said, smiling, recalling how Finn had summed up Cameron in a couple of words earlier. Entitled arse indeed.

"Grand. Well, let's cycle there together, shall we?"

As she cycled behind Finn along the main road into town, Freya's mind went into overdrive. She was trying to analyze her feelings. How had it happened that she'd gone from not wanting to even exchange good mornings with this man to agreeing to have coffee with him, appreciating the way he'd summed Cameron up, and even feeling a pang of guilt at only having described them as simply neighbors? She realized, to her surprise, that she was even looking forward to spending a little time with him, to getting to know him a bit better.

The coffee shop was steamy and noisy, packed with students who must have come straight from the lecture halls. Finn strode ahead of Freya and found a table in the corner. As they sipped their coffees, they talked about Agnes and worked out a schedule between them for popping in morning and evening once she was home. They both agreed that even though carers would be coming in, it would really help Agnes to see them regularly too.

"It will be so tough for her," said Finn. "She's been getting weaker for years, but knowing you only have months to live, that's a real blow for anyone, whatever their age."

"Poor, poor Agnes," said Freya. "It's so tragic that she's so alone in the world. So far from where she grew up, and with no family."

"I know," said Finn. "I suppose at least she's got us."

"Has she ever spoken to you about the war and what happened to her family?"

Finn stirred his coffee and looked down at the swirling liquid. "I know a bit about it."

"I wish she'd talk to me about what happened to her during the war. What did she say to you?"

"Not much, just that she'd lost a lot in the war. Which isn't hard to imagine."

"That's terrible," said Freya. "I don't know much about what happened to Lithuania during the war."

Finn looked at her, surprised. "Agnes isn't Lithuanian."

"Really? She told me she came from Lithuania."

"Yes—she came to *this* country from Lithuania in the fifties, but that's not where she's originally from. Agnes is German."

"I see. Which part of Germany?"

"I don't know. But I remember she told me when she asked me to buy her German bread one day. It just slipped out. I was quite surprised at the time."

"That's extraordinary," Freya murmured, realizing that as a German citizen, Agnes would have been on the other side from her grandfather; she would have been classed as an enemy. But she'd been a child too. How vulnerable she must have been. It struck Freya then how terrible it all was; how much everyone had been the victim of chance and of circumstances beyond their control. What difference did any of that make, either now or then? She'd just been an innocent civilian, caught up in something terrible, beyond her control or understanding.

The next morning, Freya let herself into Agnes' house. It was very early, but she wanted to make sure the place was clean and comfortable for Agnes to return to. She and Finn had spoken to the discharge nurse before they'd left the ward. She had told them that Agnes wouldn't be strong enough to get upstairs anymore.

Freya fed the cat in the kitchen, then investigated the back study, where Agnes had said she would be able to sleep. "There's a single bed in there," she'd said. "I had it for guests, traveling pianists when they came to give a concert in Cambridge sometimes slept there, but no one has slept in it for years now."

The room was dark, like all the others. Freya pulled back the heavy floral curtains and looked out at the overgrown garden. A thin layer of frost had settled over everything. It looked as if the grass and bushes had been dusted with icing sugar, like an eerie Christmas landscape. Would that remind Agnes of her home?

On an impulse, Freya went out into the hall and stood in front of the painting of the fairy-tale castle, snowbound on the top of that hill that rose steeply above the pine forest. She stared up at it, awed. She'd never had the chance to look at it for more than a few seconds before and she'd certainly never been able to peer at it close up like this. She noticed an inscription in tiny letters along the bottom: SCHLOSS ENDENBURGEN, LANDKREIS TILSIT, OSTPREUßEN.

OSTPREUßEN. Even with her almost non-existent German, Freya quickly worked out that it meant East Prussia. The castle was in East Prussia! She recalled Agnes' angry reaction when she'd pressed her about where it was: *That castle is not in Lithuania! . . . Have you forgotten that already? That place, that castle, that country, it doesn't exist. I don't know why you keep on asking about it.* Freya stared at the inscription on the picture, wondering. Her knowledge of that region and its history was so hazy, partly due to fear of stepping on her grandfather's toes.

So, was East Prussia where Agnes came from, not Lithuania after all?

Freya took out her phone and tapped the names of the

district into it, so she would be able to look them up later on, then went back into the study to clear the piles of books and boxes off the bed. In the study was a marble fireplace, a smaller version of the one in the front room. Some old photographs in frames were gathering dust on the mantelpiece. There was a black and white one of a young Agnes, dressed in a strapless ball gown, seated at a grand piano, her hair swept up into a bun. She looked glamourous, confident, but in the dark eyes that stared out of the picture at her, Freya saw a deep well of sadness. There was another one of Agnes receiving a bouquet of flowers on stage, shaking the hand of a man in a dinner jacket, and another of her dressed in an academic cap and gown, standing in front of the Senate House in Cambridge. She was smiling into the camera, but the sadness in her eyes was just the same.

Tucked in the corner of that photograph was a small card with AEROFLOT RUSSIAN AIRLINES printed in blue lettering across the top above the airline's distinctive emblem—the hammer and sickle between a pair of wings. Freya eased the ticket out of the frame and read the faded wording: VILNIUS TO LONDON AIRPORT. 9 A.M. APRIL 9th 1952. MISS AGNES PETRAKIS. Agnes Petrakis? Perhaps Agnes had changed her last name to Peters when she settled in Cambridge?

Freya put it back and reached for the last photograph. This one was right at the back, hidden from view behind the others. But unlike the others, it didn't feature Agnes. Instead, it was of three other people: a middle-aged couple flanking a young man with blond hair. The photograph was overexposed and they seemed to be blinking into blazing sunshine. All three were dressed in rough boots and work clothes and stood in front of a hayrick. The older man was holding a pitchfork, its prongs pointing toward the sky. The only one smiling was the young man; the other two looked uncomfortable in front of the camera and stood stiffly, as if to attention. Freya frowned. Who were these people? Could this be Agnes' brother, grown up? With a sigh, she tucked the photograph back on the mantelpiece. Perhaps she would never know.

All she did know was that Agnes must have escaped her hometown in 1945. It wouldn't have been safe for her to have stayed there.

NINETEEN
AGNES

East Prussia, 1945

It was over a hundred kilometers back to their home village, but she wasn't going to tell Dieter that. Silently, she took his sweaty hand in hers again and they started to walk, on through the devastated streets of the city, on through the empty outskirts.

Eventually the houses began to thin out and they were in open country at last. Here, there was little sign of the Russian army, but the sound of the battle still rumbled on in the distance behind them. The cottages and farms they passed looked shut up and empty, deserted by their inhabitants. Corpses of farm animals littered the snow-covered fields, dead horses and broken carts lay in ditches. They were used to such sights by now and passed them without a word.

By the time they were out of earshot of the city, the sky was growing dark and hunger pangs gnawed at Agnes' stomach. They hadn't eaten since the porridge doled out by the soldiers on the army base that morning before they got on the train.

How long ago that seemed. They were desperately thirsty too; they'd drunk nothing since that morning either, except mouthfuls of snow scooped up from the side of the road as they walked.

Agnes began to wonder whether to knock on the doors of the houses they passed to ask for food. Even in this desperate time, she felt nervous about approaching strangers, but there was no real choice. Every few minutes Dieter would say, "I'm hungry, when are we going to eat?," so she summoned her courage and, at the next farm, they went in through the open front gates, crossed the empty, silent farmyard, and approached the front door of the house. Agnes knocked and waited. She knocked again but there was no answer. She tried a third time. Nerves were making her stomach churn, but she tried the door handle and the door opened easily. She pushed it open and they went inside: the house was cold and dark.

"Hello?" Agnes called tentatively, but no one replied. They walked on, into an empty kitchen. The people had left in a hurry, just as they had left Aunt Hannah's farm all those weeks before. Cupboards stood open, boxes and debris were scattered about, chairs were upturned. Feeling a little guilty, Agnes started to look in the cupboards in the hope of finding food. She knew that the family must have been short for months before they left and would have taken everything they could with them when they fled, but she carried on anyway. Dieter was searching too, but it didn't take long to discover that the cupboards were empty. They wandered through the rest of the downstairs, their spirits sinking further. Through the empty rooms, where tables were upturned, cushions lay on the floor. There was a back hallway with a back door to the farmyard and off that was a scullery. They stood in the doorway. There was hardly any light in the room, but Agnes sniffed the air. There was a familiar smell, sweet and rancid.

"Apples!" she said. "There are apples here somewhere."

They rifled through empty boxes, buckets, and cupboards and finally found, on a high shelf right at the back of the room, a wooden crate filled with the apples. Agnes lifted it down, set it on the floor, and took off the newspaper that was covering the fruit. They were huge, shiny cooking apples, stored between more layers of newspaper, many of them blackened with rot or eaten through by maggots. But Agnes and Dieter picked out the best ones and ate hungrily, sitting there on the cold scullery floor of that abandoned farmhouse.

"Where are we going to sleep?" Dieter asked.

"We will sleep here."

They went back inside the chilly house and up a winding, wooden staircase. There was something deeply disturbing about being here, inside the home of a family they'd never met, especially as darkness was upon them and after everything that had happened over the past few days. It was cold in the house, but it was colder outside and Agnes knew it was better to stay here than to sleep out in the snow. At the top of the stairs was a big bedroom with a wooden bedstead. The sheets from the previous occupants were still on the unmade bed but, overcome with exhaustion, Agnes and Dieter curled up together under the eiderdown anyway. Dieter fell asleep straight away, but Agnes lay awake, listening to the creaking beams in the still house, the wind in the trees outside, imagining all sorts of horrors.

She must have eventually drifted off, but she woke with a start a few hours later. It was already light and from outside came the roar of engines on the road and men's voices shouting. Agnes' scalp tingled in alarm: they were speaking Russian. She ran to the window and her mouth went dry with shock at what she saw. A Russian tank was crawling along the road past the window, soldiers clad in greatcoats and fur hats, with guns slung over their shoulders, riding on the footplates. Agnes drew back, behind the curtain, her heart hammering. She watched in horror as the tank swung round and pulled into the farmyard.

Then the soldiers were jumping off it and running toward the house. She rushed over to Dieter and shook him.

"Wake up, wake up, we've got to hide!"

Dieter sat up, blinking.

"Come on, quick, under here."

She virtually dragged him off the bed and they crawled under it together. There were piles of blankets and old rugs stored under there and they crawled in and crouched among them, listening in terrified silence to the sound of soldiers rampaging through the downstairs of the house, banging doors, ripping furniture, shouting and laughing. Then came the sound of boots hammering up the wooden staircase; two or three pairs together. Dieter started to whimper and Agnes put her hand over his mouth to silence him. Then the soldiers were running along the passage, opening doors, knocking furniture over. When one crashed into their room, Agnes thought her heart would burst as she watched the boots cross the floor. She waited while the soldier pulled out drawers, emptied cupboards. Then he bent down to glance under the bed and the blood froze in her veins as she caught sight of his eyes peering toward them in the gloom. She could hear his labored breathing and caught the smell of alcohol on his breath. A few seconds passed. The tension was unbearable. Then one of his comrades shouted from the passageway and the soldier straightened up and walked out of the room, shouting something to the others.

Agnes let out a sob of relief and hugged Dieter to her. They lay there sobbing together. It was another ten minutes or so before the sound of footsteps in the house receded, doors banged behind the retreating Russians, and the engine of the tank roared as it moved out of the yard and rumbled on along the road under the window.

Agnes and Dieter crawled out from under the bed, their legs stiff from crouching there. The room was in chaos; drawers were flung on the floor, linens strewn around, clothes pulled from the wardrobe. They went downstairs, too shocked to speak. The same scene greeted them in every room of the house. Cupboards plundered, furniture upturned, even coal emptied from the scuttle beside the empty fireplace.

"Why did they do this?" Dieter asked, breaking the silence.

"I don't know. Perhaps they're looking for food or for jewelry."

It made Agnes wonder about their own home. Had that suffered a similar fate? Had the refugees who'd moved in finally fled? Had the Russians got there and taken what the refugees before them hadn't? A wave of overwhelming sadness passed over her as she had a sudden vivid memory of sitting at the piano and playing for the family after supper. She could see the smile on her father's face as he listened, Mutti nodding in approval. Poor, poor Mutti, still lying there abandoned, frozen on the ice. She didn't deserve to die. And where was Papa? Would they ever see him again? Or poor Aunt Hannah?

Dieter was tugging at her clothes: "I'm hungry, Agnes."

They went back through the devastated kitchen and out into the scullery, but the box of apples had been taken. Smashed crates and boxes were strewn around the room. Dieter began to cry.

"Come on, let's find some food somewhere else," Agnes told him, trying to make it sound like an adventure. She had an instinct that it wasn't safe to stay at this farm, that they needed to move on, that more Russian soldiers could come looking for loot at any time.

They left the cold house and went out into the frozen morning. They crossed the farmyard, went out onto the road, and started to walk, skidding along in the deep tracks in the snow left by the tank.

Agnes could tell they were heading in the right direction because their home was due east of Königsberg. It was shortly after sunrise and she knew the sun rose in the east, so she knew to follow it, a pale glimmer in the white sky. After a few kilometers, at a crossroads, they came across a sign to Tilsit and later, they passed stones marking the kilometers between Königsberg and Tilsit. All the time, her ears were primed for the sound of vehicles on the road, her eyes constantly checking for suitable places to hide. They'd only walked three or four kilometers before they heard the roar of engines on the road behind them. She jumped down into the ditch and pulled Dieter down beside her. The ditch was filled with icy water but they crouched there, shivering with fear and cold, as two tanks labored past. The great metal caterpillar tracks of the tanks rolled past at eye level. It seemed an age before they finally moved off.

"Can we get out now?" Dieter asked as the sound of the engines and tank tracks faded. Agnes put her head up cautiously and checked the road, but crouched down again immediately. An armored car was approaching, more quickly than the tanks had.

"Stay down!" she told Dieter and they ducked again while three vehicles crunched and skidded past on the snow, a meter or so from their faces.

When Agnes was sure there were no more vehicles approaching, they climbed out of the ditch. "It's too dangerous to walk on the road," she said. "We'll have to find another route." She stared across the undulating fields, covered in thick drifts of snow.

Dieter began to protest that the snow was too deep to walk across, but she ignored his pleas and grabbed his hand firmly.

"Come on."

They set off across the adjacent field, trying to keep within the shelter of hedges so they wouldn't be spotted by passing convoys. Soon their legs were heavy with exhaustion and they were soaked to the skin and shivering with the cold and wet. They walked for hours, sometimes struggling through forests, sometimes skirting frozen lakes. Each step was a huge effort as they sank down into the deep, drifting snow each time. There was no food and the only drink they had was the snow they scooped from the ground. At last they saw the roofs of a farmstead nestled between two hills. They stood at the crest of a hill and stared down at it.

"Look, Dieter," Agnes said, pointing. "There are people there." There was a wisp of smoke rising from the chimney.

They couldn't run through the thick snow but they walked as quickly as they could toward the house, rejuvenated by the hope that the people at the farm might help them. It crossed Agnes' mind that it could be Russian soldiers who'd lit the fire in the farmhouse, but she didn't mention that to Dieter. As they neared the farm they slowed down, more nervous now that they were drawing closer. They climbed over a wooden fence and into the farmyard. It was deserted, no animals or poultry anywhere, just like all the other farms they'd come across. At least there were no vehicles anywhere to be seen either, so Agnes relaxed a little as they approached the back door of the house. This farm was a long way from the main road, so perhaps the Russians wouldn't bother to come here.

They knocked on the shabby back door and waited. After several minutes an old woman opened it and peered out at them. She wore a long woolen skirt and was wrapped up in a black shawl.

"Please, Frau," Agnes asked. "May we come in and shelter? We've walked a long way."

"Who are you?"

"Agnes and Dieter Kass. We live in a village in Tilsit District. Our ship was sunk near Danzig . . ." Agnes could say no more. Her voice was stopped by a painful lump in her throat and she was powerless to prevent the tears from falling.

"You poor dears, come on in." The old woman pulled the door back and let them inside the kitchen. A stove was burning in the corner. "I am Frau Müller. I will make you some tea," she said. "You can warm yourselves by the stove."

"Thank you. Thank you so much."

Agnes and Dieter took off their wet coats and boots and crouched beside the stove, warming their hands.

"Where did you say you have come from?" the old woman asked, putting a large black kettle on the stove. "Most people left weeks ago."

Haltingly, Agnes told the old woman their story. She had to stop to fight back the tears as she spoke of Mother's death, of the shipwreck and the loss of Aunt Hannah.

"You poor young souls," said Frau Müller, looking at them with pitying eyes. "I can give you some meat and vegetable soup to eat. My family left for the Reich some time ago. My daughter-in-law and the children, that is. My son is in the army. They were taking a train to Berlin. I don't know if they made it. I hope and pray that they did."

"Why didn't you go?" Agnes asked.

"Oh, they pleaded with me to go with them. They delayed leaving for days, trying to persuade me. But I'm far too old to survive such a journey. I was born on this farm. My husband is buried on this land. I am East Prussian through and through and I couldn't leave this land, not for Hitler, not for the Russians. I'm not afraid of what they might do."

Agnes stared at her, impressed by the old woman's stubborn courage.

"Now, I will get you that soup. We used to raise pigs and cattle and send our quota to the army for slaughter, but we were clever and kept a few back for ourselves. Once we'd butchered them, we preserved the meat in salt. It's hidden under the floorboards. First, we hid it from the Nazi authorities and now from the Russians . . . that is, if they ever find me tucked away down here in the valley."

Later, they sat at the table and ate the soup that the old

woman had cooked. It seemed like the most delicious thing Agnes had ever tasted. It filled her groaning stomach and she actually felt warm for the first time since she could remember. After they'd eaten, Frau Müller showed them to a bedroom above the kitchen, where there were two children's beds made up with thick blankets and quilts.

"This room is where my grandchildren sleep . . . slept," she said wistfully. "But who knows if they'll ever be able to come back here. I sleep downstairs in a room off the kitchen."

Agnes closed her eyes and went straight into a deep sleep, but once again was awoken just before dawn. Frau Müller was shaking her.

"There's a Russian tank coming down the lane," she said urgently. "It's at the top of the hill now but it will be here in minutes. Take your brother, climb out of this window, and run away from here. I will keep them talking at the front door as long as I can. If you follow that track to the top of that hill, you will come to a railway. That's the Königsberg to Tilsit line."

Agnes blinked at her, groggy with sleep but instantly aware of the peril they were in.

"But what about you?" she asked.

"Don't worry about me, I'm not afraid of a few Russian boys. And take this with you. You might need it."

She handed Agnes a leather bag. "There's some food in there. For your journey."

"Oh, Frau . . ." Agnes was overwhelmed by her kindness.

"But you must hurry."

Agnes leapt out of bed. "Dieter!"

They pulled on their clothes quickly and dashed over to the back window. Already they could hear the roar of a tank in the front yard, the crunch of the tracks on the stones. Agnes fumbled with the catch. There was a loud rapping at the front door. She tried the stiff lock again and released it finally. The window was warped and she had to put her shoulder against it, but finally it gave. She heard the front door open downstairs and Frau Müller's shrill, indignant voice.

"Frau . . . Frau kommen," a man's voice said. There were a few more exchanges, then came some angry protests from Frau Müller, the sound of her screams, the scuffle of boots, and men laughing. Fear sliced through Agnes.

"Come, Dieter. We've got to jump. You go first."

He looked as terrified as she felt, but he climbed onto the windowsill, put his legs over the edge, and jumped down onto the snowy bank below. A split second later, Agnes jumped too, the leather bag over her shoulder. She felt the breath jolt from her body as she landed heavily next to Dieter. Frau Müller's screams were still coming from inside the house. Her heart thumping, Agnes took Dieter's hand and began to run away from the house and up the hill behind it, heading for the track that Frau Müller had pointed out. They'd only run a few meters when a series of gunshots rang out from the house and the screaming stopped.

They had to carry on, running across the snow toward the track on the other side of the field. Tears of pity misted Agnes' eyes at the cruelty and injustice of what was happening. Poor Frau Müller! Why did she have to die? She'd shown them such kindness and been so courageous. Killing her was a senseless, brutal act. But there was no opportunity to slow down or to stop and think, or even to cry properly. They needed to keep moving. Any of the Russian soldiers could look out of the back windows of the farmhouse and see them there. Then what would become of them? From what she'd read and heard of the brutality of the Russian soldiers, she knew that her young age wouldn't be a bar to being assaulted and probably shot afterward, like Frau Müller. Then what would happen to Dieter? She couldn't bear to think about it.

"Run faster, Dieter," she kept saying. "We're nearly there."

In a few more steps they gained the safety of the rutted farm track and slowed to a walk, breathing heavily. The track wound round the hill, away from the farmyard, and they were soon out of sight of the house and sheltered by trees. At the top of the hill, just as Frau Müller had said, they reached the railway line, bordered by hedges. They crawled under the hedge and walked onto the track. Agnes looked up and down the line, straining her eyes to see as far as she could. The track was straight in both directions and ahead of them it ran through a forest.

"We'll walk along the line to Tilsit," she told Dieter.

"What if a train comes?"

"Trains won't come from Königsberg. Not now the Russians are there. And look how the sleepers and rails are covered in snow. No train has been along here for days."

So, they started their long trek along the track eastwards toward Tilsit.

They walked for three days, stopping only to drink snow from their cupped hands and to nibble on the stale bread and salted meat Frau Müller had thrown into the bag for them. They had to make sure, on exposed sections, that they kept their heads below the level of the hedges.

The first night they slept in a deserted railwayman's hut beside the tracks and on the second night, they found an old cow barn in a field near the line and slept on the mildewed hay. On the afternoon of the third day the city of Tilsit came into view on the horizon and in another hour, they were close enough to make out the shape of buildings. Fearing the Russians may already be in the city, they left the railway behind them and crossed the snowbound fields, finding a narrow country road that meandered around the edge of the city. On this remote country lane that wound through fields and woodland, it was easy to imagine that there was no war going on, that the surrounding countryside buried under the snow was simply hibernating, just as it did every winter. Perhaps the Russians hadn't reached Tilsit?

When they came to a crossroads, Agnes paused, wondering whether to risk approaching the city. She decided to chance it, but they'd only gone a few steps when she spotted a pall of black smoke hovering above the buildings.

"We'll have to turn back."

Having to go round the edge of the city added several kilometers to their walk, but they were on familiar territory now, passing landmarks Agnes recognized from trips with Father into the town. They walked quickly, spurred on by the thought that home was close. It was late afternoon as they trudged up the last hill, through the forest toward their village.

"We'll get to the farm first," she said as they labored up the last few kilometers. With every step she took, she remembered setting off in the opposite direction on the farm wagon with Aunt Hannah and Mutti, when they had had high hopes of escaping the Red Army. The road was still scarred and rutted with the tracks of refugee wagons and debris from the fleeing convoy was strewn by the wayside but the wagons and carts were long gone, along with their terrified passengers, and the countryside was still and eerily quiet now.

They reached the top of the hill and looked down the gently sloping valley toward Aunt Hannah's farm. Dieter let out a cry and Agnes' hand flew to her mouth in shock. The farmhouse and all the barns around it glowed orange with fire, lighting up the pale afternoon. Flames licked the sky and smoke billowed around the surrounding fields. Agnes stared at it for long minutes until the sight of the flames burned into her eyes, then she sank to her knees in the snow and let the sobs rip through her body.

TWENTY

Agnes crouched on her knees in the snow beside the road, crying. They were tears of frustration and desperation; tears she hadn't been able to shed for Mother, for Aunt Hannah, for Frau Müller, and for all the desperate people she'd seen suffering and dying since the four of them had left home all those weeks ago. They were tears of fear too, for herself and for Dieter. What would they do now? Coming back to the farm had been their last and only option. She'd pinned her hopes on that ever since they'd fled from Königsberg and now those hopes were going up in smoke as the flames engulfed the farm right before her eyes. All these thoughts spun round in her mind and she cried and cried, until she felt Dieter's hand on her shoulder, shaking her urgently.

"There's something coming up the road," he was saying. "We should go into the trees."

She looked into his face and, seeing panic in his eyes, immediately reprimanded herself for giving in to her emotions when he needed her to be strong. She lifted her head and listened. He was right: a vehicle was approaching from behind them on the road. The engine was loud enough to be a tank or armored car.

She grabbed Dieter's hand and without a word, they fled into the forest. They crouched behind the thick trunk of a fir tree as a convoy of Russian tanks and armored cars labored up the hill, skidding in the snow. The vehicles passed within a few meters of where the two of them sat, holding each other, holding their breath. Above the roar of the engines, Agnes could make out the sound of the soldiers shouting to each other in Russian. Somehow hearing human voices so close, confirming the presence of Russian soldiers, was even more terrifying than the crumple of the tanks' caterpillar tracks on the snow.

When the convoy had finally passed, Agnes stood up and stretched her aching limbs. She wondered what to do, where to go.

"Can we go home?" Dieter asked, his eyes eager. "To our house? You said we could go home."

She looked into his pleading eyes. She owed it to him to keep her promise, even though it would be dangerous, even though they were certain to be disappointed.

"Come on then. Let's try."

She knew that they couldn't go anywhere near the farm and that it would be dangerous to go back onto the road now they knew the Russians were in the area. Instead, they pushed deeper into the forest, wading on through drifts of snow under the trees. When they reached the other side, they stepped out of the wood onto farmland. Their familiar valley was spread out beneath them and from where they stood, they could see the village roofs and the church tower. Agnes' heart twisted with pain. How well she knew these fields. This was where she'd explored with her friends in all weathers, feeling no fear when they ventured far from home. But this countryside no longer felt safe. And although the village where they'd spent their whole lives looked deceptively calm from this vantage point, the Russians were surely there now. She knew it couldn't be the same place that occupied her memory.

They plunged on, down the hill, skirting ponds and wood-land, eventually arriving, wet and shivering, through a gap in the hedge, onto the village street near the station.

All was unnaturally quiet and still. One or two houses were boarded up, but there was no sign of life anywhere. The station was shuttered and silent, the railway itself covered in snowdrifts.

Dieter tugged Agnes' hand. "Come on, let's go to our house. Papa might be there."

"Papa won't be there, Dieter. He is away with the army." Then she stopped and swallowed, thinking about what she'd just said. The German army must surely have been defeated, or the Russians wouldn't be pouring in through the lanes and roads of East Prussia. What had happened to dear Papa? Could he still be alive? And if he *was* alive, had he been captured? Was he a prisoner now?

She allowed Dieter to pull her along the street a little way, skidding and slipping on the snow. They passed Frau Eckert's shop, shuttered up and quiet, then rounded the bend to the main street.

"Stop!" Agnes hissed.

There in front of them, two jeeps were parked up. Russian soldiers were strolling up and down the road in fur hats and greatcoats, brandishing rifles. A row of villagers was lined up in front of the houses, hands above their heads. Terror gripped Agnes' heart as she recognized Frau Eckert among them, the stationmaster, and the refugees who'd been occupying their home. There was the old man, still in the crumpled coat he'd worn on Christmas Day, and the stout aggressive woman, now cowed and shamed, her head hanging down, her two small children clinging to her skirts, bawling.

The soldiers were shouting at them in Russian. Agnes couldn't understand what they were saying and she didn't want to witness what might happen next.

"Come, Dieter. The soldiers are there. We can't go to the house."

In fear and desperation, she ran, dragging Dieter behind her, back along the street, through the gate into the station yard, and onto the railway track.

"We have to get out of here. Now," she said, setting off beside the track. They walked as quickly as they could, not speaking, their eyes on the track in front of them. They fell into a rhythm, striding from sleeper to sleeper, just as they had for the past few days since leaving Frau Müller's farm.

In a few minutes they were clear of the village and going through the great cutting that led through the von Meyer estate. As they walked past the place where Agnes had slid down the bank to the railway all those weeks ago, leaving Liesel behind, she couldn't help looking up to see if Liesel was still standing at the top where the path through the trees ended, watching her, waving goodbye. Wherever was Liesel now? Had the Count managed to get his staff to safety somewhere in the Reich? Would she and Liesel ever see each other again? She thought of Liesel's kind eyes, of her laughter, of her constant companionship until they'd been ripped cruelly apart, and a lump rose in her throat. Those days were over now. Those carefree childhood days were gone forever.

Agnes and Dieter walked on as the track emerged from the forest and made its meandering way across the countryside. Agnes knew this track well from all the trips she'd taken into Lithuania for food, but it was different walking it. And the countryside was different now too. Still and empty. As if it was holding its breath, waiting for something to happen.

The light was fading quickly. They stopped, exhausted, in a tumbledown shed beside the track and ate the last scraps of Frau Müller's food before curling up and falling asleep together.

. . .

It was mid-morning when they reached the railway bridge across the Memel River. Dieter hung back when he saw the swirling waters between the slats of the bridge.

"Why do we have to cross?"

"It's safe on the other side. You'll see. We'll be able to get food, I promise."

"What if we fall in?"

"We won't fall in, Dieter. I've done this before. It's safe, I promise. I'll go first. Just step where I step."

It was more difficult crossing the bridge with Dieter in tow than it had been crossing alone. And it was daylight this time. As they made their slow progress across the iron bridge, stepping from girder to girder, hanging onto the steel frame, occasionally wobbling dangerously, Agnes' heart was in her mouth. She had no way of knowing if there were Russian soldiers in the town on the far bank, watching the bridge, their rifles trained on it. She half expected a shot to ring out at any time to end it all.

But no shots came and at last they reached the other side. From there it was a short walk along the line to the place where Agnes used to jump off the freight trains and roll down the bank.

"We need to get to that forest up on the hill," she said, stepping off the track and urging Dieter on. He peered up at the jagged outline of trees on the horizon. "Is there food there?"

"On the other side there is. It's where I used to come and get food for us all. It's safe inside the forest."

Dieter looked skeptical but followed her down the bank and across the field toward the forest. Agnes' stomach was grumbling and her body was weak with exhaustion but she dragged herself on, pulling Dieter along behind her. She was aware that he must be feeling the same way too, but in recent days he'd mostly given up complaining about being hungry. She knew there was little chance of finding anything to eat until morning, but at least they could find somewhere to sleep in the wood and go on to the little market town at dawn. All the time she'd been walking along the railway track, she'd been thinking of the wild-looking boy she'd met in the forest the first time she'd crossed into Lithuania to look for food. She recalled his words: *There are a few of us living in these woods . . . There's more food in Lithuania and the farmers are kind to us.* She remembered giving him a loaf of her precious bread. Would he still be here? Would he remember her?

They reached the edge of the wood and plunged in under the thick branches of the great conifers. The light had almost gone from the sky and it was even gloomier inside the forest. They'd ventured only a few yards and were already enveloped in darkness.

"I don't like it here," Dieter said. "Can't we go back?"

"There's nowhere to go, Dieter. We'll be safer in here, come on."

She pulled him off the main track and onto a side path that branched from it. This was where she'd met the wild German boy. The trees were much denser here, which meant less snow on the ground, and they were able to walk more easily than they had all day. But as the night drew in and they had to feel their way through the darkness, it became impossible to make progress.

They found themselves at the base of a huge fir tree. Someone had been there before them. Fallen branches had been leaned against the tree to make a crude shelter.

Grateful for a scrap of luck at the end of a cruel day, they crawled inside. Both shivering and soaked to the skin, they huddled together. The branches of the shelter provided enough cover to contain the heat from their bodies and gradually they grew warm enough to fall asleep.

· · ·

When Agnes awoke hours later, shafts of weak sunlight were glinting down through the gaps in the shelter. For a few seconds she had no idea where she was and then it all came back to her in a rush. The shock and pain of seeing the farm in flames, the Russian soldiers terrorizing their neighbors in the village street, the ever-present ache in her heart caused by the loss of Mutti and Hannah and countless others. Dieter was still asleep, his head heavy against her chest. She moved gradually away from him, letting his head rest on their bag, so she could sit up and listen carefully. She could hear movement outside the shelter, the sound of something or someone moving around on the dead leaves and ferns on the forest floor. Was it an animal? She knew that bears and wolves had been sighted in some of the deeper forests and her heart raced, thinking about it. Or was it a Russian soldier? That could be even worse.

She listened to the crackle of twigs for a few more minutes, then plucked up enough courage to poke her head out through a gap in the branches. She gasped. She was face to face with a boy, a little younger than herself. His face was filthy, his dark hair matted with mud. He sprang back, as surprised as she was. He reminded her of the young boy she'd met before, but this boy was taller, his face more mature.

"What are you doing here?" he asked. His tone sounded aggressive.

"We don't have anywhere else to go," Agnes said, trying to keep calm. There was a wild look in this boy's eyes and she wasn't sure he was friendly.

"Do you have any food?" he asked, looking at the bag that Dieter's head rested on.

"None. We've walked for days and all we had was some salted meat."

"Here." He took half a stale loaf from his ragged pocket and handed it to Agnes.

"Thank you," she said, surprised. "But are you sure?"

The boy shrugged. "I'm off to the town. I can get some more."

"Do you live here in the forest?" she asked.

"Yes. There are lots of us, but much deeper in. It goes on for miles, this place. You can get lost. No one ever goes deep into this forest. Only us kids. No soldiers, nobody."

"How do you survive?"

The boy shrugged again. "Some of us work on farms around here, some just steal or beg for food. Sometimes we trap rabbits. If you go a couple of kilometers into the forest, you'll find a lot of German children hiding in there. Orphans mostly. Some are friendly, some not."

"Oh."

It was what the other boy had told her. She imagined bands of feral children, separated from their loved ones by this terrible war, striving to survive in the harshest of conditions.

"I have to go now. Good luck."

And then he was gone, slipping between the trees, disappearing from view.

When Dieter awoke, they shared the bread the boy had given Agnes. She watched her little brother anxiously as he ate, wondering how she was going to feed him from now on. She'd planned to go down to the market as she used to, but this time she'd nothing to sell apart from the tiny silver ear studs that Mutti had given her for Christmas. They had been in her ears since that day; she'd never taken them out, not even to sleep. They'd survived the trek to Danzig, the shipwreck, and the long walk from Königsberg to Lithuania. It would break her heart to part with them—they were her last reminders of Mutti and their beloved home—but she knew her mother would want her to sell them to feed herself and Dieter.

When they'd finished the bread, they left the shelter, made their way back through the undergrowth to the main path, and walked through the forest to the edge nearest the village. The route was familiar to Agnes, but she was wary of walking down the road with Dieter. There could be locals on horses or driving carts coming to the market; or, worse than that, Russian soldiers. She remembered with a shiver being challenged by the soldier and how the kind farmer had come to her rescue. So they walked along inside the hedge that bordered the road and, when they neared the village, they skirted around the back of the buildings until they came out a little way down from the market square.

"Wait," Agnes told Dieter and they hung back behind a wall until she was sure there were no Russian soldiers among the thin crowd. When she was satisfied, she led Dieter forward into the crowd, keeping their heads down, and approached a stall selling loaves of *rugine duona*, dark rye bread. The large, red-faced woman behind the trestle table smiled at her. Agnes recognized her from her previous trips and it was easy to negotiate four loaves of bread in return for the earrings. But just as she was slipping them into Frau Müller's bag, a Russian jeep loaded with soldiers swung into the market square. The woman's eyes widened with fear and her expression changed. Quickly concealing the earrings in her pocket, she began shouting in panic at Agnes, gesturing to her to leave quickly.

Agnes grabbed Dieter's hand and they ran back round the corner of the buildings before the jeep had come to a standstill. It was a tense walk back through the snow-covered fields to the forest. All the time Agnes' ears were fine-tuned, listening out for the whistle or shout of a Russian soldier, her heart pounding, her palms sweating. Dieter didn't complain, or even ask why they were hurrying. He seemed to know instinctively now when their lives were in danger. Being fugitives on the run was second nature to them both now.

At last they reached the edge of the forest and entered it by the wide path. Once under the shelter of the trees, they slowed down, breathing heavily, still too out of breath to speak. They took the small path that branched off to the right and made their way toward the shelter, but as they approached it, Agnes stopped and froze.

"There's someone in there," she whispered. Between the slats she could make out movement. Her mind was racing, trying to work out what to do, which way to turn, but her eyes were glued to the shelter and on whatever was moving in there. Was it an animal? Was it the boy who'd given them bread? As she watched, paralyzed with indecision, a face suddenly poked out of the entrance and someone emerged and stood in front of it. This time it was a girl, about her own age. Like the boy from that morning, her face was filthy. Her hair was in matted plaits, her clothes in rags. She stared at Agnes and Dieter, arms folded. Then another child came out behind her: a skinny little boy slightly older than Dieter, as grubby and ragged as the girl. Part of Agnes felt relief, but the looks on their faces weren't friendly.

"Hey, you!" the girl shouted. "You can't stay in this place."

Agnes didn't reply. Her mouth was dry. The girl was taller than her and, although very thin, she looked tough and wiry. Agnes had never had a fight with anyone in her life.

"I'm talking to you! I said you can't stay here."

"We'll find somewhere else, then," Agnes replied evenly, her voice cracking with nerves.

The girl stepped forward. "You can't just stay anywhere, you need to come with us. We'll show you where you can sleep."

Agnes hesitated. "It's all right. We'll just go somewhere else."

She turned to walk away but the girl shouted, "No, you don't!" She ran forward and grabbed Agnes' arm. "You're not listening to me." Her fingers were pinching Agnes' flesh and close up, she could see that the girl's teeth were coated in filth. Her breath was foul. "If you're in this forest, there are rules. You need to come with us and we will help you. We know how to get food."

Agnes glanced down at Dieter.

"Let's just go with them," he said.

"Your brother is right. Come with us, we'll show you the way. You'll be safe with us. We have food and there's somewhere for you to sleep. I'm Gunhild and this is Kurt. Who are you?"

Agnes told them their names and they set off along a narrow path that led deeper into the forest. It was so narrow, they had to walk in single file. Kurt went first, then Agnes and Dieter, with Gunhild bringing up the rear. All the time she walked, Agnes felt uneasy. She was aware that Gunhild was walking behind them to stop them trying to make a run for it. Kurt walked quickly, virtually running, like a woodland creature; he obviously knew the route well, darting off between trees, taking sharp turns.

"Go quicker, can't you?" Gunhild kept shouting from behind. "We'll lose him."

Agnes was struggling to keep up with Kurt, tripping over roots and stones on the uneven forest floor. As she stumbled along, she was aware that they were going deeper and deeper into the great wood, that it was closing around them. Once a rabbit sprang across their path, another time a startled deer jumped into the undergrowth as they approached. There was little snow on the ground here, the ancient branches forming a canopy above the dead floor of the forest. The trees they moved through were becoming ever more gnarled and ancient. It was like a primeval place, where time had stood still, where nature was rampant and human beings weren't meant to venture.

Agnes had lost track of how long they'd been walking when at last the trees thinned out and opened up into a great clearing. Kurt stopped and turned.

"This is it. You stay here and I'll tell Theo."

"Theo?"

"Theo is our leader," said Gunhild. "He'll help you."

A small fire smoldered in the middle of the clearing and

four young children crouched in front of it, warming their hands. A few battered pots and pans were stacked beside the fire. Shelters like the one they'd slept in were built from branches leaning around the trunks of several trees. In a couple of places tarpaulins were strung out between branches to form tents. Agnes became aware of several pairs of eyes watching them from inside the shelters.

A tall, rangy boy swaggered toward them from the other side of the clearing. Kurt and two other smaller boys walked beside him. He had dark eyes in a grubby face, wild black hair and, like all the others, was dressed in rags. He stopped in front of Agnes and ran his eyes up and down her.

"I'm Theo," he said. "I look after everyone here. You can stay if you want."

Agnes looked up into his face. His eyes with their arrogant look were intimidating. In fact, everyone here and this whole place made her feel afraid. She wished she'd been firmer with Gunhild at the shelter. Whyever had she agreed to come along? She swallowed.

"It's all right," she said. "I think we're OK. We can look after ourselves."

Theo's eyes widened and he barked out a humorless laugh.

"Listen to her! It isn't that easy, you know. Some of us have been in these woods for months. We know how to survive, we look after each other."

"I'm sure. It's just . . ."

"Look, come and sit by the fire. Have a drink with us. Boys! Boil some water!"

The little ones sitting beside the fire sprang into action. One of them scurried to one corner of the clearing and fetched a metal canister back to the fire, slopping water from it as he ran.

"Don't spill it!" bellowed Theo, menace in his tone. Then he turned to Agnes: "Come on, sit down. These boys will make us some tea."

Feeling uneasy, Agnes went to the fire and sat down on the bare earth. Dieter sank down beside her. Theo sat down too, cross-legged. To her surprise he pulled out some tobacco, rolled himself a cigarette, and lit it from the fire.

"Want a puff?" he asked, eyeing her. She shook her head.

"I didn't think you would," he said in a mocking tone, blowing smoke in her face. "Where have you come from?"

"We've walked from Königsberg," she said.

He raised his eyebrows. "A long way. Was that your home?"

"No. Our home was in a village about thirty kilometers this side of Tilsit."

"So, why were you in Königsberg?"

Reluctantly and hesitantly, she told him their story, just as she'd told Frau Müller a few days before. While she spoke, the small boys brought her and Dieter cups of steaming black tea in dirty, chipped mugs, then sat down to listen. Theo watched her, puffing on his roll-ups, shaking his head at some points, tutting and exclaiming at others. This time, she found that she was able to speak about Mother and Aunt Hannah without the tears stopping her.

When she'd finished, Theo said, "All the kids in here have similar stories. Most have lost at least one parent, many both. You see that little boy who brought you tea?" He nodded toward one of the small children, who looked at Agnes with huge, waif-like eyes. "Everyone in his village was rounded up by the Russian army, the women and the men were separated and marched off to Russia. Siberia probably. People say they will be going to work camps and be used as slaves. The kids were just left to fend for themselves."

"That's terrible," murmured Agnes, her heart going out to all those wild-looking children, separated from their families, having no one to care for them.

"What about your family?" she asked Theo.

"The Red Army came to my village. The soldiers went from

house to house. They were brutes. The women were raped in their homes, their families forced to watch, then they were put in lorries and driven away. The men who were left were lined up and shot. My mother stood at the door, trying to stop them coming into our house, but they raped and shot her anyway. I ran out the back way and managed to escape into these woods."

Agnes stared at him in horror, hoping that none of the smaller children could understand his words, but from the beaten, defeated look in their eyes, she suspected that they were all too familiar with the scenes he'd just described.

"Some of these kids just got separated from their parents on the long march when they were trying to escape to the ports. You know what it was like."

Agnes nodded and sipped the earthy tea. It warmed her insides, but her stomach still rumbled, craving the bread for which she'd sold her grandmother's earrings. As if he could read her thoughts, Theo said, "What have you got in that bag? You've been to the market, haven't you?"

"It's nothing . . ." she began, terrified that he would take the food she'd sacrificed so much to get hold of.

"Don't give me that," he sneered. "It doesn't look like nothing."

He lunged at her, grabbing the bag and yanking it off her shoulder. He opened the flap and laughed. "Bread. I knew it! Come on, kids. Plenty to eat for lunch."

He began tearing great lumps off the bread and passing them to the children, who flocked around him, holding their grubby hands out for morsels, jostling and pushing each other.

"It's ours." Agnes' outrage fueled a sudden burst of courage. She stood up and yelled at him: "I sold my grandmother's earrings for that. Give it back!"

Theo jumped up too, grabbed her by the collar, and twisted it hard, his knuckles pressing into her neck. Soon she was gagging and choking. She heard Dieter crying out, then saw the blur of his blond head as he ran at Theo and heard the dull thump as Theo kicked him away. Dieter was left sprawling in the earth. Theo pulled Agnes' face close to his. Her heart froze as she felt the prick of something sharp against her stomach. He had a knife! The breath left her body. The shock had made her limbs turn to jelly.

"We share our food here," he said through gritted teeth. "Do you hear me? All these kids go out every day to the farms and villages and get food. Some of them work for it, some steal. It doesn't matter. They bring it back here and we share it. I look after them. We all look after each other. That's the way things work. And now you're here, that's the way things will work for you, too."

TWENTY-ONE

FREYA

Cambridge, Present Day

All day, as Freya worked in the library, her mind kept returning to the photographs and also to the inscription on the picture of the castle. Her own research couldn't hold her attention and it wasn't long before she was searching for information about East Prussia. She was aghast at what she read; the province was cut off from the rest of Germany by the Polish corridor and its border with Russia meant it would be the first place to be invaded by the advancing Red Army as the German army began to retreat on the Eastern Front. The population was prevented from evacuating by the Nazi *Gauleiter,* Erich Koch, until it was too late to do so safely. But people left anyway, terrified by the propaganda about the reprisals the brutal Russians would exact upon them for the cruelty the Wehrmacht had itself used against the Russian population. In January 1945, thousands of civilians streamed toward East Prussian ports on the Baltic coast, some dying on the ice of the Frisches Haff, others perishing in ships that were torpedoed by Russian submarines.

Freya went home, her mind filled with those stories, wondering where Agnes had fit into the picture, what fate had befallen her. She'd told Finn she would look in on Agnes on her way home, so she let herself into the house and made her way through to the back study.

Agnes was sitting up in bed and looked up when Freya entered. She looked tired and frail, in her old, frayed dressing gown. Freya noticed that the little silver photograph of her brother was now on the table next to the bed.

"It's kind of you to come and see me," she said. "One of the carers has already been, just after the ambulancemen left. A very nice lady. Come and sit down." She nodded toward the armchair beside the bed.

"How are you feeling?" Freya asked.

Agnes shrugged and didn't speak for a few moments. Then she said, "To tell you the truth, rather weak."

"Can I get you anything? Water? Tea?"

Agnes shook her head. "I don't want to drink too much, it's not that easy getting to the bathroom."

"I can help you, Agnes," said Freya, but Agnes shook her head.

"Thank you for tidying the room, though. It was a dreadful mess. So much clutter."

"It's no problem," said Freya. "I was happy to do it."

Agnes sighed and there was a long silence, interrupted only by Claus bounding in and jumping up on the bed, curling himself up beside Agnes. The silence wasn't awkward, but rather companionable, the only sound that of traffic passing on Chesterton Road, distant clocks in the colleges striking six o'clock.

"You know, I've been very lucky really," Agnes said, finally breaking the silence. "I've had a long life. And I've still got a few months to prepare myself . . ."

"Oh, Agnes." Freya wanted to tell her not to talk like that, that she would get better, but she knew that Agnes was speaking the truth and facing the inevitable bravely.

"It's true, my dear. There's no hiding from it."

She lifted her face to Freya's. Her lips were trembling and her eyes were glistening with tears. "Tell me, did you write to your brother in the end?"

Freya was silent for a moment, wondering why Agnes had returned to the subject at this particular time. Why was it so important to her?

"I can't. Not yet. I don't feel ready," she finally admitted, dropping her gaze.

Agnes sat forward, her eyes startled. "But I thought you had. You told me that you would. You really should, you know. It's so important!"

"But why do you say that? I saw the picture of you. The one up there on the mantelpiece of you and your brother. You stayed together, you protected each other. My brother let me down and we fell out. It is such a different situation."

"You really don't know what you're talking about," Agnes said, her lips quivering. "You should get in touch with your brother like you promised and make it up. You don't know how important and precious that bond is, believe me. You have no idea what it means to truly lose a brother."

"Do you want to tell me about it?" ventured Freya tentatively. She was a little worried that like all the times before, Agnes might shut down and get defensive with her, but somehow she sensed this time was going to be different.

"If you'd like to hear it? I think the time has come for me to talk about it."

"Of course."

"Well . . ." Agnes settled back against her pillows and her eyes took on a dreamy look, as if she was transported thousands of miles away into a different time and place. "I grew up in a little village. In Tilsit province in East Prussia. My father was the village schoolteacher and we were happy, the four of us: Father, Mother, my little brother Dieter, and I. We didn't have much, but life was good. We didn't know how good it was, of course, at the time. It was simple, there, deep in the countryside in that remote farming community. We had friends and we had freedom. Until the war engulfed us and ended that world forever . . ."

TWENTY-TWO

AGNES

East Prussia, 1945

The next morning when Agnes awoke, lying on her back, staring up through the slats of a different forest shelter, she was immediately aware of the pain in her throat and the bruises on her neck where Theo had tried to choke her. Dieter was lying beside her on the bare earth. He was so still that at first, she thought he was asleep, but then she noticed that his eyes were wide open. He was staring up at the white sky through the gaps in the wood and with a jolt, she noticed tears running down his cheeks. With a rush of guilt, she slid her arm around him.

"Please don't cry, Dieter. I'm here."

"I want Mutti and Papa," he sobbed.

"I know . . . I know you do."

"Why did they have to leave us? If Papa had been with us yesterday, that horrible boy wouldn't have hurt you like he did."

"I wasn't badly hurt," she said, struggling to find some words of comfort when she herself was craving the touch of Mutti's arms around her, the soothing sound of Papa's jovial voice to reassure her that everything would be all right. Missing them was an ever-present ache in her chest, weighing her down wherever she went. Sometimes it almost overwhelmed her, stopping the breath in her throat so she could neither breathe nor swallow.

"They are here with us though, Dieter," she said, burying her face in his filthy hair. "If you stay still and listen carefully, you'll see that Mutti and Papa are with you all the time, looking after you, guiding you, helping you."

He didn't reply and they both lay there in silence, staring up at the sky beyond the pine branches, aching for the safety of home and for the embrace of those they had lost. But soon came the sound of shambling footsteps close to their shelter and the rattle and scrape of wood as one of the branches was shoved aside. Theo's face appeared in the gap, leering down at them, revealing blackened teeth.

"Time to get up, you two. There's breakfast to eat. Bread and tea."

Agnes sat up and glowered at him. She wanted to tell him that they didn't want his food, that they could take care of themselves. But then she stopped herself, remembering how he'd pressed the knife into her stomach, how she'd thought he would kill her. It pained her that she'd had to agree to give up her loaves of bread. She'd been prepared to stand up to him, to let him harm her or kill her rather than succumb to his bullying, but she'd finally given in. It was partly through fear of what would happen to Dieter if Theo did kill her and partly through compassion for the other young orphans under Theo's control. Didn't they deserve to eat too, those children with their stick-like limbs and their sad eyes?

When Theo had let her go, she'd helped Dieter to his feet and dazed and shaken by what had happened, they'd wandered over to the fire to sit with the other children. Through sheer hunger, they accepted the share of their own bread that Theo handed out. As Agnes was chewing the delicious, moist hunk, she couldn't stop thinking of her grandmother's earrings and of the danger she and Dieter had risked just for those few mouthfuls.

When they'd finished their meager portions, Theo nodded toward one of the makeshift shelters leaning against one of the ancient pines that fringed the clearing.

"You can sleep in there. That one can be yours."

"It's all right," muttered Agnes. "We can manage by ourselves."

Theo let out a snorting laugh, "You don't listen, do you? You're staying here with us now."

She looked around her at the skinny children with the bewildered, defeated look in their eyes, tucking into the bread she'd brought. Even as she'd said the words she knew she would have a fight on her hands to get away. Perhaps it would be better if she gave in for the time being, she told herself, and went along with Theo's suggestions while she figured out a safe way of leaving.

"You can help prepare the meal this evening and tomorrow you can go out looking for food like everyone else."

The meal consisted of potatoes, carrots, and some indeterminate scraps of smoked meat, all of which Theo produced from under a pile of logs. Two of the younger children peeled the vegetables with blunt knives and passed them to Agnes to chop up on a stone with another blunt knife and boil in a battered saucepan over the fire. The peelings weren't thrown away, they were passed round the group, each child grabbing a handful and munching on them.

As she was working, children began to drift into the clearing through the trees from all directions. They came alone or in groups of two or three, and by the time the meal was ready, she counted twenty of them sitting around the fire. Most were very young and all looked skinny and unhealthy, their faces pale under the dirt, their skin a mass of sores, their cheekbones hollow. Some were clearly from the same family, sticking together, holding hands, the older children taking care of the younger ones. All wore equally ragged clothes and carried knapsacks or bags. Some had coats, others were wrapped in blankets. As each one arrived, they made straight for Theo, who sat cross-legged by the fire like a king holding court. Agnes noticed that none of the children lifted their eyes to his or uttered a word. They just handed Theo whatever food they were carrying in their bags and scuttled away.

Now, she got to her feet and stretched her aching limbs. "Come on, Dieter. Let's do as he says for now," she whispered. "Let's go and eat some breakfast. I'll think of a way of getting out of here."

The other children were already sitting by the fire, tucking into chunks of bread and taking it in turns to sip tea from the three battered tin mugs that were being passed around. Agnes and Dieter took their places among them. Theo was already giving orders to each of the children, telling them which path he wanted them to take out of the wood and where to go looking for food or money. The children headed off in all directions as he spoke. Then he turned to Agnes.

"*You* can go that way." He pointed across the clearing, in the opposite direction from the village she knew. "If you take the path that goes more or less straight through the trees that way for about two kilometers, then strike out to the right and find a way out of the forest, you'll come to a hamlet on the edge of it with a couple of farms. If you get there early enough, you might be able to take some eggs from the hen coop before the farmer gets up. They've got a dog, so be careful."

"We'll try," muttered Agnes. "Come on, Dieter."

"Hey! Not so fast." Theo grabbed Dieter by the shoulders. "You're going on your own, girl. Do you think I'm stupid? Your little brother's going to stay here with me, or you won't come back. And if you go by yourself and don't come back, I can't promise he'll be safe."

Agnes felt anger boil inside her, but at the same time she was overwhelmed by a sense of powerlessness.

"That's not fair. All the others are all going together," she protested. Theo's face clouded over with anger and he grabbed Dieter to him, pulling back his arms. Dieter yelped, his eyes wide with fear.

"I don't trust you," Theo shouted and others around him shrank away, melting into the trees without a sound. Then Agnes saw the flash of a blade as Theo pulled out his knife and held it to Dieter's throat. "Now get going, girl," he growled. "Get off to that farm and bring back the eggs, like I told you."

"Stop doing that! I'll go," she said, panic-stricken. "Please don't hurt him. I'll be as quick as I can."

She had to tear herself away to leave Dieter there with Theo's knife at his throat. She set off through the forest alone, her stomach churning with fear, her eyes blinded by tears. She ran along the narrow path, not sure that she was going in the right direction, pushing through the undergrowth, stumbling and slipping as she ran, snagging her coat on branches, her skin scratched by brambles. All the time her panicked mind wondered how she would ever find her way back to the clearing. But she followed Theo's directions and eventually emerged from the forest in roughly the place he had indicated, and there was a farm right in front of her. The wooden buildings were run-down and shabby; the thatched roofs of the barns and house were falling in. But unlike the deserted farms they'd passed in East Prussia, this one was clearly occupied. From where she stood, she could see cows moving about in one of the sheds and hear their mournful lowing. A thin line of smoke rose from the chimney of the house into the pale winter sky.

Taking a deep breath, she plunged across the patch of land

between the forest and the farmyard. Her heart pounded as she walked. What if someone was watching from the house? What if the farmer was already out and about? It was surely morning milking time? But she reached the farmyard and slipped in through an opening in the broken fence, skidding on the puddles of slush and cow dung, which must have been accumulating for years. Once inside the yard, she looked about for a chicken coop, exchanging glances with the cows. Their heads hung over the door of the cowshed and they stared at her with soulful brown eyes. This was a run-down, neglected farm, with piles of rusting machinery and rubbish strewn about the yard. What a contrast to Aunt Hannah and Uncle Tomas' place, where in the old days the yard was always immaculate and the animals sleek and well-fed.

Spotting a wooden chicken coop with a rusting iron roof in the opposite corner, she went quickly to it, knelt down in the mud, slid up one of the wooden hatches, and peered inside. Her heart sped up. There were four or five skinny ginger hens in there, roosting on a perch. Four brown eggs covered in white droppings lay together in the straw. But as she put her hand in to take the eggs, the hens set up a terrible cackling. She tried to hush them, but they jumped off the perch and rushed about the coop squawking and clucking, puffing their feathers. As quickly as she could, she grabbed the eggs and put them inside her bag, taking care to wrap each one in as much straw as she could get. But as she took the last one, she heard the squeak of a door opening somewhere behind her and then the fierce barking of a dog. She slammed the door of the coop down, did up her bag with shaking fingers, and dashed across the farmyard.

"Hey, you! Stop, you little thief!" came the farmer's voice but she didn't turn around. "I've had enough of you thieving Germans. You'll pay for this!"

She ran on, out of the farmyard, and struggled across the snow toward the looming pine trees on the edge of the forest.

She didn't look back but she could hear the dog behind her, gaining on her, panting and growling as it bounded after her. She'd almost reached the cover of the trees when it was upon her and she felt a searing pain in her calf as it sank its teeth into her flesh. With a cry, she wrenched her leg away and kicked the dog hard on the nose. It all happened in a matter of seconds. The dog yelped and slunk away, but the farmer was still running up the hill behind her. With a supreme effort of will, she pushed herself on and into the trees, struggling to catch her breath, battling forward through the thickets of brambles, the dead bracken, and ferns.

She was in such a panic, she didn't notice that she wasn't on the path and forgot that she had no idea where she was heading. Despite the throbbing pain in her leg, she didn't stop running until she'd covered some distance and was buried in the deepest part of the forest. She was finally forced to stop and bend over to catch her breath. Straightening up, she looked around her and with a shiver saw that the trees here were thicker and even more gnarled and ancient than those around the clearing. She had no idea where she was. She sat down in the snow under a great conifer, utterly exhausted, and let the tears fall.

It took her hours to find her way back onto the path she'd come along that morning. First, she tried retracing her steps, but quickly lost her way. Then she tried striking out in the direction she thought the clearing was in, but had many false starts before she finally hit the right path. All the time her mind was going over and over what Theo might do to Dieter if she was late back. The boy was ruthless and brutal, she knew that from his eyes and the way he'd treated her and Dieter and all the other children. The fear that he would harm her brother drove her on, despite the pain in her leg and her increasing exhaustion. When she finally came within sight of the clearing, it was late morning. There was no one about as she approached the smoldering fire and she began to fear the worst. Then Gunhild emerged from one of the shelters and walked toward her.

"You're late," she said with a cold stare.

"The dog bit me and I got lost."

"Give me your bag," was all Gunhild said and grabbed the knapsack from Agnes' shoulder. "Theo's resting now. I'm in charge."

"Where's Dieter? Is he all right?" Agnes asked.

Gunhild smiled; an evil sort of smile: "Theo thought you wouldn't come back."

"What do you mean? Dieter's all right, isn't he? Theo hasn't hurt him?"

"Not yet, but he was getting close. Another half an hour and your precious little brother would have suffered badly because of you."

"Where is he now?" Agnes was desperate. She knew there were tears in her eyes but she didn't care if Gunhild saw them and thought her weak.

"He's in your shelter, of course. He's fine at the moment, but don't try that trick again."

Agnes limped over to the shelter and ignored Gunhild's indignant shout of, "Hey, one of these eggs is broken!"

Dieter was lying curled up inside, his arms around his knees; his eyes were red from crying. She lay down beside him and cuddled him to her.

"I'm so sorry, Dieter," she said, thinking of her promise to Mutti. "I'm so, so sorry."

They lived in that clearing deep in the forest among the feral children for more weeks than Agnes cared to count. At night, they slept on the bare earth in their shelter and by day, Dieter stayed in the camp under Theo's watchful eye and Agnes followed his orders, making her way back through the wood on tiny paths, either to the village or to local farms. After that first time, she was never late back. Theo stopped threatening to harm Dieter but Agnes knew he wouldn't hesitate if she didn't play by his rules.

They were beginning to know and understand the forest; Agnes was familiar with all the wild creatures: the rabbits and hares, the deer and badgers. She even knew how to spot the tracks of wild boar when a herd had rampaged through the undergrowth, stripping bark off the trees, to recognize the approach of a giant elk, and to press herself against a tree trunk so as not to get trampled underfoot. She and Dieter had even seen a spotted lynx slink between the trees behind their shelter on one occasion. That had sent her pulse racing, but she quickly realized that the great cat was a shy creature, like all the other wild animals in the forest. Sometimes, she would lie awake in a cold sweat in the dead of night, listening to the baying of distant wolves, imagining what might happen to all the vulnerable little girls and boys living in the clearing if the pack was ever to discover them there.

But of course, it wasn't the forest creatures that frightened her most: it was Theo and the iron control he exercised over all the children he claimed to protect. She feared Gunhild too, who was equally ruthless and followed Theo's lead in everything.

From that first day, when Theo had forced Agnes at knife-point to give up her bread, she'd watched how he controlled and manipulated those around him through fear and threats and intimidation. The routine was the same each and every day. Every morning, he would select a group of children to set off to the nearby villages to scavenge for food, or to offer their services to the local farmers. Others would stay behind in the clearing to tidy and guard the camp, fetch water, tend the fire, and generally fetch and carry for Theo. Every afternoon, the children who'd been dispatched in the morning would return and give whatever they'd pilfered or earned that day to Theo. Agnes saw how they trembled and cast their eyes down through fear when he spoke to them. If he thought anyone had eaten food on the way back to the clearing, or cheated him in any way, he would beat them with a thin stick in front of the whole group.

Agnes grew increasingly afraid of him and tried to think of ways of escaping his control, but there was little choice. He kept Dieter under his watchful eye in the camp and she knew he wouldn't hesitate to harm him if they tried anything. She also knew that by now the Red Army must be occupying all the towns, villages, and farms on the East Prussian side of the forest, brutalizing any civilians who hadn't already fled, raping the women, killing the men, evicting them from their homes, or marching them off to Siberia to work as slave labor. Although there was less military presence on the Lithuanian side, Russian soldiers were frequently to be seen in the towns and villages, and although the farmers and villagers seemed content to let the German children work for them, they too were terrified of being discovered and there was no guarantee that they wouldn't be given up if discovery threatened.

One day, on her return from a trip to a farm just outside the market village, Dieter was nowhere to be seen. He was not in their shelter and he wasn't sitting beside the fire or working with the children who'd stayed back in the clearing that day.

Theo and Gunhild were lounging beside the fire. Theo clicked his fingers at her and automatically, she went over to him.

"Where's Dieter?" she asked in alarm.

Theo and Gunhild exchanged glances. "Give me what you've got today, then I'll tell you," Theo said, clicking his fingers again. As she'd been conditioned to do, she put her knapsack down in front of him.

"Where's Dieter?" she repeated.

"He's sulking," Theo said, waving vaguely behind him. "Somewhere in the trees. I had to use the stick on him."

"Stick?" She stared at him in horror.

He looked back at her, defiant. "Yes. And not before time," he said. "He's a lazy little shit. I told him to chop some wood and I found him sitting around resting every time I went to check on him."

"How could you? He's only eight years old, he's weak and sick."

Theo shrugged. "He knows the rules here. I do the same to any of the kids if they're lazy. He's a lot older than some of the others but he doesn't pull his weight like they do. That's your fault, girl. You pander to him."

"Where did he go?"

Again, Theo shrugged and smirked at Gunhild, who giggled. Agnes left them and ran into the trees where Theo had pointed. "Dieter, Dieter," she called. She went from tree to tree, searching in the bushes, in the hollows made by roots, under fallen branches. He surely couldn't have strayed far, but the longer she looked, the more desperate she became. The light was fading when she eventually came across him, hiding behind a fallen tree trunk. The first sign of him was his mop of wild hair sprouting up above the log like an exotic plant.

"Dieter!" She ran to him and grabbed him to her, holding him tight.

"Theo beat me with his whip," he said bitterly. "He's beastly, he's a monster."

This time Dieter hadn't been crying and Agnes saw the glint of anger in his eyes. Anger and defiance. She had a sudden image of him cuddled on Mutti's lap as they sat in front of the fire, clean and scrubbed before bed, sharing a fairy tale. How he had changed, how this terrible war had altered them both, stolen their childhood and robbed them of their innocence.

"Are you hurt?"

He nodded, biting back the tears. Then he stood up and turned round to show her his backside. Agnes gasped. His trousers were torn to shreds and covered in blood. Blood was oozing from open wounds on his legs.

"Oh, Dieter! We need to get back to the camp and clean you up."

"I'm not going back there."

"But if we don't, Theo will . . ."

"Theo will what?"

As she looked into Dieter's eyes she realized that now could be just the opportunity they'd been waiting for to run away. It might be the only one they would ever have. They'd never been out of the camp together like this before, away from Theo's watchful eye, not in all the months they'd been living in the forest. But Theo had no way of knowing how long it would take her to find Dieter and he was unlikely to come looking for her just yet.

"Why don't we just leave now?" she said breathlessly. "We can go in the opposite direction, toward the village. Some of the people down there are kind. They might help us. We'd have to make sure there were no soldiers about, that's all. Come on, do you think you can walk?"

He nodded and they set off, away from the camp, in the direction of the village where Agnes used to come to get food for Aunt Hannah and Mother. They walked as fast as they could through the damp, dense undergrowth, knowing that at any time Theo or Gunhild or any of the others might come looking for them. It didn't matter that they had left behind the few belongings they'd accumulated over the weeks they'd been in the shelter; a knitted blanket that a farmer's wife had given Agnes when she'd gone begging for food; a metal mug each, and an old pillowslip Agnes had found on a rubbish heap, which they'd stuffed with leaves to rest their heads on at night. And she'd left the knapsack Frau Müller had given them in the clearing with Theo too. All they had were the rags they stood up in; the same clothes that they had been wearing since they'd boarded that ill-fated liner at Danzig. They had slept on the earth in them, sweated in them, and bled in them. It was too cold in the forest to ever think about undressing, but Agnes felt as if the clothes were welded to her body with dirt and yearned to strip them off and bathe in fresh water. She sometimes dreamed she was standing in front of the mirror back in her bedroom at home, her hair neatly braided, her face and body clean, dressed for church in her best red velvet dress. Oh, how she longed for those simpler times.

At last, they reached the familiar path where Agnes used to cut across the forest from the railway track to the village market. They hurried along it and were soon out of the trees on the other side.

"Look! The snow is melting," said Dieter and as they set off across the open field toward the village, Agnes looked around her. It was true. She'd been so preoccupied and hurried in her daily forays for food since they'd been living in the forest, she'd barely noticed the gradual passing of winter, the drip, drip of melting snow from the trees, and the sweet sound of birdsong in the hedgerows. But this was the first time Dieter had been out of the forest since they'd first arrived, back in the depths of winter. He looked around him in wonder at the open fields, at the towering clouds in the vast, darkening sky.

"It will soon be spring," she said, taking his hand, and they ran down the field toward the road.

They were used to keeping to the field side of the hedge instead of walking on the road and as before, they skirted the buildings on the edge of the village and found a gap between two barns to slip through once they were nearing the center. The market square was empty but for debris from the morning market; collapsed wooden trestle tables were stacked beside the wall, rubbish was strewn about, wooden pallets, straw, and horse manure.

"We'll have to wait until morning to find food." Agnes sighed.

They went back between the two barns and trudged around the edge of the village, checking in stables and outhouses, searching for somewhere to sleep. Most were too close to human habitation to be safe, but a little way outside the village they found a hay barn beside some stables a long way from the farm-house. Agnes found a dented bucket in the corner, fetched some water from a trough in the yard, and washed Dieter's wounds. He winced, screwing up his face with the pain, but he didn't cry out once.

Then they made a bed of loose hay between two bales and settled down to sleep. But Agnes lay awake for a long time staring out of the open barn door at the stars making pinpricks in the midnight sky, listening for footsteps, and thinking back over the horrors of the past months. After falling asleep in the small hours, she was awoken shortly before dawn by a cock crowing. She quickly shook Dieter awake.

"We'll have to get going. The farmer might come soon."

They scrambled up, rubbing their eyes and stretching, and went out into the chilly morning.

"Hey, you! Stop right there!"

Agnes looked up. A man was approaching across the yard. He was roughly dressed and walked with a shambling gait. A gun was slung across his shoulder. Agnes had had many brushes with farmers during her weeks scavenging for food for Theo. She was normally able to get away without coming to any harm, but Dieter was with her this time and she knew he would slow them down.

"Who do you think you are, hanging around in there? This is private property." The man was coming closer, his face threatening.

"I'm sorry," Agnes said. It was one of the short phrases of Lithuanian she'd had to learn to get by. There was something about this man that made her feel uneasy. He looked bleary-eyed and was unshaven. Was he drunk? But then he stepped forward and peered at her. To her astonishment, his face creased up with laughter and he started to speak in broken German.

"I remember you," he said. "*Vokietukai*—Little Germans, you are! You came to the market months ago, didn't you, *Fraulein*? I offered you work, but you ran away. Well, I still need workers. There is planting to do and I have no one to help me. My workers have fled or been killed by the Russians."

Agnes stared at him and it came back to her. It was the man who had frightened her the first time she'd made the journey across the border for food. She hadn't liked the look of him then and she didn't now. She tightened her grip on Dieter's hand.

"It's all right," she said, lifting her chin, looking him straight in the eye. "We will go now. You must be mistaken."

The man shook his head and reached out to pinch her chin with his rough fingers. "Oh no, I'm not mistaken. I would know your pretty face anywhere. Now, come to my house and clean up. You can work for me on my farm and I'll feed you and give you lodgings. I will shelter you from the Russian army. But if you don't work, or if you try to run away, I will have no choice but to give you up as enemy aliens."

TWENTY-THREE

Agnes straightened up and wiped a muddy hand across her brow. Her arms and shoulders ached, her head was swimming from the constant bending and stretching. Sweat streamed down her forehead and into her eyes, making them sting. There was no shade in the field and it was backbreaking work, bending down and planting the turnip seeds in the soil, line after line of them. Dieter worked beside her, taking handfuls of seed from the shoulder bag the farmer had given them, digging a little hole in the ground with a trowel, dropping the seeds into it, and smoothing the soil back over the top. They'd been working in the same field since early morning and the sun was high in the sky now. Agnes glanced at Dieter and tried to give him an encouraging look, but he just turned away, scowling. She couldn't blame him. He was thinner than ever now, the skin under his eyes was permanently bruised, his lips were cracked, and his face was a mass of sores and insect bites.

"It's almost lunchtime," Agnes said. "Only a few more minutes."

Up ahead the farmer, Darius Balkus, was leading the black carthorse which dragged a flat metal harrow behind it to break up the soil. A curl of smoke rose from the cigarette he was smoking. All morning, the clank, clank, clank of the harrow a few yards ahead of them was the only sound they'd heard, apart from the mournful cawing of crows from the trees around the farm buildings.

Now Balkus turned round and, spotting Agnes standing still, cupped his hands to his mouth and yelled at her: "Keep on working. Haven't I told you to keep up with me? We should have finished this field by now."

Agnes didn't reply, but bent down again to take more seeds from the bag. It was useless to argue, she'd learned that through bitter experience.

They had been working on the same field for days, first clearing the worst of the coarse weeds and grass by hand, then plowing it, Dieter leading the horse and Agnes following behind to keep the plow straight. At first it had made a change from tending the pigs and cattle in the farmyard, mucking out their filthy pens, feeding them, watering them, but they quickly learned that working in the open fields in early summer was even more grueling.

They had been at the farm for almost two months. At first, Agnes had been relieved to be here rather than at the mercy of Theo and Gunhild in the forest, but she quickly realized that they had exchanged one frightening and exploitative situation for another.

That first morning, Darius had taken them into the farmhouse and introduced them to his wife, Martina, a podgy, downtrodden-looking woman. She was chopping vegetables at the kitchen table and didn't stop or lift her eyes from her task when they entered. Darius had said something to her and the woman had scowled at him and snapped in response. She barely looked at them.

Agnes had hoped to be shown to a room in the house to stay in, but instead, Darius produced some threadbare blankets and said they could sleep in the barn where they'd hidden the first night.

"There's running water in the yard where you can wash and you can do your business in the muckheap behind the barn."

Agnes' face must have dropped, because Darius had started glowering then.

"Not good enough for you, *Fräulein?*" he'd yelled, lunging toward her. "You're German, remember? You kids have no rights here. You're *lucky* I'm taking you in. If you complain, or if you don't work hard, I won't hesitate. I'll speak to the Russian officers straight away."

Agnes knew he was right: they weren't safe. Darius showed them how to clean out the animal pens, where to dump the muck, where the hay and straw were stored, where their feed was kept.

"If you work hard, you will be well rewarded," he said. But no rewards had ever come their way, other than three meager meals a day and a bed on the straw in the barn where the rats scurried around at night and there was little protection from the freezing temperatures. But at least they had blankets, they were hidden from the Russians, and they were being fed, albeit with leftovers or food that Balkus and his wife would normally have set aside for the pigs.

Gradually the snow melted from the fields and the night frosts were no more. The countryside was bursting into bloom; new leaves clothed the hedgerows again and wildflowers grew among the grass and dotted the crops in the fields with color. It reminded Agnes of the countryside around their home village and although the passing of winter made life slightly more comfortable, it brought home to her that time was moving on and renewed her grief for Mother and Aunt Hannah. She thought with horror of the ice slowly melting on the Frisches Haff. Mother's body, which must have lain there, frozen, for months with all the other unfortunates who'd met their end during that terrible exodus, would slip into the depths to be eaten by the fish. And Aunt Hannah too, her decaying body trapped inside that sunken ship, being eaten by sea creatures. Agnes often imagined their faces, lit up with laughter, and the thought that she would never see them again, or hear their mirth, brought unbearable pain.

Again and again, Mother's last words rang in her head: *Promise you'll look after your brother for me, Agnes.*

She was doing her best, but Dieter was unhappy and hungry, bone thin, and being worked like a slave. His childhood had been snatched from him. He should have been running around, laughing and having fun, playing with other boys. Would she ever be able to honor the promise she'd made? The guilt plagued her constantly but how could she even begin to do that while they were enemy aliens in a hostile land, living as slaves under the constant threat of discovery?

Now, she watched as the farmer turned the horse around and ambled back toward them.

"Lunchtime," he said, throwing his cigarette down and grinding it into the earth with his boot. "This afternoon, you will work harder."

Agnes and Dieter trudged behind him, back across the mud to the farmyard. There, they washed their hands in the trough and went into the kitchen to eat as they always did. Today, Martina had a smile on her face for the first time since they'd arrived. Her eyes lit up as they entered, as if she'd been waiting for them. She said something to Darius, her voice brimming with excitement. He turned to Agnes and she saw the triumphant look in his eyes.

"The war is over," he said, beaming. "Hitler is dead. Germany is defeated."

Agnes sat down heavily at the table, her mind swirling. Martina placed the food on the table and she and Darius talked excitedly in Lithuanian, but Agnes couldn't look at them. She didn't believe anything he said and just because the war was over, it didn't mean she and Dieter were safe. Soldiers were everywhere, she was still the enemy. She swallowed hard, thinking about it more, remembering what she and Dieter had witnessed on the walk from Königsberg; the stories Theo and the orphans in the wood had told them about how brutally East Prussian civilians had been treated at the hands of the advancing Red Army. Women and old men had been shown no mercy; they had been shot or taken away to work as slave labor in camps in the Soviet Union.

Was that what had happened to Father? If he'd even survived the war, that was. She could hardly bear to contemplate his fate and normally pushed it to the back of her mind, but now an image forced itself forward. Emaciated and prematurely aged, still wearing his threadbare overcoat, he was being forcibly marched to Russia, shuffling along in a great column with thousands of others, his soul and his hopes crushed forever. She glanced at Dieter, who had already started munching his way through the lump of bread Martina had put on his plate. Did he understand what this meant?

"Eat, girl," Darius said, pushing Agnes' plate toward her. "There is cheese here too. Tomorrow, you will come with me on the cart to the market. I have vegetables to sell there."

Agnes dropped her eyes to the table and shuddered inwardly. She dreaded being alone with Darius. If he'd ever found her separated from Dieter in one of the barns or in a corner of the farmyard, he would trap her against a fence or wall and try to feel her chest or kiss her on the mouth, forcing his tongue between her teeth. She would push him away and if she screamed, he would scowl and leave her alone, afraid no doubt that Martina would hear. But she did her best to avoid ever being alone with him and the revulsion of those moments and the smell of the tobacco and alcohol on his breath never left her.

"Can Dieter come too?" she ventured now, her eyes on Martina's face.

"He must stay and work on the farm," Darius said, but Martina cut in with a sharp question to Darius and, shamefaced, his eyes sidled back toward Agnes. He shrugged and said, "But perhaps he may come, he is not needed here after all."

So, in the morning after breakfast, Darius harnessed the horse and hitched him up to a shabby wooden cart he kept in the barn and ordered Agnes and Dieter to load sacks of vegetables onto the back. They were heavy, but Agnes didn't mind the work. Going to market meant a trip away from the farm. Seeing the countryside, seeing some other people. They hadn't been off the farm since they'd arrived and the only visitors to the farm had been Russian soldiers. She and Dieter had had to climb up into a stuffy loft above the stable and cower there until the soldiers had finished searching the property.

"You'll need to keep quiet, you know," Darius instructed as he flicked the whip and they pulled off in the jolting cart. "If there are soldiers in the market square . . . or even if not."

They set off out of the farmyard and down the road. "You never know who might report you," he went on. "No one can be trusted nowadays. Not friends, nor neighbors, nobody."

The farm wasn't far out of the village and within a few minutes they were trotting into the old familiar market square. Agnes' spirits rose a little to see the stalls laid out, farmers unloading produce from carts onto them, people wandering about, chatting in groups. She looked around for faces she knew, especially the jovial stallholder who'd helped her to escape from the Russian soldier, but he wasn't there. No one she recognized from her visits in the winter of 1944 was there.

Darius pulled the cart up beside an empty stall and nodded toward it.

"Unload the vegetables onto that table," he ordered, then lit a cigarette. "Well, go on, then," he added when they didn't jump to attention immediately. Agnes and Dieter climbed down from the cart and Darius swung to the ground and ambled off toward a group of men who were gathered around a beer stall.

"Come on, Dieter," said Agnes. "We'd better do as he says."

They hauled the sacks down from the back of the cart and began taking the vegetables out to lay out on the stall. As they worked, Agnes looked around her at the other stall-holders. She was enjoying the sound of people gossiping, the vibrant colors and movement of the marketplace after so long cooped up away from humanity. She was so enthralled with what was going on that she barely noticed what she was doing. She emptied the sacks, laying out potatoes, swedes, carrots caked in mud on the slatted wooden table. Some of the vegetables were moldy or damaged, shriveled by frost or nibbled by rodents.

She'd almost emptied all the sacks when she felt Darius' hand on her shoulder.

"What do you think you're doing, girl?" He was holding a beer tankard in one hand, slopping the contents.

"What?" She automatically cowered away from him.

"You've taken no care. No one will buy any of this stuff like this!"

He pushed her against the hard, wooden stall and she felt the crack of the wood as it jarred against her spine. Then he grabbed her by the shoulders and pulled her face toward his. She tried to turn away, the smell of his breath revolted her so much.

"Are you listening to me?" She felt his spittle on her face. "Do your job properly! Hide the moldy ones in the sacks or under the good ones. Clean the mud off with a rag so people can see them. There's one on the cart."

Then he let her go and she staggered, grabbing the stall for support. She watched him walk away and rejoin the group of men at the beer stall. Her eyes were smarting with tears of shame and humiliation. Dieter was staring at her, his eyes wide with fear.

"Don't worry, Dieter," she muttered, swallowing her tears. "It'll be OK. Go and find the rag from the cart, like he said."

She busied herself again, trying not to think about what had just happened, putting some of the moldy vegetables back in the sacks, hiding others under the good ones, just as Darius had ordered. Suddenly, there was a different voice at her shoulder:

"Does he often shout at you like that?"

She turned in surprise that someone else here could speak German and looked up into the earnest blue eyes of a teenage boy, a few years older than herself. His skin was tanned and his nose covered in freckles. His blond hair was tousled and from the way he was dressed, she could tell he was a farm worker. But his eyes were full of concern. She could barely remember the last time anyone had looked at her like that. After quickly glancing over at Darius to check he wasn't watching her and then back at the young man, she shrugged. "Sometimes," she said.

"I've heard a lot of stories about how Lithuanian farmers take in German children who have no homes or family. Some are good to them but others not so good and work them too hard. It looks as though our friend over there is one of those."

"I'm not a child," Agnes protested and the young man smiled, which lit up his whole face.

"Maybe not. But this young boy here is and I bet you wouldn't be working for that oaf if you had any choice?"

"Of course not," she muttered.

Now it was the boy's turn to look surreptitiously round at Darius.

"My name is Lukas, by the way. I'm just passing through this village," he said. "I've been to take some calves to my uncle in the next district. I live with my parents thirty kilometers or so from here. Why don't you come back with me? We could do with more help on the farm and my parents are kind. They would treat you well."

"What?" She stared at him, open-mouthed. This was hard to process. Was it a trick?

"Would they be safe from the war there? From the soldiers?" she blurted, before she'd thought about it.

The boy laughed. "You'd just have to trust me, I suppose. Look, the offer is there. If you want to, I will be waiting for you with my cart behind the church over there. Come and find me when you can get away. Bring the boy too. But if you don't come by twelve o' clock, I can't wait. I'll need to get going."

Agnes stared at him again. "But . . ."

"All you have to do is wait until he's had too much to drink, then you can creep away. It won't take long by the look of how he's drinking."

Agnes glanced across at the group of men. They were growing rowdier by the minute. Darius had his head back and was draining the contents of his tankard.

"See you before twelve then," said Lukas and then he was gone, walking toward the churchyard.

"Can we go with him?" Dieter was looking at her with pleading eyes.

"I don't know, let me think," Agnes said.

Just then an old woman came up to buy potatoes. She was saying something in Lithuanian, holding out some coins. Agnes barely understood what she was saying, but she didn't want to call Darius over, so she smiled and nodded and used the few phrases she'd picked up. The woman seemed happy with the bargain, loaded several kilos of potatoes into her basket, and moved on.

"Well?" Dieter was pulling at her clothes. "Can we go with that boy?"

Again, Agnes looked over at the beer stall. Darius was drinking another beer, laughing loudly, and looking unsteady on his feet. She looked back at Dieter. He was waiting for her to reply, pleading with his eyes. Her heart went out to him and she made her decision. How could she deny him this after all they'd been through? There was a chance that life might be better with the boy and his parents. He seemed educated; at least he could speak German. It couldn't be worse than life with Darius and Martina, surely?

"All right, we'll go. When it is safe, we will just walk away."

For the next hour, Agnes went through the motions of minding the stall, helping people who came to buy vegetables, putting the money in a pile on the table. It was a strain trying to play the part of a Lithuanian with her limited language. If they tried to engage her in conversation, she pretended not to have heard. She had no interest in making sure she was getting a fair price for the produce, she just wanted to get through the morning and get away from there safely now the decision had been made. She watched the clock on the church tower as the hands crawled round. Part of her wanted this hour to be over, the other part was worrying that Darius would still be on his feet at twelve o'clock and they wouldn't be able to get away.

Darius was still at the beer stall at a quarter to twelve. Agnes wondered if he would notice if they just walked away. The time ticked by and he was still standing there, but at about five to twelve, he broke away from the others and staggered over to the cart, clambered on board with a loud belch, and then lay down among the empty sacks. Agnes glanced at Dieter.

"Now," she mouthed.

She glanced at the pile of coins she'd tucked under a large potato on the stall, looking at them longingly. That amount of money could make all the difference to her and Dieter, but she couldn't bring herself to take it. Just the thought of Papa and Mutti and the values they had instilled in her stopped her from contemplating it too long. Instead, she took Dieter's hand and they walked away from the stall and along the back of the market square until they reached a path that led through the churchyard. As they walked past the church, the clock in the tower began to strike the hour. Agnes started to run: "It's twelve o'clock. Come *on*," she said, pulling Dieter along behind her. They reached the road on the other side of the churchyard and her heart leapt. There was a cart, harnessed up to a smart, black horse, and there was Lukas on the driving seat, shielding his eyes from the sun, peering across the churchyard. He was still there, he'd waited for them!

TWENTY-FOUR

Lukas patted the seat next to him and first Dieter, then Agnes climbed up and settled down beside him.

"You came, then," he said, grinning. "I wasn't sure you would, but I'm really glad you did. Let's get going before he realizes you're missing." He flicked the reins and they moved off.

As the cart rumbled through the village street, Agnes kept looking over her shoulder, fearful she'd see Darius running down the road after them, his red face full of thunder.

"It's all right," Lukas reassured her. "He won't come after us. And even if he did, what could he say? You are free to come with me, he doesn't own you."

"He wouldn't see it that way," muttered Agnes, but she felt a little comforted by Lukas' words and as they left the outskirts of the village behind them, her fears started to melt away. She looked about her, enthralled by the beauty all around, the fields of newly sown crops, the spring flowers in the hedgerows, the sound of birdsong. But soon they were trotting along the country highway that led past the entrance to the great forest she knew so well.

"Did you come that way through the woods from East Prussia?"

Lukas asked. He must have seen her looking with trepidation in the direction of the forest.

Agnes nodded.

"There are lots of German kids living wild in that wood," he said. "Everyone for miles around knows about them. The poor things are abandoned and desperate. They move about in gangs, stealing food from farms on the edge of the wood. Some of them get work with the locals. It's the only place where they can be safe from the Russians."

"I know," said Agnes bitterly, looking down at her hands.

There was a short silence between them, the only sound the clip-clop of the pony's hoofs on the road and the rumble of the metaled wheels.

"Hey, you two didn't *live* in that forest, did you?" Lukas asked.

"For a while, yes," she said.

"Oh," Lukas said. "So, you are wolf children, *Vokietukai?* I thought you'd come straight through to that village from the railway line. I didn't realize . . . That must have been tough."

Agnes stared up the hill at the dense, brooding evergreens, remembering how huge the forest was: kilometer upon kilometer of towering conifers and untamed undergrowth, the horrors it harbored in its depths. She wished the road would bend away from the edge of the wood so that she could try to put it out of her mind. As the cart jogged on, the gentle swaying motion and the rhythmic clop, clop of the horse's hoofs was mesmerizing. Agnes felt Dieter's body grow heavy against hers, his head slump down on her shoulder. She put her arm around him and held him tightly to her.

"What are your names?" Lukas asked.

"Agnes and Dieter."

"Well, Agnes, you will need to be called Agne from now on and your brother can be Dimitri. You can't be German anymore. Can you speak any Lithuanian?"

"A little bit. Not very much," she replied, in stumbling Lithuanian.

Lukas laughed. "That's very good, but I'll have to teach you. If you're going to stay on our farm, we will have to pretend you're my cousins and that I've brought you back with me to help with the harvest so you'll have to learn our language. Otherwise, you won't be safe."

Agnes felt the familiar flutter of nerves in her stomach. When could they stop running? When would they ever be safe?

"I thought, with the war ending, things might be different for us now," she said.

Lukas shook his head. "Things will tighten up, if anything. Lithuania is occupied by the Soviet army. They will do their best to root out any Germans and deport them, or punish them. We will need to be very careful."

Fear coursed through Agnes afresh. She swallowed hard, but her eyes were flooded with unbidden tears.

"Oh, I'm sorry!" said Lukas. "I didn't mean to upset you. It's just that we need to face reality. But we will be careful. My parents are kind, like I said. We will keep you safe."

Agnes watched the countryside roll by, sheep and cattle in a nearby field, a stone farmhouse, its garden a riot of roses and geraniums. How she ached for home.

"Why are you doing this?" she asked. "You could be punished too."

He didn't reply for a while, then he said, "I saw you being brutalized by that oaf and I felt sorry for you. I can't bear cruelty, especially to animals and children. And because, when I came over, I saw the spirit in your eyes. You are a fighter, Agnes. I could see that straight away and I wanted to help you."

Agnes felt the color rise in her cheeks and for a moment she couldn't look at him.

"Do you want some *lasiniai,* by the way?" Lukas broke the silence. "I bought some at the market. I don't think we should stop to eat, we need to get on, but if you're hungry, tuck in." And he passed her a hunk of fatty, cured meat, wrapped in grease-proof paper. She smiled her thanks.

It was dusk as they finally rolled into the village that Lukas told them was his home. There were picturesque cottages, a neat village square, a little church. It was achingly similar to her own home village. People tending animals outside their homes or watering vegetables in neat plots waved to Lukas as they passed. He waved back, shouting something in Lithuanian.

"What are you saying?"

"I'm saying you are my cousins, here to visit and help on the farm. Look! They are waving at you. You need to smile and wave back."

So, Agnes did as he said and nudged Dieter, who did the same.

On the far edge of the village, Lukas guided the cart through a pair of green-painted gates and into a neat farmyard. It couldn't have been more different from Darius' shambolic establishment. The yard was swept clean, a few plump chickens pecked around in a pen, and in another pen on clean straw, four or five cows suckled young calves. A gray-haired man in a boiler suit emerged from one of the sheds, wiping his hands on his clothes.

"Lukas!" His face was wreathed in smiles.

"My father, Emilis," Lukas explained quietly to Agnes in German. The man had begun walking across the yard toward the cart, but when his eyes alighted on Agnes and Dieter, he stopped and frowned. There followed a rapid exchange in Lithuanian, of which Agnes could only pick out a few words, but she sensed the sight of her and Dieter was not an altogether welcome one for Lukas' father. The surge of relief she'd felt when they'd pulled into the yard was rapidly evaporating.

The exchange ended with the father shaking his head and

sighing. Then he approached the cart with a rueful smile and held his hand out for Agnes to take.

"*Sveiki*," he said.

"It means welcome," said Lukas.

"*Aciu*," Agnes thanked him in Lithuanian, which earned her a grin from the old man.

"Is everything all right?" she asked Lukas, clambering down from the cart.

"All is good," said Lukas, lifting Dieter down. "My father is a little worried, that's all. Sometimes Russian officials come to the farm to check up on us, sometimes soldiers come too. But Father is a good man. He says you can stay here, but we must keep you away from others until you know enough of the language."

Agnes nodded, her eyes on Dieter, who had gone to look at the calves. "We are quick learners."

"That's good." Lukas smiled. "Now come on inside and meet my mother. Come, Dimitri!"

Dieter looked round, amusement in his eyes at being addressed by this new name, and they both followed Lukas round the edge of the barn and into the neat, wooden house that was surrounded by a riot of colorful flowerbeds.

A woman stood at the kitchen sink, her back to the door, peeling vegetables. The kitchen was filled with the delicious aroma of meat cooking; onions and garlic and root vegetables all mixed in with it, and suddenly Agnes was transported back to the kitchen at the family farm and those happy Sundays spent with Aunt Hannah, Uncle Tomas, and the cousins before the war.

"Mama?" Lukas said and the woman turned round and her face momentarily lit up at the sound of his voice. It was clear Lukas took after his mother. She was a tall, strong-looking woman, with streaks of gray in her blonde hair that was plaited around her head. Her eyes were the same cornflower blue as Lukas', but her face was careworn and lined. When she saw

Agnes and Dieter, just like her husband's a few minutes before, her expression fell and she said a few sharp words to her son. Agnes squeezed Dieter's hand and the two of them stood there awkwardly, watching mother and son as they argued. But at last the woman sighed and her face took on a look of resignation.

"Come, then," she said suddenly, acknowledging Agnes and Dieter in German, but she didn't smile. "I am Lina." She ushered them toward a large, square kitchen table.

"She says you can stay," said Lukas, pulling out chairs for the two of them to sit down. He was beaming, but Agnes was unsettled by the reception both parents had given them.

Emilis came in from the farmyard, pulling off his boots in the doorway. He sat down at the head of the table and Lina put plates of steaming stew and dumplings in front of them.

"Eat," she said.

Dieter attacked the food, shoveling it into his mouth, but Agnes ate more slowly, savoring the wonderful tastes, chewing every mouthful many times. At Darius and Martina's there had never been enough food for them; Martina had saved most of it for herself and her husband. She was a terrible cook and what she had given them was tasteless and unappetizing.

"Slow down, Dieter," Agnes said under her breath, worried that he would make himself sick, but he took no notice. She caught Lukas' eye across the table and they both giggled. She saw his parents exchanging glances, tight-lipped, and looked back down at her food.

When the meal was over, Lina said something to Lukas, who got up from his chair.

"Come, I will show you where you can sleep," he said. "Follow me."

They were about to get up from the table when there was a knock at the door. Everyone froze. Lukas' parents looked flustered and Emilis whispered something to him.

"He says for you to keep quiet and still," Lukas said.

Wiping her hands on her apron, Lina went to the door and opened it. From where she was sitting at the kitchen table, Agnes could just see the visitor. It was a man dressed in dark overalls, with cropped hair and pebble glasses. Holding a clipboard, he was firing questions at Lukas' mother and writing her stumbling answers down. From the tone of his voice, it was clear he wasn't satisfied with the answers she was giving. Each time he looked up from his clipboard, he tried to peer behind Lina and into the kitchen. Agnes felt chills run through her each time he did this. She had no idea what this was all about, but it made her feel uneasy. Finally, the conversation ended and Lina closed the door and turned back into the kitchen, her face ashen. She came and sat down at the table and spoke slowly and quietly to Lukas and Emilis.

"That man, Ponas Shimkus, is a local Soviet official," Lukas explained to Agnes. "They are always coming here now the Russians are in control. They check up on the farm all the time; what we are producing, where we are selling our produce. They are trying to persuade my parents to join a collective farm, but my father is resisting. He has always been his own boss and he doesn't want to give up control."

Emilis looked up and said something to Lukas. A little shamefaced, Lukas looked back at Agnes.

"What did he say?" she asked.

"He says he doesn't want more trouble from the authorities. That you and your brother must learn Lithuanian quickly or you'll have to leave . . . but please don't worry about that. He doesn't mean it. And like I said, I will teach you the language. Now . . . I was going to show you your room."

They followed Lukas through into a hallway and toward a wooden staircase at the end of it. As they passed the open door of a living room, Agnes stopped and stared inside.

"What is it?" Lukas asked.

"You have a piano," she said softly, awed at the sight of the polished wooden upright piano, with a lace cloth laid over the top with vases and ornaments displayed on it.

"It belonged to my grandmother. None of us play, but Mother won't get rid of it. She says it reminds her of her childhood."

Those words struck such a chord with Agnes, she had to steady herself against the doorpost.

"Are you all right?" asked Lukas, his voice gentle.

The sight of the old instrument standing there under the window and Lukas' words had brought back such a sharp memory of her own that she was brought up short. She was reminded of her own childhood. The childhood that she should still be living, but which had been snatched from her by the war.

"Can you play?" Lukas asked.

"I'm not sure anymore," she said. Because it was true. It seemed several lifetimes since she'd last sat down at the piano in her old home and played the pieces she used to play for Papa and Mutti. She wiggled her fingers. Those same fingers that had kindled fires in the forest, scraped the muck out of chicken houses and pigpens, grown red raw with frostbite, gathering snow to drink on their long trek from Königsberg, and planting and harvesting vegetables on Darius' farm.

"You *can* play, Agnes." It was Dieter's voice. He was gently pushing her toward the piano.

"It is Agne now," said Lina. She was standing in the doorway, drying a plate with a cloth. "You can't say Agnes anymore. Not even with us, child. It will bring danger on us all."

Dieter looked away. He seemed crushed by her words.

"Go on then, Agne," said the woman. "Play for us. The instrument may be a little out of tune. I had it tuned regularly until the Russians came."

Agnes walked across the room toward the piano, her eyes fixed on the polished wooden surface, the lace cloth on the top, the family ornaments and photographs. Everything else in the room seemed to fade away as she moved toward it and it was as if she was back at home, walking toward her old familiar piano, with Papa and Mutti looking on. She stopped in front of it and with trembling fingers, lifted the lid and stared down at the ivory and ebony keys. It was as if they were beckoning her, calling her to touch them.

"Sit down, girl," said Lukas' mother. Agnes pulled out the stool and sat down. It was a little too high and she had to stretch her toes to touch the pedals, but that didn't matter. Suddenly nervous, she glanced over her shoulder. They were all standing in the doorway, waiting. Emilis had joined them now, his expression expectant. So, she put her fingers on the keys and played.

First, she played "Für Elise" and the notes came back to her immediately. They must have lain dormant in her memory throughout those terrible, hard months. The melody flowed from her fingers as sweetly and delicately as it used to all those times she'd played it for Papa. And as she played, she lost herself in the music. It was as if it was just her and the notes, as if nothing else mattered in the world. When she'd finished that piece, she didn't stop. She carried on, rattling through all the sonatas she'd learned. Mozart, Beethoven, Chopin . . . she remembered them all. She'd always had a good ear for music and once she'd learned a piece, she had no need for the sheet music.

When she'd exhausted her repertoire, she stopped and looked down at her bony fingers on the keys and reality came flooding back to her. She remembered where she was and everything that had happened over the past few months. She remembered too that she wasn't playing for Mutti and Papa in the living room at home. But the sound of enthusiastic clapping behind her interrupted her memories. She turned round and saw that as she'd been playing, everyone had come into the room. They were sitting in the armchairs listening to her. Dieter sat on Lukas' knee, his face brimming with pride—it was the biggest smile she'd seen on his face for a long time.

"You have talent, young Agne," said Lina, smiling herself for the first time. Then she turned to Lukas and said something rapidly in Lithuanian.

"My mother says that I must take you to the village teacher's house one day. He is a musician as well as a teacher. You must play for him and he might offer to give you lessons. She says such a talent must be nurtured."

"But—" Agnes was about to ask whether that might be dangerous.

"The teacher is a good man," Lina cut her off. "He can be trusted not to give you away to the Russians."

Later, Lukas showed Agnes and Dieter to their room under the eaves of the farmhouse. There was a big, saggy bed piled with soft blankets and colorful quilts. He handed them clean pajamas. "These used to be mine," he said. "Tomorrow we will heat some water downstairs and you can have a proper wash."

When he'd gone, they pulled off their filthy clothes, changed into Lukas' pajamas, and sank into the cozy bed. Dieter fell asleep immediately, but despite her exhaustion Agnes lay awake, staring at the ceiling. She listened to the night-time sounds of the farm and reflected on the extraordinary quirk of fate that had changed everything that morning and how, in twenty-four short hours, their lives had been transformed from drudgery and danger to being given a glimmer of hope for their safety.

TWENTY-FIVE

The weeks passed and Agnes and Dieter quickly got used to the rhythm of the new routine on Lina and Emilis' farm. Each morning, they would rise as the first cockerels crowed in the yard. They would go down to the kitchen, where Lina would have already cooked them eggs and porridge for breakfast. Afterward, Lukas would take them out to help him with the early-morning chores on the land. When they came back to the farm, they would wash at the pump in the yard, sit back down at the kitchen table and, for the rest of the morning, Lukas would give them lessons in the Lithuanian language. Agnes loved that part of the morning, as the summer sun moved gradually round in the sky, sending shafts of golden light through the kitchen windows.

Lukas was a good teacher. Intelligent and patient, but always with a twinkle in his eye and ready with a joke or a funny story to entertain them and bring the lessons to life.

"How do you speak such good German?" Agnes asked him one day after he'd explained something to them in their own language. "Your mother speaks a little bit too."

Lukas was quiet for a moment and then he said, "You know,

before the Russians came here, the German army occupied our country. The Nazis. We had to learn German at school for a while, until the Soviets came back last year and threw them out."

"Do you still go to school?" she asked and he shook his head.

"I loved learning and I was a good student, but my father needs me here on the farm. I left school last year. I still go to visit my old teacher, though: Jurgis Klukas. He gives me books to read and we talk about history and literature. One day, perhaps, when I'm not needed so badly here, I will go back to my studies . . ."

The two of them learned Lithuanian rapidly, especially Dieter, who absorbed the lessons like a sponge. They practiced the language throughout each day as well, only lapsing into German when they were alone together.

The only thing that marred those first few weeks for Agnes and Dieter was the daily visit of Ponas Shimkus, the Soviet official. Sometimes he just came to the kitchen door, as he had on the first day, with his clipboard, to ask questions. On other days, he came with two soldiers bearing rifles. On those days, Emilis' shoulders would droop and he would shrug and give Lina a desperate look and go with the soldiers and the official out into the farmyard.

"What do they want?" Agnes asked Lukas, unsettled by the presence of the soldiers. She understood now why Emilis and Lina had been so insistent that they should become fluent in Lithuanian as quickly as they could.

"They come to check production on the farm. We have to give up a certain amount of everything we farm to the state. Every Friday, Father and I make a delivery of milk, and whatever else we've produced, to the cooperative in the market town a few kilometers away. Some farmers try to get round the rules, so the Soviets send officials and soldiers round the farms to stop that happening."

"It doesn't seem fair," Agnes murmured. It reminded her of what had happened to East Prussian farmers during the war, being forced to give up their yield to feed the war effort and how Aunt Hannah had cleverly kept back some of the food to keep the family from starving.

"That's not the only thing that's unfair about what they're doing to farmers here." There was bitterness in Lukas' voice and he clenched his fists as he said the words. Agnes glanced at him in surprise. She'd never seen him so serious before.

"They've confiscated some of our land already to distribute to other people. There was nothing Father could do about it. He had too many acres to escape the decree. The Soviets have brought poor people out from the cities to work the land. The village is full of them now. Most of them know nothing about farming and the land is going to rack and ruin. And they are the people we can't trust not to speak to the authorities about whatever we do."

Agnes shuddered, remembering how when they'd arrived in the village, some of the villagers had peered intently at her and Dieter as they passed through in the cart. How could they be sure that none of them had already spoken to the Russians about her and Dieter being at the farm?

"So, you see, it's not safe in this village. Nowhere is safe from informers, from people who want to do us harm. Father is fighting a constant battle to keep his land. Some of his friends who resisted the reforms have disappeared overnight and all of their land has been taken by the Soviets and absorbed into collective farms."

"That's dreadful, Lukas," she said, fear rolling through her. "Where do you think your father's friends went?"

He shrugged. "Taken off to Siberia, to work camps. It happens."

Agnes fell silent, thinking of the stories of East Prussian civilians who hadn't been able to get away before the Russian invasion and who had suffered the same fate. And of her father. Was that where he was now? If he'd survived the fighting. Her mouth quivered as she thought once again of him trudging away from the house in the snow, carrying his battered suitcase.

One day when they had been at the farm about a month, Lukas harnessed the horse and cart and took Agnes to see the village teacher, Jurgis Klukas. Dieter stayed behind to help Lina catch and pluck a chicken and prepare vegetables for supper. He stood in front of her and waved them goodbye from the kitchen doorway. Agnes felt a pang of anxiety mingled with guilt as the cart rolled out of the yard and Dieter disappeared from view. He'd rarely been out of her sight for all the months they had been fugitives and it felt strange to be setting off without him. He seemed happy enough with Lina, though, and in that short month had smiled and laughed more than in all the long, hard months since they'd lost Mutti and Aunt Hannah. Already his eyes were clearer, his cheeks were filling out, and flesh was beginning to cover his bony limbs.

"He'll be all right. Don't worry about him," Lukas said as they set off out of the village in the opposite direction from the way they'd arrived on their first day.

"I'm not worried. He looks happy. It's just . . . I'm not used to being without him, that's all."

"I understand."

Agnes stole a glance at Lukas but he wasn't looking at her, he was concentrating on the road ahead, guiding the horse with the reins. She took in his tanned face, the way his blond hair curled around his ears and neck, the muscles on his arms, his capable hands. She felt a rush of gratitude toward this farm boy with his sunny nature, for rescuing them from their life of drudgery and for persuading his parents to take them in. She felt safe there, sitting beside him on the cart rolling through the flat endless fields, watching the sun play on the ripening corn.

And she realized then that Lukas was the first person who'd offered her friendship, through all the hardship and loss.

"Why are you doing this, Lukas?" she asked.

"Doing what? Taking you to see Jurgis Klukas?"

"No, not that. All of it. Why are you doing this for me and Dieter—giving us a home, taking risks for us?"

"I told you before, didn't I? I couldn't bear the way that man was treating you in the market."

"But to bring us to your home . . . it's . . . it's very kind. And we are grateful. But it's so risky for you. Most people would have just looked the other way. Most people did."

Lukas shrugged, still staring ahead at the horse's rippling flanks as it trotted on. Agnes thought that was the end of the conversation until he started speaking again a few minutes later.

"I had a little sister once," he said. "Marija. She was a few years younger than me. She would have been about your age. But she died of typhus fever when she was five years old. She had a lot of spirit. I suppose you reminded me of her when I saw you in that marketplace. That's why I wanted to help you."

"Oh . . . that's terrible," Agnes said quietly, trying to imagine the pain of the whole family. Was that why Lina was sometimes prickly and defensive, why Emilis was withdrawn and preoccupied?

"We just had to carry on," he said. "But Mother and Father sometimes need help to keep positive. They have never really got over their grief."

"I can understand that," murmured Agnes.

"I noticed though, this month since you arrived, Mother has seemed a lot happier . . . but of course, you have lost family too, haven't you? Or you wouldn't have gone into the forest to fend for yourselves."

"We lost our whole family," she said quietly. "My mother and aunt died when we were trying to escape the fighting. My cousins were conscripted into the Wehrmacht to fight the

Russians. Father and Uncle were taken too—to serve in the *Volkssturm*. I don't know where they are now. They might have been taken to a work camp in Russia. I really don't know—"

She stopped. She realized that she was twisting her hands together until the nails dug into the palms. She couldn't go on. She'd never said those words out loud before, but hearing them coming from her own mouth suddenly made her feel disloyal to Papa. But then she felt Lukas' arm slipping around her shoulders. He pulled her to him and she put her head on his shoulder. There was no need to say anything and she was glad he hadn't tried to comfort her with words. This way was so much simpler and spoke directly to her heart.

The road took them through a long stretch of forest, then on through acres of farmland that stretched for miles on either side. After a kilometer or so, Lukas pulled the cart off onto a side road that took them through another spinney. A little house was nestled there among the trees. It was a one-story, white painted cottage. Beyond the trees was a river, fast-flowing, but shallow-looking, with gravel beaches.

"This is a long way from the village," Agnes said as they drew up outside the house.

Lukas smiled.

"Jurgis loves the countryside and being beside the river. He grew up in this house. And he likes to be away from his pupils, I think."

Jurgis Klukas appeared at the door wearing a baggy white shirt and paint-spattered trousers. He had wild gray hair and gold-rimmed glasses. "Lukas, my friend, how are you?" he exclaimed, coming forward, his arms outstretched.

"I have brought a friend," Lukas said in German and introduced Agnes.

"Come inside, come inside!" the teacher said, switching effortlessly to German. "I've just been working on my latest picture. The river at sunset. Come and see . . ."

They followed him through to a cluttered studio, where a large window overlooked the river. The room was stacked with dusty books, ornaments, canvases. A half-finished oil painting stood on an easel beside the window. It was vibrant and the colors startling. But Agnes' eyes were drawn to a small grand piano in the corner.

"My mother thought you should hear Agne playing," Lukas said. "She wondered if you might be prepared to give her lessons."

"Be my guest . . ." beamed the teacher.

Agnes sat down, lifted the lid of the piano, and played, just as she had the first night they'd arrived at the farm. She played and played, pouring her heart and soul into the music. When she'd finished, she looked round. Lukas was smiling broadly, but Jurgis Klukas had tears in his eyes.

"You have suffered a lot these past few months, my child, haven't you?" he asked, and when Agnes nodded, he said, "I can tell, I can tell. Your suffering came to me through the music. I will teach you, Agne, of course I will. I will gladly teach you for nothing. If I have anything to teach you at all, that is."

TWENTY-SIX

Agnes and Dieter stayed on Emilis and Lina's farm throughout that long, hot summer. As the crops ripened from green to golden in the huge, flat fields that surrounded the farmstead, they spent their days helping Lukas and Emilis with the harvest and tending to the pigs and cattle. Lina taught them all about rearing hens for maximum egg yield and how to milk the dairy cows by hand, which they did twice a day. This work was different from any other farm work they'd done before. Emilis was a diligent farmer and knew everything there was to know about animal and crop husbandry, and Lukas was a great companion and took genuine pleasure in teaching them about his work.

Agnes loved spending her days following Lukas around on the farm, helping him with anything he asked her to do: scything crops, loading hay on the back of the wagon, following the plow, planting vegetables, herding animals. Working with him was no hardship, no matter how hard or strenuous the work was. She loved to hear his stories and to see his face light up in a broad smile when her work pleased him, and her heart was warmed by the way he took Dieter under his wing, showed him what to do, was endlessly patient when the little boy was slow to learn or made mistakes.

Within a couple of months, both Agnes and Dieter were speaking the Lithuanian language fairly confidently, but Lina and Emilis were still nervous when anyone came to the door. They would usher them upstairs or tell them to keep quiet until the visitor had gone. The atmosphere was tense both during and after those visits, especially if it was one of the newcomers to the village who knocked on the door asking for work. Often, they would try to peer inside the kitchen, as the official had done on the first day.

"They're just looking for information to sneak on us to the authorities," Lina would say once they'd gone, her forehead knitted into an anxious frown. "They're not interested in working for us at all."

"Try not to worry, Lina," Emilis would reply. "You're reading too much into it. They're just simple people. What good would it do them to inform on us like that?"

"They're jealous that we still own and work our land. They'd love to see our farm confiscated and us reduced to the status of laborers on our own land."

Agnes would listen to these exchanges with fear in her heart. She knew that if the Soviet officials found out that the family had been harboring enemy children, not only would Lina and Emilis lose their land, they would be punished too. And she had seen first-hand how brutal Russian soldiers could be. Every time something like this happened, she would spend sleepless nights worrying that Lina or Emilis would lose their nerve and tell her and Dieter that they must leave the farm. She was conscious that their future was poised on a knife-edge; that only Lukas stood between them and being cast out in an inhospitable world to take their chances alone again. She began to regard Lukas as her protector, to worship him as an older-brother figure, as well as her best friend.

In the evenings, she would practice her scales and exercises on the old upright piano in the living room and once a week, Lukas would drive her out of the village for a lesson with Jurgis Klukas. She loved those rides out on the cart in the blistering sunshine, sitting beside Lukas as he drove, enveloped in the cloud of dust that rose from the horse's hoofs on the dry road. Lukas would tell her stories about people in the village or about his school-days, and in return, he would ask her to tell him about her old life in East Prussia. At first, she found it difficult to tell him much about those days—it was far too painful to remember—but after a few attempts it became easier, and she found herself gradually opening up, able to describe everything about her family, her schooldays, her village, and her friends. When she spoke to him about Liesel, though, she started to cry.

"You don't have to tell me if it's too difficult," Lukas said gently.

"It's just that . . . I have no idea where poor Liesel ended up, whether the Count and all the estate workers got to where they were going, or whether Liesel is even still alive. Everyone just had to leave their homes and run away in the middle of winter. But even running away was dangerous . . ." She thought of her mother, of Aunt Hannah.

Lukas shook his head. "War is a terrible, terrible thing. Perhaps one day, when things have calmed down, you will be able to go back to your home."

She stared at him wordlessly through the tears. It was something she no longer even dared to hope for.

Jurgis would be standing in the door of his cottage when they arrived. He always greeted them effusively, plied them with fruit juice. Lukas would wait in Jurgis' small living room, or walk down to the riverbank, while Agnes had her piano lessons. Jurgis was an inspirational teacher; he encouraged her to perfect her technical skills as well as to play more and more advanced pieces. He had an instinctive feel for the music and seemed to be able to draw inspiration from the notes on the page that her old teacher never had.

One day, Dieter came along with them for the ride. When Jurgis saw him climbing down from the cart he exclaimed, "How alike you two are! Such beautiful children. You know, I'd love to paint your portraits, if you would permit me?"

"I'm not sure Dieter would be able to sit still long enough for that," Agnes said, laughing.

"Oh, there would be no need for him to sit still for more than a second," Jurgis replied emphatically. "I could take your photographs and work on them myself later. I have a camera in the studio for this very purpose. Come, come . . ."

He ushered them through the cottage and into the studio, where he produced a brown leather case and pulled a portable camera out of it.

"Wow!" Dieter exclaimed, his eyes lighting up, as Jurgis pulled the folding lens out and held the camera up proudly.

"Stand over there . . . near the window, please. You first, little boy."

Dieter stood in front of the window and grinned broadly while Jurgis snapped away. Then it was Agnes' turn. She felt shy standing in front of the camera and found it difficult to lift her eyes to the lens. But it was over before she knew it.

"Next time you come, I will have developed these and I will have started painting your portraits. Now come, Agnes, sit down and play what you have been practicing this week for me."

So the days rolled by, and soon the leaves were turning on the trees and there was a new chill in the air as summer moved rapidly into autumn. Agnes realized with a jolt that it was almost a year since Papa had been taken away to join the *Volkssturm*. Not an hour went by without her thinking about him and Mutti, but although they were constantly in her mind, she allowed herself to feel occasional moments of happiness now. Was that disloyal to her parents, she wondered as she lay awake one night, listening to the distant hoot of a barn owl. But she only had to think about it for a moment to be sure that they would want her and Dieter to be happy, not to spend their days mourning and miserable. But despite these glimpses of happiness, there was always that dark cloud hovering over them; they were here in hiding. If anyone disloyal discovered their identity, the consequences would be unthinkable. One day they might speak the language well enough to pass as Lithuanians, but if anyone was really intent on finding out their true identity, they would have nowhere to hide.

On their weekly deliveries of farm produce to the nearby depot, Emilis and Lukas heard rumors in the local town that now the war with Germany was over, the enforcement of Soviet rules and regulations against the local population was about to be stepped up. The collectivization of farms would be accelerated as part of that. Once, on their way home from the depot, they saw Russian soldiers ransacking a farm, the farmer and his wife being bundled into a lorry.

"They won't take my land," Emilis said when he related the story on their return home. "Not over my dead body."

One evening, the inevitable happened. The Soviet official Ponas Shimkus knocked on the door just as the family had finished supper. Everyone fell silent and exchanged anxious glances. Emilis got up and went to the door, telling Agnes and Dieter to stay at the table but to keep quiet. He opened the door and answered all the usual questions about milk and egg yield, how many animals were ready for slaughter, and the state of the harvest. The official scribbled down the answers on his clipboard and from the tone of his voice it sounded as though he was satisfied and the conversation was at an end, but just as he was about to go, he turned on his heel and faced Emilis once again.

"I have had reports of you refusing to employ peasant workers on your farm."

There was a short silence, then Emilis' voice came, firm and defiant.

"We have no need of extra workers, sir. We have enough help here on the farm already."

"So, who exactly is it that works on your farm?"

"Myself, my wife, and son."

Shimkus pushed back the door and stared past Emilis into the kitchen.

"And who is that, sitting at your table?"

"Er . . . my young nephew and niece. They are here for the summer, from my brother's farm in the next district."

"I will need to see their identity documents," said the man sharply.

Agnes could barely control her nerves. She'd been sipping some water, but now her hands were shaking so much she couldn't hold the glass steady. She put it down and clasped her hands on her lap out of sight. Emilis cleared his throat.

"Their papers are not to hand at this moment. I'm not sure in fact if they brought their papers with them at all," he answered bravely. "I'm sorry, sir, but as you can see, they are only children."

"That is not good enough," the official barked. "I need to see those documents. I will come back tomorrow and you had better be able to produce them then or the consequences will be severe. Some farmers have taken in enemy aliens to work their land. That is a criminal act that we need to do everything we can to stamp out."

"But I told you, I am not at all sure that they brought their papers with them."

"And I told *you*, I need to see them. Now, good night. I will be back tomorrow."

Emilis turned back into the room, his face ashen.

"Why did you tell them that? We should have hidden the children from view," Lina said, her voice sharp.

"He has seen the children before, many times, my dear. It was a test."

"But what are we going to do now? They have no papers, Emilis! Didn't you think of that?"

Emilis slumped down at the table, head in his hands.

"Don't worry, Papa. I have an idea," said Lukas.

The next morning, after breakfast, Lukas harnessed the horse and hitched him up to the cart and Agnes and Dieter climbed up beside him on the driver's seat. Emilis came out of the house lugging a large suitcase, which he tied with string to the back of the cart. Then, with much clattering of hoofs and loud "Goodbyes," they set off out of the farmyard. Emilis and Lina followed the cart a little way down the road, blowing kisses and waving goodbye. Lukas trotted the horse and cart straight down the village street. It was a busy time of day, with people out doing their morning chores, sweeping their front paths, feeding chickens, gossiping in front of their houses. As the cart clattered past the cottages, people shaded their eyes to see who it was, then, seeing Lukas, waved enthusiastically.

"Where are you off to, Lukas, my boy?" shouted an old man, shuffling down the road, carrying some tiny piglets in a crate.

"Just taking my cousins home; they need to go back to school."

The old man waved and the cart trotted on. They reached the row of narrow dwellings where the temporary workers from the city were housed. Lukas slowed the cart down and walked the horse past the cramped cottages. Agnes glimpsed more than one pair of eyes peering out from the windows, watching them pass. Her heart was thumping hard against her ribs. She'd had hardly any sleep the night before. She'd lain awake worrying about being taken away by the Russians. She couldn't help but think back to what had happened to Frau Müller, to all the times she and Dieter had had to hide in fear for their lives. Sweat poured off her as her mind was filled with images of what might have become of them if Ponas Shimkus had pursued his line of inquiry that evening.

They carried on along the highway for two or three kilometers out of the village, then Lukas turned the cart off the road and headed down a dusty track between two fields. The surface was bumpy here and they had to proceed slowly, the cart bucking and jolting over the ruts. When they reached a gate beside a small barn, he pulled the horse to a halt.

"Here's the barn I told you about. You can walk back to the farm by following that hedge there." He pointed to a meandering boundary that ran between fields. "Take your time, though. You'll have to make sure no one sees you. There shouldn't be anyone on our land, but you never know."

"Come on, Dieter." Agnes jumped down from the cart and held out her hand to help her brother down.

"Aren't you coming with us?" Dieter asked Lukas.

"Not right now," said Lukas. "I explained before. I'm going to pull the horse and cart into this barn, sleep here overnight, and drive back to the farm tomorrow without the suitcase. People will think I've taken you back home again. Now off you go, see you tomorrow!"

Agnes and Dieter set off back across the fields, keeping under the cover of the hedge. They were used to walking out of sight like this and this time it was far easier than dragging their feet through freezing snow. Soon the farmyard came into view and Agnes was careful to make sure they kept hidden behind the bushes as they made their way round to the back door of the house. Lina was in the kitchen, peeling potatoes at the sink. She looked up as they entered and in her expression Agnes caught a mixture of relief and resignation.

"Come and sit down. I've made you some soup for lunch,"

Lina said. "And when you're done, I'll show you where you can hide."

Later, she took them across the farmyard to the hay barn.

"Wait there," she said. Then she climbed nimbly to the top of the stack and threw down a couple of bales, revealing a wooden door set high up the wall. She pushed it open.

"There's a loft up here," she said. "It goes over the top of the cowshed. You can stay in there until the official has been back tonight. Then we'll have to think about what to do. I'll bring you some pillows and blankets. Come on, up you come. It's not so bad in there."

Dieter was keen to go first. He scrambled up the bales quickly and hauled himself inside the loft behind Lina. Agnes followed. As she climbed, she remembered that today she was meant to go for her lesson with Jurgis. What would he think when they didn't arrive? Last time they'd gone, he'd shown her the painting of Dieter he'd started. It captured her brother's tousled hair and mischievous eyes perfectly. Sadness washed over her at the thought that this happy interval in their lives might be drawing to a close.

The loft was cramped and stuffy, full of dust and cobwebs. There was only a tiny opening at the far gable for light and air.

"Don't worry, Agnes," Lina said with a sympathetic smile, her eyes on Agnes' face. "It won't be for long. Once the official has been this evening, you can come back into the house to sleep. Things will be fine, we'll just have to make sure he doesn't see you again, that's all. Now I'll pop back to the house and get your things."

There was nothing to do in the loft and it was difficult keeping Dieter entertained through the long day. Lina brought some picture books from the house, but they'd soon finished looking at them and the hours dragged. Darkness was gathering when they heard footsteps marching into the yard outside. Agnes crept over to the opening in the gable. On tiptoe, she could just see out into the yard. There was the Soviet official, flanked by two Russian soldiers, rifles slung over their shoulders. Her heart in her mouth, she watched as Emilis opened the door and spoke to the official. She couldn't hear what was being said, but from the tone of the voices and the body language of the official, it sounded as though the man wasn't happy with Emilis' answers. Agnes watched in horror as a scuffle broke out, the official pushed Emilis aside, and he and the two soldiers barged into the kitchen and slammed the door behind them.

"What's happening?" Dieter asked.

"Nothing to worry about," Agnes said, trying to sound brave. She put her arms around him and held him to her. "Let's sit down and look at that book again, shall we?"

"It's boring. Can't we go down and play on the hay?" he said, breaking away from her and running toward the door.

"No, Dieter! I've told you before. We must stay here until Lina comes to get us."

She watched the farmhouse anxiously, jumping at the sound of banging doors coming from inside the house. Eventually, after the yard was enveloped in darkness, the back door burst open and the official followed by the two soldiers came out into the yard. The official said something to the soldiers and then the three of them split up and went in different directions into the buildings in the farmyard. Agnes froze when she heard one of them in the haybarn below and another in the cowshed directly underneath them. She held her finger up to her mouth to Dieter to signal to him to keep quiet. He crouched in the corner, under the cobwebbed beams, hugging his knees. She knew he wouldn't need telling twice—he was well aware of the danger of making a sound.

The search went on for a terrifying half an hour, during which gates were slammed, sheds ransacked, animals and poultry disturbed, the hens cackling and fluttering around angrily. Agnes and Dieter had no choice but to remain frozen where they were, hoping against hope that their hiding place wouldn't be discovered.

Agnes breathed again as she saw the three men gather back in the farmyard and finally march out through the gates, shaking their heads.

A while later, Lina appeared in the loft doorway. Her shoulders drooped and her face was drained of color: "You can come back to the house now."

As they climbed down and crossed the yard, Lina told them in hushed tones that the official hadn't been satisfied with the explanation that Lukas had taken the two of them home that day. He had been suspicious and insisted on searching the house and farm for them.

"They will come back again, I'm sure," she said. "The official told us that they are clamping down on the whole district. Looking for Germans who've been hiding here. They are also forcing more and more farmers to give up their land to the state."

In the kitchen, Emilis sat at the table, his face drained of color.

"From now on, you two youngsters must keep out of sight," he said. "No one but us must know you're here. You can only go outside in the farmyard if the gates are shut. Each evening, you must hide in the loft until the official has made his rounds."

Agnes nodded and swallowed hard. She was still trembling from the fear of discovery. This meant an end to the trips out in the cart with Lukas, to her piano lessons. Even practicing could be dangerous; people might hear her from the road. She and Dieter probably wouldn't even be able to help Lukas in the fields anymore in case someone spotted them from afar.

When Lukas came home the next day, driving the horse and empty cart, Agnes rushed to him and as he got down from the driver's seat, threw her arms around him.

"What happened?" he asked and when Lina told him about the search, he shook his head: "The whole district is crawling with them. I saw two armored cars full of soldiers just on my way back through the village."

Life resumed an uneasy new routine. Agnes and Dieter now slept in their old bedroom as before, but sleep was never easy to come by. As well as thinking about her old life and mourning the loss of her family, there was now a fresh new terror to keep her awake. During the daytime, she and Dieter were allowed to help with the milking and the animals in the yard, but it was far too risky to go out on the land with Lukas. Agnes missed working alongside him. She especially missed those evening trips out to Jurgis' cottage in the beauty of the late afternoon.

She and Dieter no longer ate supper with the family. Lina would give them an early tea, then they would have to go and hide in the hayloft until after the official's visit. Sometimes Shimkus was late and Agnes and Dieter would grow tired. They would curl up together and fall asleep on the blankets in the loft.

Lukas still gave them language lessons in the kitchen in the mornings though and this was the part of the day Agnes most looked forward to. When they were sitting round the table practicing their vocabulary, listening to Lukas' jokes and stories, it almost seemed as if life on the farm had never changed from the early days.

But after one of the lessons, when Dieter had gone out with Lina to collect some eggs, Lukas closed the book they had been reading, cleared his throat, and looked straight at Agnes, his eyes deadly serious.

"I want you to promise me something," he said. "Will you do that for me?"

She nodded, dreading what he was about to say.

"If anything happens, and you and Dieter are ever left alone here, I want you to promise me that you will get away from this village. That you will try to make it to the next district. There aren't so many soldiers there and you would be far safer."

She stared at him, trying to process what he'd just said. If they were ever alone? If that happened, where would he be? Where would Lina and Emilis be?

"I don't even know how to get to the next district," she said.

"It's across the river. You know, the one near Jurgis' house? You would need to cross the river to get there. There aren't any bridges nearby but it's very shallow in places. You'd have to be very careful."

"We could go to Jurgis instead," she replied, trying to stop tears coming. "He would help us."

Lukas shook his head. "Please don't go there. It might not be safe at his house either, not now the Russians are clamping down. Jurgis has been taken in for questioning more than once. He worked against Soviet rule before the Nazis came. He's on their list of agitators. It would be wiser to get out of this area altogether."

She wanted to ask him more, to understand what he was trying to tell her, but Lina and Dieter's footsteps could be heard on the path outside.

"We got six eggs, Agnes, look!" Dieter was saying.

Lukas said quietly to Agnes under his breath, "Don't breathe a word to anyone about this."

It was only a fortnight or so later that the soldiers came to the farm with Ponas Shimkus again. They arrived early in the morning while Agnes and Dieter were helping Lina milk the cows in the shed. This time they didn't arrive on foot, they came in an army truck and there were four of them. It had been raining steadily for days and the soldiers wore rubber boots and sou'westers, their hoods pulled up to hide their faces.

"Get up into the loft," whispered Lina, panic in her eyes. "Quick. I will stack the bales behind you. Hurry now."

They scrambled over a wooden partition, into the hay barn, and climbed the bales up into the loft as quickly as they could. Before Lina closed the door, she put her hands on Agnes' shoulders and held her gaze for a moment. She said, "You're a good girl, Agne. You need to be strong now."

Then Agnes and Dieter were inside the loft and there was the familiar thump and scratch of hay on wood as Lina piled the bales up to hide the door.

"What's happening?" Dieter asked. "What do the soldiers want this time?"

Agnes couldn't answer him, her throat was so dry and taut with fear. She crept over to the gap in the gable and looked down into the yard, but all she could see was the lorry parked up, the rain lashing its tarpaulin, and the driver waiting in the cab, cigarette smoke rising from his open window.

This time, the sound of the rain beating on the barn roof made it impossible to hear whether any noise was coming from the house. Agnes closed her eyes, trying to blot it all out, to pretend this wasn't happening. When she opened them and dared to look down at the house again, all the breath went from her body.

Down below in the farmyard, first Emilis, then Lina, and finally Lukas were being marched out of the house, holding their hands in the air. A soldier was following behind each one, prodding his rifle at their backs. When they reached the back of the lorry, they were forced to climb up the steps, over the tailgate. Then they disappeared from view under the tarpaulin. Tears flooded Agnes' eyes and, in the pain of the moment, her fingernails dug into her palms. Then came the sound of the lorry engine revving up. The driver maneuvered carelessly, then swung the lorry round. It was too big for the yard and it knocked over some of Lina's potted plants as it turned. Then it moved slowly out through the farm gates and stopped, the engine idling. Before it moved away, though, Shimkus appeared in Agnes' line of sight again. She watched as he slammed the farm gates shut, padlocked them together, and hung an official-looking notice from the chain.

Agnes sank down on the bare floorboards of the barn, hardly able to think. Whatever would happen to Lina, Emilis, and Lukas? The little family who had shown them such kindness and who she'd begun to think of as her own. Again and again, the image of Lukas climbing into the back of the lorry went through her mind. He must have known she'd be watching from the loft, but he hadn't once looked up at the gable end. She knew he would have said goodbye if he could.

"What's the matter? What's happened, Agnes?" Dieter was pulling at her clothes.

She shook her head. "I don't know, but we need to get out of here." Her promise to Lukas rang in her head.

"I don't want to go," said Dieter, his bottom lip wobbling, "Can't we stay? I like it here at the farm."

"No, Dieter. The soldiers will come back, I'm sure of it, and this time they might find our hiding place. Let's go, now."

"I'm hungry. Can't we get some breakfast first?"

She looked into his pleading eyes, wondering, remembering how hard it had been to find food when they were on the run before. It could be even more difficult now, with Russian soldiers patrolling the area and the villages full of people who were all too keen to inform the authorities.

"All right," she said slowly. "We'll go back into the house and get some food to take with us, but we'll have to be quick."

It was the first time they'd had to climb down from the loft alone and Lina had wedged the bales so firmly against the door that it was hard for them to push it open. They both leaned their shoulders against the door and shoved until they could feel the bale outside shifting. With a few more pushes it finally toppled over and the door burst open. They stood in the doorway, looking down. They'd dislodged the three top layers of hay and it was a long drop to the floor of the barn.

"You go first," Agnes said and Dieter took the plunge immediately. As soon as she'd seen he'd landed safely, she followed and landed beside him on an upturned bale. The force of the impact grazed her knees, but she hardly felt it. Her blood was pumping in her ears. What if the soldiers returned now?

They emerged from the barn and slid along the walls of the sheds. It was still raining hard and within seconds, they were soaked through, rainwater dripping down their faces. The cows stared at them as they passed, lowing in protest. Some hadn't been milked that morning and their udders would be uncomfortable by now.

They reached the edge of the building and crouched down to pass the front gate. Once on the other side, it was only a few steps up the path to the back door.

They stopped in the kitchen doorway, aghast at what they saw. Chairs were upturned and smashed crockery littered the floor. Lukas' language books had been ripped apart, the pages strewn about the room. Agnes' scalp prickled. She knew they had to get out of there.

"Quick, get some food from the larder. I'll find a bag."

She ran through to the inner hall where coats and bags were hung on a peg. Through the living room door, she saw cushions thrown on the floor, pictures torn from the walls. The piano looked bare. The lace cloth and all the family photos had been pulled off the top and dashed to the ground. On an impulse she bent down and picked one up. The glass was shattered, but still in place. It was a photograph of Lukas, Lina, and Emilis standing in front of the hay barn. Lukas' smile shone out from the picture, but his parents looked awkward and a little stern. Agnes shook out the glass and took the photo out. Then, shoving the photo in her pocket, she grabbed Lukas' knapsack from a hook in the passage.

Dieter had gathered cheese, bread, and cold meat from the larder. They loaded it all into the bag, together with a small blanket. Agnes hoisted it onto her back and they left the house.

They ran, keeping to the shelter of the hedges on Emilis' land until they reached the pine woods on its boundary. Agnes knew that the road to Jurgis' house and the river beyond it ran through these woods, so they carried on, running between the trees parallel to the road, careful to keep out of sight in the under-growth. They could see the road from where they were and twice, they glimpsed army vehicles pass. Each time they spotted them, they stopped running and hid behind trees while they passed. This terror, this panic, this sadness felt all too familiar to Agnes, but this time she felt angry and thwarted too. Angry that those good people, Lina, Emilis, and Lukas, had been taken away at gunpoint and thwarted because the home she and Dieter had made there had been cruelly snatched away.

It took them a couple of hours to reach the river. They had to cross the field on the edge of the wood to get down to the river-bank. As they ran across the muddy earth of the field, their shoes clogging with mud, Agnes glanced across at Jurgis' house and recalled Lukas' warning. Should they really not go there? Surely Jurgis would help them? But even as she looked at the house, her heart stood still. There was an army vehicle parked in front of it; three soldiers stood at the front door.

It was still pouring when they reached the riverbank. They scrambled down onto one of the pebble beaches on a bend in the river and stood there staring at the fast-flowing water. There was another pebble beach beneath a sandy bank on the other side.

"We have to get across," Agnes told Dieter. "Lukas said we'd be safe from the soldiers on the other side."

From where they stood, although the current was running

faster than normal today in the rain, the river appeared shallow at this point; the pebbly beach on the other side looked tantalizingly close. It would only be a few steps across, then they would be safe.

Agnes hitched the knapsack tight to her shoulder, gripped Dieter's hand, and stepped into the current. He stepped in too, happy to follow her as he'd always done, trusting her implicitly. She looked down at him and he smiled up at her, his eyes sparkling with adventure. She waded a few steps further and he waded alongside her, but it was deeper than she'd imagined. The water was up to her waist quickly and the force of the current was stronger now. It pressed against her, pushing her downstream, and suddenly she was struggling to keep her footing on the slippery rocks. She lost her balance and tripped, splashing down into the cold water, her arms flailing, beating against the current, trying to keep her balance and save herself as she was swept downriver, the heavy knapsack dragging her down. She went under again and again, her body bouncing against rocks, her knees scraping on jagged surfaces. She gasped and swallowed gulps of water and struggled to come up for air. When she did, the far bank was at a strange angle and Dieter's hand was no longer in hers.

She was swimming now, looking around desperately for her brother.

"Dieter," she cried. "Dieter!"

Then she glimpsed his bedraggled blond head, bobbing away from her, plunging away downriver on the current. Sick with panic, she finally reached the far bank and scrambled up onto the grass. Shrugging off the knapsack, she ran, as fast as her trembling legs would take her, sobbing and screaming and gasping for air, but even as she ran, she knew he was lost, that the river had taken him and that she had failed in her promise. Finally, she sank to her knees, sobbing.

"I'm sorry," she gulped. "I'm sorry, Mutti. I'm so, so sorry."

TWENTY-SEVEN

FREYA

Cambridge, Present Day

When Agnes finally stopped speaking, tears were glistening in her eyes. Freya felt her own eyes moisten again as they had so many times while Agnes was telling her story. Agnes had related it all to Freya over the course of three days after her return from hospital. Freya had worried that the emotional and physical effort might exhaust her, but Agnes was insistent that she *must* tell her story, no matter how tiring or painful it might be. And once she'd started, the floodgates had opened and there was no stopping her. After each session, Freya had gone away shaken by the details of the shocking ordeal Agnes had been harboring in her memories. On more than one occasion, she'd been so affected by what she'd been told that, against her better nature, she'd knocked on Finn's door and he'd invited her in and listened while she told him what Agnes had just told her. Finn would give her some tea or a beer and sit down opposite her. He would barely say a word while she spoke, but she knew he understood that she needed to share what she'd heard. He would just shake his head gravely and say, "Poor, poor Agnes. I knew things had been tough for her, but I didn't know quite how tough."

Gradually, it had become clear to Freya why Agnes had wanted to put her past to the back of her mind and just how difficult it had been for her to face it. Often, when Agnes had reached a particular point in her story, she would falter and pause, grasping for words. At those moments, Freya's heart went out to her and she would reach for her hand and say gently, "You don't have to go on, if you don't want to..." But Agnes would dab her eyes with a handkerchief, shaking her head.

"I need to talk about it now," she'd say, finding her voice. "It has to be told! I have bottled it up for so long, so many years, it has to come out."

"Oh, Agnes..." Freya would protest, but she knew there was no point denying the truth that Agnes was bravely facing. And Freya could tell that she was doing it in part for her too, to reinforce the importance of family. To explain why that had been so important to her.

"I haven't got long, dear. You know that, so I need to tell you before it's too late."

Now, with the image of Dieter being carried away downstream by the swollen river and Agnes, distraught, desperate and alone, stumbling along the riverbank after him, Freya understood why the photograph of her little brother that Agnes carried with her everywhere was so important to her.

What had happened to Agnes after that, though? Had Dieter drowned? Had she managed to find him? Had she found another family to take her in? Freya waited for Agnes to go on, but realized that it would be difficult for her.

"Would you like another cup of tea?" she offered and when Agnes nodded, she went through to the kitchen and put the kettle on the stove. She glanced at the kitchen clock. It was six o'clock and she was due at the pub at seven thirty. She bit her nail, wondering. She really should go home and get ready for her shift, but how could she say that to Agnes at this momentous point in her story? She couldn't get out of working this evening either; it was her last shift at the pub for a few days.

She was worried about leaving Agnes like this. Not until she had finished telling her story and Freya was sure she was going to be all right.

Freya made two mugs of tea and took them to the study. In the few minutes she'd been out of the room, Agnes had recovered her composure. She'd dried her eyes and was sitting up straight, looking determined and ready to speak again. Freya put a mug down on the table beside her.

"I expect you need to be getting off soon, don't you? To your bar job?" Agnes asked, perceptive as ever.

"Not for half an hour or so."

Freya sat down in the chair beside Agnes' bed. It was where she'd sat throughout all those hours to listen to her story. She lifted her eyes to the mantelpiece and the photograph of the three farm workers that had puzzled her so much when she'd first seen it. When Agnes had first spoken about Lukas and his parents, she'd asked Freya to take the photograph down and they'd looked at it together. And when Freya finally put it back, Agnes had asked her to give it pride of place beside the photograph of her on the stage at the grand piano.

"I still think about them every day," she'd said. "I think about them all. Every one of them. Mutti and Papa, Uncle Tomas, Aunt Hannah, and the cousins. Lukas, Lina, and Emilis. And Dieter, of course. Poor, poor little Dieter. I never *stop* thinking about him."

"What happened to you, Agnes? After you crossed the river?" Freya asked gently.

Agnes drew a long, deep breath, but her face dropped, tragedy etched on every line.

"My life was over then. When I lost Dieter, I might as well have died myself. I wandered up and down that riverbank for two days, sleeping under bushes at night. Somewhere, I found the drenched knapsack that had been carried down the river and dried the blanket on a bush. I had to eke out the sodden food that we'd taken from Lina's larder. I walked many, many kilometers, trying to find Dieter, dreading all the time that I would stumble across his little body washed up on the bank. But I never did. I never saw him again.

"On the third day, I ran out of food. I had no idea what to do or where to go, but I found myself walking back upriver in the direction I'd come from and finally, I reached the place where Dieter and I had tried to cross. It had stopped raining by then and the water levels had dropped. I remember thinking that if we had tried to cross together that day, we would have made it easily. I decided to go back across, I wanted to retrace my steps. I wasn't thinking straight and I must have thought that if I did that, I might find Dieter that way.

"It was easy to reach the other side. The water only came up to my thighs and I waded back across easily. Once I reached the other side, I sat down on the little beach and cried my heart out. I must have fallen asleep eventually, because when I woke up, someone was leaning over me, shaking me gently, peering at me. I looked up and started. I knew those eyes: it was Jurgis, my piano teacher. He'd come down to the river to watch the sunset as he often did and there I was.

"I owe my life to Jurgis and everything that followed. He took me back to his house, fed me, and cleaned me up, but he would only let me stay hidden there for a couple of days. He told me that the Russians were always coming to check up on his activities, so it wasn't safe for me to stay there. I don't know how he did it, but he managed to arrange for me to go and stay in the capital, Vilnius, with a friend of his who worked at the university, Professor Gabriel Petrakis and his wife. They had no children and they welcomed me and gave me a home. Someone, somewhere in their network of like-minded, liberal friends produced some identity papers for me. I became Agne Petrakis, a distant relative who had come from Southern Lithuania to study piano with the professor. When I left Jurgis' house for Vilnius, he gave me that photograph. The one he'd taken of Dieter. It is all I have left of my dear little brother.

"I never found out what happened to Lukas and his parents. They disappeared, as did many Lithuanians at that time; their land was confiscated for the collective farm. And I became Lithuanian. I could speak the language more or less fluently by then and it wasn't so hard to pass for a local. Everything German about me was simply scrubbed away, just as East Prussia was removed from the map after the war. German Agnes was left behind, drowned in that river with Dieter.

"The Petrakises were kind and very brave to take me in. I was extremely grateful to them, but they could never replace the family I'd lost. I worked hard at my studies and won a place at Vilnius University to study music. Funnily enough, I saw Theo once, in a backstreet in Vilnius. I was in my first year at the university and he was working on a market stall, selling food. I went right up to him and spoke to him. I could see from his eyes that he'd recognized me but he didn't even acknowledge me. It was too risky for either of us to do that. He'd scrubbed away his past, just as I had.

"But I was a shell of the girl I'd once been. I went through my days with an everlasting pain deep inside my heart and even though success came to me in one sense, and I'm grateful for that, that pain has never left me."

"I'm so sorry, Agnes," Freya said, not knowing what else to say, but knowing no words were adequate.

"I never found out what happened to my father. I tried to research it years ago. I did get as far as tracing his unit in the *Volkssturm* as being involved in one of the last battles against the Red Army on the Baltic coast. Most German soldiers in that unit were either killed or captured and taken to Siberia. Lost without trace in work camps there. I have no idea what happened to my cousins and uncle either. A similar fate, perhaps. But I know they didn't go home."

"How do you know that?"

"Because if they ever had gone back, they would have been evacuated from East Prussia along with the rest of the German civilians who remained after the war. The province was divided between Poland and the USSR and repopulated with Polish people and Russian citizens . . . and I also know because I went back there once."

"Oh *really*?" Freya sat forward, eager to hear more.

Agnes nodded. "In the mid-nineties. After perestroika and the fall of the Berlin Wall, it became possible for Westerners to travel to that region. I was a bit worried about going back in case I was still on some list somewhere."

"On a list? What do you mean?" Freya's scalp prickled.

Agnes smiled tentatively for the first time since she'd described Dieter's drowning. "Yes, my dear. Didn't you know about that?"

"About what?"

Agnes pointed at her old bureau. "Open the second drawer down and you'll see why. I've kept all the newspaper clippings. There's a box full of them."

Intrigued, Freya did as Agnes said, pulled open the drawer and slid out a battered old shoebox and opened it. There was a pile of yellowing newspaper clippings inside. She lifted the top one out carefully and read the headline:

Talented pianist defects to the West.

Underneath was a photograph of a young Agnes framed in the archway of one of the Cambridge colleges, looking startled at being snapped. Freya's eyes scanned the article.

A music student from Lithuania, on an exchange to Cambridge from Vilnius University, has decided to make England her home. Agne Petrakis, a talented pianist, has already thrilled concert audiences nationwide with her music and now more Britons will have a chance to hear her play.

Freya looked up at Agnes, who was now smiling broadly.

"You came to the UK as a defector!"

Agnes nodded. "Well, that's another story of course, but the chance of a new life came and I seized the opportunity. I won a place in Vilnius on a university exchange program and when I arrived in Cambridge I loved the place instantly. I came with five other musicians and we were taken around the country in a minibus to give concerts. At one of these, in London, we were approached by a man, I'm not quite sure who he was now, and asked if we'd like to become British citizens and stay here. I was the only one who took up the offer. And I've never regretted it.

"I never, ever felt Lithuanian, you know. I was East Prussian, German at heart, but I could never speak my language or admit who I was while I lived there. It was all far too close to what had happened during the war. Coming to England gave me a chance to try to forget and to start again."

"That's amazing, Agnes," Freya said. "Truly amazing. I had no idea."

"You're far too young to remember that era, of course. There was a flurry of interest in the press at the time, but it all died down very quickly and then I was able to get on with life at the university here. I buried myself in my music."

"But you said you went back in the nineties?"

Agnes nodded. "To Königsberg first." Her face fell. "It's called Kaliningrad now. It wasn't the place I remembered. Many of the old buildings were destroyed during the war and there has been so much rebuilding. Stark, Soviet architecture." She shook her head. "It made me very sad to see it then and remember how beautiful it had once been.

"I got a taxi to our old village too. Different people lived there. Strangers from Russia, most of them. It was strange to see the old cottages lived in by completely different people. I tried to ask them if they knew anything about my father, my uncle, and cousins, but the names meant nothing to them.

"I went back to the farm, too, but there was nothing there. Just tumbledown buildings covered in nettles and strewn with rubbish."

"How sad that must have been for you."

Agnes shrugged. "I needed to go there, just to make sure that none of my family had returned. It confirmed it to me. I'd done my grieving already. I was glad to leave. I never want to go back." She smiled wistfully.

"But you have the picture of the castle," Freya ventured, cautiously, remembering how mention of the castle had been such a source of irritation to Agnes before.

"Yes. I saw it in a junk shop in London. It was such a shock to see it there, but I wanted it straight away. It reminded me of the beauty that surrounded me as a child, and of dear Liesel, of course."

"And?"

Agnes shook her head again. "I have no idea what became of her or where she ended up. She may still be alive and well in another part of Germany . . . I got the taxi driver to drive me up to the estate when I was there. The cottages were derelict. The castle is used as some sort of conference center now . . ."

She trailed off. Freya got to her feet. "You must be exhausted. I'm sorry to have asked so many questions."

"I am a little tired, but I'm so pleased to have told you everything. Thank you for listening to me."

"Thank you, Agnes. It means so much to me." And in that moment Freya knew what she had to do when she got home. She was ready to press SEND on the email she'd drafted so many times to Matthew, but had not yet felt able to forward on to him.

Agnes lay back on her pillows, her face tired and gray. Freya went over to her and kissed her cold cheek. "One of the carers will be here soon. I'd better get going to the pub, or I'll be late."

Freya left Agnes' house and dashed back to her own. Up in the flat, she quickly got ready for work, then got out her laptop. Now was the time. She found the email she'd drafted and pressed SEND before logging off. Then she ran back down to the hallway to collect her bike. As she pushed it out of the front door, she realized the front tire was completely flat. Cursing, she took it back into the hall and tried to pump the tire, but it kept going down again. With a sigh, she realized the only other option was to walk. Texting Amber to let her know she would be late, she set off at a run to cross Jesus Green to the other side of town.

"Everything OK? How's Agnes?" Amber asked, glancing up from pulling a pint, when Freya arrived in the pub, out of breath and flustered, twenty minutes later.

"She's frail, but she's in good spirits. Thanks so much for covering for me," Freya replied, slipping behind the bar.

It was crowded in the pub that night. Freya was kept busy all evening serving drinks, clearing tables, washing glasses. She barely had a chance to pause for breath, or to speak to Amber.

But every so often, snippets from Agnes' story would surface in her mind, so shocking that she had to stop and take a moment. She checked her phone a few times, her heart in her mouth, to see if Matthew had replied to her email. Finally, around ten o'clock, his response came through. Her heart soared when she read it:

Dear Sis,

I was so happy to get your email. The trek was amazing, Freya, the Annapurna mountains are magical and we were staying in villages where they have no roads so everything has to be brought in by donkey or carried by Sherpas. But the people are so generous and welcoming, even though they are incredibly poor. All this really made me think hard about what has happened recently, and how the most important thing in life is the people you love. You're so right. Let's put all that behind us, Freya. Jah-Dek was very bitter in his old age, but he always loved both of us to the end, it's just that he found it so hard to express it. I'm sure he didn't intend to upset either of us, he just wasn't thinking properly when he drew up his will.

You and Mum mean the world to me, as you know. We've all been through so much together and nothing can pull us apart. I'm on my way home now. I had to come back via Delhi to report on the India-Africa Summit. As soon as I'm home, you must come back to London for the weekend and we will go through all Jah-Dek's personal effects together. As far as I'm concerned, it's as much yours as it is mine.

I'm sorry too if I've been intransigent over this, or if anything I've said has upset you. I didn't mean that to happen. Looking forward to seeing you,

Love, Matt

She stared at it, tears in her eyes. At last! She couldn't wait to see him now.

Toward the end of the evening, the crowds began to thin out. As Freya pulled the last pints, she suddenly remembered about her bike.

"I'd better call a taxi," she said to Amber, reaching for her phone.

Amber smiled, conspiratorially. "I don't think you need to," she said, and nodded in the direction of a table in the corner. "Someone's here to take you home."

"Oh!" Freya felt the blood rush to her cheeks as she looked over and there was Finn sitting in the corner, holding a pint up to her, smiling at her with his dark eyes.

"Is he your neighbor? The Irish one?"

Freya nodded.

"I thought you said you didn't like him? He seems great to me. He's really friendly."

"Oh, well. We've got to know each other a bit now," Freya said quickly. "We've had to. For Agnes' sake."

Amber laughed. "Who are you kidding? From the way he's been looking at you, I'd say he's in love with you."

Freya stared at her, irritation and disbelief rising in her. "Don't be ridiculous."

"Not ridiculous at all. And from the way you just reacted when you saw him sitting there, I'd say you're pretty keen on him too."

"Oh, Amber! You sound like my mum," Freya said, laughing. "Be quiet now. He's coming over."

"I saw your bike had a flat tire," Finn said, leaning on the bar, "And I knew you were working this evening, so I brought the van over to give you a lift home."

"That's really kind of you, Finn, but I could have got a taxi," Freya said.

"There's gratitude for you," he said to Amber, who laughed. "I was worried you'd try to walk across the gardens on your own."

"I can look after myself, Finn," Freya said, her emotions fighting with each other. Part of her was grateful and flattered that he was looking out for her; another part, the part that had told her she didn't want to get close to anyone, was telling her that this was a step too far. That it was an imposition and a presumption on his part.

"I know you can, Freya. I was just worried about you, that's all," he replied, his eyes serious now.

"I'll get my things," she said.

Amber followed her through to the lobby behind the kitchen and touched her shoulder as she took her coat down from the peg.

"Don't be frosty with him, Freya. He cares about you, it's obvious. Don't push him away."

"I'm not! It's just that . . . Well, you know, after Cameron . . ."

"I know, but you've got a chance to put that behind you now."

Freya stared into her friend's eyes. It was on the tip of her tongue to tell Amber to mind her own business, but she stopped herself. Amber cared about her and just wanted the best for her, she knew that.

"I know. You're right really, and I *am* trying," she said and went back through to the bar, where Finn was waiting for her.

"All ready?" he asked.

She nodded.

"All ready. Oh, and Finn . . ." she added, looking into his eyes, "thanks for coming to get me. I do appreciate it, really I do."

TWENTY-EIGHT

"It's so wonderful that we're all together again," Monica said, smiling around the dinner table, taking in both Freya and Matthew in one loving look. Freya smiled back and squeezed Monica's hand on the table. She was glad to see her mother looking so happy. Brother and sister were reunited again and the three of them were just finishing the first meal they'd shared together for months. Monica had cooked spaghetti Bolognese, which had been a favorite of both Freya and Matthew's during their childhood. They'd shared a bottle of red wine with the meal and conversation, anecdotes, and old family jokes had flowed between them as if nothing had ever happened to disrupt their closeness.

Freya had arrived in London by train from Cambridge in the middle of the afternoon. When she'd opened the front door of her old home and called out "Hello?," Matthew had come bounding down the stairs to hug her tight. There had been no need for either of them to say much at all. Freya's letter had already said everything she needed to, and from the way he greeted her, Freya could tell that, like her, Matthew just wanted to put their disagreements and misunderstandings behind him and move on.

All three of them had gone for a walk together in the afternoon on Hampstead Heath, exchanging news and catching up on the time they'd been apart. Then, when they'd returned to the house for tea, Matthew had shown Freya and Monica some of the pictures he'd taken in Nepal and India.

Now, pouring out the last dregs of wine from the bottle, Matthew said, "Let's help Mum clear up, then shall we go to Jah-Dek's room and go through his things?"

"No need to help. I can manage the dishes," Monica said brightly. "You two go on through."

"Aren't you coming, too, Mum?" asked Freya.

Monica shook her head quickly and began to clear the table. "Not right now. I'll let you two take a look first. Come and tell me if you find anything interesting."

Freya glanced at Matthew, each of them understanding that Monica might prefer to be alone when she first looked through whatever her secretive father had hidden in that chest.

"If you're quite sure, Mum," he said. "Come on then, Freya. Are you ready?"

She nodded and followed Matthew into her grandfather's room. She glanced up at the picture of the fortified farm, thinking how when she'd first seen Agnes' picture of the castle on the hill the similarity had struck such a chord with her. The woods surrounding the farm in this painting looked virtually identical to the forest in Agnes' picture and the atmosphere of the two paintings was similar too: fairy-tale buildings amid snowbound forests. Freya knew now that the two forests weren't so far apart geographically—no wonder she'd made that connection.

The room felt empty and forlorn, and Freya shivered as she sat down in her grandfather's old armchair, although it wasn't cold. His presence was palpable; she could almost hear his voice.

"That information you found out about Jah-Dek from your research was amazing," Matthew said. "Incredible that now we know which RAF unit he was in and the town he came from in Poland. Thanks so much for sending me the links. I couldn't believe it when I read that airman's memories."

"I know, it was incredible. I was stunned when I read it. I was so lucky to find it too. As I said, one of my students stumbled across it."

"You look as though you're enjoying being back in Cambridge again," Matthew said. "You look so much better than you did back in the summer. More relaxed. Like life is really suiting you."

She smiled. "Life is suiting me there. That's partly because of Agnes," she said.

"Agnes? A new friend?"

"Yes, she is a wonderful new friend. She lives in the next house. She's over eighty years old and her health is failing fast, but she's an extraordinary woman."

She didn't tell Matthew that it had been Agnes who had persuaded her to write to him to heal the rift between them. Neither did she say that it wasn't just Agnes who was making her happy now, that she was enjoying life; working with her students, her job in the pub . . . her growing closeness with Finn. She smiled inwardly, thinking back to that morning. Finn had given her a lift to the station because her bike was still out of action. They had chatted easily all the way and when he'd dropped her off, he'd said, "I could always come down to London to pick you up tomorrow if you like? I haven't got much on this weekend."

She'd stood there on the pavement at the station drop-off point with the van door open, wondering what to say, while impatient drivers sounded their horns behind. She swallowed and took the plunge. "All right," she'd said, looking into Finn's eyes and noticing that they didn't have that teasing look for once. "That would be nice. I'll call you."

She said to Matthew now, "Agnes has had an incredible life. She escaped from the advance of the Red Army into East Prussia in 1945. She had to look after her little brother. Her whole family died."

"That *does* sound incredible," said Matt and Freya could see the journalist's curiosity burning in his eyes. "Why don't you tell me a bit about it? Shall we look in Jah-Dek's wardrobe first, before we open his chest?"

So, as Matthew opened the sliding doors to their grandfather's wardrobe and began to take out his old suits and shirts and lay them out on the bed, Freya began to tell him a little of Agnes' story. As she spoke, she watched their grandfather's old clothes piling up on the bed: the threadbare but once-smart suits he used to wear to the Polish club, the checked shirts he would wear around the house, a couple of tattered jumpers. Just seeing them lying there brought a lump to her throat. The sight of the old clothes brought home the fact that his death was so recent and so real.

"Hey, look at this," Matthew said, taking out a hanger with a suit cover. He unzipped the cover to reveal an old uniform: an airman's navy-blue jacket with brass buttons, colors across the breast pocket. Tucked inside it was a peaked cap, marked AIRMAN J. KOWALSKI.

"His RAF uniform!"

Beside it hung a moth-eaten sheepskin jacket. It smelled a little musty.

"It's incredible to imagine him wearing these, as a young man," Freya said.

Matthew reached inside the cupboard and pulled out yet

another bulky suit cover. He laid it on the bed and unzipped it. Another uniform lay inside. This one was gray, with the word POLAND embroidered on the epaulet.

"His Polish air force uniform."

"To think what he went through," Freya said. "You know, just talking to him, you'd never have known. And he wanted to keep it all buried away. He was so much like Agnes—it took a lot for her to tell me her story."

"And her story is so fascinating," said Matt. "You must tell me the rest later. Shall we look through Jah-Dek's chest now?"

"If you're sure?"

She went over to join him beside their grandfather's secret chest and as he turned the key and lifted the lid, Freya was back in the past—an impulsive teenager, sneaking a quick look at its contents while he was out at the clinic. Even now she was half afraid of him stumbling through the door, shaking his stick at them as they opened up his box of secrets, his face clouded with anger.

Matthew began to lift out the treasured mementos and hand them to Freya. On the top were those faded black and white photographs of impossibly young pilots smiling in front of a flimsy-looking aircraft on a bleak airfield. They were the ones Freya had seen before and they were exactly as she remembered them. Beneath them were more photographs, even more faded and dog-eared. These were of their grandfather in school uniform, in front of some school gates; as a very young man, standing in front of a stone farmhouse. Then another one that Matthew stared at in disbelief. It was definitely him, a young man in his early twenties, standing beside a pretty young woman with blonde hair, about his own age. She was holding a chubby little boy, no more than a baby really, who stared out with huge, inquisitive eyes at the camera.

"Who are they?" Matthew asked and Freya shook her head.

"That's definitely Jah-Dek," she said slowly. She didn't feel ready to voice what the picture was suggesting to her.

Underneath the photograph was an envelope addressed to Janick Kowalski at an address in Warsaw.

Matthew slid the letter out of the envelope and opened it up. The paper was brittle and yellowing. He looked up at Freya. "It's in Polish, of course," he said. "I only know a few words . . . I suppose I could ask someone at work. Some of the foreign correspondents speak good Polish."

"Or Mum?" suggested Freya. "Don't you remember? She went to lessons at the Polish club to learn when we were young. Jah-Dek didn't really approve, but she insisted."

"Of course! How could I have forgotten that?" Then he hesitated. "But I got the feeling that she didn't want to go through the things in the chest yet. She might not want to . . ."

"Who might not want to do what, Matthew?"

Monica was standing in the doorway. "I just popped through to see if either of you would like tea or coffee and I see you're taking my name in vain."

"We've found this letter to Jah-Dek," Matthew said. "It's dated October 1939 and looks fairly official, but it's in Polish, Mum. Freya was just remembering that you took Polish classes for a while. I know this might be difficult for you, but do you think you know enough to be able to translate it?"

Their mother hesitated momentarily, then seemed to square her shoulders. She came into the room and sat down on the bed beside the mound of clothes. She sighed. "All right. You know, I made quite good progress in Polish, but your grandfather Jah-Dek would never speak the language to me. He said he was rusty after all these years. But I used to hear him chatting away at the bar with his friends. Give me the letter, Matthew. I'll have a go."

Matthew handed Monica the letter and she peered at it

closely for a few minutes, her eyes running along the lines. Then she dropped the letter to her lap and looked up, her face suddenly pale.

"What does it say, Mum?" asked Freya, dreading the answer.

"It says that Jah-Dek's wife and child, a little boy aged three, were killed by a bomb in their home when the German army took the town of Hajnowka. It is written by the mayor of the town. He sends Jah-Dek his heartfelt condolences."

There was silence in the room as all three struggled to digest this new, heartbreaking information. Finally, Freya spoke.

"So . . . the baby and the young woman in the photo with him are Jah-Dek's wife and child," she murmured, not being able to lift her eyes from the photo.

"Let me see the photo, Freya." It was her mother's voice, dry with shock. Freya handed it to her.

"So, he was married before the war and his wife and baby were killed," Monica said slowly, her eyes on the photograph. When she lifted them, they were glistening with tears. "This is such a shock. Why did he never tell us about it? How could he have kept that a secret for more than seventy years?"

"Perhaps he just didn't want to remember," Matthew ventured, his voice gentle. "He was always saying that he wanted a new start when he came to England, that he would never go back to Poland."

"It's unbelievable. Poor, poor Dad," whispered Monica. "No wonder he was sometimes so grouchy and bad-tempered. Deep down, it must always have been with him. How could he ever have been able to forget such a tragic loss?"

Freya went and sat down on the bed beside Monica and put her arm around her. At the same time, Matthew sat down beside their mother on her other side. All three sat there together, comforting each other, coming to terms, each in their own way, with this revelation about the man they had known and loved their whole lives, that perhaps they didn't know him as fully as they'd thought.

It took Freya, Matthew, and Monica most of the evening to go through the rest of Jah-Dek's memories. There were more photographs of Polish airmen, their names scribbled on the back in Jah-Dek's scrawling hand, some wartime medals on ribbons, some letters and timetables, printed weather reports from the summer of 1940. At the very bottom of the chest lay a faded sepia photograph of a thatched cottage, surrounded by pine trees. On the back, in Jah-Dek's writing, was scrawled: *Dom, Bialowieza.*

"*Dom* means home," said Monica quietly. "Perhaps that cottage is where he grew up."

"And Bialowieza is the huge, primeval forest near his hometown of Hajnowka. I looked into it when I read that account by the Polish airman who knew him," Freya added. "It looks as though his home was either on the edge of the forest, or actually right in the heart of it."

"Maybe we should go there someday?" Monica said, brightening. "To Poland. Just the three of us. We haven't been away together since you were both at school. We could go back to where Jah-Dek started out. Try to find out more about him?"

Freya and Matthew agreed instantly and they all promised each other that they would make that journey to Poland in the coming months to honor Jah-Dek's memory and to try to understand more about his past.

After their mother had gone upstairs to bed, Freya and Matthew sat up talking into the small hours, remembering their grandfather, his traits and his idiosyncrasies, laughing over old anecdotes about him. They were now able to put everything into some context, to view his difficult behavior in a different light. And gradually, naturally, the conversation moved on to the subject of Agnes. Matthew was fascinated by what Freya had told him about Agnes' wartime plight and curious to hear more of her story. Freya did her best to remember exactly what Agnes had told her and to do her story justice, but Matthew had many questions.

Eventually, Freya said, "Look, why don't you come back with me to Cambridge? Perhaps you could talk to Agnes yourself? She's ready to tell her story now. She would be able to answer all your questions, fill in the gaps that I can't . . . You're thinking about writing about it, aren't you?"

Matthew smiled. "How well you know me, Freya. Yes. I'll come back with you, and if Agnes will let me, I'll write an article about her for the paper. I'm sure I'll be able to persuade my editor to feature it soon. It sounds like a story that needs to be told."

"It would be wonderful if you came and spoke to her. And, I haven't said this before, but thank you for letting me go through Jah-Dek's things with you. It meant so much to me, you know. Especially after the words we had over it, back in the summer."

Matthew squeezed her arm. "All that's behind us now, Freya. There's no need to thank me. I wouldn't have wanted to do it alone. Having you and Mum here has made it so much easier for me. And we *had* to do it together. Jah-Dek didn't just belong to me, you know. We were all his family."

"You're right. But even so, thank you." Freya got to her feet. "I suppose I should be going to bed now. It's almost o'clock and I don't want to be exhausted tomorrow."

"What time train are you getting back to Cambridge?"

"Oh, didn't I tell you?" she said, feeling color creeping into her cheeks. "I'm not going by train. A friend is coming to pick me up in his van. I'm sure he won't mind you coming along too."

"A friend?" Matthew said, amusement creeping into his gaze. "Must be a pretty committed friend to drive all this way in a van to pick you up when you could easily get the train."

"He's actually my downstairs neighbor. He and I have been helping Agnes. That's how we know each other."

"I see . . . and you're absolutely sure he won't mind me tagging along? I wouldn't want to play gooseberry, you know."

"Matt! Please, it's not like that. Anyway, he's coming at ten in the morning, so I'm off to bed now."

In her old childhood bedroom, Freya slept heavily that night, and when she awoke the next morning and glanced at the clock, it was already nine thirty: she had slept in. Cursing under her breath, she dragged herself out of bed. An engine was revving in the street, so she went over to the window to see what the noise was about. Finn's battered Transit van was being maneuvered into a parking space outside the house.

Oh my God, he's early! She dashed to the bathroom just as the front doorbell rang and showered as quickly as she could, but above the sound of the water she heard her mother's voice exclaiming in surprise and welcoming Finn into the house. When she'd thrown on some clothes, applied some perfunctory makeup, and got herself downstairs, Finn was sitting at the kitchen table looking completely at home and Monica was handing him some coffee and a large plate of bacon and eggs. A warm feeling stole over her as she saw him sitting there and she couldn't help noticing that Finn's eyes lit up as she entered the room.

"Finn and I have been chatting, Freya," Monica said, smiling. "I told him you must have overslept so I gave him your breakfast, I'm afraid. I can quickly make some more egg and bacon for you."

"I'm sorry . . . we had a bit of a late night," she said, sitting down opposite him.

"Your mother explained. And I've already met Matt briefly too. He said he's coming back to Cambridge with us."

"If you don't mind? He wants to talk to Agnes."

"Of course I don't mind. It will be great to have him along."

Freya stole a quick glance at Finn and saw that half-teasing look in his eyes again. Was that a twinge of disappointment she was feeling that he hadn't expressed regret that they wouldn't be alone on the journey? But she smiled back at him and sat down opposite him, admonishing herself for such a ridiculous thought.

They set off about an hour later, Freya sitting in the middle between Finn and Matt. Conversation flowed easily between the three of them on the two-hour journey and the time passed in a flash. They discussed Agnes and how best to broach the subject of her speaking to Matthew. They wondered how best to do that so she wouldn't feel her privacy was being invaded, or clam up, as she used to do when things got difficult.

In the end, Freya decided that it was best to simply ask Agnes outright. So, when they got back to Chesterton Road, after she'd shown Matthew around her flat and they'd had a cup of tea, she took him round to Agnes' house. She opened the front door and called out down the passage.

"Agnes, it's me, Freya."

"Oh, come in, dear." Agnes' voice sounded tremulous. "I've been waiting for you. Finn told me he was going to London to collect you this morning."

"I've brought someone to meet you . . ."

Freya paused at the half-open door of Agnes' room.

"Who is it, Freya?"

"It's my brother, Matthew."

"Your brother? That's marvelous. Come in, Matthew. I've heard so much about you. Come in and sit down beside me. I want to get a good look at you."

Freya stood in the doorway, smiling inwardly, as Matthew went and shook Agnes' hand and sat down in the chair beside the bed.

"I've heard a lot about you too, Miss Peters," he said. "It's wonderful to meet you. Freya is so fond of you."

"And I of her." Agnes switched her gaze toward Freya. "Freya, my dear, would you be able to put the kettle on? We could have some tea while we talk."

Freya closed the door and left them to get to know each other while she went through to the kitchen and made some tea. She took her time, sitting at the table, stroking Claus, who had jumped onto her lap, purring. When she finally went back through to Agnes' room with the tray of tea and a plate of biscuits, Agnes was in the middle of telling Matthew how she'd sat at the window and watched her father walking through the snow with his suitcase to join the *Volkssturm*.

"It was the last time I ever saw him," she said, tears in her eyes. "My wonderful papa. Though he is with me every day."

Freya walked carefully across the room and placed the tea tray down on the table beside Agnes.

"Oh, Freya! Thank you, dear. Your brother has asked if he can write about me for his newspaper."

"And are you happy for him to do that?"

"Yes, of course. What happened to East Prussia is so little known about. And us abandoned children—Little Germans. People need to know."

"It's so kind of you," Matthew said. "But I don't want to tire you out. If now isn't a good time, I can come back another day."

"No, no. Now is as good a time as any."

Freya left them to it and closed the door quietly behind her. She left the house and went back to her own. She entered the hall and was about to go upstairs when she hesitated. Then she took the plunge and knocked on Finn's door.

"How did it go?" he asked. "I take it that she agreed to speak to Matt?"

"She did. I didn't think they needed me so I left them to it."

"Do you need some company?"

She nodded. "If you're not busy, that is. Maybe we could go for a walk? It's a beautiful afternoon."

Finn smiled broadly, then stepped forward and put his arms around her to hug her tight. "I thought you'd never ask! I'll just get my coat."

EPILOGUE

Freya got up early and cycled as quickly as she could to the newsagent's in Magdalen Street. She was already waiting on the pavement when they opened the shop at seven o'clock. Matt's article was in the color supplement of the Sunday edition of his paper. She bought three copies: one for herself, one for Finn, and one for Agnes. The newspapers were heavy and slippery, wrapped in plastic and containing many different sections. She slipped them into her pannier, managing to resist the temptation to rip one open right there and then.

As soon as she got back to the house, she leaned her bike against the wall, pulled out one of the bundles, ripped open the plastic wrapping, and let the other parts of the paper cascade to the floor, flicking through the color supplement until she came to Matt's article.

The feral orphans of East Prussia: Human tragedies of the Eastern Front during WW2.

And beside the headline, a black and white photograph of Agnes taken by Matthew the day she'd told him her story, the lines on her face bearing testament to her tragedy, her sad eyes staring into the camera. And beneath that, the oval photograph of Dieter, taken by Jurgis Klukas, inset into the text, and on the middle of the facing page, the picture of Lukas and his parents, standing in front of that barn in rural Lithuania in their farm workers' overalls. Matt had shown Freya the first draft of the article, but seeing it in print for the first time took her breath away. Her eyes ran eagerly through it. She was so engrossed in the story that she hardly heard the click of Finn's front door as it opened, but she did feel his arms around her waist and the touch of his stubble on her cheek as he kissed her. She lowered the magazine, looked into his eyes, and kissed him back.

"I didn't hear you get up," he said. "When I realized you weren't in bed, I freaked out for a second. Then I remembered what day it was and that you must have gone to the newsagents . . . How's the article?"

"It's brilliant. So moving. Here's your copy."

"Thanks, I can't wait to read it. Let's get some coffee on and we can do just that."

She followed him inside and slumped down on his shabby but comfortable sofa, burying her nose back in the article while Finn busied himself in the kitchenette. Delicious aromas of freshly brewed coffee and toast were soon wafting in her direction. She looked up and smiled at him fondly, and as if sensing her eyes on him, he looked up from buttering the toast and met her gaze.

She'd been staying over with him on and off since that first weekend when they'd come back from London with Matt and had walked around Jesus Green together, arm in arm, to watch the sun set over the colleges. The walk had been partly designed to give Agnes and Matt the space for her story to be told, but neither of them had wanted to go home, finding excuses to prolong the walk, loving the new closeness they were discovering and the feeling of warmth where their arms touched. Their conversation had lost that stilted edge it had had when they'd first met, when Freya had been trying to keep Finn at arm's length. They'd wandered happily to a pub near the river and had sat there drinking and talking until Freya's phone buzzed with a text from Matt, saying that he and Agnes had finished talking and he needed to get back into Freya's flat.

Matt had gone back to London on the train the next morning to speak to his editor and write the article, and that evening, Finn had asked Freya out properly for the first time. They'd eaten Italian in a candlelit bistro in Regent Street, holding hands over the table, so engrossed in each other's company that they hardly tasted the food; then they'd wandered back arm in arm through the quiet, lamplit streets, back across the moonlit river to Finn's flat, where he'd made coffee and they'd eventually graduated from the sofa to his bedroom and made love for the first time.

That was only a few weeks ago, but to Freya it seemed as though she'd known Finn for a lifetime and she couldn't imagine an existence without him now. Everything else had gradually fallen into place too: her students were blossoming with her help, especially Lewis, who now spoke up in supervisions and had completely lost his initial shyness. Freya had told him her grandfather's story and he had used Michal Nowak's account of the battle in which Jah-Dek had been shot down in his dissertation. Freya had been very careful to give as much attention to all the students' dissertations, not wanting them to think she was favoring Lewis, and they had each rewarded her by giving their best efforts.

She'd been brimming with pride when she'd spoken to Dan about their progress during their weekly meetings.

"It's fantastic how they've all responded to your input," Dan said, leaning back in his chair. "I'm looking forward to reading the fruits of their labors, but what about your own research?"

"Oh," she said. "That's stalled a bit lately, to tell you the truth, but I've been thinking . . ."

She felt awkward about broaching the subject with Dan. He'd been so supportive and she didn't want to disappoint him. But he was looking at her, waiting for her to go on, his eyebrows raised. Now was the time.

"I've got very interested in another subject, actually, and I was wondering if I could run some ideas past you about it?"

"Really? I'm all ears."

"Yes . . . I'm interested in researching the fall of East Prussia and the impact on the civilian population, particularly the children . . ."

"That's certainly a fascinating subject. Very different to your current thesis, though. Could you tell me how you became interested in it?"

"Yes, of course. Through my neighbor: Agnes Peters."

"Agnes Peters? That name rings a bell. She was an academic here, wasn't she?"

"Yes. A music professor. I've got to know her very well recently. Her health is failing fast, but she's told me what happened to her during the war. It's an incredible story. She was orphaned and had to escape from East Prussia with her little brother. They survived for a time in the forests on the border with Lithuania. In Lithuania, they were known as Vokietukai."

"Ah, *wolfskinder* in German, of course. Yes, quite extraordinary. I believe some academics have explored the plight of those children, but it would be a fascinating subject for research, I agree."

"So, I was wondering if I might start my thesis again? With that subject matter?" She leaned forward, looking earnestly into Dan's eyes. "I know it's a lot to ask, but I was always fascinated by the Second World War. As I told you, my grandfather was in the Polish air force, but he wanted to forget the war. It was a taboo subject in our house. But now—"

"I understand, Freya," Dan cut in. "I'm pleased that you've found something that truly sparks your interest. I always wondered if the Inclosure Acts would do that for you." He pondered, rubbing his chin. "It's a bit late to start afresh with a completely new subject although, I suppose we're still only in Michaelmas term."

As he was speaking, she remembered how she'd sat there in this very chair, pouring her heart out to him, when Cameron had walked out on her. And how patient and kind he had been to her then. She held her breath. Finally, Dan looked up and said, "I'll have to clear it with the faculty and we will have to apply to the Degree Committee for approval, but I think there's probably time for you to make alterations to your area of study."

"Are you sure, Dan? That's so good of you."

"Not at all. I believe in you, Freya. And I think you may have finally found your niche. I wouldn't agree to it otherwise."

She and Finn had carried on taking it in turns to look in on Agnes two or three times a day, to sit with her and talk, sip tea together, listen to the news together, sometimes to read to her. Finn had tried to persuade Freya to hand her notice in on her own flat and move in with him, but she'd held back.

"Why are you waiting, Freya?" Amber had asked as they served together one evening in the pub. "You're so right together. And he's kind and generous—not to mention gorgeous."

"I know. You're right. He's all those things, but the fact is, I'm not quite ready," she'd replied, thinking of Cameron. "I need to be sure. You must understand that?"

Agnes was more contented now, less demanding than Freya

had ever known her, but she was fading fast. When she read the article, she seemed content with it, but Freya worried about how quickly she might deteriorate afterward. Was she just holding out to read it?

One morning, Freya was cycling across town to college for a regular appointment with Dan when her phone rang. Thinking it might be Dan calling to cancel or postpone, she stopped her bike and took out the phone. But it was Matt's name flashing on the screen.

"Are you sitting down? I've got some incredible news," he said as soon as she answered. He sounded breathless, brimming with excitement.

"No, I'm not sitting down, Matt." She laughed. "I'm in the middle of Cambridge on my bike. There's a lot of traffic about so it's difficult to hear. It's not bad news, is it?" she asked with a sudden prickle of worry. A van was edging past her bike on the narrow, cobbled street, so she pulled it onto the pavement and wheeled it along until she found a low wall to perch on.

"I'm sitting down now. What is it, Matt?"

"Well, I had a call yesterday evening from the editor of a magazine in Lithuania. I think I told you before that the article about the *wolfskinder* was syndicated, didn't I? It was taken up by magazines and newspapers all over the world. Well, this editor in Lithuania had a call yesterday from an old man. His name is Dimitri Dobis. He had read the article and recognized the photographs. To cut a long story short, he says he is Agnes' brother, Dieter."

"Dieter?" Freya's mouth dropped open. She couldn't believe what she was hearing. Everything around her seemed to go into a strange slow-motion blur. The traffic, the church opposite where she was sitting, the people passing on foot or by bike. "Did you say *Dieter*? But . . . but Dieter died. He was drowned in the river."

"I know. That's what I told the editor. But this old gentleman is adamant. The editor gave me his number. Although he doesn't speak English and I can't speak Lithuanian."

Freya swallowed. "Agnes can speak Lithuanian, of course, but . . . well, what if this old gentleman isn't for real? What if he's . . . well, I'm not sure why anyone would make something like that up, but what if he's mistaken or something?"

The line went silent for a few seconds, then Matt said, "Yes. It would be terrible to get her hopes up if this person turns out not to be Dieter. I've been wondering. Is there something we could get the editor to ask him that wasn't in the article, that only *he* would know?"

Freya thought for a while, then it came to her: "He was only a little boy. He might not remember much at all. He might have blotted it all out. But the article didn't mention the names of the cousins—Joachim and Gunter. He might remember them. Oh, and they had a cat called Claus. Agnes named her current cat after him."

"Let me write that down . . . I'll give it a try and call you back. I don't know how long it will take, though."

Freya was late now. She dashed to college, locking her bike outside the porter's lodge and running through Front Court and up the stairs to Dan's familiar room under the eaves.

Dan was as welcoming and enthusiastic about seeing her as ever, but she had difficulty concentrating during their discussion; her mind kept flitting back to her extraordinary conversation with Matt. She had to resist the temptation to keep glancing at her phone to check if he'd called or texted. But she didn't want Dan to get the impression that she wasn't fully engaged; after all, he'd fought her cause with the faculty and the examination board and got them to agree to her change of subject. At the same time, she didn't want to tell him the news about Dieter in case it all turned out to be a misunderstanding.

When they'd finished reviewing her students' work and the

progress she was making on her own research, she got up to leave.

"Won't you stay for a cup of tea, Freya? I should have offered you one before. Apologies."

"I'm sorry, Dan, not today," she said. "There's something I need to do."

He laughed. "How mysterious! I thought you seemed a little distracted. Well, off you go then. And I'll see you next week."

As she clattered down the wooden staircase and back into Front Court, her phone rang again.

"Hi Freya, it's me again," Matt said. "You'll never believe it, the editor has checked, and the old man answered both questions. He knew the names of the cousins and the cat. No hesitation apparently. And he wants to come over to Cambridge to see Agnes. As soon as he can."

Freya stopped in her tracks. "It has to be him! It has to be Dieter. Matt, I need to go and tell Agnes straight away."

Breathless from pedaling at breakneck speed across Jesus Green, Freya ran up the steps to Agnes' house and let herself in. Agnes had been fading even more over the past weeks and when she called out, "Hello?" now, her voice sounded weak and tremulous.

"It's me, Freya."

Agnes was lying back on the pillows, her eyes closed. The curtains were drawn. Freya crept forward.

"Agnes, I have some news for you," she said gently.

Agnes' eyes blinked open. Freya sat down beside the bed and took the old woman's hand.

"This might be a bit of a shock, so prepare yourself," she began.

"I'm prepared for anything, my dear." She smiled a wan smile. "Nothing can shock me at my age."

"It's about Dieter. Your brother. He's alive and well, and

living in Lithuania. He saw Matthew's article in a magazine and got in touch with the editor."

Agnes gasped. "Oh, my . . ."

Freya looked at Agnes anxiously. The old woman was gazing vacantly ahead of her. She wasn't smiling, she wasn't responding.

"Are you all right?" Freya asked, alarmed.

Slowly, Agnes turned to look at her, her eyes moist. "For all these years I have grieved for him, tortured myself with guilt that I didn't keep my promise to Mutti, and all the time, he was out there. Alive."

"Yes, he is alive. Fit and well. You *did* save him, Agnes. And he wants to come and see you as soon as he can."

Agnes swallowed, took some breaths, fought back the tears.

"It's strange. It feels almost as if I've finally come home after all these years. Thanks to you, my dear. It wouldn't have happened without you."

The little old man who wandered through the glass doors at Stansted Airport with a small plastic suitcase had a shock of white hair and a slight stoop. He stopped and peered at the waiting crowd through round glasses. Catching sight of Freya's handwritten sign, proclaiming "Dimitri Dobis," his eyes lit up and he waved and came across to where she and Finn were waiting.

"Miss Carey?" he asked, holding out his hand. Freya nodded, took the hand, and shook it warmly.

"This is my friend, Finn," she said. "He's driving us back to Cambridge."

"No understand," the old man replied.

It didn't seem to bother him, though, and he smiled broadly, nodding, as Freya ushered him out of the arrivals lounge and toward the car park. Conversation was difficult, if not impossible, but they got by with smiles and Google Translate.

Finn had hired a car, deeming the battered Transit van unsuitable for such a momentous occasion. Dimitri—Dieter—insisted on sitting in the back. As soon as they were clear of the airport roads and were speeding toward Cambridge on the M11, the old man fell asleep on the back seat, slumping sideways against the seatbelt.

"I still can't believe this is happening," said Finn as he drove. "And I don't think Agnes can either."

"Well, she'll believe it soon," said Freya, staring out at the brown winter fields. "We'll be there in less than an hour."

They were silent for a time, then Finn returned to an old and familiar subject. He hadn't mentioned it for a while, but Freya knew he'd just been holding back.

"You know, it would be great if we were together all the time, Freya. Have you given that any more thought?"

"We are together all the time," she said. "Would it make a lot of difference?"

"It would to me," he said and Freya could hear the disappointment in his voice. He didn't mention it again, though, and quickly moved on to talk about something else.

It was late afternoon and the light was fading fast as they drew up outside Agnes' house. Dieter had awoken as they drove through the outskirts of Cambridge and had peered out of the window keenly, taking everything in, exclaiming to himself in his own language.

Finn parked in front of the house and switched off the engine. "We shouldn't really stop here, but a few minutes won't hurt. Do you want to show Dieter inside, Freya?"

Freya found she was tingling with nerves. "You come too, Finn."

He smiled sideways at her, that teasing look again, got out of the car, and opened the back door for Dieter to get out. Then he took Dieter by the arm and helped him out of the car and up the steps. Freya darted ahead and opened the front door. All three of them walked along the passage together and Dieter paused for a second and looked up at the picture of the castle in the forest, a flash of recognition in his eyes. Freya went ahead and pushed open the door to Agnes' room. She was sitting forward, her eyes fixed on the door, her cheeks flushed for the first time in months.

Freya could hardly say anything, the words she wanted to say caught in her throat.

Agnes held out her arms and Dieter gave a short cry, then rushed forward to embrace her. Freya quickly backed out of the room and shut the door quietly.

Finn was standing in the passage, tears in his eyes. Freya went to him and felt his arms encircle her. Neither of them could speak for a while.

It was Freya who finally broke the silence. She looked up into his eyes and said, "I've been thinking about what you asked me in the car, Finn, and the answer is yes. I've made a decision and on Monday, I'm going to the agent to give notice on my flat. I love you and I do want to be with you. I want to be with you all the time."

YOUR BOOK CLUB RESOURCE

READING GROUP GUIDE

THE WRITING BEHIND THE CHILD WITHOUT A HOME

I've always been fascinated by history, partly because it has always fired my imagination. Partly, too, because my father died when I was a child, and as I grew older, finding out about his past seemed to bring me closer to him. And he had a fascinating past.

He served in the Indian Army in British India in the 1930s, signing up during the Great Depression, when there were very few jobs in London. He was sent out to India and stationed on the North-West Frontier (now the border between Pakistan and Afghanistan) for several years. Later, he volunteered to serve in the Malayan Campaign at the start of World War II. He was taken prisoner by the Japanese at the fall of Singapore, along with a hundred thousand other Allied soldiers. He spent the rest of the war as a prisoner, starting his incarceration in the Changi POW camp in Singapore.

He was sent to work on the Thai-Burma Railway in November of 1942, where he spent three and a half years, and finally ended the war in Taiwan. He suffered brutal treatment, malnutrition, disease, and the sinking of his transport ship, the *Hōfuku Maru*, by the US Navy off the Philippine coast. Researching his story inspired me to write my first book, originally published as *Bamboo Heart* and subsequently as *A Daughter's Quest*, based on his experiences, followed by five more books set in Southeast Asia during World War II.

The inspiration for *The Child Without a Home* came to

me out of the blue when I was researching something else. I stumbled across the story of the *Wolfskinder*—children who had become orphaned during the fall of East Prussia and had found refuge in the huge, untamed forests that straddled the borders between East Prussia and Lithuania. I read about how they had struggled to survive, older siblings caring for younger ones, living in gangs, and some going out into Lithuanian villages to beg or steal from local farmers for survival. Many were taken in by Lithuanian families, but when the iron curtain came down after the war, their German roots could never be revealed. They were cut off from their original families forever.

I also read about how the civilians of East Prussia were ordered by their Gauleiter (Erich Koch) not to evacuate, even though the eastern front was moving closer and closer to their homes. Evacuation would have been seen as an admission of defeat. When the order finally came, it was too late, and many were overtaken by the advance of the Red Army. They evacuated in carts and sleighs, or on foot, through driving snow and in freezing temperatures, sharing their retreat with the German army, the Wehrmacht. Many perished en route or were shot down by enemy aircraft. They were all bound for ports on the Baltic Sea, from where they hoped to board ships bound for the Reich.

When they reached the inland sea of the Vistula Lagoon, it was frozen over. Many risked life and limb to cross it, but the ice gave way in places and lives were lost, still more shot and killed by Russian planes. Once at the Baltic Sea ports, including Danzig, modern-day Gdańsk, they boarded overcrowded boats. One in particular, the *Wilhelm Gustloff*, was torpedoed by a Russian submarine with great loss of life.

The loss of innocent German lives seems to have been glossed over, at least for people growing up in the United Kingdom, due to the tendency to associate all German people with the Nazis. But many Germans had lived under Nazi persecution themselves for years, forced to live under Nazi rule against their will.

This angle interested me, because I like to research and write about aspects of the second world war that are out of the mainstream and not generally written about.

I devoured books on the subject: *The Death of East Prussia* by Peter B. Clark; *Forgotten Land: Journeys Among the Ghosts of East Prussia* by Max Egremont; together with memoirs of children caught up in the fall of East Prussia, notably *Ruined by the Reich: Memoir of an East Prussian Family* by Christabel Weiss Brandenburg; *Abandoned and Forgotten: An Orphan Girl's Tale of Survival in World War II* by Evelyne Tannehill; and *Skating at the Edge of the Wood: Memories of East Prussia, 1931–1945* by Marlene Yeo.

East Prussia itself is intriguing in that it no longer exists—its borders obliterated at the end of the war—but echoes of it still remain. I wanted to convey that sense of a forgotten land on the edge of a dying empire, and the turmoil of its passing.

To convey modern Cambridge, little research was necessary. I was a student there in the early eighties, taking some of my supervisions in the room under the eaves in Emmanuel College that is Dan's office in the book, going to student parties in big old houses on Chesterton Road, and taking misty early-morning rowing lessons on the River Cam. Some things have changed, of course. There are new buildings, such as the very modern Squire Law Library, and the town is much busier nowadays, but the magical atmosphere and the beautiful, historic buildings have remained the same.

The idea for the relationship between Agnes and Freya came from watching my sister care for an elderly neighbor years ago, and the friendship and love that grew between them. Freya's grandfather's tale was inspired by stories from my wider extended family, whose roots are in pre-war Poland.

I loved researching and writing *The Child Without a Home* (for which I used the working title *The Bend in the River*), and I really hope readers enjoy reading it as much.

DISCUSSION QUESTIONS

1. One of the themes in the book is regret for past actions. Agnes has regrets from the war years, and Freya regrets things that happened in her relationship with her grandfather. Do you think there are parallels between their two stories?

2. Both characters are lonely and coming to terms with their loss. How far do you think their experiences may be compared?

3. How do you think the growing friendship between Agnes and Freya helps each woman to come to terms with her life and to find the strength to look for the truth and face the past?

4. How well do you think the book portrays the struggle for survival among the evacuees of East Prussia?

5. The landscape and setting are very important in the book. Do you think the book evokes the atmosphere of East Prussia well? What about Cambridge, in the modern portion?

6. The sense of place and time is important in both strands of this book. Which one did you find you related to best?

7. Agnes and her family have been living under Nazi rule for some time, but they don't identify with the regime. Do you think this comes across in the book and in what ways?

8. How well did you think the two different stories came together at the end?

AUTHOR Q&A

Was there a place you visited in Cambridge that you used as inspiration for any scene in this story?

Many scenes in the book were inspired by places I visited when I was a student in Cambridge in the early eighties. For example, I have set some scenes in Emmanuel College, in a room on the top floor of a building overlooking Front Court. This room, which is occupied by Freya's thesis advisor in the book, and where she goes to discuss her dissertation, is modeled on the room of one of my own tutors, in which I myself attended supervisions on Constitutional and Administrative Law. I remember the wooden staircase up to the room being very narrow and the room itself being under the eaves, with exposed beams and a low ceiling. It was furnished with an odd assortment of comfortable old armchairs. The whole place felt very historic and going through that magnificent courtyard and up those stairs to be grilled on a weekly basis felt very daunting too. However, I was just a nervous fresher then, whereas Freya is a postgraduate student and has a good relationship with her thesis advisor.

The Free Press pub was a favorite haunt at weekends. Some friends of mine—medical students—lived in a little terraced house in Grafton Street, just round the corner from the pub, so we would often pop in there for a pint before moving on to other pubs in the town or on the river. I remember it as very traditional—low-ceilinged, cozy, and atmospheric.

The River Cam is ever-present in the book, as it was for me

as a student. I remember walks out to Grantchester to picnic on the banks, punting with friends on summer evenings, and that magical mist that used to rise from the river in the winter at dusk.

Agnes' house, on Chesterton Road, is modeled on an old student house where I used to go to parties. It was a huge Victorian terraced house with a big bay window at the front overlooking the river. Of course, it was run down and neglected like a lot of student houses in those days, but it had so much character it has stayed in my mind for forty years.

Are there any particular places of historical events in the story that you'd like to visit?

I have never been to the former East Prussia, and researching the story made me yearn to go there. It would be fascinating to see the countryside that I tried to depict, where Agnes traveled to escape the fighting. I would love to travel to the frozen wastes of the lagoons near the Baltic, the enormous evergreen forests on the Lithuanian border, and the port of Danzig, now Gdańsk, and of course, Königsberg, where so much of the fighting and action in the book took place.

Is there a particular supporting character in the story that resonates most with you?

Agnes' mother is a character that resonates with me. She does everything she can to feed her family and keep them safe from the war, taking them to the farm when supplies are running out and making the decision to flee the country when she realizes it is no longer tenable to stay there. She has to put on a brave face for the sake of her children, and even though the odds are stacked against them, she never gives up. Though sometimes her frustration and sense of justice come to the surface, for example, when she finds squatters in her home and when she sees the Nazi soldiers meting out cruelty to Jewish prisoners.

Why do you believe there are so many people passionate about learning more about the historic events that occurred during World War II?

World War II looms over us, and I don't think I've met anyone whose life wasn't shaped in some way by it. For example, my own father was in the British Indian Army in Malaya, taken prisoner at the fall of Singapore, and suffered starvation, disease, and brutal treatment at the hands of the Japanese on the Thai-Burma railway. His transport ship was torpedoed by US planes off the Philippines, and he was one of very few survivors. He met my mother when he was being treated in a London hospital and she was a student nurse there. Like so many other people, my parents met as a direct result of the war, and I've always been fascinated by their experiences. The fact that it is such recent history, that so many unbelievably brutal events took place as well as so many sacrifices and acts of heroism, means that we want to learn from what happened then, to ensure that it doesn't happen again.

ACKNOWLEDGMENTS

Huge thanks to Jennifer Hunt, to my friend and writing buddy Siobhan Daiko for all her support, to everyone who has read my books and encouraged me on my writing journey.

About the Author

Ann Bennett was born in a small village in Northamptonshire, UK, on the same street as William Carey, one of the first Baptist missionaries to work in India in the early nineteenth century. She read law at Cambridge, but was always inspired by history, travel, and great stories. Her first book, *A Daughter's Quest*, originally published as *Bamboo Heart*, was written after researching her father's experience as a prisoner of war on the Thai-Burma Railway. *The Planter's Wife* (originally *Bamboo Island*), *A Daughter's Promise*, *The Homecoming* (formerly *Bamboo Road*), *The Tea Planter's Club*, and *The Amulet* are also about the war in Southeast Asia. She has traveled to India and Southeast Asia many times.

The idea for *The Orphan House* came partly from researching William Carey's story, but also from reading into family history. Her great-grandfather, Brice Bennett, was headmaster of a county school for pauper children in Wargrave-on-Thames, Berkshire, England.

Ann is married with three grown-up sons and works as a lawyer.

You can learn more at:
BambooHeart.co.uk
Twitter @AnnBennett71
Facebook.com/AnnBennettAuthor